P9-DMS-589

Faithful Place

ALSO BY TANA FRENCH

The Likeness
In the Woods

TANA FRENCH

Faithful Place

VIKING

VIKING
Published by the Penguin Group
Penguin Group (USA) Inc., 375 Hudson Street, New York, New York 10014, U.S.A.
Penguin Group (Canada), 90 Eglinton Avenue East, Suite 700, Toronto, Ontario, Canada M4P 2Y3
(a division of Pearson Penguin Canada Inc.)
Penguin Books Ltd, 80 Strand, London WC2R 0RL, England
Penguin Ireland, 25 St. Stephen's Green, Dublin 2, Ireland (a division of Penguin Books Ltd)
Penguin Books Australia Ltd, 250 Camberwell Road, Camberwell, Victoria 3124, Australia
(a division of Pearson Australia Group Pty Ltd)
Penguin Books India Pvt Ltd, 11 Community Centre, Panchsheel Park, New Delhi - 110 017, India
Penguin Group (NZ), 67 Apollo Drive, Rosedale, North Shore 0632, New Zealand
(a division of Pearson New Zealand Ltd)
Penguin Books (South Africa) (Pty) Ltd, 24 Sturdee Avenue, Rosebank,
Johannesburg 2196, South Africa

Penguin Books Ltd, Registered Offices: 80 Strand, London WC2R 0RL, England

First published in 2010 by Viking Penguin, a member of Penguin Group (USA) Inc.

10 9 8 7 6 5 4 3 2 1

Copyright © Tana French, 2010
All rights reserved

Excerpts from "The Rare Ould Times" and "The Ferryman" by Pete St. John. Reprinted by kind permission
of Pete St. John.

PUBLISHER'S NOTE: This is a work of fiction. Names, characters, places, and incidents either are the product of
the author's imagination or are used fictitiously, and any resemblance to actual persons, living or dead, business
establishments, events, or locales is entirely coincidental.

LIBRARY OF CONGRESS CATALOGING-IN-PUBLICATION DATA
French, Tana.
Faithful Place : a novel / Tana French.
    p. cm.
ISBN 978-0-670-02187-1
1. Missing persons—Fiction.   2. First loves—Fiction.   3. Dublin (Ireland)—Fiction.   I. Title.
PR6106.R457F35   2010
823'.92—dc22   2010003212

Printed in the United States of America

Without limiting the rights under copyright reserved above, no part of this publication may be reproduced,
stored in or introduced into a retrieval system, or transmitted, in any form or by any means (electronic,
mechanical, photocopying, recording or otherwise), without the prior written permission of both the
copyright owner and the above publisher of this book.

The scanning, uploading, and distribution of this book via the Internet or via any other means without the
permission of the publisher is illegal and punishable by law. Please purchase only authorized electronic editions
and do not participate in or encourage electronic piracy of copyrightable materials. Your support of the
author's rights is appreciated.

For Alex

Faithful Place

Prologue

I n all your life, only a few moments matter. Mostly you never get a good
look at them except in hindsight, long after they've zipped past you: the
moment when you decided whether to talk to that girl, slow down on
that blind bend, stop and find that condom. I was lucky, I guess you could
call it. I got to see one of mine face-to-face, and recognize it for what it was.
I got to feel the riptide pull of my life spinning around me, one winter
night, while I waited in the dark at the top of Faithful Place.

I was nineteen, old enough to take on the world and young enough to
be a dozen kinds of stupid, and that night as soon as both my brothers were
snoring I slid out of our bedroom with my rucksack on my back and my
Docs hanging from one hand. A floorboard creaked and in the girls' room
one of my sisters murmured in her sleep, but I was magic that night, riding
high on that surge tide, unstoppable; my parents didn't even turn over on
the pullout bed as I moved through the front room, close enough to touch.
The fire had burned down to nothing but a muttering red glow. In the
rucksack was everything important I owned: jeans, T-shirts, a secondhand
wireless, a hundred quid and my birth cert. That was all you needed to go
over to England, back then. Rosie had the ferry tickets.

I waited for her at the end of the road, in the shadows outside the foggy
yellow circle of lamplight. The air was cold as glass, with a savory burnt edge
from the hops up at Guinness's. I had three pairs of socks under the Docs,
and I stuffed my hands deep into the pockets of my German army parka
and listened one last time to my street alive and moving down the long currents of the night. A woman laughing, *Ah now who said you could,* a window
slamming down. Scrabble of a rat along brickwork, a man coughing, the

whoosh of a bike around the corner; the low fierce grumble of Mad Johnny Malone, in the basement of Number 14, talking himself to sleep. Couple-noises somewhere, muffled whimpers, rhythmic bumps, and I thought about the smell of Rosie's neck and grinned up at the sky. I heard the bells of the city chime for midnight, Christchurch, St. Pat's, St. Michan's, huge round notes tumbling down from the sky like a celebration, ringing in our own secret New Year.

When they rang one I was afraid. A trail of faint rustles and thumps all down the back gardens, and I straightened up ready, but she didn't come climbing over the end wall; probably someone sneaking home, late and guilty, in at a window. In Number 7 Sallie Hearne's newest kid cried, a thin defeated wail, till she dragged herself awake and sang to it. *I know where I'm going . . . Painted rooms are bonny . . .*

When they rang two, the mix-up hit me like a kick in the hole. It cata-pulted me right over the end wall into the garden of Number 16, con-demned since before I was born, colonized by us kids ignoring the awful warnings, littered with beer cans and fag ends and lost virginities. I leaped up the rotten stairs four at a time without caring who heard. I was so sure, I could already see her, furious copper curls and fists on hips, *Where the fuck have you been?*

Splintered floorboards, holes punched in plaster, debris and cold dark drafts and no one. In the top front room I found the note, just a page ripped out of a kid's school copy. On the bare floor, fluttering in the pale rectangle of light from the window, it looked like it had been there for a hundred years. That was when I felt that riptide change, jackknife and turn deadly, much too strong to fight and not on my side any more.

I didn't take the note with me. By the time I left Number 16 I knew it by heart, and I had the rest of my life to try to believe it. I left it where it was and went back to the end of the road. I waited there in the shadows, watching the plumes of smoke that my breath sent into the lamplight, while the bells tolled three and four and five. The night faded to a thin sad gray and round the corner a milk cart clattered over cobblestones towards the dairy, and I was still waiting for Rosie Daly at the top of Faithful Place.

1

My father once told me that the most important thing every man should know is what he would die for. *If you don't know that, he said, what are you worth? Nothing. You're not a man at all.* I was thirteen and he was three quarters of the way into a bottle of Gordon's finest, but hey, good talk. As far as I recall, he was willing to die a) for Ireland, b) for his mother, who had been dead for ten years, and c) to get that bitch Maggie Thatcher.

All the same, at any moment of my life since that day, I could have told you straight off the bat exactly what I would die for. At first it was easy: my family, my girl, my home. Later, for a while, things got more complicated. These days they hold steady, and I like that; it feels like something a man can be proud of. I would die for, in no particular order, my city, my job, and my kid.

The kid is well behaved so far, the city is Dublin, and the job is on the Undercover Squad, so it may sound obvious which one I'm most likely to wind up dying for, but it's been a while since work handed me anything scarier than a paperwork megaturd. The size of this country means a field agent's shelf life is short; two ops, maybe four, and your risk of being spotted gets too high. I used up my nine lives a long time back. I stay behind the scenes, for now, and run operations of my own.

Here's the real risk in Undercover, in the field and out: you create illusions for long enough, you start thinking you're in control. It's easy to slide into believing you're the hypnotist here, the mirage master, the smart cookie who knows what's real and how all the tricks are done. The fact is you're still just another slack-jawed mark in the audience. No matter how good you are, this world is always going to be better at this game. It's more cunning than you are, it's faster and it's a whole lot more ruthless. All you can do is try to keep up, know your weak spots and never stop expecting the sucker punch.

The second time my life geared up for the sucker punch, it was a Friday afternoon at the beginning of December. I had spent the day doing maintenance work on some of my current mirages—one of my boys, who would not be getting any cookies from Uncle Frank in his Christmas stocking, had got himself into a situation wherein, for complex reasons, he needed an elderly lady whom he could introduce to several low-level drug dealers as his granny—and I was heading over to my ex-wife's place to pick up my kid for the weekend. Olivia and Holly live in a jaw-droppingly tasteful semi-d on a manicured cul-de-sac in Dalkey. Olivia's daddy gave it to us for a wedding present. When we moved in, it had a name instead of a number. I got rid of that fast, but still, I should have copped right then that this marriage was never going to work. If my parents had known I was getting married, my ma would have gone deep into hock at the credit union, bought us a lovely floral living-room suite and been outraged if we took the plastic off the cushions.

Olivia kept herself bang in the middle of the doorway, in case I got ideas about coming in. "Holly's almost ready," she said.

Olivia, and I say this hand on heart with the proper balance of smugness and regret, is a stunner: tall, with a long elegant face, plenty of soft ash-blond hair and the kind of discreet curves you don't notice at first and then can't stop noticing. That evening she was smoothed into an expensive black dress and delicate tights and her grandmother's diamond necklace that only comes out on big occasions, and the Pope himself would have whipped off his skullcap to mop his brow. Me being a less classy guy than the Pope, I wolf whistled. "Big date?"

"We're going for dinner."

"Does 'we' involve Dermo again?"

Olivia is way too smart to let me yank her chain that easily. "His name's Dermot, and yes, it does."

I did impressed. "That's four weekends running, am I right? Tell me something: is tonight the big night?"

Olivia called up the stairs, "Holly! Your father's here!" While she had her back turned, I headed on past her into the hall. She was wearing Chanel No. 5, same as she has ever since we met.

Upstairs: "Daddy! I'm coming I'm coming I'm coming, I just have to . . ." and then a long intent stream of chatter, as Holly explained her complicated little head without caring whether anyone could hear her. I yelled, "You take your time, sweetheart!" on my way into the kitchen.

Olivia followed me. "Dermot will be here any minute," she told me. I wasn't clear on whether this was a threat or a plea.

I flipped open the fridge and had a look inside. "I don't like the cut of that fella. He's got no chin. I never trust a man with no chin."

"Well, fortunately, your taste in men isn't relevant here."

"It is if you're getting serious enough that he'll be spending time around Holly. What's his surname again?"

Once, back when we were heading for the split, Olivia slammed the fridge door on my head. I could tell she was thinking about doing it again. I stayed leaning over, to give her every opportunity, but she kept her cool. "Why do you want to know?"

"I'll need to run him through the computer." I pulled out a carton of orange juice and gave it a shake. "What's this crap? When did you stop buying the good stuff?"

Olivia's mouth—subtle nude lipstick—was starting to tighten. "You will *not* run Dermot through any computer, Frank."

"Got no choice," I told her cheerfully. "I have to make sure he's not a kiddie-fiddler, haven't I?"

"Sweet Lord, Frank! He is not—"

"Maybe not," I acknowledged. "*Probably* not. But how can you be sure, Liv? Wouldn't you rather be safe than sorry?" I uncapped the juice and took a swig.

"Holly!" Olivia called, louder. "Hurry up!"

"I can't find my *horse*!" A bunch of thumps, overhead.

I told Olivia, "They target single mammies with lovely little kids. And it's amazing how many of them don't have chins. Have you never noticed that?"

"No, Frank, I haven't. And I won't have you using your job to intimidate—"

"Take a good look next time there's a pedo on the telly. White van and no chin, I guarantee you. What does Dermo drive?"

"*Holly!*"

I had another big gulp of juice, wiped off the spout with my sleeve and stuck the carton back in the fridge. "That tastes like cat's piss. If I up the child support, will you buy decent juice?"

"If you tripled it," Olivia said sweetly and coldly, glancing at her watch, "not that you could, it might just about cover one carton a week." Kitty has claws, if you keep pulling her tail for long enough.

At this point Holly saved both of us from ourselves by shooting out of her room calling, "Daddydaddydaddy!" at the top of her lungs. I made it to the bottom of the stairs in time for her to take a flying leap at me like a little spinning firework, all gold cobweb hair and pink sparkly things, wrapping her legs round my waist and whacking me in the back with her schoolbag and a fuzzy pony called Clara that had seen better days. "Hello, spider monkey," I said, kissing the top of her head. She was light as a fairy. "How was your week?"

"Very busy and I'm not a spider monkey," she told me severely, nose to nose. "What's a spider monkey?"

Holly is nine and the fine-boned, easy-bruised spit of her mother's family—us Mackeys are sturdy and thick-skinned and thick-haired, built for hard work in Dublin weather—all except for her eyes. The first time I ever saw her she looked up at me with my own eyes, great wide bright-blue eyes that hit me like a Taser zap, and they still make my heart flip over every time. Olivia can scrape off my surname like an out-of-date address label, load up the fridge with juice I don't like and invite Dermo the Pedo to fill my side of the bed, but there's not a thing she can do about those eyes.

I told Holly, "It's a magic fairy monkey that lives in an enchanted wood." She gave me a look that was perfectly balanced between *Wow* and *Nice try*. "What has you so busy?"

She slid off me and landed on the floor with a thump. "Chloe and Sarah and me are going to have a band. I drew you a picture in school because we made up a dance and can I have white boots? And Sarah wrote a song and . . ." For a second there Olivia and I almost smiled at each other, across her head, before Olivia caught herself and checked her watch again.

In the drive we crossed paths with my friend Dermo, who—as I know for a fact, because I snagged his plate number the first time he and Olivia went out to dinner—is an impeccably law-abiding guy who has never even parked his Audi on a double yellow, and who can't help looking like he lives life on the verge of a massive belch. "Evening," he said, giving me an electrocuted nod. I think Dermo may be scared of me. "Holly."

"What do you call him?" I asked Holly, when I had fastened her into her booster seat and Olivia, perfect as Grace Kelly, was kissing Dermo's cheek in the doorway.

Holly rearranged Clara's mane and shrugged. "Mum says to call him Uncle Dermot."

"And do you?"

"No. Out loud I don't call him anything. In my head I call him Squid-face." She checked in the rearview mirror, to see if I was going to give out about that. Her chin was all ready to turn stubborn.

I started to laugh. "Beautiful," I told her. "That's my girl," and I did a handbrake turn to make Olivia and Squidface jump.

Since Olivia got sense and kicked me out, I live on the quays, in a massive apartment block built in the nineties by, apparently, David Lynch. The carpets are so deep that I've never heard a footstep, but even at four in the morning you can feel the hum of five hundred minds buzzing on every side of you: people dreaming, hoping, worrying, planning, thinking. I grew up in a tenement house, so you would think I'd be good with the factory-farm lifestyle, but this is different. I don't know these people; I never even see these people. I have no idea how or when they get in and out of the place. For all I know they never leave, just stay barricaded in their apartments, thinking. Even in my sleep I've got one ear tuned to that buzz, ready to leap out of bed and defend my territory if I need to.

The decor in my personal corner of Twin Peaks is divorcé chic, by which I mean that, four years on, it still looks like the moving van hasn't arrived yet. The exception is Holly's room, which is loaded with every fluffy pastel object known to man. The day we went looking for furniture together, I had finally managed to wrestle one weekend a month out of Olivia, and I wanted to buy Holly everything on three floors of the shopping center. A part of me had believed I'd never see her again.

"What are we doing tomorrow?" she wanted to know, as we headed up the padded corridor. She was trailing Clara on the carpet by one leg. Last I'd looked, she would have screamed bloody murder at the thought of that horse touching the floor. Blink and you miss something.

"Remember that kite I got you? Finish all your homework tonight, and if it's not raining I'll bring you to the Phoenix Park and teach you to fly it."

"Can Sarah come?"

"We'll ring her mum after dinner." Holly's mates' parents love me. Nothing feels more responsible than having a detective take your kid to the park.

"Dinner! Can we get pizza?"

"Sure," I said. Olivia lives an additive-free, organic, high-fiber life; if I don't do a little counterbalancing, the kid will grow up twice as healthy as all her mates and feel left out. "Why not?" and then I unlocked the door and got my first hint that Holly and I weren't getting any pizza tonight.

The voice-mail light on my phone was going apeshit. Five missed calls. Work rings me on my mobile, field agents and confidential informants ring me on my other mobile, the lads know they'll see me in the pub when they see me, and Olivia sends me text messages when she has to. That left family, which meant my kid sister Jackie, seeing as she was the only one I'd talked to in a couple of decades. Five calls probably meant one of our parents was dying.

I told Holly, "Here," and held out my laptop. "You take that to your room and annoy your mates on IM. I'll be in to you in a few minutes."

Holly, who knows well that she isn't allowed to go online in private till she's twenty-one, gave me a skeptical look. "If you want a cigarette, Daddy," she told me, very maturely, "you can just go out on the balcony. I know you smoke."

I steered her towards her room with a hand on her back. "Oh, yeah? What makes you think that?" At any other time I would have been seriously curious. I've never smoked in front of Holly, and Olivia wouldn't have told her. We made her mind, the two of us; the idea of it containing things we didn't put there still blows me away.

"I just know," Holly said, dumping Clara and her bag on her bed and looking lofty. The kid'll make a detective yet. "And you shouldn't. Sister Mary Therese says it turns all your insides black."

"Sister Mary Therese is dead right. Smart woman." I switched on the laptop and hooked up the broadband line. "There you go. I've to make a phone call. Don't be buying any diamonds on eBay."

Holly asked, "Are you going to ring your girlfriend?"

She looked tiny and way too wise, standing there in her white padded coat that came halfway down her skinny legs, wide eyes trying not to look scared. "No," I said. "No, sweetheart. I don't have a girlfriend."

"Swear?"

"I swear. I'm not planning on getting one anytime soon, either. In a few years maybe you can pick one out for me. How's that?"

"I want Mum to be your girlfriend."

"Yeah," I said. "I know." I put my hand on her head for a second; her hair felt like petals. Then I closed her door behind me and went back to the living room to find out who had died.

It was Jackie on the voice mail, all right, and she was going like an express train. Bad sign: Jackie brakes for good news ("You'll never guess what happened. Go on, have a guess") and floors the pedal for bad. This was Formula 1 stuff. "Ah, Jaysus, Francis, would you ever pick up your bleeding phone, I need to talk to you, I'm not just ringing you for the laugh, do I ever? Now before you go getting a fright, it's not Mammy, God forbid, she's grand, a bit shook up but sure aren't we all, she was having palpitations there at first but she had a sit-down and Carmel gave her a drink of brandy and she's grand now, aren't you, Mam? Thank God Carmel was there, she does call round most Fridays after the shopping, she rang me and Kevin to come down. Shay said not to be ringing you, what's the point, he said, but I told him to feck off for himself, it's only fair, so if you're at home would you ever pick up this phone and talk to me? Francis! I swear to God—" The message space ran out with a beep.

Carmel and Kevin and Shay, oh my. It sounded very much like the entire family had descended on my parents' place. My da; it had to be. "Daddy!" Holly yelled, from her room. "How many cigarettes do you smoke every day?"

The voice-mail lady told me to press buttons; I followed orders. "Who says I smoke?"

"I need to *know*! Twenty?"

For a start. "Maybe."

Jackie again: "Bleeding machines, I wasn't finished! Come here, I should've said right away, it's not Da either, he's the same as ever, no one's dead or hurt or nothing, or anyway we're all grand. Kevin's a bit upset but I think that's because he's worried about how you'll take it, he's awful fond of you, you know, he still is. Now it might be nothing, Francis, I don't want you losing the head, right, it could all be a joke, someone messing, that's what we thought at first, although pretty shite joke if you ask me, excuse my language—"

"Daddy! How much exercise do you get?"

What the hell? "I'm a secret ballet dancer."

"Noooo, seriously! How much?"

"Not enough."

"—and sure, none of us have a clue what to be doing with it an' anyway, so would you ever ring me as soon as you get this? Please, Francis. I'll have my mobile in my hand, now."

Click, beep, voice-mail babe. Looking back, I should have figured it out by that point, or at least I should have got the general idea. "Daddy? How much fruit and vegetables do you eat?"

"Truckloads."

"You do not!"

"Some."

The next three messages were more of the same, at half-hour intervals. By the last one, Jackie had reached the point where only small dogs could hear her.

"Daddy?"

"Give me a sec, sweetie."

I took my mobile out on the balcony, above the dark river and the greasy orange lights and the running snarl of the traffic jams, and phoned

Jackie. She answered on the first ring. "Francis? Jesus, Mary and Joseph, I've been going mental! Where were you?"

She had slowed down to about eighty miles an hour. "Picking up Holly. What the hell, Jackie?"

Background noise. Even after all that time, I knew the quick bite of Shay's voice straight away. One note of my ma caught me right in the throat.

"Ah, God, Francis . . . Would you sit down for me, now? Or get yourself a glass of brandy, something like that?"

"Jackie, if you don't tell me what's going on, I swear I'm going to come over there and strangle you."

"Hang on, hold your horses . . ." A door closing. "Now," Jackie said, into sudden quiet. "Right. D'you remember I was telling you a while back, some fella's after buying up the three houses at the top of the Place? To turn into apartments?"

"Yeah."

"He's not doing the apartments after all, now everyone's after getting all worried about property prices; he's leaving the houses a while and see what happens. So he got the builders in to take out the fireplaces and the mold ings and that, to sell—there's people pay good money for those yokes, did you know that? mentallers—and they started today, on the one up on the corner. D'you remember, the derelict one?"

"Number Sixteen."

"That's the one. They were taking out the fireplaces, and up behind one of them they found a suitcase."

Dramatic pause. Drugs? Guns? Cash? Jimmy Hoffa? "Fuck's sake, Jackie. *What?*"

"It's Rosie Daly's, Francis. It's her case."

All the layers of traffic noise vanished, snapped right off. That orange glow across the city turned feral and hungry as forest fire, blinding, out of control.

"No," I said, "it's not. I don't know where the hell you got that, but it's a load of my arse."

"Ah, now, Francis—"

Concern and sympathy were pouring off her voice. If she'd been there,

I think I would have punched her lights out. "'Ah, now, Francis,' nothing. You and Ma have yourselves worked up into some hysterical frenzy over sweet fuck-all, and now you want me to play along—"

"Listen to me, I know you're—"

"Unless this is all some stunt to get me over there. Is that it, Jackie? Are you aiming for some big family reconciliation? Because I'm warning you now, this isn't the fucking Hallmark Channel and that kind of game isn't going to end well."

"You big gobshite, you," Jackie snapped. "Get a hold of yourself. What do you think I am? There's a shirt in that case, a purple paisley yoke, Carmel recognizes it—"

I'd seen it on Rosie a hundred times, knew what the buttons felt like under my fingers. "Yeah, from every girl in this town in the eighties. Carmel'd recognize Elvis walking down Grafton Street for a bit of gossip. I thought you had better sense, but apparently—"

"—and there's a birth cert wrapped inside it. Rose Bernadette Daly."

Which more or less killed that line of conversation. I found my smokes, leaned my elbows on the railing and took the longest drag of my life.

"Sorry," Jackie said, softer. "For biting your head off. Francis?"

"Yeah."

"Are you all right?"

"Yeah. Listen to me, Jackie. Do the Dalys know?"

"They're not in. Nora moved out to Blanchardstown, I think it was, a few years back; Mr. Daly and Mrs. Daly go over to her on Friday nights, to see the baba. Mammy thinks she has the number somewhere, but—"

"Have you called the Guards?"

"Only you, sure."

"Who else knows about this?"

"The builders, only. A couple of Polish young fellas, they are. When they finished up for the day they went across to Number Fifteen, to ask was there anyone they could give the case back to, but Number Fifteen's students now, so they sent the Polish fellas down to Ma and Da."

"And Ma hasn't told the whole road? Are you sure?"

"The Place isn't the same as you remember it. Half of it's students and yuppies, these days; we wouldn't even know their names. The Cullens are still here, and the Nolans and some of the Hearnes, but Mammy didn't want to say anything to them till she'd told the Dalys. It wouldn't be right."

"Good. Where's the case now?"

"It's in the front room. Should the builders not have moved it? They had to get on with their work—"

"It's grand. Don't touch it any more unless you have to. I'll be over as fast as I can."

A second of silence. Then: "Francis. I don't want to be thinking anything terrible, God bless us, but does this not mean that Rosie . . ."

"We don't know anything yet," I said. "Just sit tight, don't talk to anyone, and wait for me."

I hung up and took a quick look into the apartment behind me. Holly's door was still shut. I finished my smoke in one more marathon drag, tossed the butt over the railing, lit another and rang Olivia.

She didn't even say hello. "No, Frank. Not this time. Not a chance."

"I don't have a choice, Liv."

"You begged for every weekend. *Begged.* If you didn't want them—"

"I do want them. This is an emergency."

"It always is. The squad can survive without you for two days, Frank. No matter what you'd like to think, you're not indispensable."

To anyone more than a foot away, her voice would have sounded light and chatty, but she was furious. Tinkling cutlery, arch hoots of laughter; something that sounded like, God help us, a fountain. "It's not work this time," I said. "It's family."

"It is, of course. Would this have anything to do with the fact that I'm on my fourth date with Dermot?"

"Liv, I would happily do a lot to wreck your fourth date with Dermot, but I'd never give up time with Holly. You know me better than that."

A short, suspicious pause. "What kind of family emergency?"

"I don't know yet. Jackie rang me in hysterics, from my parents' place; I can't work out the details. I need to get over there fast."

Another pause. Then Olivia said, on a long tired breath, "Right. We're in the Coterie. Drop her down."

The Coterie has a TV-based chef and gets hand-jobbed in a lot of weekend supplements. It badly needs firebombing. "Thanks, Olivia. Seriously. I'll pick her up later tonight, if I can, or tomorrow morning. I'll ring you."

"You do that," Olivia said. "If you can, of course," and she hung up. I threw my smoke away and went inside to finish pissing off the women in my life.

Holly was sitting cross-legged on her bed, with the computer on her lap and a worried look on her face. "Sweetheart," I said, "we've got a problem."

She pointed at the laptop. "Daddy, look."

The screen said, in big purple letters surrounded by an awful lot of flashing graphics, YOU WILL DIE AT THE AGE OF 52. The kid looked really upset. I sat down on the bed behind her and pulled her and the computer onto my lap. "What's all this?"

"Sarah found this quiz online and I did it for you and it said this. You're *forty-one*."

Oh, Jesus, not now. "Chickadee, it's the internet. Anyone can put anything on there. That doesn't make it real."

"It *says*! They figured it all *out*!"

Olivia was going to love me if I gave Holly back in tears. "Let me show you something," I said. I reached around her, got rid of my death sentence, opened up a Word document and typed in, YOU ARE A SPACE ALIEN. YOU ARE READING THIS ON THE PLANET BONGO. "Now. Is that true?"

Holly managed a watery giggle. "Course not."

I turned it purple and gave it a fancy font. "How about now?"

Head-shake.

"How about if I got the computer to ask you a bunch of questions before it said that? Would it be true then?"

For a second I thought I'd got through, but then those narrow shoulders went rigid. "You said a problem."

"Yeah. We're going to have to change our plans just a little bit."

"I have to go back to Mum's," Holly said, to the laptop. "Don't I?"

"Yep, sweetie. I'm really, really sorry. I'll come get you the second I can."

"Does work need you again?"

That *again* felt worse than anything Olivia could dish out. "No," I said, leaning sideways so I could see Holly's face. "It's nothing to do with work. Work can take a long walk off a short pier, am I right?" That got a faint smile. "You know your auntie Jackie? She's got a big problem, and she needs me to sort it out for her right now."

"Can't I come with you?"

Both Jackie and Olivia have tried hinting, occasionally, that Holly should get to know her dad's family. Sinister suitcases aside, over my dead body does Holly dip a toe in the bubbling cauldron of crazy that is the Mackeys at their finest. "Not this time. Once I've fixed everything, we'll bring Auntie Jackie for an ice cream somewhere, will we? To cheer us all up?"

"Yeah," Holly said, on a tired little breath exactly like Olivia's. "That'd be fun," and she disentangled herself from my lap and started putting her stuff back into her schoolbag.

In the car Holly kept up a running conversation with Clara, in a subdued little voice too quiet for me to hear. At every red light I looked at her in the rearview mirror and swore to myself that I'd make it up to her: get hold of the Dalys' phone number, dump the damn suitcase on their doorstep and have Holly back at El Rancho Lyncho by bedtime. I already knew it wasn't going to work out that way. That road and that suitcase had been waiting for me to come back for a long time. Now that they'd got their hooks in, what they had saved up for me was going to take a lot more than one evening.

The note had the bare minimum of teen-queen melodrama; she was always good that way, was Rosie. *I know this is going to be a shock and I'm sorry but please don't be feeling like I messed you around on purpose, I never wanted to do that. Only I've thought about it really hard, this is the only way I'll ever have a decent chance at the kind of life I want. I just wish I could do it and not hurt you/upset you/disappoint you. It would be great if you could wish me luck in my new life in England!! but if you can't I understand.*

I swear I'll come back someday. Till then, loads and loads and loads of love, Rosie.

In between the moment when she left that note on the floor of Number 16, in the room where we had our first kiss, and the moment when she went to heave her suitcase over some wall and get the hell out of Dodge, something had happened.

2

You won't find Faithful Place unless you know where to look. The Liberties grew on their own over centuries, without any help from urban planners, and the Place is a cramped cul-de-sac tucked away in the middle like a wrong turn in a maze. It's a ten-minute walk from Trinity College and the snazzy shopping on Grafton Street, but back in my day, we didn't go to Trinity and the Trinity types didn't come up our way. The area wasn't dodgy, exactly—factory workers, bricklayers, bakers, dole bunnies, and the odd lucky bastard who worked in Guinness's and got health care and evening classes— just separate. The Liberties got their name, hundreds of years ago, because they went their own way and made their own rules. The rules in my road went like this: no matter how skint you are, if you go to the pub then you stand your round; if your mate gets into a fight, you stick around to drag him off as soon as you see blood, so no one loses face; you leave the heroin to them down in the flats; even if you're an anarchist punk rocker this month, you go to Mass on Sunday; and no matter what, you never, ever squeal on anyone.

I parked my car a few minutes away and walked; no reason to let my family know what I drove, or that I had a booster seat in the back. Night air in the Liberties still felt the same, warm and restless, crisp packets and bus tickets whirling in updrafts, a rowdy hum spilling out from the pubs. The junkies hanging on corners had started wearing bling with their tracksuits, for your truly suave fashion statement. Two of them eyed me up and started drifting my way, but I gave them a big shark smile and they changed their minds.

Faithful Place is two rows of eight houses, old redbricks with steps going up to the main hall door. Back in the eighties each one had three or four households, maybe more. A household was anything from Mad Johnny Malone, who had been in World War I and would show you his Ypres tattoo, through Sallie Hearne, who wasn't exactly a hooker but had to support all those kids somehow. If you were on the dole, you got a basement flat and a Vitamin D deficiency; if someone had a job, you got at least part of the first floor; if your family had been there a few generations, you got seniority and top-floor rooms where no one walked on your head.

Places are supposed to look smaller when you go back to them, but my road just looked schizoid. A couple of the houses had had nifty little makeovers involving double glazing and amusing faux-antique pastel paint; most of them hadn't. Number 16 looked like it was on its last legs: the roof was in tatters, there was a pile of bricks and a dead wheelbarrow by the front steps, and at some point in the last twenty years someone had set the door on fire. In Number 8, a window on the first floor was lit up, gold and cozy and dangerous as hell.

Carmel and Shay and I came along straight after my parents got married, one a year, just like you'd expect in the land of the contraband condom. Kevin was almost five years later, once my parents got their breath back, and Jackie was five years after that, presumably in one of the brief moments when they didn't hate each other's guts. We had the first floor of Number 8, four rooms: girls' room, boys' room, kitchen, front room—the toilet was in a shed down the back of the garden, and you washed in a tin bath in the kitchen. These days Ma and Da have all that space to themselves.

I see Jackie every few weeks and she keeps me up to speed, depending on your definition of the term. She feels I need to know every detail of everyone's life, while I feel I need to know if someone dies, so it took us a while to find that happy medium. When I walked back into Faithful Place, I knew that Carmel had four kids and an arse like the 77A bus, Shay was living upstairs from our parents and working in the same bike shop he left school for, Kevin was selling flat-screen TVs and had a new girlfriend every month, Da had done something unclear to his back, and Ma was still Ma. Jackie, to round out the picture, is a hairdresser and lives with this guy Gavin who she says she might marry someday. If she had been following orders, which I doubted, the others knew sweet fuck-all about me.

The hall door was unlocked, so was the flat door. No one leaves doors open in Dublin any more. Jackie, tactfully, had arranged things so I could make my entrance my own way. There were voices coming from the front room; short sentences, long pauses.

"Howyis," I said, in the doorway.

A ripple of cups going down, heads turning. My ma's snappy black eyes and five bright-blue pairs exactly like mine, all staring at me.

"Hide the heroin," Shay said. He was leaning against the window with his hands in his pockets; he'd watched me coming down the road. "It's the pigs."

The landlord had finally put in a carpet, a flowery green and pink thing. The room still smelled of toast, damp and furniture polish, with a faint dirty undercurrent I couldn't place. There was a tray full of doilies and digestive biscuits on the table. My da and Kevin were in the armchairs; my ma was on the sofa, with Carmel and Jackie on either side, like a war leader showing off two prize prisoners.

My ma is your classic Dublin mammy: five foot nothing of curler-haired, barrel-shaped don't-mess-with-this, fueled by an endless supply of disapproval. The prodigal son's welcome went like this:

"Francis," Ma said. She eased back into the sofa, folded her arms where her waist would have been and eyed me up and down. "Could you not be bothered putting on a decent shirt, even?"

I said, "Howya, Ma."

"Mammy, not Ma. The state of you. The neighbors'll think I raised a homeless."

Somewhere along the way I swapped the army parka for a brown leather jacket, but apart from that I still have much the same fashion sense I left home with. If I'd worn a suit, she would have given me hassle for having notions of myself. With my ma you don't expect to win. "Jackie sounded like it was urgent," I said. "Howya, Da."

Da was looking better than I'd expected. Back in the day, I was the one who took after him—same thick brown hair, same rough-edged features—but the resemblance had faded a lot along the way, which was nice. He was starting to turn into an old fella—white hair, trousers up above his ankles—but he still had enough muscle that you'd think twice before taking him on.

He looked stone cold sober, although with him you never could tell till it was too late. "Nice of you to honor us," he said. His voice was deeper and hoarser; too many Camels. "You've still got a neck like a jockey's bollix."

"So they keep telling me. Howya, Carmel. Kev. Shay."

Shay didn't bother to answer. "Francis," Kevin said. He was staring at me like I was a ghost. He'd turned into a big guy, fair and solid and good-looking; bigger than me. "Jaysus."

"Language," Ma snapped.

"You're looking very well," Carmel informed me, predictably. If the Risen Lord appeared to Carmel one morning, she'd tell him he was looking very well. Her arse was in fact pretty high-impact, and she had developed a genteel meet-my-sinuses accent that didn't surprise me one bit. Things around here were more like they used to be than they ever had been. "Thanks very much," I said. "So are you."

"Come here, you," Jackie said to me. Jackie has complicated peroxide hair and she dresses like something out of a Tom Waits diner; that day she was wearing white pedal pushers and a red polka-dot top with ruffles in bewildering places. "Sit down there and have a cup of tea. I'll get another cup." She got up and headed for the kitchen, giving me an encouraging little wink and a pinch on her way.

"I'm grand," I said, stopping her. The thought of sitting next to Ma made the hair go up on the back of my neck. "Let's have a look at this famous suitcase."

"Where's your rush?" Ma demanded. "Sit down there."

"Business before pleasure. Where's the case?"

Shay nodded to the floor at his feet. "All yours," he said. Jackie sat down again with a thump. I picked my way around the coffee table and the sofa and the chairs, under all those eyes.

The suitcase was by the window. It was a pale-blue thing with rounded corners, spotted over with big patches of black mold, and it was a crack open; someone had forced the pathetic tin locks. What got to me was how small it was. Olivia used to pack just about everything we owned, including the electric kettle, for a weekend away. Rosie had been heading for a whole new life with something she could carry one-handed.

I asked, "Who's touched this?"

Shay laughed, a hard sound at the back of his throat. "Jaysus, lads, it's Columbo. Are you going to take our fingerprints?"

Shay is dark and wiry and restless, and I'd forgotten what it was like, getting too near him. It's like standing next to a power line; it makes you edgy all over. He had sharp fierce grooves going from nose to mouth, these days, and between his eyebrows. "Only if you ask me nicely," I said. "Did you all touch it?"

"I wouldn't go near it," Carmel said promptly, doing a little shudder. "The dirt of it." I caught Kevin's eye. For a second it was like I'd never been away.

"Me and your da tried opening it," Ma said, "only it was locked, so I called Shay down and I got him to take a screwdriver to it. We'd no choice, sure; there was nothing on the outside to tell us who owned it."

She gave me a belligerent look. "Dead right," I said.

"When we saw what was in it . . . I'm telling you, I got the shock of my life. The heart was leaping out of me; I thought I was having a heart attack. I said to Carmel, thank God you're here with the car, in case you've to bring me to the hospital." The look in Ma's eye said this would have been my fault, even if she hadn't figured out how yet.

Carmel told me, "Trevor doesn't mind giving the children their tea, not when it's an emergency. He's great that way."

"Me and Kevin both had a look inside once we got here," Jackie said. "We touched bits, I don't remember what ones—"

"Got your fingerprint powder?" Shay inquired. He was slouching against the window frame and watching me, eyes half closed.

"Some other day, if you're a good boy." I found my surgical gloves in my jacket pocket and put them on. Da started to laugh, a deep, nasty rasp; it collapsed into a helpless coughing fit that shook his whole chair.

Shay's screwdriver was on the floor beside the suitcase. I knelt down and used it to lift the lid. Two of the boys in the Tech Bureau owed me favors, and a couple of the lovely ladies fancied me; any of them would run a few tests for me on the QT, but they would appreciate me not fucking up the evidence any more than I had to.

The case was stuffed with a heavy tangle of fabric, stained black and half-shredded with mold and age. A dark, strong smell, like wet earth, came up off it. That undercurrent I'd caught in the air, when I first came in.

I lifted things out slowly, one by one, and stacked them in the lid where they wouldn't get contaminated. One pair of baggy blue jeans, with plaid patches sewn under the rips in the knees. One green woolen pullover. One pair of blue jeans so tight they had zips at the ankles, and Jesus Almighty I knew them, the swing of Rosie's hips in them punched me right in the gut. I kept moving and didn't blink. One man's collarless flannel shirt, fine blue stripes on what used to be cream. Six pairs of white cotton knickers. One long-tailed purple and blue paisley shirt, falling to pieces, and when I picked it up the birth cert fell out.

"There," Jackie said. She was leaning over the arm of the sofa, peering anxiously at me. "See? Up until then, we thought it might've been nothing, I don't know, kids messing or someone who'd robbed some gear and needed to hide it, or maybe some poor woman whose fella was hurting her and she was keeping her things ready for when she got the courage to leave him, you know how they tell you to do in the magazines?" She was starting to rev up again.

Rose Bernadette Daly, born 30 July 1966. The paper was on the verge of disintegrating. "Yep," I said. "If that's kids messing, they're pretty thorough about it."

One U2 T-shirt, probably worth hundreds, if it hadn't been pockmarked with rot. One blue-and-white-striped T-shirt. One man's black waistcoat; the Annie Hall look was in then. One purple woolen pullover. One pale-blue plastic rosary. Two white cotton bras. One off-brand Walkman that I spent months saving for; I got the last two quid a week before her eighteenth birthday, by helping Beaker Murray sell bootleg videos down at the Iveagh Market. One spray can of Sure deodorant. A dozen home-taped cassettes, and I could still read her round handwriting on some of the inserts: REM, *Murmur*; U2, *Boy*; Thin Lizzy, the Boomtown Rats, the Stranglers, Nick Cave and the Bad Seeds. Rosie could leave everything else behind, but her record collection was coming with her.

At the bottom of the case was a brown envelope. The bits of paper inside had been mashed into a solid lump by twenty-two years' worth of damp; when I pulled delicately at the edge, it came apart like wet jacks roll. One more favor for the Bureau. A few blurred words of type still showed through the plastic window in the front of the envelope.

. . . *LAOGHAIRE–HOLYHEAD* . . . *DEPARTING* . . . *:30AM* . . . Wherever Rosie had gone, she had got there without our ferry tickets.

Everyone was staring at me. Kevin looked genuinely upset. "Well," I said. "That appears to be Rosie Daly's suitcase, all right." I started to transfer stuff from the lid back into the case, leaving the papers till last so they wouldn't get crushed.

"Will we call the Guards?" Carmel asked. Da cleared his throat, spectacularly, like he was going to spit; Ma shot him a ferocious look.

I asked, "And say what?"

Clearly no one had thought about this. "Someone stuck a suitcase behind a fireplace, twenty-odd years ago," I said. "It's hardly the crime of the century. The Dalys can ring the Guards if they want, but I'm warning you now, I wouldn't expect them to bring out the big guns for the Case of the Blocked Chimney."

"But Rosie, sure," Jackie said. She was tugging at a piece of hair and gazing at me, all bunny-teeth and big worried blue eyes. "She's missing. And that yoke there, that's a clue, or evidence, or whatever you call it. Should we not . . . ?"

"Was she reported missing?"

Glances back and forth: nobody knew. I seriously doubted it. In the Liberties, cops are like the jellyfish in Pacman: they're part of the game, you get good at avoiding them, and you definitely don't go looking for them. "If she wasn't," I said, shutting the case with my fingertips, "it's a little late now."

"But," Jackie said. "Hang on. Does this not look like . . . ? You know. Like she didn't go off to England after all. Does it not seem like maybe someone might have . . . ?"

"What Jackie's trying to say here," Shay told me, "is it looks like someone knocked Rosie off, shoved her in a bin liner, hauled her round to the piggeries, dumped her in, and put that case up a fireplace to get it out of the way."

"Seamus Mackey! God bless us!" from Ma. Carmel crossed herself.

This possibility had already occurred to me. "Could be," I said, "sure. Or she could have been abducted by aliens and dropped off in Kentucky by mistake. Personally, I'd go for the simplest explanation, which is that she stuck that case up the chimney herself, didn't get a chance to take it back out, and headed over to England without a change of undies. But if you need a little extra drama in your life, feel free."

"Right," said Shay. There are plenty of things wrong with Shay, but stupid isn't one of them. "And that's why you need that shite"—the gloves, which I was stuffing back into my jacket. "Because you don't think there's any crime here."

"Reflex," I said, grinning at him. "A pig is a pig twenty-four seven, know what I mean?" Shay made a disgusted noise.

Ma said, with a nice blend of awe, envy and blood lust, "Theresa Daly'll go mental. Mental."

For a wide variety of reasons, I needed to get to the Dalys before anyone else did. "I'll have a chat with her and Mr. Daly, see what they want to do. What time do they get home, Saturdays?"

Shay shrugged. "Depends. Sometimes not till after lunch, sometimes first thing in the morning. Whenever Nora can drop them back."

This was a pisser. I could tell by the look of Ma that she was already planning to pounce on them before they got their key in the door. I considered sleeping in my car and cutting her off at the pass, but there was no parking within surveillance range. Shay was watching me and enjoying himself.

Then Ma hitched up her bosom and said, "You can stay the night here, Francis, if you like. The sofa still pulls out."

I didn't assume this was a reunion burst of the warm and fuzzies. My ma likes you to owe her. This is never a good idea, but I couldn't come up with a better one. She added, "Unless you're too posh for that nowadays," in case I thought she was going soft.

"Not at all," I said, giving Shay a big toothy grin. "That'd be great. Thanks, Ma."

"Mammy, not Ma. I suppose you'll be wanting breakfast and all."

"Can I stay as well?" Kevin asked, out of the blue.

Ma gave him a suspicious stare. He looked as startled as I was. "I can't stop you," she said, in the end. "Don't be wrecking my good sheets," and she hoisted herself up off the sofa and started collecting teacups.

Shay laughed, not nicely. "Peace on Walton's Mountain," he said, nudging the suitcase with the toe of his boot. "Just in time for Christmas."

Ma doesn't allow smoking in the house. Shay and Jackie and I took our habit outside; Kevin and Carmel drifted after us. We sat on the front steps, the way we used to when we were kids sucking ice pops after tea and waiting for something interesting to happen. It took me a little while to realize that I was still waiting for the action—kids with a football, a couple yelling, a woman hurrying across the road to swap gossip for tea bags, anything—and that it wasn't coming. In Number 11 a couple of hairy students were cooking something and playing Keane, not even that loudly, and in Number 7 Sallie Hearne was ironing and someone was watching TV. This was apparently as active as the Place got, these days.

We'd gravitated straight to our old spots: Shay and Carmel at opposite ends of the top step, Kevin and me below them, Jackie at the bottom between us. We had personal arse-prints worn in those steps. "Jaysus, it's warm, all the same," Carmel said. "It's not like December at all, sure it's not? Feels all wrong."

"Global warming," Kevin said. "Someone give us a smoke?"

Jackie handed up her packet. "Don't be starting on them. Filthy habit."

"Only on special occasions."

I flicked my lighter and he leaned across to me. The flame sent the shadows of his lashes down his cheeks so that for a second there he looked like a kid asleep, rosy and innocent. Kevin worshipped me, back in the day; followed me everywhere. I gave Zippy Hearne a bloody nose because he took Kevin's Jelly Tots off him. Now he smelled of aftershave.

"Sallie," I said, nodding up at her. "How many kids did she have in the end?"

Jackie reached a hand over her shoulder to take her smokes back off Kevin. "Fourteen. Me fanny's sore just thinking about it." I snickered, caught Kevin's eye and got a grin off him.

After a moment Carmel said, to me, "I've four of my own now. Darren and Louise and Donna and Ashley."

"Jackie told me. Fair play to you. Who do they look like?"

"Louise is like me, God help her. Darren's like his daddy."

"Donna's the spit of Jackie," Kevin said. "Buckteeth and all."

Jackie hit him. "Shut up, you."

"They must be getting big now," I said.

"Ah, they are, yeah. Darren's doing his Leaving Cert this year. He wants to do engineering at UCD, if you don't mind."

No one asked about Holly. Maybe I'd been underrating Jackie; maybe she did know how to keep her mouth shut. "Here," Carmel said, rummaging in her bag. She found her mobile phone, fiddled with it and held it out to me. "D'you want to see them?"

I flipped through the photos. Four plain, freckly kids; Trevor, the same as always, except for the hairline; a pebble-dashed seventies semi-d in I couldn't remember which depressing sub-suburb. Carmel was exactly what she'd always dreamed of being. Very few people ever get to say that. Fair play to her, even if her dream did make me want to slit my throat.

"They look like great kids," I said, handing the phone back. "Congrats, Melly."

A tiny catch of breath, above me. "Melly. God . . . Haven't heard that in years."

In that light they looked like themselves again. It erased the wrinkles and the gray streaks, fined the heaviness off Kevin's jaw and wiped the makeup off Jackie, till it was the five of us, fresh and cat-eyed and restless in the dark, spinning our different dreams. If Sallie Hearne looked out her window she'd see us: the Mackey kids, sitting on their steps. For one lunatic second I was glad to be there.

"Ow," Carmel said, shifting. Carmel was never good with silence. "Me arse is killing me. Are you sure that's what happened, Francis, what you said inside? About Rosie meaning to come back for that case?"

A low hiss that might have been a laugh, as Shay sent out smoke through his teeth. "It's a load of shite. He knows that as well as I do."

Carmel smacked his knee. "Language, you." Shay didn't move. "What are you on about? Why would it be a load of shite?" He shrugged.

"I'm not sure about anything," I said. "But yeah, I think there's a good chance she's over in England living happily ever after."

Shay said, "With no ticket and no ID?"

"She had money saved up. If she couldn't get hold of her ticket, she could've bought another one. And you didn't need ID to go to England, back then." All of which was true enough. We were bringing our birth certs along because we knew we might need to sign on the dole while we looked for work, and because we were going to get married.

Jackie asked quietly, "Was I right to ring you, all the same? Or should I have just . . . ?"

The air tightened up. "Left well enough alone," Shay said.

"No," I said. "You were dead right all the way, babe. Your instincts are diamond, you know that?"

Jackie stretched out her legs and examined her high heels. I could only see the back of her head. "Maybe," she said.

We sat and smoked for a while. The smell of malt and burnt hops was gone; Guinness's did something eco-correct back in the nineties, so now the Liberties smell of diesel fumes, which apparently is an improvement. Moths were looping the loop around the street lamp at the end of the road. Someone had taken down the rope that used to be tied to the top of it, for kids to swing on.

There was one thing I wanted to know. "Da looks all right," I said.

Silence. Kevin shrugged.

"His back's not great," Carmel said. "Did Jackie . . . ?"

"She told me he's got problems. He's better than I expected to find him."

She sighed. "He gets good days and bad days, sure. Today's a good day; he's grand. On bad days . . ."

Shay drew on his smoke; he still held it between thumb and finger, like an old-movie gangster. He said flatly, "On bad days I've to carry him to the Jacks."

I asked, "Do they know what's wrong?"

"Nah. Maybe something he did on the job, maybe . . . They can't work it out. Either way, it's getting worse."

"Is he off the drink?"

Shay said, "What's that got to do with you?"

I said, "Is Da off the drink?"

Carmel moved. "Ah, he's all right."

Shay laughed, a sharp bark.

"Is he treating Ma OK?"

Shay said, "That's none of your fucking business."

The other three held their breath and waited to see if we were going to go for each other. When I was twelve Shay split my head open on those same steps; I still have the scar. Not long afterwards, I got bigger than him. He's got scars too.

I turned round, taking my time, to face him. "I'm asking you a civil question," I said.

"That you haven't bothered asking in twenty years."

"He's asked me," Jackie said, quietly. "Loads of times."

"So? You don't live here either, any more. You've no more of a clue than he has."

"That's why I'm asking you now," I said. "Does Da treat Ma all right these days?"

We stared each other out of it, in the half dark. I got ready to throw my smoke away fast.

"If I say no," Shay said, "are you going to leave your fancy bachelor pad and move in here to look after her?"

"Downstairs from you? Ah, Shay. D'you miss me that much?"

A window shot up, above us, and Ma shouted down, "Francis! Kevin! Are yous coming in or not?"

"In a minute!" we all yelled back. Jackie laughed, a high, frantic little sound: "Listen to us . . ."

Ma slammed the window down. After a second Shay eased back and spat through the railings. The moment his eyes moved off me, everyone relaxed.

"I've to go anyway," Carmel said. "Ashley likes to have her mammy there when she goes to bed. She won't go for Trevor; gives him terrible hassle. She thinks it's funny."

Kevin asked, "How are you getting home?"

"I've the Kia parked round the corner. The Kia's mine," she explained, to me. "Trevor has the Range Rover."

Trevor always was a depressing little fucker. It was nice to know he'd turned out according to spec. "That's lovely," I said.

"Give us a lift?" Jackie asked. "I came straight from work, and today was Gav's turn for the car."

Carmel tucked in her chin and clicked her tongue disapprovingly. "Will he not pick you up?"

"Not at all. The car's at home by now, and he's in the pub with the lads."

Carmel hauled herself up by the railing and tugged her skirt down primly. "I'll drop you home, so. Tell that Gavin, if he's going to let you work, he could at least buy you a car of your own to get you there. What are yous lot laughing at?"

"Women's lib is alive and well," I said.

"I never had any use for that carry-on. I like a good sturdy bra. You, missus, stop laughing and come on before I leave you here with this shower."

"I'm coming, hang on—" Jackie stuffed her smokes back into her bag, threw the strap over her shoulder. "I'll call round tomorrow. Will I see you then, Francis?"

"You never know your luck. Otherwise we'll talk."

She reached up a hand and caught mine, squeezed it tight. "I'm glad I rang you, anyway," she said, in a defiant, semiprivate undertone. "And I'm glad you came down. You're a gem, so you are. Look after yourself. All right?"

"You're a good girl yourself. Seeya, Jackie."

Carmel said, hovering, "Francis, will we . . . ? Are you going to call round again, like? Now that . . ."

"Let's get this thing over with," I said, smiling up at her. "Then we'll see where we are, yeah?"

Carmel picked her way down the steps and the three of us watched them head up the Place, the taps of Jackie's spike heels echoing off the houses, Carmel clumping along next to her, trying to keep up. Jackie is a lot taller than Carmel, even before you add hair and heels, but on the other hand Carmel has her beat several times over on circumference. The mismatch made them look like some goofy cartoon team, off to have painful comic accidents till they finally caught the villain and saved the day.

"They're sound women," I said quietly.

"Yeah," Kevin said. "They are."

Shay said, "If you want to do those two a favor, you won't call round again."

I figured he was probably right, but I ignored him anyway. Ma did her window number again: "Francis! Kevin! I've to lock this door. Yous can come in now, or yous can sleep where yous are."

"Go in," Shay said. "Before she has the whole road awake."

Kevin got up, stretching and cracking his neck. "Are you coming?"

"Nah," Shay said. "Having another smoke." When I shut the hall door, he was still sitting on the steps with his back to us, snapping his lighter and watching the flame.

Ma had dumped a duvet, two pillows and a bunch of sheets on the sofa and gone to bed, to make a point about us dawdling outside. She and Da had moved into our old room; the girls' room had been turned into a bathroom, in the eighties, judging by the attractive avocado-green fixtures. While Kevin was splashing around in there, I went out onto the landing—Ma hears like a bat—and rang Olivia.

It was well after eleven. "She's asleep," Olivia said. "And very disappointed."

"I know. I just wanted to say thanks again, and sorry again. Did I completely wreck your date?"

"Yes. What did you think would happen? The Coterie would bring out an extra chair and Holly could discuss the Booker Prize list with us over salmon *en croute?*"

"I've got some stuff to do around here tomorrow, but I'll try and pick her up before dinnertime. Maybe you and Dermot can reschedule."

She sighed. "What's going on there? Is everyone OK?"

"I'm not sure yet," I said. "I'm still trying to figure it out. Tomorrow I should have a better idea."

A silence. I thought Liv was pissed off with me for being cagey, but then she said, "What about you, Frank? Are you all right?"

Her voice had softened. In all the world, the last thing I needed that night was Olivia being nice to me. It rippled my bones like water, soothing and treacherous. "Never better," I said. "Gotta go. Give Holly a kiss from me in the morning. I'll ring you tomorrow."

Kevin and I made up the sofa bed and arranged ourselves head to foot, so we could feel like two party animals crashing out after a wild night instead of two little kids sharing a mattress. We lay there, in the faint patterns of light coming through the lace curtains, listening to each other breathe. In the corner, Ma's Sacred Heart statue glowed lurid red. I pictured the look on Olivia's face if she ever saw that statue.

"It's good to see you," Kevin said quietly, after a while. "You know that?"

His face was in shadows; all I could see was his hands on the duvet, one thumb rubbing absently at a knuckle. "You too," I said. "You're looking good. I can't believe you're bigger than me."

A sniff of a laugh. "Still wouldn't want to take you on."

I laughed too. "Dead right. I'm an expert at unarmed combat, these days."

"Seriously?"

"Nah. I'm an expert at paperwork and getting myself out of trouble."

Kevin rolled onto his side, so he could see me, and tucked an arm under his head. "Can I ask you something? Why the Guards?"

Cops like me are the reason why you never get posted where you're from. If you want to get technical, everyone I grew up with was probably a petty criminal, one way or another, not out of badness but because that was how people got by. Half the Place was on the dole and all of them did nixers, specially when the beginning of the school year was coming up and the kids needed books and uniforms. When Kevin and Jackie had bronchitis one winter, Carmel brought home meat from the Dunne's where she worked, to build up their strength; no one ever asked how she paid for it. By the time I was seven, I knew how to fiddle the gas meter so my ma could cook dinner. Your average career counselor would not have pegged me for an officer in the making. "It sounded exciting," I said. "Simple as that. Getting paid for the chance of some action; what's not to like?"

"Is it? Exciting?"

"Sometimes."

Kevin watched me, waiting. "Da threw a freaker," he said eventually. "When Jackie told us."

My da started out as a plasterer, but by the time we came along he was a full-time drinker with a part-time sideline in things that had fallen off the backs of lorries. I think he would have preferred me to be a rent boy. "Yeah, well," I said. "That's just icing. Now you tell me something. What happened the day after I left?"

Kevin rolled over onto his back and folded his arms behind his head. "Did you never ask Jackie?"

"Jackie was nine. She's not sure what she remembers and what she imagined. She says a doctor in a white coat took Mrs. Daly away, stuff like that."

"No doctors," Kevin said. "Not that I saw, anyway."

He was staring up at the ceiling. The lamplight through the window made his eyes glitter like dark water. "I remember Rosie," he said. "I know I was only a kid, but . . . Like, really strongly, you know? That hair and that laugh, and the way she walked . . . She was lovely, Rosie was."

I said, "She was that." Dublin was brown and gray and beige all over, back then, and Rosie was a dozen bright colors: an explosion of copper curls right down to her waist, eyes like chips of green glass held up to the light, red mouth and white skin and gold freckles. Half the Liberties fancied Rosie Daly, and what made her even more fanciable was that she didn't give a damn; none of it made her think she was anything special. She had curves that could give you vertigo, and she wore them as casually as she wore her patched jeans.

Let me show you Rosie, back when the nuns had convinced girls half as pretty that their bodies were a cross between cesspools and bank vaults and that boys were filthy little burglars. One summer evening when we were about twelve, before we ever copped that we were in love with each other, the two of us played I'll-show-you-mine. The closest I'd ever got to seeing a naked woman before was black-and-white cleavage, and then Rosie tossed her clothes in a corner like they were just getting in her way and spun around in the dim light of Number 16, palms up, luminous, laughing, almost close enough to touch. The thought still knocks the wind out of me. I was too young even to know what I wanted to do about her; I just knew nothing in the world, not the Mona Lisa walking through the Grand Canyon with the Holy Grail in one hand and a winning Lotto ticket in the other, was ever going to be that beautiful.

Kevin said quietly, to the ceiling, "We didn't even think anything was up, at first. Shay and I noticed you weren't there when we woke up—obviously, like—but we just thought you'd gone out somewhere. Only then we were having breakfast and Mrs. Daly came roaring in, looking for you. When we said you weren't there, she practically had a bleeding coronary—Rosie's stuff was all gone, and Mrs. Daly was screaming that you'd run off with her, or kidnapped her, I don't know what she was on about. Da started roaring back at her, and Ma was trying to make the both of them shut up before the neighbors heard—"

"Good luck with that," I said. Mrs. Daly's form of crazy is different from my ma's, but at least as loud.

"Yeah, I know, right? And we could hear someone else yelling across the way, so me and Jackie had a look out. Mr. Daly was chucking the rest of Rosie's gear out the window, and the whole street was coming out to see what was up . . . I've got to be honest with you, I thought it was bleeding hilarious."

He was grinning. I couldn't help grinning too. "I'd have paid good money to watch that."

"Oh, yeah. It almost turned into a catfight. Mrs. Daly called you a little gouger and Ma called Rosie a little slapper, like mother like daughter. Mrs. Daly went through the roof."

"See, now, my money'd be on Ma. The weight advantage."

"Don't let her hear you say that."

"She could just sit on Mrs. Daly till she surrendered."

We were laughing, under our breath in the dark, like two kids. "Mrs. Daly was armed, though," Kevin said. "Those fingernails—"

"Fuck me. Has she still got those?"

"Longer. She's a human—what do you call those?"

"Garden rake?"

"No! The ninja yokes. Throwing stars."

"So who won?"

"Ma, give or take. She shoved Mrs. Daly out onto the landing and slammed the door. Mrs. Daly yelled and kicked the door and all, but in the end she gave up. She went and had a row with Mr. Daly about Rosie's stuff, instead. People were practically selling tickets. Better than *Dallas*."

In our old bedroom, Da went into a coughing fit that made the bed rattle off the wall. We froze and listened. He got his breath back in long wheezes.

"Anyway," Kevin said, lower. "That was sort of the end of it. It was major gossip for like two weeks, and then everyone forgot about it, more or less. Ma and Mrs. Daly didn't talk for a few years—Da and Mr. Daly never did anyway, sure, so no big change there. Ma gave out shite every Christmas when you didn't send a card, but . . ."

But it was the eighties and emigration was one of your three main career paths, along with Daddy's firm and the dole. Ma had to have been expecting at least one of us to end up with a one-way ferry ticket. "She didn't think I was dead in a ditch?"

Kevin snorted. "Nah. She said whoever got hurt, it wouldn't be our Francis. We didn't call the cops or report you missing or anything, but that wasn't . . . Not that we didn't care, like. We just figured . . ." The mattress moved as he shrugged.

"That Rosie and I had run off together."

"Yeah. I mean, everyone knew the two of yous had been mad into each other, right? And everyone knew what Mr. Daly thought about that. So why not, you know what I mean?"

"Yeah," I said. "Why not."

"Plus, there was the note. I think that was what blew Mrs. Daly's fuse: someone was messing about in Number Sixteen and they found this note. From Rosie, like. I don't know if Jackie told you—"

"I read it," I said.

Kevin's head turned towards me. "Yeah? You saw it?"

"Yeah."

He waited; I didn't elaborate. "When did . . . ? You mean before she left it there? She showed it to you?"

"After. Late that night."

"So—what? She left it for you? Not for her family?"

"That's what I thought. We were meant to meet up that night, she didn't show, I found the note. I reckoned it had to be for me."

When I finally figured out that she meant it, that she wasn't coming because she was already gone, I put on my rucksack and started walking. Monday morning, coming up to dawn; town was frosty and deserted, just me and a street sweeper and a few tired night-shift workers heading home in the icy half-light. Trinity clock said the first ferry was leaving Dun Laoghaire.

I ended up in a squat, off Baggot Street, where a bunch of smelly rockers lived with a wall-eyed mutt named Keith Moon and an impressive amount of hash. I sort of knew them from gigs; they all figured another one had invited me to stay for a while. One of them had a nonsmelly sister who lived in a flat in Ranelagh and would let you use her address for the dole if she liked you, and it turned out she liked me a lot. By the time I put her address on my application to cop college, it was practically true. It was a relief when I got accepted and had to go off to Templemore for training. She had started making noises about marriage.

That bitch Rosie, see; I believed her, every word. Rosie never played games; she just opened her mouth and told you, straight out, even if it hurt. It was one of the reasons I loved her. After life with a family like mine, someone who didn't do intrigue was the most intriguing thing of all. So when she said *I swear I'll come back someday,* I believed her for twenty-two years. All the time I was sleeping with the smelly rocker's sister, all the time I was going out with feisty, pretty, temporary girls who deserved better, all the time I was married to Olivia and pretending to belong in Dalkey, I was waiting for Rosie Daly to walk through every door.

"And now?" Kevin asked. "After today. What do you reckon now?"

"Don't ask me," I said. "At this point, I honestly don't have a clue what was going on in Rosie's head."

He said quietly, "Shay thinks she's dead, you know. So does Jackie."

"Yeah," I said. "Apparently they do."

I heard Kevin take a breath, like he was gearing up to say something. After a moment he let it out again.

I said, "What?"

He shook his head.

"What, Kev?"

"Nothing."

I waited.

"Just . . . Ah, I don't know." He moved, restlessly, on the bed. "Shay took it hard, you leaving."

"Because we were such great pals, you mean?"

"I know yous fought all the time. But underneath . . . I mean, you're still brothers, you know?"

Not only was this obvious bullshit—my first memory is of waking up with Shay trying to jam a pencil through my eardrum—but it was obviously bullshit that Kevin was making up to distract me from whatever he had been going to say. I almost pushed it; I still wonder what would have happened if I had. Before I got there, the hall door clicked shut, a faint, deliberate sound: Shay coming in.

Kevin and I lay still and listened. Soft steps, pausing for a second on the landing outside, then moving on up the next flight of stairs; click of another door; floorboards creaking above us.

I said, "Kev."

Kevin pretended to be asleep. After a while his mouth fell open and he started making little huffing sounds.

It was a long time before Shay stopped moving softly around his flat. When the house went silent I gave it fifteen minutes, sat up carefully—Jesus, glowing away in the corner, gave me a stare that said he knew my type—and had a look out the window. It had started to rain. All the lights in Faithful Place were out except one, throwing wet yellow streaks on the cobblestones from above my head.

3

I have a camel-type approach to sleep: I stock up when I get the chance, but I can go without for a long time if something else needs doing. I spent that night staring at the dark lump of the suitcase under the window, listening to Da snore and getting my head in order, ready for the next day.

The possibilities were tangled up like spaghetti, but two stuck out. One was the line I'd fed my family, a minor variation on the same old theme. Rosie had decided to fly solo, so she stashed the suitcase early, for a quick getaway with less chance of being snared by her family or by me; when she went back to pick it up and drop off the note, she had to go through the back gardens, because I was watching the road. Hoisting the suitcase over walls would have made too much noise, so she left it where she'd hidden it and headed off—the rustles and thumps I'd heard, moving down the gardens—to her shiny new life.

It almost worked. It explained everything except one thing: the ferry tickets. Even if Rosie had been planning to skip the dawn ferry and lie low for a day or two, in case I showed up at the harbor in full Stanley Kowalski mode, she would have tried to do something with her ticket: swap it, sell it. Those things had cost us the best part of a week's wages each. There was no way in hell she would have left them to rot behind a fireplace, unless she had no choice.

The other main possibility was the one that Shay and Jackie, on their different levels of charm, had gone for. Someone had intercepted Rosie, either on her way to Theory One or on her way to meet me.

I had a truce with Theory One. Over more than half my life it had worn itself a nice little corner in my mind, like a bullet lodged too deep to dig out; I didn't feel the sharp edges, mostly, as long as I didn't touch. Theory Two blew my mind wide open.

It was Saturday evening, just over a day before Zero Hour, the last time I saw Rosie Daly. I was heading out to work. I had this mate called Wiggy who was the night guard in a car park, and he had this mate called Stevo who was a bouncer in a nightclub; when Stevo wanted a night off, Wiggy did his job, I did Wiggy's, everyone got paid in cash and everyone went away happy.

Rosie was leaning on the railings of Number 4 with Imelda Tierney and Mandy Cullen, in a sweet giggly bubble of flowery smells and big hair and glittery lip gloss, waiting for Julie Nolan to come down. It was a cold evening, fog blurring the air; Rosie had her hands pulled up into her sleeves and was blowing on them, Imelda was jigging up and down to keep warm. Three little kids were swinging off the lamppost at the top of the road, "Tainted Love" was blaring out of Julie's window and the air had that Saturday-night charge, a fizzle and musk like cider, tantalizing. "There's Francis Mackey," Mandy said to the air, nudging the other two in the ribs. "The hair on him. He thinks he's only gorgeous, doesn't he?"

"Howyis, girls," I said, grinning at them.

Mandy was little and dark, with a puff of fringe and a lot of stone-washed denim. She ignored me. "If he was ice cream he'd lick himself to death," she told the others.

"I'd rather someone else did it for me," I said, wiggling my eyebrows. The three of them screamed.

"Come here, Frankie," Imelda called, flipping her perm. "Mandy wants to know—"

Mandy shrieked and dived to clap a hand over Imelda's mouth. Imelda ducked away. "Mandy said to ask you—"

"Shut up, you!"

Rosie was laughing. Imelda caught Mandy's hands and held them away. "She said to ask if your brother fancies going to the pictures and not watching the film."

She and Rosie dissolved into giggles. Mandy clapped her hands over her face. "Imelda, you wagon! I'm scarlet!"

"So you should be," I told her. "Cradle robbing. He's only started shaving, do you know that?"

Rosie was doubled over. "Not him! Not Kevin!"

"She means Shay!" Imelda gasped. "Would Shay fancy going to the—" She was laughing too hard to finish. Mandy squeaked and dived back behind her hands.

"I doubt it," I said, shaking my head ruefully. The Mackey men have never had any trouble with the ladies, but Shay was in a class of his own. By the time I was old enough for action I took it for granted, from watching him, that if you wanted a girl she came running. Rosie once said Shay only had to look at a girl and her bra snapped open. "I think our Shay might be more into the fellas, you know what I mean?"

The three of them screamed again. God but I love gangs of girls on their way out, rainbow-colored and perfect as wrapped presents; all you want to do is squeeze them and see if one of them is for you. Knowing for sure that the best one was all mine made me feel like I was Steve McQueen, like if I had a motorbike I could sweep Rosie up behind me and leap it straight over the rooftops. Mandy called, "I'm telling Shay you said that!"

Rosie caught my eye, a tiny secret glance: by the time Mandy told Shay anything, the two of us would be a sea's width out of reach. "Feel free," I said. "Just don't tell my ma. We'll need to break it to her gently."

"Mandy'll convert him, won't you?"

"I swear, 'Melda—"

The door of Number 3 opened and Mr. Daly came out. He hitched up his trousers, folded his arms and leaned against the door frame.

I said, "Evening, Mr. Daly." He ignored me.

Mandy and Imelda straightened up and looked sideways at Rosie. Rosie said, "We're waiting for Julie."

"That's grand," Mr. Daly said. "I'll wait with yous, so." He pulled a squashed cigarette out of his shirt pocket and started carefully smoothing it into shape. Mandy picked a bit of fluff off her jumper and examined it; Imelda pulled her skirt straight.

That night even Mr. Daly made me happy, and not just the thought of his face when he woke up Monday morning. I said, "You're looking very well dressed tonight, Mr. Daly. Are you off out to the discos yourself?"

A muscle flickered in his jaw, but he kept watching the girls. "Bleedin'
Hitler," Rosie said, under her breath, shoving her hands into the pockets of
her jeans jacket.

Imelda said, "We'll go see what's keeping Julie, will we?"

Rosie shrugged. "Might as well."

"Bye-bye, Frankie," Mandy said, giving me a cheeky dimpled grin. "Say
howya to Shay from me, now."

As Rosie turned to go, one eyelid drooped and her lips pursed, just a
fraction: a wink and a kiss. Then she ran up the steps of Number 4 and
vanished, into the dark hallway and out of my life.

I spent hundreds of nights lying awake in a sleeping bag, surrounded by
smelly rockers and Keith Moon, picking those last five minutes to shreds looking for a hint. I thought I was losing my fucking mind: there had to have been
something there, had to, but I would have sworn on every saint in the calen-
dar that I'd missed nothing. And all of a sudden it looked like I might not have
been off my nut after all, might not have been the world's most gullible all-day
sucker; I might have been just plain right. There's such a fine line.

There had been nothing in that note, not one thing, that said it was
meant for me. I had taken it for granted; I was the one she was ditching,
after all. But our original plan had involved ditching a lot of other people,
that night. The note could have been for her family, for her girls, for the
whole of Faithful Place.

In our old room Da made a noise like a water buffalo being strangled;
Kevin muttered in his sleep and rolled over, flinging out an arm and whacking me in the ankles. The rain had turned even and heavy, settled in.

Like I said, I do my best to stay one step ahead of the sucker punch. For
the rest of the weekend, at least, I had to work off the assumption that
Rosie had never made it out of the Place alive.

In the morning, as soon as I had convinced the Dalys that they wanted
to leave the suitcase in my capable hands and that they didn't want to call
the Guards, I needed to talk to Imelda and Mandy and Julie.

Ma got up around seven; I heard the bedsprings creaking, through the rain,
as she stood up. On her way to the kitchen she stopped in the doorway of

the front room for a long minute, looking down at me and Kevin, thinking God only knows what. I kept my eyes shut. Eventually she sniffed, a wry little noise, and kept moving.

Breakfast was the full whammy: eggs, rashers, sausages, black pudding, fried bread, fried tomatoes. This was clearly some kind of statement, but I couldn't work out whether it was *See, we're doing just grand without you*, or *I'm still slaving my fingers to the bone for you even though you don't deserve it*, or possibly *We'll be even when this lot gives you a heart attack*. No one mentioned the suitcase; apparently we were playing happy family breakfast, which was fine with me. Kevin shoveled down everything in reach and sneaked glances at me across the table, like a kid checking out a stranger; Da ate in silence, except for the occasional grunt when he wanted a refill. I kept one eye on the window and went to work on Ma.

Direct questions would just get me the guilt trip: *All of a sudden you want to know about the Nolans, you didn't care what happened to any of us for twenty-two years*, rinse and repeat. The way into my ma's info bank is by the disapproval route. I'd noticed, the night before, that Number 5 was painted a particularly darling shade of baby-pink that had to have caused a conniption or two. "Number Five's been done up nicely," I said, to give her something to contradict.

Kevin gave me a startled are-you-mental stare. "Looks like a Teletubby puked on it," he said, through fried bread.

Ma's lips vanished. "Yuppies," she said, like it was a disease. "They're working in the IT, the pair of them, whatever that means. You won't believe me: they've an au pair. Did you ever hear the like? A young one from Russia or one of them countries, she is; it'd take me the rest of my life to pronounce her name. The child's only a year old, God love him, and he never sees his mammy or daddy from one weekend till the next. I don't know what they wanted him for, at all."

I made shocked noises at the right points. "Where did the Halleys go, and Mrs. Mulligan?"

"The Halleys moved out to Tallaght when the landlord sold the house. I raised five of yous in this flat right here, and I never needed any au pair to do it. I'd bet my life your woman had an epidural, having that child." Ma smacked another egg into the frying pan.

Da looked up from his sausages. "What year do you think it is?" he asked me. "Mrs. Mulligan died fifteen years back. The woman was eighty-bleeding-nine."

This diverted Ma off the epidural yuppies; Ma loves deaths. "Come here, guess who else died." Kevin rolled his eyes.

"Who?" I asked obligingly.

"Mr. Nolan. Never ill a day in his life and then dropped down dead in the middle of Mass, on his way back from the Communion. Massive heart attack. What d'you think of that?"

Nice one, Mr. Nolan: there was my opening. "That's terrible," I said. "God rest him. I used to hang around with Julie Nolan, way back when. What happened to her?"

"Sligo," Ma said, with gloomy satisfaction, like it was Siberia. She scraped the martyr's share of the fry-up onto her plate and joined us at the table. She was starting to get the bad-hip shuffle. "When the factory moved. She came up for the funeral; she's a face like an elephant's arse on her, from doing the sun beds. Where do you go to Mass now, Francis?"

Da snorted. "Here and there," I said. "What about Mandy Cullen, is she still about? The little dark one, used to fancy Shay?"

"They all used to fancy Shay," Kevin said, grinning. "When I was coming up, I got all my practice off girls who couldn't get their hands on Shay."

Da said, "Little whoremasters, the lot of yous." I think he meant it in a nice way.

"And look at the state of him now," Ma said. "Mandy married a lovely fella from New Street, she's Mandy Brophy now; they've two young ones, and a car. That could've been our Shay, if he'd bothered his arse. And you, young fella"—she aimed her fork at Kevin—"you'll end up the same way as him if you don't watch yourself."

Kevin concentrated on his plate. "I'm grand."

"You'll have to settle down sooner or later. You can't be happy forever. What age are you now?"

Being left out of this particular salvo was a little disturbing; not that I felt neglected, but I was starting to wonder about Jackie's mouth again. I asked, "Does Mandy still live around here? I should call in to her, while I'm about."

"Still in Number Nine," Ma said promptly. "Mr. and Mrs. Cullen have the bottom floor, Mandy and the family have the other two. So she can look after her mammy and daddy. She's a great girl, Mandy is. Brings her mammy to her appointment at the clinic every Wednesday, for her bones, and the one on Friday for—"

At first all I heard was a faint crack in the steady rhythm of the rain, somewhere away up the Place. I stopped listening to Ma. Footsteps splashing closer, more than one set; voices. I put down my knife and fork and headed for the window, fast ("Francis Mackey, what in God's name are you at?"), and after all this time Nora Daly still walked just like her sister.

I said, "I need a bin liner."

"You haven't eaten what I cooked for you," Ma snapped, pointing her knife at my plate. "You sit down there and finish that."

"I'll have it later. Where do you keep the bin liners?"

Ma had all her chins tucked in, ready for a fight. "I don't know what way you live these days, but under my roof you won't waste good food. Eat that and then you can ask me again."

"Ma, I don't have time for this. That's the Dalys." I pulled open the drawer where the bin liners used to live: full of folded lacy God-knows-whats.

"Shut that drawer! Acting like you live here—"

Kevin, smart boy, had his head right down. "What makes you think the Dalys want to see your ugly mug?" Da wanted to know. "They probably think this is all your fault."

"—strolling in like Lord Muck—"

"Probably," I agreed, whipping open more drawers, "but I'm still going to show them that case, and I don't want it getting rained on. Where the *fuck*—" All I could find was industrial quantities of furniture polish.

"*Language!* Thinking you're too good for a fry-up—"

Da said, "Hang on till I get my shoes and I'll come with you. I'd love to see Matt Daly's face."

And Olivia wanted me to introduce Holly to this. "No, thanks," I said.

"What d'you have for your breakfast at home? Caviar?"

"Frank," Kevin said, hitting his limit. "Under the sink."

I pulled open the cupboard and, thank Christ, there was the Holy Grail: a roll of bin liners. I ripped one off and headed for the front room. On the way I asked Kevin, "Want to come along for the ride?" Da was right, the Dalys weren't likely to be fans of mine, but unless things had changed, nobody hated Kevin.

Kevin shoved back his chair. "Thank fuck," he said.

In the front room I worked the bin liner around the suitcase, as delicately as I could. "Jesus," I said. Ma was still going ("Kevin Vincent Mackey! You get your arse back in here *right now* and . . ."). "It's even more of a nuthouse than I remembered."

Kevin shrugged and pulled on his jacket. "They'll settle once we're gone."

"Did I say you could leave the table? Francis! Kevin! Are yous listening to me?"

"Shut the *fuck up*," Da told Ma. "I'm trying to eat here."

He wasn't raising his voice, not yet anyway, but the sound of it still made my jaw clench, and I saw Kevin's eyes snap shut for a second. "Let's get out of here," I said. "I want to catch Nora before she heads."

I carried the case downstairs balanced flat on my forearms, lightly, trying to go easy on the evidence. Kevin held doors for me. The street was empty; the Dalys had disappeared into Number 3. The wind came barreling down the road and shoved me in the chest, like a huge hand daring me to keep on coming.

As far back as I can remember, my parents and the Dalys hated each other's guts, for a vast tapestry of reasons that would burst a blood vessel in any outsider trying to understand them. Back when Rosie and I started going out I did some asking, trying to figure out why the idea sent Mr. Daly straight through the ceiling, but I'm pretty sure I only scratched the surface. Part of it had to do with the fact that the Daly men worked at Guinness's, which put them a cut above the rest of us: solid job, good benefits, the chance of going up in the world. Rosie's da was taking evening classes, talking about working his way up off the production line—I knew from Jackie that these days he had some kind of supervisor job, and that they had bought Number 3 off their landlord. My parents didn't like people with Notions; the Dalys didn't like unemployed alcoholic wasters. According to my ma, there was also an element of jealousy involved—she had popped out the five of us easy as pie, while Theresa Daly had only managed the two girls and no son for her fella—but if you stayed on this line for too long, she started telling you about Mrs. Daly's miscarriages.

Ma and Mrs. Daly were on speaking terms, most of the time; women prefer to hate each other at close range, where you get more bang for your buck. I never saw my da and Mr. Daly exchange two words. The closest they got to communication—and I wasn't sure how this related to either employment issues or obstetrical envy—was once or twice a year, when Da came home a little more thoroughly tanked than usual and staggered straight past our house, down to Number 3. He would sway in the road, kicking the railings and howling at Matt Daly to come out and fight him like a man, until Ma and Shay—or, if Ma was cleaning offices that night, Carmel and Shay and I—went out there and convinced him to come home. You could feel the whole street listening and whispering and enjoying, but the Dalys never opened a window, never switched on a light. The hardest part was getting Da around the bend in the stairs.

"Once we get in there," I said to Kevin, when we had legged it through the rain and he was knocking on the door of Number 3, "you do the talking."

That startled him. "Me? Why me?"

"Humor me. Just tell them how this thing showed up. I'll take it from there."

He didn't look happy about it, but our Kev always was a people-pleaser, and before he could come up with a nice way to tell me to do my own dirty work, the door opened and Mrs. Daly peered out at us.

"Kevin," she said. "How are—" and then she recognized me. Her eyes went round and she made a noise like a hiccup.

I said smoothly, "Mrs. Daly, I'm sorry to disturb you. Could we come in for a moment?"

She had a hand up to her chest. Kev had been right about the finger-nails. "I don't . . ."

Every cop knows how to get in a door past someone who's not sure. "If I could just bring this in out of the rain," I said, juggling the case around her. "I think it's important for you and Mr. Daly to have a look at it."

Kevin trailed after me, looking uncomfortable. Mrs. Daly screeched "Matt!" up the stairs without taking her eyes off us.

"Ma?" Nora came out of the front room, all grown up and wearing a dress that showed it. "Who— Jaysus. *Francis?*"

"In the flesh. Howya, Nora."

"Holy God," Nora said. Then her eyes went over my shoulder, to the stairs.

I had remembered Mr. Daly as Schwarzenegger in a cardigan, but he was on the short side of medium, a wiry, straight-backed guy with close-cut hair and a stubborn jaw. It got tighter while he examined me, taking his time. Then he told me, "We've got nothing to say to you."

I cut my eyes sideways at Kevin. "Mr. Daly," he said, fast, "we really, really need to show you something."

"You can show us anything you like. Your brother needs to get out of my house."

"No, I know, and he wouldn't have come, only we didn't have a choice, honest to God. This is important. Seriously. Could we not . . . ? Please?"

He was perfect, shuffling his feet and shoving his floppy fringe out of his eyes, all embarrassed and clumsy and urgent; kicking him out would have been like kicking a big fluffy sheepdog. No wonder the kid was in sales. "We wouldn't bother you," he added humbly, for good measure, "only that we don't know what else to do. Just five minutes?"

After a moment, Mr. Daly gave a stiff, reluctant nod. I would have paid good money for a blow-up Kevin doll that I could carry around in the back of my car and whip out in emergencies.

They brought us into the front room, which was barer than Ma's and brighter: plain beige carpet, cream paint instead of wallpaper, a picture of John Paul II and an old trade-union poster framed on the wall, not a doily or a plaster duck in sight. Even when we were all kids running in and out of each other's houses, I had never been in that room. For a long time I wanted to be invited in there, in the hot, vicious way you want something when you've been told you're not good enough. This wasn't how I'd pictured the circumstances. In my version, I had my arm around Rosie and she had a ring on her finger, an expensive coat on her back, a bun in the oven and a huge smile straight across her face.

Nora sat us down around the coffee table; I saw her think about tea and biscuits, and then think twice. I put the suitcase on the table, made a big deal about pulling on my gloves—Mr. Daly was probably the only person in the parish who would rather have a cop in his front room than a Mackey—and peeled the bin liner away. "Have any of you seen this before?" I asked.

Silence, for a second. Then Mrs. Daly made a sound between a gasp and a moan, and reached to grab the case. I got a hand out in time. "I'm going to have to ask you not to touch that."

Mr. Daly said, roughly, "Where . . ." and took a breath between his teeth. "Where did you get that?"

I asked, "Do you recognize it?"

"It's mine," Mrs. Daly said, into her knuckles. "I brought it on our honeymoon."

"*Where did you get that,*" Mr. Daly said, louder. His face was turning an unhealthy shade of red.

I gave Kevin the eyebrow. He told the story pretty well, all things considered: builders, birth cert, phone calls. I held up various items to illustrate, like an air hostess demonstrating life jackets, and watched the Dalys.

When I left, Nora had been maybe thirteen or fourteen, a round-shouldered, lumpy kid with a head of frizzy curls, developing early and not looking one bit happy about it. It had worked out well for her, in the end: she had the same knock-your-eye out figure as Rosie, getting soft around the edges but still va-va-voom, the kind of figure you don't see any more now that girls starve themselves into size zero and permanent narkiness. She was an inch or two shorter than Rosie and her coloring was a lot less dramatic—dark-brown hair, gray eyes—but the resemblance was there; not when you looked at her full-face, but when you caught a fast glimpse out of the corner of your eye. It was an intangible thing, somewhere in the angle of her shoulders and the arch of her neck, and in the way she listened: absolutely still, one hand cupping the opposite elbow, eyes straight on Kevin. Very few people can sit still and listen. Rosie was the queen of it.

Mrs. Daly had changed too, but not in a good way. I remembered her feisty, smoking on her steps, cocking a hip against the railings and calling double entendres to make us boys blush and scurry away from her throaty laugh. Rosie leaving, or just twenty-two years of life and Mr. Daly, had knocked the stuffing out of her: her back had curved over, her face had fallen in around the eyes and she had a general aura of being in need of a Xanax milk shake. The part that got to me, the thing I had missed about Mrs. Daly back when we were teenagers and she was ancient, was this: under the blue eye shadow and the explosive hair and the low-level crazy, she was the image of Rosie. Once I had spotted the resemblance I couldn't stop seeing it, hanging in the corner of my eye, like a hologram flicking into view and then gone. The chance that Rosie might have turned into her ma, over the years, gave me a whole fresh layer of heebie-jeebies.

The longer I watched Mr. Daly, on the other hand, the more he looked like his very own free-spirited self. A couple of buttons had been resewn on his fashion-crime sweater-vest, his ear hair was neatly clipped and his shave was brand-new: he must have taken a razor with him to Nora's, the night before, and shaved before she drove them home. Mrs. Daly twitched and whimpered and bit down on the side of her hand, watching me go through that suitcase, and Nora took deep breaths a couple of times, flicked her head back, blinked hard; Mr. Daly's face never changed. He got paler and paler, and a muscle jumped in his cheek when I held up the birth cert, but that was all.

Kevin wound down, glancing at me to see if he had done it right. I folded Rosie's paisley shirt back into the case and closed the lid. For a second there was absolute silence.

Then Mrs. Daly said, with her breath gone, "But how would that be in Number Sixteen? Rosie brought it with her to *England*."

The certainty in her voice made my heart skip. I asked, "How do you know that?"

She stared. "It was gone after she went."

"How do you know for a fact that she went to England?"

"She left us a note, sure. To say good-bye. The Shaughnessy young fellas and one of Sallie Hearne's lads brought it round, the next day; they found it in Number Sixteen. It said right there, she was off to England. At first we thought the two of yous . . ." Mr. Daly moved, a stiff, angry little jerk. Mrs. Daly blinked fast and stopped talking.

I pretended not to notice. "I think everyone did, yeah," I said easily. "When did you find out we weren't together?"

When no one else answered, Nora said, "Ages ago. Fifteen years, maybe; it was before I got married. I ran into Jackie in the shop one day and she said she was after getting back in touch with you, and you were here in Dublin. She said Rosie had gone over without you." Her eyes went from me to the suitcase and back again, widening fast. "Do you think . . . Where do you think she is?"

"I'm not thinking anything yet," I said, in my best pleasant official voice, just like this was any missing girl. "Not till we know a little more. Have you heard anything at all from her since she left? A phone call, a letter, a message from someone who ran into her somewhere?"

Mrs. Daly said, in one impressive burst, "Sure, we'd no phone when she left, how would she ring us? When we got the phone in, I wrote down the number and I went to your mammy and your Jackie and Carmel and I said to them, I said, come here to me, if you ever hear anything from your Francis, you give him that number and you tell him to tell Rosie to ring us, even if it's only for a minute at Christmas or— But, sure, once I heard she wasn't with you I knew she wouldn't ring, she hasn't got the number after all an' anyway, has she? She could still write, but Rosie, sure, she always did things in her own time. But I've my sixty-fifth coming up in February and she'll send a card for that, she wouldn't miss that—"

Her voice was getting higher and faster, with a brittle edge on it. Mr. Daly put out a hand and clasped it around hers for a moment, and she bit down on her lips. Kevin looked like he was trying to ooze down between the sofa cushions and disappear.

Nora said, quietly, "No. Not a word. At first we just thought . . ." She glanced fast at her father: she'd thought Rosie was taking it for granted that she was cut off, for running away with me. "Even once we heard you weren't with her. We always thought she was in England." Mrs. Daly tipped her head back and swiped off a tear.

So that was that: no quick out, no waving bye-bye to my family and erasing yesterday evening from my mind and going back to my personal approximation of normal, and no chance of getting Nora langered and coaxing Rosie's phone number out of her. Mr. Daly said heavily, without looking at any of us, "We'll have to ring the Guards."

I almost hid a dubious look. "Right. You could, yeah. That was my family's first instinct, too, but I thought you should be the ones to decide if you really want to go that way."

He gave me a suspicious stare. "Why wouldn't we?"

I sighed and ran a hand through my hair. "Look," I said. "I'd love to tell you the cops will give this the attention it deserves, but I can't. Ideally I'd like to see this tested for fingerprints and for blood, just for starters"—Mrs. Daly made a terrible squeaking sound, into her hands—"but before that can happen, it would need to be given a case number, the case would need to be assigned to a detective, and the detective would need to submit a request for testing. I can tell you right now, it's not going to happen. No one's going to throw valuable resources at something that might not even be a crime to begin with. Missing Persons and Cold Cases and the General Unit will bounce this back and forth between them for a few months, until they get bored, give up and file it in a basement somewhere. You need to be prepared for that."

Nora asked, "But what about you? Could you not put in the request?"

I shook my head ruefully. "Not officially, no. No matter how far you stretch it, this definitely isn't something my squad would deal with. Once it goes into the system, there's nothing I can do about it."

"But," Nora said. She was sitting up straighter, alert, watching me. "If it wasn't in the system, like; if it was just you. Could you . . . is there not a way to . . . ?"

"Call in a few favors, on the QT?" I raised my eyebrows, had a think about that. "Well. I guess it could be done. You'd all need to be positive that that's what you want, though."

"I do," Nora said, straight off. A fast decider, same as Rosie. "If you'd do that for us, Francis; if you could. Please."

Mrs. Daly nodded, fished in her sleeve for a tissue and blew her nose. "Could she not be in England, after all? Could she not?"

She was begging me. The note in her voice hurt; Kevin flinched. "She could," I said gently, "yeah. If you want to leave this with me, I suppose I could try to check that out, too."

"Ah, God," Mrs. Daly said, under her breath. "Ah, God . . ."

I asked, "Mr. Daly?"

There was a long silence. Mr. Daly sat there with his hands clasped between his knees, staring at the suitcase, like he hadn't heard me.

Finally he said, to me, "I don't like you. You or your family. No point pretending."

"Yeah," I said. "I noticed that, along the way. But I'm not here as one of the Mackeys. I'm here as a police officer who might be able to help you find your daughter."

"On the QT, under the table, through the back door. People don't change."

"Apparently not," I said, giving him a bland smile. "But circumstances do. We're on the same side this time."

"Are we?"

"You'd better hope so," I said, "because I'm the best you've got. Take it or leave it."

His eyes came up to mine then, a long raking stare. I kept my back straight and did my respectable face from parent-teacher meetings. Finally he nodded, one sharp jerk, and said—not all that graciously—"Do it. Whatever you can. Please."

"Right," I said, and got out my notebook. "I'll need you to tell me about Rosie leaving. Start from the day before. In as much detail as you can, please."

They knew it by heart, just like every family that's lost a child—I once had a mother show me which glass her son drank out of, the morning before he took his overdose. A Sunday morning in Advent, cold, with a gray-white sky and breath hanging in the air like fog. Rosie had come in early the night before, so she had gone to nine o'clock Mass with the rest of the family, rather than sleeping in and getting the noon Mass, the way she did if she'd been out late on Saturday night. They had come home and made a fry-up for breakfast—back then, eating before Holy Communion earned you a string of Hail Marys at your next confession. Rosie had done the ironing while her mother washed up, and the two of them had discussed when to buy the ham for Christmas dinner; it grabbed my breath for a second, the thought of her calmly talking about a meal she had no plans to eat and dreaming about a Christmas that would be just hers and mine. A little before noon the girls had walked over to New Street to pick up their nana Daly for Sunday dinner, after which they had all watched the telly for a while—that was another thing that had put the Dalys a cut above us peasants: they actually owned their own TV. Reverse snobbery is always fun; I was rediscovering subtle nuances that I'd almost forgotten existed.

The rest of the day was more nothing. The girls had walked their nana home, Nora had headed out to hang around with a couple of her mates, and Rosie had gone to their room to read, or possibly to pack or to write that note or to sit on the edge of her bed and take a lot of deep breaths. Tea, more housework, more telly, helping Nora with her maths homework; there hadn't been a single sign, anywhere in that day, that Rosie had anything up her sleeve. "An angel," Mr. Daly said grimly. "All that week, she was an angel. I should've known."

Nora had gone to bed around half past ten, the rest of the family a little after eleven—Rosie and her da had to be up for work in the morning. The two girls shared one back bedroom, their parents had the other; no pullout sofas for the Dalys, thanks very much. Nora remembered the rustle of Rosie changing into her pajamas and the whisper of "Night" as she slid into bed, and then nothing. She hadn't heard Rosie get out of bed again, hadn't heard her get dressed, hadn't heard her slip out of the room or out of the flat. "I slept like the dead, back then," she said, defensively, like she had taken a lot of flak about this along the way. "I was a teenager, you know what they're like . . ." In the morning, when Mrs. Daly went to wake the girls, Rosie was gone.

At first they didn't worry, any more than my family were worrying across the road—I got the sense Mr. Daly had been a bit snotty about inconsiderate modern youth, but that was all. It was Dublin in the eighties, it was safe as houses; they thought she had headed out early to do something, maybe meet the girls for some mysterious girl reason. Then, around the time Rosie was missing breakfast, the Shaughnessy boys and Barry Hearne had shown up with the note.

It was unclear what the three of them had been doing in Number 16 bright and early on a cold Monday morning, but I would have bet on either hash or porn—there were a couple of precious magazines doing the rounds, smuggled in by someone's cousin who had been over to England the year before. Either way, that was when all hell had broken loose. The Dalys' account was a little less vivid than Kevin's—his eyes slid sideways to catch mine, once or twice, while they were giving us their version—but the general outline was the same.

I nodded at the case. "Where was that kept?"

"The girls' room," Mrs. Daly said, into her knuckles. "Rosie had it to hold her spare clothes and her old toys and all—we didn't have the fitted wardrobes then, sure, no one did—"

"Think back. Do any of you remember the last time you saw it?"

No one did. Nora said, "It could have been months before. She kept it under her bed; I'd only see it when she brought it out to get something."

"What about the things inside it, can you remember when you last saw Rosie using any of that stuff? Playing those tapes, wearing any of those clothes?"

Silence. Then Nora's back snapped straight and she said, her voice going up a notch, "The Walkman. I saw that on the Thursday, three days before she went. I used to take it out of her bedside locker, when I got home from school, and listen to her tapes till she got in from work. If she caught me she'd give me a clatter round the ear, but it was worth it—she had the best music . . ."

"What makes you so sure you saw it on the Thursday?"

"That's when I'd borrow it. Thursdays and Fridays, Rosie used to walk to work and back with Imelda Tierney—do you remember Imelda? She did the sewing with Rosie, down at the factory—so she wouldn't take the Walkman. The rest of the week, Imelda had a different shift, so Rosie walked in on her own, and she'd bring the Walkman to listen to."

"So you could've seen it on either Thursday or Friday."

Nora shook her head. "Fridays we used to go to the pictures after school, a gang of us. I went that Friday. I remember because . . ." She flushed, shut up and glanced sideways at her father.

Mr. Daly said flatly, "She remembers because, after Rosie ran off, it was a long time before I let Nora out gallivanting again. We'd lost one by being too lax. I wasn't going to risk the other."

"Fair enough," I said, nodding away like that was perfectly sane. "And none of you remembers seeing any of those items after Thursday afternoon?"

Head-shakes all round. If Rosie hadn't been packed by Thursday afternoon, she had been cutting it a little close to find a chance of hiding that suitcase herself, specially given Daddy's Doberman tendencies. The odds were starting to shade, ever so slightly, towards someone else doing the hiding.

I asked, "Had you noticed anyone hanging around her, giving her hassle? Anyone who worried you?"

Mr. Daly's eye said, *What, apart from you?* but he managed not to share. He said evenly, "If I'd noticed anyone bothering her, I'd have sorted it out."

"Any arguments, problems with anyone?"

"Not that she told us about. You'd probably know about that kind of thing better than we would. We all know how much girls tell their parents, at that age."

I said, "One last thing." I fished in my jacket, pulled out a bunch of envelopes just big enough to hold a snapshot, and handed out three of them. "Do any of you recognize this woman?"

The Dalys gave it their best shot, but no hundred-watt bulbs lit up, presumably because Fingerprint Fifi is a high-school algebra teacher from Nebraska whose photo I pulled off the internet. Wherever I go, Fifi goes. Her picture has a nice wide white border so you won't feel the need to hold it delicately by the edges, and since she may be the most nondescript human being on the planet, it'll take you a close look—probably involving both thumbs and index fingers—to be sure that you don't know her. I owe my girl Fifi many a subtle ID. Today, she was going to help me find out whether the Dalys had left prints on that suitcase.

What had my antennae wiggling at this lot was the mind-bending off chance that Rosie had been heading to meet me, after all. If she was sticking to our plan, if she didn't need to dodge me, she would have taken the same route I had: out the door of the flat, down the stairs, straight into the Place. But I had had a perfect view of every inch of the road, the whole night through, and that front door had never opened.

Back then, the Dalys had the middle floor of Number 3. On the top floor were the Harrison sisters, three ancient, easily overexcited spinsters who gave you bread and sugar if you did their messages for them; the basement was sad, sick little Veronica Crotty, who said her husband was a traveling salesman, and her sad, sick little kid. In other words, if someone had intercepted Rosie on her way to our rendezvous, that someone was sitting across the coffee table from me and Kevin.

All three of the Dalys looked genuinely shocked and upset, but that can swing so many ways. Nora had been a big kid at a difficult age, Mrs. Daly was somewhere on the crazy spectrum, and Mr. Daly had a five-star temper, a five-star problem with me, and muscles. Rosie was no lightweight; her da might not be Arnie after all, but he had been the only one in that house strong enough to dispose of her body.

Mrs. Daly asked, peering anxiously over the photo, "Who's she, now? I've never seen her about. Do you think she might have hurt our Rosie? She looks awful small for that, does she not? Rosie was a strong girl, she wouldn't—"

"I'd say she has nothing to do with it," I told her truthfully, retrieving the photo envelopes and slipping them back into my pocket, in order. "I'm just exploring every possibility."

Nora said, "But you think someone hurt her."

"It's too early to assume that," I said. "I'll set some inquiries in motion and keep you posted. I think I've got enough to start with. Thanks for your time." Kevin leaped out of his seat like he was on springs.

I took off my gloves to shake their hands good-bye. I didn't ask for phone numbers—no sense in pushing my welcome—and I didn't ask if they still had the note. The thought of seeing it again made my jaw clench.

Mr. Daly walked us out. At the door he said abruptly, to me, "When she never wrote, we thought it was you that wouldn't let her."

This could have been some form of apology, or just one final dig. "Rosie never let anyone stop her from doing what she wanted to do," I said. "I'll get back to you as soon as I have any information." As he closed the door behind us, I heard one of the women starting to cry.

4

The rain had slackened off to a faint damp haze, but the clouds were getting denser and darker; there was more on the way. Ma was pressed up against the front-room window, sending out curiosity rays that practically burned my eyebrows off. When she saw me looking in her direction, she whipped up a J-cloth and started furiously cleaning the glass.

"Nicely done," I said to Kevin. "I appreciate that."

He shot me a quick sideways glance. "That was weird."

His own big brother, the same one who used to nick crisps from the shop for him, in full cop mode. "Didn't show," I told him approvingly. "You worked it like a pro. You've got a knack for this, do you know that?"

He shrugged. "Now what?"

"I'm going to put this in my car before Matt Daly has a change of heart," I said, balancing the case on one arm and giving Ma a wave and a big grin, "and then I'm going to go have a little chat with someone I used to know. Meanwhile, you're going to wrangle Ma and Da for me."

Kevin's eyes widened in horror. "Ah, Jaysus, no. No way. She'll still be raging about the breakfast."

"Come on, Kev. Tighten up your jockstrap and take one for the team."

"Team, my arse. You're the one pissed her off to begin with, and now you want me to go back in there and take all the flak?"

His hair was sticking up with outrage. "Bingo," I said. "I don't want her hassling the Dalys, and I don't want her spreading the word, at least not right away. All I need is an hour or so before she starts doing damage. Can you give me that?"

"What am I supposed to do if she starts heading out? Rugby-tackle her?"

"What's your phone number?" I found my mobile, the one my boys and my informants use, and sent Kev a text that said HI. "There," I said. "If Ma escapes, you just reply to that and I'll come rugby-tackle her myself. Fair enough?"

"Fucking hell," Kevin muttered, staring up at the window.

"Nice one," I said, clapping him on the back. "You're a trooper. I'll meet you back here in an hour and I'll get you a few pints tonight, how's that?"

"I'll need more than a few," Kev said gloomily, and he squared up his shoulders and headed off to face the firing squad.

I stashed the suitcase safely in the boot of my car, ready to take to a lovely lady in the Technical Bureau whose home address I happened to know. A handful of ten-year-olds with underprivileged hair and no eyebrows were slouched on a wall, scoping out the cars and thinking wire hangers. All I needed was to come back and find that suitcase gone. I leaned my arse on the boot, labeled my Fingerprint Fifi envelopes, had a smoke, and stared our country's future out of it until the situation was clear all round and they fucked off to vandalize someone who wouldn't come looking for them.

The Dalys' flat had been the mirror image of ours; there was nowhere to stash a body, at least not long-term. If Rosie had died in that flat, then the Dalys had had two options. Assuming Mr. Daly was the proud owner of one serious set of cojones, which I didn't rule out, he could have wrapped her up in something and carried her out the front door and away: into the river, onto some abandoned site, into the piggeries as per Shay's charming suggestion. But, the Liberties being the Liberties, the odds were high that someone would have seen it, remembered it, and talked about it. Mr. Daly didn't strike me as a gambling man.

The nongambler's option was the back garden. Probably nowadays half the gardens had been dolled up with shrubs and decking and various wrought-iron doodads, but back then they were neglected and ragged: scrawny grass, dirt, boards and broken furniture and the odd wrecked bike. Nobody went out there except to use the toilet or, in summer, to hang washing; all the action was out front, in the street. It had been cold, but not cold enough to freeze the ground. An hour one night to start digging a grave, maybe another hour the next night to finish it, another the third night to fill it in. No one would spot you; the gardens didn't have lighting, on dark nights you needed a torch just to find your way to the jacks. No one would hear you; the Harrison sisters were deaf as a pair of fence posts, the back windows of Veronica Crotty's basement were boarded up to keep the heat in, everyone else's windows would have been shut tight against the December cold. Cover the grave, during the days and when you were all finished, with a sheet of corrugated iron or an old table or whatever was lying around. No one would look twice.

I couldn't get into that garden without a warrant, and I couldn't get one of those without something that bore a passing resemblance to probable cause. I threw my smoke away and headed back to Faithful Place, to talk to Mandy Brophy.

Mandy was the first person who was unequivocally, unmistakably glad to see me. The scream out of her nearly lifted the roof off; I knew it would send my ma scurrying for the window again. "Francis Mackey! Jesus, Mary and holy Saint Joseph!" She pounced and caught me in a hug that left bruises. "You nearly gave me a heart attack; I never thought I'd see you around these parts again. What are you doing here?"

She was mammy-shaped these days, with mammy hair to match, but the dimples were still the same. "This and that," I said, smiling back. "It seemed like a good moment to see how everyone was getting on."

"About fecking time, is all I can say. Come in out of that. Here, yous"— two dark-haired, round-eyed little girls were sprawled on the front-room floor—"go on upstairs and play in your room, give me some peace while I talk to this fella here. Go on!" She shooed the girls out with her hands.

"They're the image of you," I said, nodding after them.

"They're a pair of little wagons, so they are. They've me worn out, I'm not joking you. My ma says it's my comeuppance, for all the times I put the heart crossways in her when I was a young one." She whipped half-dressed dolls and sweet wrappers and broken crayons off the sofa. "And come here to me, I hear you're in the Guards now. Very respectable, you're after getting."

She was holding the armful of toys and smiling up at me, but those black eyes were sharp and watchful: she was testing. "You'd think," I said, dropping my head and giving her my finest bad-boy grin. "I grew up, is all. Same as yourself."

She shrugged. "I'm the same as ever, sure. Look around you."

"So am I. You can take the fella out of the Place . . ."

"But you can't take the Place out of the fella." Her eyes stayed wary for another second; then she nodded, a quick little snap, and pointed a Bratz's foot at the sofa. "Sit down there now. You'll have a cup of tea, yeah?"

And I was in. There's no password more powerful than your past. "Ah, Jaysus, no. I'm only after my breakfast."

Mandy tossed the toys into a pink plastic toy box and slammed the lid. "Are you sure? Then d'you mind if I fold the washing, while we're talking? Before those two little madams come back and have the place turned upside down again." She plumped down on the sofa next to me and pulled a washing basket closer. "Did you hear I married Ger Brophy? He's a chef now. He always did love his food, Ger did."

"Gordon Ramsay, yeah?" I said, and gave her a wicked grin. "Tell me something, does he bring his spatula home with him, in case you're bold?"

Mandy squealed and smacked my wrist. "You dirty bastard. You are the same as ever, aren't you? Ah, he's no Gordon Ramsay, he's at one of them new hotels up by the airport. He says it does be mostly families that missed their flights and businessmen looking to take their fancy women somewhere they won't be snared; nobody minds about the food. One morning, I swear, he was that bored he put bananas in the breakfast fry-ups, just to see what would they do. No one said a fecking word."

"They must've thought it was nouvelle cuisine. Fair play to Ger."

"I don't know what they thought it was, but all of them ate it. Egg and sausage and banana."

I said, "Ger's a sound man. You both did well there."

She shook out a little pink sweatshirt with a snap. "Ah, sure, he's all right. He's a good laugh. It was always on the cards, anyway; when we told my ma we were engaged, she said she'd seen it coming since we were in diapers. Same as with . . ." A quick glance up. "Same as with most of the weddings round here."

Back in the day, Mandy would have heard all about that suitcase by this time, complete with detailed gory speculation. The decayed grapevine, plus my man Kevin's sterling work with Ma, meant that she wasn't tense and she wasn't being careful; just a little tactful, so as not to hurt my wounded feelings. I relaxed back into the sofa and enjoyed it while it lasted. I love messy homes, homes where a woman and kids have left their mark on every inch: sticky finger marks down the walls, trinkets and nests of pastel hair-gadgets on the mantelpiece, that smell of flowery things and ironing.

We shot the breeze for a while: her parents, my parents, various neighbors who had got married or had kids or moved out to the suburbs or developed intriguing health problems. Imelda was still around, a two-minute walk away on Hallows Lane, but something at the corners of Mandy's mouth told me they didn't see as much of each other any more, and I didn't ask. Instead I made her laugh: get a woman laughing and you're halfway to getting her talking. She still had the same round bubbly giggle that exploded out of her and made you want to laugh too.

It took ten minutes or so before Mandy asked, casually, "So tell us, d'you ever hear anything from Rosie?"

"Not a dicky bird," I said, just as easily. "You?"

"Nothing. I thought . . ." That glance again. "I thought you might have, that's all."

I asked, "Did you know?"

Her eyes were down on the socks she was rolling, but her lashes flickered. "What d'you mean?"

"You and Rosie were close. I thought she might have told you."

"That yous were eloping, like? Or that she . . . ?"

"Either one."

She shrugged. "Ah, Jaysus, Mandy," I said, putting a humorous twist on it. "It's been twenty-odd years. I can promise you, I'm not going to throw a wobbler because girls talk to each other. I only wondered."

"I hadn't a notion she was thinking of breaking it off. Honest to God, not a clue. I have to tell you, Francis, when I heard yous two weren't together, I was only gobsmacked. I thought for definite you'd have been married, with half a dozen kids to put a stop to your gallop."

"So you did know we were planning on heading off together."

"Yous went off the same night, sure. Everyone figured."

I grinned at her and shook my head. "'Breaking it off,' you said. You knew we were still seeing each other. We'd been keeping that under wraps for almost two years, or at least I thought we had been."

After a moment Mandy made a wry little face at me and tossed the socks into the washing basket. "Smart-arse. It's not that she was spilling her guts to us, or nothing—she never said a word, right up until . . . Did you and Rosie meet up for a few drinks, about a week before yous left? Somewhere in town, I think it was?"

O'Neill's on Pearse Street, and all the college boys' heads turning as Rosie made her way back to our table with a pint in each hand. She was the only girl I knew who drank pints, and she always stood her round. "Yeah," I said. "We did."

"That was what did it. See, she told her da she was going out with me and Imelda, but she never said it to us so we could cover for her, know what I mean? Like I said, she'd been keeping you very quiet; we hadn't a notion. But that night the pair of us got home early enough, and Mr. Daly was watching out the window and he saw us come in, without Rosie. She didn't get in till late." Mandy dimpled up at me. "Yous must have had loads to talk about, did you?"

"Yeah," I said. Good-night kiss pressed up against the wall of Trinity, my hands on her hips, pulling her close.

"Mr. Daly waited up for her, anyway. Rosie called round to me the next day—the Saturday, it was—and she said he went *ballistic*."

And we were right back to big bad Mr. Daly again. "I bet he did," I said.

"Me and Imelda asked her where she'd been, but she wouldn't say. All she would say was that her da was livid. So we guessed she must've been meeting you."

"I always wondered," I said. "What the hell did Matt Daly have against me?"

Mandy blinked. "God, I wouldn't have a clue. Himself and your old fella don't get on; I'd say it might be that. Does it matter, sure? You're not round here any more, you never see him . . ."

I said, "Rosie dumped me, Mandy. She dumped me flat on my arse, out of the clear blue sky, and I've never known why. If there's an explanation, somewhere out there, I'd love to know what it is. I'd like to know if there was something, anything, I could've done to make things turn out different."

I gave it plenty of the strong-but-suffering, and Mandy's mouth went soft with sympathy. "Ah, Francis . . . Rosie never gave a tinker's damn what her da thought of you. You know that."

"Maybe not. But if she was worried about anything, or hiding something from me, or if she was scared of someone . . . How livid did he use to get with her, exactly?"

Mandy looked baffled or wary, I couldn't tell which. "How d'you mean, like?"

"Mr. Daly had a temper," I said. "When he first found out Rosie was seeing me, the whole Place heard him roaring. I always wondered if it stopped there, or if . . . well. If he used to hit her."

Her hand went to her mouth. "Jaysus, Francis! Did she say something?"

"Not to me, but she wouldn't have, not unless she wanted me punching her da's lights out. I thought she might have talked to you and Imelda, though."

"Ah, no, God, no. She never said a word about anything like that. I think she would've, but . . . you never know for definite, sure you don't?" Mandy thought, smoothing a blue school-uniform tunic in her lap. "I'd say he never laid a finger on her," she said, in the end. "And I'm not just saying that because you want to hear it, now. Half Mr. Daly's problem was that he never copped that Rosie had grown up, d'you know what I mean? That Saturday when she called round to me, after he'd caught her coming home late—the three of us were meant to be going to the Apartments that night, and Rosie couldn't go because, I'm not joking you, her da had taken her keys away. Like she was a kid, instead of a grown woman putting her wages on the table every week. He said he was locking the door at eleven sharp, and if she wasn't in by then, she could sleep on the street—and you know yourself, by eleven the Apartments were only getting started. See what I mean? When he got annoyed with her, he didn't give her the slaps; he sent her to sit in the corner, the way I'd do with one of my little young ones if she was bold."

And just like that, Mr. Daly no longer had the spotlight all to himself, getting a search warrant for his garden was no longer top priority, and snuggling up in Mandy's cozy little corner of domestic bliss wasn't as much fun any more. If Rosie hadn't come out the front door of her house, it didn't have to be because she was dodging me, or because Daddy had caught her in the act and had a melodrama moment involving a blunt object. It could have been just because he had left her no choice. Front doors were locked at night; back doors had a bolt on the inside, so you could go to the jacks shed without needing a key or locking yourself out. Without her keys, it didn't matter whether Rosie was running away from me or into my arms: she had had to go out the back door, over walls and down the gardens. The odds were spreading out, away from Number 3.

And the chances of pulling prints off that case were going down. If Rosie had known she was going to be monkeying around with garden walls, she would have hidden the case in advance, ready to pick up on her way out of town. If someone had got his hands on her, along the way, he might never even have known the suitcase existed.

Mandy was watching me, a little worried, trying to work out if I got what she meant. "Makes sense," I said. "I can't see Rosie taking well to being sent to the corner, though. Was she planning on trying something? Nicking her keys back from her da, maybe?"

"Not a thing. That's what tipped us off something was up, sure. Me and Imelda said to her, 'Fuck him, come out with us anyway, if he locks you out you can sleep here.' But she said no, she wanted to keep him sweet. We said, 'Why would you be arsed?'—like you said, it wasn't her style. And Rosie said, 'Sure, it's not for much longer.' That got our attention, all right. The pair of us dropped everything and jumped on her, wanting to know what she was on about, but she wouldn't say. She acted like she just meant her da would give the keys back soon enough, but both of us knew it was more than that. We didn't know what, exactly; just that something big was happening."

"You didn't try for more details? What she had planned, when, whether it was with me?"

"God, yeah. We went on at her for ages—I was poking her in the arm and all, and Imelda smacked her with a pillow, trying to make her talk—

but she just ignored us till we gave up and went back to getting ready. She was . . . Jaysus." Mandy laughed, a soft, startled little catch, under her breath; her brisk hands on the washing had slowed to a stop. "We were just through there, in that dining room—that used to be my room. I was the only one of us had my own room; we always met up there. Me and Imelda were doing our hair, backcombing away—God, the state of us, and the turquoise eye shadow, d'you remember? We thought we were the Bangles and Cyndi Lauper and Bananarama all rolled into one."

"You were beautiful," I said, and meant it. "All three of you. I've never seen prettier."

She wrinkled her nose at me—"Flattery'll get you nowhere"—but her eyes were still somewhere else. "We were slagging Rosie, asking her was she joining the nuns, telling her she'd look lovely in a habit and was it because she fancied Father McGrath . . . Rosie was lying on my bed, looking up at the ceiling and biting her nail—you know the way she used to do? Just the one fingernail?"

Right index fingernail; she bit at it when she was thinking hard. Those last couple of months, while we made our plans, she'd drawn blood a few times. "I remember," I said.

"I was watching her, in the mirror on my dressing table. It was *Rosie*, I knew her since the lot of us were babas together, and all of a sudden she looked like a new person. Like she was older than us; like she was already halfway gone, somewhere else. I felt like we should give her something—a good-bye card, or a St. Christopher medal, maybe. Something for a safe journey."

I asked, "Did you mention this to anyone?"

"No way," Mandy said, fast, with a snap in her voice. "No way would I have squelt on her. You know better than that."

She was sitting up straighter, starting to bristle. "I do, babe," I said, smiling across at her. "I'm only double-checking, out of habit. Don't mind me."

"I talked to Imelda, all right. We both figured yous were eloping. We thought it was dead romantic—teenagers, you know yourself . . . But I never said a word to anyone else, not even after. We were on your side, Francis. We wanted yous to be happy."

For one split second I felt like if I turned around I would see them, in the next room: three girls, restless on that edge where everything was just about to happen, sparking with turquoise and electricity and possibilities. "Thanks, honey," I said. "I appreciate that."

"I haven't a clue why she changed her mind. I'd tell you if I did. The two of yous were perfect for each other; I thought for sure . . ."

Her voice trailed off. "Yeah," I said. "So did I."

Mandy said softly, "God, Francis . . ." Her hands were still holding the same little uniform tunic, not moving, and there was a long invincible current of sadness under her voice. "God, it's an awful long time ago, isn't it?"

The road was quiet, only the singsong murmur of one of the little girls explaining something to the other, upstairs, and the rush of wind sweeping a gust of fine rain past the windows. "It is," I said. "I don't know how it got to be so long."

I didn't tell her. Let my ma do it; she would enjoy every second. We hugged good-bye at the door and I kissed Mandy's cheek and promised to call round again soon. She smelled of sweet safe things I hadn't smelt in years, Pears soap and custard creams and cheap perfume.

5

Kevin was slumped against our railings, looking the way he used to when we were kids and he got left behind for being too little, except that now he had a mobile and he was texting away at top speed. "Girlfriend?" I said, nodding at the phone.

He shrugged. "Sort of, I guess. Not really. I'm not into settling down yet."

"That means you've got a few of them on the go. Kev, you dirty dog."

He grinned. "So? They all know the story. They're not into settling down either; we're just having a laugh. Nothing wrong with that."

"Nothing at all," I agreed, "except I thought you were wrangling Ma for me, not playing Fingers of Love with today's laugh. What happened to that?"

"I'm wrangling her from here. She was doing my head in. If she'd tried to go across to the Dalys, I'd've caught her."

"I don't want her ringing the world and his wife."

"She won't ring anyone, not till she's called round to Mrs. Daly and got all the sca. She's doing the washing up and giving out. I tried to give her a hand and she threw a freaker because I put a fork in the drainer wrong way up and someone was gonna fall on it and lose an eye, so I split. Where were you? Were you in with Mandy Brophy?"

I said, "Let's say you wanted to get from Number Three to the top of the Place, but you couldn't go out the front door. What would you do?"

"Back door," Kevin said promptly, going back to texting. "Over the garden walls. Did it a million times."

"Me too." I aimed a finger along the line of houses, from Number 3 up to Number 15 at the top. "Six gardens." Seven, counting the Dalys'. Rosie could be still waiting for me in any one of them.

"Hang on." Kevin looked up from his phone. "Do you mean now, or way back when?"

"What's the difference?"

"The Halleys' bloody dog, that's the difference. Rambo, remember him? The little bastard bit the arse out of my trousers that time?"

"Jesus," I said. "I'd forgotten that little fucker. I drop-kicked him once." Rambo was, naturally, some kind of terrier-based mutt that weighed about five pounds soaking wet. The name had given him a Napoleon complex, complete with territorial issues.

"Now that Number Five's those eejits and their Teletubby paint, I'd go the way you said"—Kevin pointed along the same line I'd drawn—"but back then, with Rambo waiting to rip me a new one, not a chance. I'd go that way." He turned, and I followed his finger: down past Number 1, along the high wall at the bottom of the Place, up the even-numbered gardens, over the wall of Number 16 to that lamppost.

I asked, "Why not just come back over the bottom wall and straight up the road? Why would you be arsed with the gardens on our side?"

Kevin grinned. "I can't believe you don't know this shit. Did you never go throwing rocks up at Rosie's window?"

"Not with Mr. Daly in the next room. I like having testicles."

"I was buzzing off Linda Dwyer for a while, when we were like sixteen—remember the Dwyers, in Number One? We used to meet in her back garden at night, so she could stop me putting my hand up her top. That wall"—he pointed to the bottom of the road—"on the other side, it's smooth. No footholds. You can only get over it at the corners, where you can use the other wall to pull yourself up. That takes you into the back gardens."

"You're a fountain of knowledge," I said. "Did you ever get into Linda Dwyer's bra?"

Kevin rolled his eyes and started explaining Linda's complex relationship with the Legion of Mary, but I was thinking. I had a hard time picturing a random psycho killer or sex attacker hanging around back gardens on a Sunday night, hoping forlornly that a victim would stroll by. If someone had nabbed Rosie, he had known her, he had known she was coming, and he had had at least the basics of a plan.

Over the back wall was Copper Lane: a lot like Faithful Place, only bigger and busier. If I had wanted to arrange any kind of clandestine meeting or ambush or what-have-you along the route Kevin had pointed out, especially a clandestine meeting that might involve a struggle or a body dump, I would have used Number 16.

Those noises I had heard, while I waited under the lamppost shifting from foot to foot to keep from freezing. A man grunting, stifled squeaks from a girl, bumping sounds. A teenage guy in love is a walking pair of nads wearing rose-colored glasses: I'd taken it for granted that love was everywhere. I think I believed Rosie and I were so wild about each other that it got in the air like a shimmering drug, that night when everything was coming together, and swirled through the Liberties sending everyone who breathed it into a frenzy: wrecked factory workers reaching for each other in their sleep, teenagers on corners suddenly kissing like their lives depended on it, old couples spitting out their falsies and ripping off each other's flannel nighties. I took it for granted that what I was hearing was a couple doing the do. I could have been wrong.

It took a mind-bending effort to assume, just for a second, that she had been coming to me after all. If she had, then the note said she had very probably made it along Kevin's route as far as Number 16. The suitcase said she had never made it out.

"Come on," I said, cutting off Kev, who was still going (" . . . wouldn't have bothered, only she had the biggest rack in the . . ."). "Let's go play where Mammy said we shouldn't."

Number 16 was in even worse shape than I'd thought. There were big gouges all the way down the front steps where the builders had dragged the fireplaces away, and someone had nicked the wrought-iron railings on either side, or maybe the Property King had sold them too. The whacking great sign announcing "PJ Lavery Builders" had fallen down the well by the basement windows; nobody had bothered to retrieve it.

Kevin asked, "What are we doing?"

"We're not sure yet," I said, which was true enough. All I knew was that we were following Rosie, feeling our way step by step and seeing where she led us. "We'll find out as we go, yeah?"

Kevin poked the door open and leaned forward, gingerly, to peer in. "If we don't end up in hospital first."

The hallway was a tangle of crisscrossing shadows, layered half a dozen deep where faint light seeped in from every angle: from the empty rooms with their doors pulled half off, through the filthy glass of the landing window, down the high stairwell along with the cold breeze. I found my torch. I may be out of the field, officially, but I still like being ready for the unexpected. I picked my leather jacket because it's comfortable enough that it almost never comes off, and it has enough pockets to hold all the basics: Fingerprint Fifi, three small plastic evidence bags, notebook and pen, Swiss Army knife, cuffs, gloves, and a slim, high-powered Maglite. My Colt Detective Special goes in a specially made harness that keeps it snug at the small of my back, under my jeans waistband and out of sight.

"I'm not joking," Kevin said, squinting up the dark stairs. "I don't like this. One sneeze and the whole place'll come down on top of us."

"The squad has a GPS tracker implanted in my neck. They'll come dig us out."

"Seriously?"

"No. Man up, Kev. We'll be fine." And I switched my torch on and stepped into Number 16. I felt the decades' worth of dust specks hanging suspended in the air, felt them shift and stir, rising up to whirl in cold little eddies around us.

The stairs creaked and flexed ominously under our weight, but they held. I started with the top front room, where I had found Rosie's note and where, according to Ma and Da, the Polish boys had found her suitcase. There was a great jagged hole where they had ripped out the fireplace; the wall around it was crowded with faded graffiti explaining who loved who, who was gay and who should fuck off. Somewhere on that fireplace, on their way to someone's Ballsbridge mansion, were my initials and Rosie's.

The floor was littered with the same old predictable stuff, cans and butts and wrappers, but most of it was thick with dust—kids had better places to hang out, these days, and enough money to get into them—and, attractively, used condoms had been added to the mix. In my day those were illegal; if you were lucky enough to get into a situation that called for one, you took your chances and spent the next few weeks shitting bricks. All the high corners were clotted with cobwebs, and there was a thin cold wind whistling through the gaps around the sash windows. Any day now those windows would be gone, sold to some merchant wanker whose wife wanted an adorable little touch of authenticity. I said—the place made me talk softly—"I lost my virginity in this room."

I felt Kevin glance at me, wanting to ask, but he held back. He said, "I can think of a lot more comfortable places for a ride."

"We had a blanket. And comfort isn't everything. I wouldn't have swapped this dive for the penthouse of the Shelburne."

After a moment Kevin shivered. "God, this place is depressing."

"Think of it as atmosphere. A trip down Memory Lane."

"Fuck that. I stay as far from Memory Lane as I can. Did you hear the Dalys? How bloody *miserable* were Sundays in the eighties? Mass, and then the shite Sunday dinner—how much do you want to bet it was boiled bacon, roast potatoes and cabbage?"

"Don't forget the pudding." I ran the torch beam along the floorboards: a few minor holes, a few splintered ends, no mended patches—and in here anything mended would have stuck out like a sore thumb. "Angel Delight, every time. Tasted like strawberry-flavored chalk, but if you didn't eat it, you were making the black babies starve."

"God, yeah. And then nothing to do all day long except hang out on the corner in the cold, unless you could bunk into the cinema or unless you wanted to put up with Ma and Da. Nothing on the telly except Father Whoever's sermon about contraception making you go blind, and even for that you had to spend hours messing around with those bloody rabbit ears trying to get the reception . . . By the end of some Sundays, I swear I was so bored I was looking forward to school."

Nothing where the fireplace had been, or up the chimney; just a bird's nest at the top, and years' worth of white droppings streaked down the sides. The chimney was barely wide enough to fit the suitcase. There was no way anyone could have got a grown woman's body up there, even temporarily. I said, "I'm telling you, mate, you should've come in here. This was where all the action was. Sex, drugs and rock and roll."

"By the time I was old enough for the good action, nobody came in here any more. There were rats."

"There always were. They added atmosphere. Come on." I headed into the next room.

Kevin trailed after me. "They added *germs*. You weren't here for it, but someone put down poison or something—I think it was Mad Johnny, you know how he had a total thing about rats, because of being in the trenches or whatever? Anyway, a bunch of the rats crawled into the walls and died, and Jesus, I'm not kidding, the *smell* of them. Worse than the piggeries. We'd have died of typhoid."

"Smells fine to me." I did the routine with the torch again. I was starting to wonder if I was on the world's stupidest wild-goose chase. One night of my family, and the loony was already rubbing off all over me.

"Well, yeah, obviously it went away after a while. But by that time we'd all switched to hanging around in that empty lot up at the corner of Copper Lane, you know the one? It was shite too—in winter you froze your balls off, and there were nettles and barbed wire all over the place—but all the kids from Copper Lane and Smith's Road hung out there too, so you had a better chance of getting a drink or a snog or whatever you were after. So we never really came back here."

"You missed out."

"Yeah." Kevin glanced around dubiously. He had his hands in his pockets, keeping his jacket wrapped tightly around himself so it wouldn't touch anything. "I'll live. This kind of stuff is why I can't stand it when people get nostalgic about the eighties. Kids bored to death, or playing with barbed wire, or shagging in bloody *rat* holes . . . What's to miss?"

I looked at him, standing there in his Ralph Lauren logos and his snazzy watch and his slick upmarket haircut, all full up with righteous indignation and looking a thousand miles out of place. I thought of him as a skinny, cowlicky kid in my patched hand-me-downs, running wild in and out of this house without ever realizing it wasn't good enough. I said, "There was an awful lot more to it than that."

"Like what? What's so great about losing your virginity in a shit hole?"

"I'm not saying I'd bring the eighties back if I had the choice, but don't shove the baby down the plughole with the bathwater. And I don't know about you, but I was never bored. Never. You might want to have a think about that."

Kevin shrugged and mumbled something that sounded like, "I don't have a clue what you're on about."

"Keep thinking. It'll come to you." I headed for the back rooms without bothering to wait for him—if he put his foot through a rotten floorboard in the shadows, that was his problem. After a moment he came sulking after me.

Nothing interesting in the back, nothing interesting in the hall-floor rooms, except a huge stash of vodka empties that someone had apparently preferred not to put out with their rubbish. At the top of the basement steps, Kevin balked. "No way. I'm not going down there. Seriously, Frank."

"Every time you say no to your big brother, God kills a kitten. Come on."

Kevin said, "Shay locked us down there once. You and me—I was only little. Do you remember that?"

"Nope. Is that why this place gives you the vapors?"

"It does not give me the fucking vapors. I just don't see why we're trying to get ourselves buried alive for no bloody reason at all."

I said, "Then wait for me outside."

After a moment he shook his head. He followed me for the same reason I had wanted him there to begin with: old habits last.

I had been down in that basement maybe three times, total. The local urban legend claimed that someone called Slasher Higgins had slit his deaf-mute brother's throat and buried him down there; if you invaded Gimpy Higgins's territory he would come for you, waving his rotting hands and making terrible grunting sounds, cue demonstration. The Higgins brothers had probably been invented by worried parents and none of us believed in them, but we still stayed out of the basement. Shay and his mates sometimes hung out down there to show what hard men they were, and a couple might go there if they were truly desperate for a shag and all the other rooms were otherwise occupied, but the good stuff happened upstairs: the ten-packs of Marlboros and the cheap two-liter bottles of cider, the matchstick-thin spliffs and the games of strip poker that never got more than halfway. Once when Zippy Hearne and I were about nine we dared each other to touch the back wall of the basement, and I had a vague memory of bringing Michelle Nugent down there a few years later, in the hope that it would scare her enough to make her grab hold of me and possibly snog me. No such luck; even at that age I went for girls who didn't scare easy.

The other time had been when Shay locked the two of us in. He'd left us there for what was probably an hour; it felt like days. Kevin had been two or three, and he had been too terrified even to scream. He had pissed his kacks instead. I had told him it would be OK, tried to kick the door down, tried to pry the boards off the windows with my fingers, and sworn to myself that someday I would beat the living shit out of Shay.

I moved the torch in a slow sweep. The basement was a lot like I remembered it, except that now I could see exactly why our parents might have had issues with us hanging out here. The windows were still boarded up, badly, with thin stripes of pale light falling in between the slats; the ceiling was bulging in a way I didn't like, and great chunks of plaster had fallen away so that the beams showed, bent and splintering. The dividing walls had buckled and crumbled till it was basically all one huge room, and in places the floor was collapsing in on itself, sagging into the foundations—subsidence, maybe, with nothing to prop the house up on the end-of-terrace side. A very long time ago someone had made an unimpressive effort, before giving up on the place altogether, to patch up a few of the more major holes by shoving slabs of concrete into them and hoping for the best. The place smelled like I remembered—piss, mold and dirt—only more so. "Ah, man," Kevin muttered unhappily, hovering at the bottom of the stairs. "Ah, man . . ." His voice echoed off into the far corners, bouncing off walls at odd angles so that it sounded like someone was murmuring, away in the dark. He winced and shut up.

Two of the concrete slabs were man-sized, and whoever had put them in had slapped lumpy cement around the edges, for the satisfaction of a job well done. The third one was even more half-arsed: just a lopsided chunk, maybe four feet by three, and fuck the cement.

"Right," Kevin said, a notch too loudly, behind me. "There you go. The gaff is still here and it's still a dive. Can we go now, yeah?"

I moved carefully into the middle of the floor and pressed a corner of the slab with the toe of my boot. There were years of grime holding it in place, but when I put my weight down I felt a very faint shift: it was rocking. If I had had some kind of lever, if there had been an iron bar or a chunk of metal in one of the heaps of debris in the corners, I could have lifted it.

"Kev," I said. "Think back for me. Those rats that died in the walls: was that the winter I left?"

Kevin's eyes slowly widened. The sickly gray bands of light made him look transparent, like a projection flickering on a screen. "Ah, Jaysus, Frank. Ah, no."

"I'm asking you a question. Just after I split, rats in the walls, yes or no?"

"Frank . . ."

"Yes or no."

"It was only *rats*, Frank. They were all over this place. We *saw* them, a load of times."

So that, by the time the weather warmed up, there would have been nothing left to cause a serious stink and start people complaining to the landlord or the Corpo. "And smelled them. Rotting."

After a moment Kevin said, finally, "Yeah."

I said, "Come on." I got hold of his arm—too hard, but I couldn't loosen my grip—and steered him up the stairs ahead of me, fast, feeling boards twist and splinter under our feet. By the time we got out onto the steps, into the sweep of cool damp breeze and fine rain, I had my phone in my other hand and I was dialing the Tech Bureau.

The tech I got hold of was not a happy bunny, either about working the weekend shift or about being dragged out of his nice warm geek-pen. I told him that I had information indicating that a body had been dumped under a concrete slab in the basement of Number 16 Faithful Place—I didn't go into minor details, like dates—that I needed a Bureau team and a couple of uniforms, and that I might or might not be on scene by the time they arrived. The tech made weaselly noises about search warrants, till I informed him that any possible suspect would have been an intruder on the premises and therefore could have had no expectation of privacy, and— when he kept whining—that in any case the house had been in public use for at least thirty years and therefore counted as a de facto public place by right of seisin, no warrant needed. I wasn't sure how well either of these would hold up in court, but that was some other day's problem, and it shut the tech up. I filed him in my mental database under Useless Prick, for future reference.

Kevin and I waited for the tech and his buddies on the steps of the student gaff at Number 11, close enough to give me a good view, far enough that with a little luck no one would associate me with what was going to be happening. If this went down the way I thought it would, I needed the Place to see me as their homecoming homeboy, not as a cop.

I lit a smoke and pointed the packet at Kevin, who shook his head. "What are we doing?" he asked.

"Staying out of the way."

"Do you not need to be there?"

"The techs are big boys," I said. "And girls. They can do their job without me holding their hands."

He still looked unsure. "Should we not . . . ? You know. Check if there's even something there, before we get the Guards out?"

Surprisingly enough, that very option had already occurred to me. It was taking every ounce of willpower I had not to haul up that slab, with my fingernails if necessary. I managed not to bite his head off. "Evidence," I said. "The techs have the equipment to collect it properly, and we don't. The last thing they need is us fucking things up. That's assuming there's anything in there."

Kevin shifted his weight to examine the seat of his trousers; the steps were wet, and he was still wearing his good work clothes from the day before. He said, "You sounded pretty definite on the phone."

"I wanted them down here. Today, not sometime next week when they were in the mood for an afternoon out."

Out of the corner of my eye I saw Kev's sideways glance at me, bewildered and a little wary. After that he stayed quiet, flicking dust and cobwebs off his trousers, head down, which suited me fine. Patience comes with the job and I'm generally considered to have a gift for it, but after what felt like a week I was considering taking a trip over to the Bureau and dragging the tech away from World of Warcraft by his stunted little gonads.

Shay came out onto the front steps, picking his teeth, and sauntered over to us. "Story?" he inquired.

Kevin started to say something, but I cut him off. "Not much."

"I saw you go into Cullens'."

"You probably did."

Shay glanced up and down the road; I saw the door of Number 16, still swinging half open, catch his eye. "Waiting for something?"

"Stick around," I said, grinning up at him and patting the step beside me. "Maybe you'll find out."

Shay snorted, but after a moment he headed up the steps and sat at the top, with his feet in my face. "Ma's looking for you," he told Kevin. Kevin groaned; Shay laughed and flipped up his collar against the cold.

That was when I heard tires on cobblestones, up around the corner. I lit another smoke and slumped down on the steps, going for anonymous and vaguely disreputable—Shay was sweet enough to help me out with that, just by being there. As it turned out, there was no need: two uniforms in a patrol car and three Bureau boys jumping out of their van, and I didn't know any of them. "Jaysus," Kevin said, softly and uneasily. "There's loads of them. Are there always . . . ?"

"This is about the minimum. They might call more in later, depending." Shay let out a long, mock-impressed whistle.

It had been a while since I'd watched a crime scene from outside the tape line, like a field undercover or a civilian. I'd forgotten just how the machinery looks in motion. The Bureau boys wrapped in their head-to-toe white, swinging their heavy boxes of sinister tricks, snapping their masks into place as they headed up the steps and vanished into Number 16, made the hairs on the back of my neck go up like a dog's. Shay sang softly to himself: "Three big knocks came knocking at the door, weela weela waile; two policemen and a Special Branch man, down by the River Saille . . ."

By the time the uniforms had unrolled their crime-scene tape along the railings, even before they had it secured, people smelled blood in the air and came looking for a taste. Old ones in curlers and head scarves materialized out of doorways and clumped up to swap commentary and juicy speculation ("Some young one's after having a baby and leaving it there." "God forgive you, that's terrible! Come here, Fiona Molloy's after putting on a load of weight, d'you think maybe . . . ?"). Men suddenly decided they needed a smoke on the front steps and a look at the weather; spotty young fellas and pram-faced young ones slouched against the end wall, pretending not to care. A handful of razor-headed little kids on skateboards zipped back and forth, staring at Number 16 with their mouths open, till one of them banged into Sallie Hearne and she gave him a smack across the back of the legs. The Dalys were out on their steps; Mr. Daly had an arm out across Mrs. Daly, holding her back. The whole scene made me edgy. I'm not happy when I can't keep track of how many people are around me.

The Liberties always did have a piranha sense for gossip. Back in Dalkey, if a crime-scene team had had the nerve to appear on the road without planning permission, no one would have been caught dead showing anything as vulgar as curiosity. One adventurous soul might have felt a sudden urge to trim the flowers in her front garden, and relayed anything she heard to her friends over herbal tea, but on the whole they would have found out the story when the newspaper was delivered the next morning. The Place, on the other hand, went straight for the information jugular. Old Mrs. Nolan had one of the uniforms firmly by the sleeve and looked to be demanding a full explanation. He looked like basic training had not equipped him for this.

"Francis," Kevin said. "There's probably nothing there."

"Maybe not."

"Seriously. I probably imagined it. Is it too late to—"

Shay asked, "Imagined what?"

"Nothing," I said.

"Kev."

"*Nothing.* That's what I'm *saying*. I probably imagined—"

"What are they looking for?"

"My bollix," I told him.

"Hope they brought a microscope."

"Fucking hell," Kev said unhappily, rubbing one eyebrow and staring at the uniforms. "I don't like this game any more, lads. I wish I'd just . . ."

"Sketch," Shay said suddenly. "Ma."

The three of us slid down on the steps, fast and in perfect sync, getting our heads well below the crowd horizon. I caught a glimpse of Ma, between bodies: standing on our front steps with her arms folded tight under her bosom, raking the street with a gimlet eye, like she knew well that this mess was all my fault and she was going to make me pay. Da was behind her, pulling on a smoke and watching the action with no expression at all.

Noises inside the house. One of the techs came out, jerking a thumb over his shoulder and saying something smart-arsed to make the uniforms snicker. He unlocked the van, messed around inside and ran back up the steps holding a crowbar.

Shay said, "He uses that in there, the whole gaff'll come down around his ears."

Kevin was still shifting, like the step made his arse ache. "What happens if they find nothing?"

"Then our Francis goes in the bad books," Shay said. "For wasting everyone's time. Wouldn't that be a pity?"

I said, "Thanks for caring. I'll be grand."

"Yeah, you will. You always are. What are they looking for?"

"Why don't you ask them?"

A hairy student in a Limp Bizkit T-shirt wandered out of Number 11, rubbing his head and looking impressively hungover. "What's the story?"

I said, "Go inside."

"It's our steps."

I showed him my ID. "Ah, *man*," he said, and dragged himself back inside, weighed down by the massive unfairness of it all.

"That's right," Shay said, "use the badge to intimidate him," but it was just reflex. His eyes, narrowed against the fading light, were on Number 16.

A great deep boom like cannon fire echoed through the street and off the houses, out over the Liberties. That concrete slab, dropping. Nora flinched and made a small, wild noise; Sallie Hearne pulled the neck of her cardigan tighter and crossed herself.

That was when I felt the shiver in the air, the electric charge starting deep down in the guts of Number 16 and rippling outwards: the techs' voices rising and then falling away, the uniforms turning to stare, the people swaying forwards, the clouds tightening over the rooftops.

Behind me Kevin said something with my name in it. I realized we were standing up and he had a hand on my arm. I said, "Get off."

"Frank . . ."

Inside the house someone called out an order, a sharp fast bark. I had stopped caring who knew I was a cop. "Stay there," I said.

The uniform in charge of defending the railings was pudgy, with a prissy face like someone's auntie. "Move along, sonny," he told me. His accent was six foot deep in bog. "Nothing to see."

I showed him my ID, which he read with his lips moving. Feet on stairs inside the house, a flash of a face past the landing window. Somewhere Mr. Daly shouted something, but his voice sounded faraway and slowed-down, like it was traveling through a long metal pipe.

"That there," the uniform told me, handing back the ID, "is Undercover. I wasn't informed of any undercover presence on the scene."

"You're being informed now."

"You'll have to speak to the investigating officer. That might be my sergeant or it might be one of the lads from the Murder Squad, depending on what—"

I said, "Get out of my way."

His mouth puckered up. "There's no need to take that tone with me. You can wait over there, where you were, until you're cleared to enter by the—"

I said, "Get out of my way or I'll punch your teeth in."

His eyes bugged, but I meant it and he moved. He was still telling me what he was going to report me for when I took the stairs three at a time and shouldered past his startled buddy, in the door.

Have a good laugh at this: deep down, I never for a second thought they would find anything. Me, Mr. Street-Smart Cynic giving newbies my savvy little spiel about how the world is always two steps more vicious than you plan for, I never believed it would do this; not when I opened that suitcase, not when I felt the concrete slab rocking in that dim basement, not when I felt that charge magnetizing the evening air. Right deep down, deeper than everything I'd learned before or since, I still believed Rosie. I believed her all the way down the crumbling stairs to the basement and I believed her when I saw the circle of masked faces turning upwards to me in the white glare of their lights, the concrete slab uprooted and skewed at a wild angle on the floor between cables and crowbars, when I smelled the rich underground reek of something horribly wrong. I believed her right up until I pushed between the techs and saw what they were crouched around: the jagged hole, the dark mat of tangled hair, the shreds that could have been denim and the slick brown bones scored with tiny toothmarks. I saw the delicate curl of a skeleton hand and I knew that when they found the fingernails, somewhere in the layers of muck and dead insects and rotten sludge, the right index one would be bitten down to the quick.

My jaw was clenched so tight I was sure my teeth were going to break. I didn't care; I wanted to feel that snap. The thing in the hole was curled up like a kid asleep, face tucked down in its arms. Maybe that saved my mind. I heard Rosie's voice say *Francis*, clear and amazed by my ear, our first time.

Someone said something snippy about contamination and a hand shoved a mask in my face. I backed away and ran my wrist over my mouth, hard. The cracks in the ceiling were skidding, jumping like a telly screen gone bad. I think I heard myself say, very softly, "Ah, shit."

One of the techs asked, "Are you OK?"

He was on his feet, way too close to me, and he sounded like he had asked it a couple of times. I said, "Yeah."

"Gets to you at first, yeah?" one of his team said smugly. "We've seen way worse."

"Are you the one who called it in?" the tech asked me.

"Yeah. Detective Frank Mackey."

"Are you Murder?"

It took me a second to work out what he was talking about. My mind had slowed down to a standstill. "No," I said.

The tech gave me a weird look. He was a geeky little object about half my age and half my size, probably the useless prick from earlier. "We called Murder," he said. "And the pathologist."

"Safe enough her," said his sidekick cheerfully. "She didn't get in here all by herself."

He was holding an evidence bag. If one of them touched her in front of me I knew I would batter the living shit out of him. "Good for you," I said. "I'm sure they'll be along any minute. I'll go give the uniforms a hand."

On my way up the stairs I heard the geek say something about the natives getting restless, and a spatter of snickers from his team. They sounded like a bunch of teenagers, and for one last shard of a second I would have sworn that it was Shay and his mates down in that basement smoking spliff and laughing at dark-edged jokes, that the hall door opened onto the life I had been born in, that none of this was happening.

Outside, the circle of people had thickened and closed in tighter, necks stretching, only a few feet away from my friend the guard dog. His mate had come down from the door to stand next to him at the railings. The clouds had moved in lower over the rooftops and the light had changed, turned a bruised, dangerous purplish-white.

Something moved, at the back of the crowd. Mr. Daly was coming through, straight-arming people out of the way like he barely saw them, eyes fixed on me.

"Mackey—" He was trying to shout, but his voice cracked and came out hoarse and hollow. "What's in there?"

The bogmonster said snippily, "I'm in charge of this scene. Step back."

The only thing I wanted in the world was for one of them, I didn't care which one, to try and hit me. "You couldn't take charge of your dick with both hands," I told the uniform, inches from his big soft pudding of a face, and when his eyes fell away from mine I shoved him out of my way and went to meet Mr. Daly.

The second I got through that gate he grabbed my collar and reefed me in hard, chin to chin. I felt a red zip of something like joy. He had more balls than the uniform or he wouldn't back down for a Mackey, and either one worked for me. "What's in there? What did you find?"

An old one squealed ecstatically and there were monkey hoots from the hoodies. I said, loud enough that plenty of people could hear me warn him, "You want to get your hands off me, pal."

"Don't you, you little bastard, don't you tell me to— Is that my Rosie in there? Is it?"

"*My* Rosie, pal. My girl. Mine. I'm telling you one more time: get your hands off me."

"This is your fault, you dirty little knacker. If she's in there, it's because of you." His forehead was grinding against mine and he was strong enough that my shirt was slicing the back of my neck. The hoodies had started chanting, "Fight! Fight! Fight!"

I got a good grip on his wrist and I was about to break it when I smelled him, his sweat, his breath: a hot, rank, animal smell that I knew by heart. The man was terrified, almost out of his mind. In that second I saw Holly.

All the red went out of my muscles. Something felt like it broke, deep down under my ribs. "Mr. Daly," I said, as gently as I could manage, "as soon as they know anything, they'll come and tell you. Until then, you need to go home."

The uniforms were trying to pull him off me, with a lot of loud bogger noise. Neither of us cared. There were wild white rings around Mr. Daly's eyes. *"Is that my Rosie?"*

I got my thumb on the nerve in his wrist and dug in. He gasped and his hands leaped off my collar, but in the second before the sidekick uniform dragged him away he jammed his jaw against mine and hissed in my ear, close as a lover, "Your fault."

Mrs. Daly came out of somewhere, making shapeless whimpering noises, and launched herself onto him and the sidekick. Mr Daly slumped and together they hauled him away, back into the gibbering crowd.

For some reason the bogmonster was attached to the back of my jacket. I elbowed him off, hard. Then I leaned back against the railings, readjusted my shirt and massaged my neck. My breath was coming fast.

"You haven't heard the last of this, sonny," the bogmonster informed me ominously. He was an unhealthy shade of purple. "I'm telling you now, I'll be filing a report."

I said, "Frank Mackey. That's E-Y. Tell them to put it on the pile."

The uniform gave an outraged old-maid snort and flounced off to take it out on the rubberneck posse, shouting at them to get back, with plenty of sweeping arm gestures. I caught a glimpse of Mandy with a little girl on her hip and one by the hand, three pairs of round stunned eyes. The Dalys stumbled up the steps of Number 3, holding on to each other, and disappeared inside. Nora leaned against the wall beside the door with a hand pressed over her mouth.

I went back to Number 11, which seemed like as good a place as any. Shay was lighting another cigarette. Kevin looked sick.

"They found something," he said, "didn't they?"

The pathologist and the morgue van would be rolling up any minute. "Yeah," I said. "They did."

"Is it . . . ?" A long silence. "What is it?"

I found my cigarettes. Shay, in what might have been a gesture of sympathy, held out his lighter. After a while Kevin asked, "Are you OK?"

I said, "I'm just dandy."

None of us said anything for a long time. Kevin took one of my smokes; the crowd settled down, gradually, and started swapping police-brutality stories and discussing whether Mr. Daly could sue. A few of the conversations were in undertones, and I caught the odd over-the-shoulder glance at me. I stared back without blinking, until there got to be too many of them to keep up with.

"Look out," Shay said softly, up to the heavy sky. "Old Mackey's back in town."

6

Cooper the pathologist, a narky little bollix with a God complex, got there first. He pulled up in his big black Merc, stared severely over the heads of the crowd till the waters parted to let him through, and stalked into the house, fitting on his gloves and leaving the murmurs to boil up louder behind him. A couple of hoodies drifted up around his car, but the bogmonster shouted something unintelligible at them and they sloped away again, without changing expression. The place felt too full and too focused, buzzing hard, like a riot was just waiting for its moment to kick off.

The morgue guys came next. They got out of their grimy white van and headed into the house with their blue canvas stretcher slung casually between them, and just like that, the crowd changed. The collective lightbulb had switched on: this wasn't just better entertainment than whatever pseudo-reality show was playing on the telly, this was the real thing, and sooner or later someone was coming out on that stretcher. Their feet stopped shifting and a low hiss ran down the street like a thin breeze, ebbed away to silence. That was when the Murder boys, with their usual impeccable timing, showed up.

One of the many differences between Murder and Undercover is our attitudes to subtlety. Undercovers are even better at it than you think, and when we feel like a giggle we do love watching the Murder boys loving their entrances. These two swung around the corner in an unmarked silver BMW that didn't need markings, braked hard, left the car at a dramatic angle, slammed their doors in sync—they had probably been practicing—

and swaggered off towards Number 16 with the music from *Hawaii Five-0* blasting through their heads in full surround sound.

One of them was a ferret-faced blond kid, still perfecting the walk and trying hard to keep up. The other one was my age, with a shiny leather brief-case swinging from one hand, and he wore his swagger like it was part of his El Snazzo suit. The cavalry had arrived, and it was Scorcher Kennedy.

Scorcher and I go back to cop college. He was the closest mate I made in training, by which I don't necessarily mean that we liked each other. Most of the lads came from places I had never heard of and didn't want to; their main goals, careerwise, were a uniform that didn't include wellies and a chance to meet girls who weren't their cousins. Scorcher and I were both Dubs and we both had long-term plans that involved no uniforms at all. We picked each other out on the first day, and spent the next three years trying to wipe the floor with each other at everything from fitness tests through snooker.

Scorcher's real name is Mick. The nickname was my doing, and person-ally I think I let him off lightly. He liked winning, our Mick; I'm pretty fond of it myself, but I know how to be subtle. Kennedy had a nasty little habit, when he came top at anything, of pumping his fist in the air and murmuring "Goal!" almost but not quite under his breath. I put up with it for a few weeks and then started taking the piss: You got your bed made, Mikey, is that a goal? Is it a good one, yeah? Is it a real scorcher? Did you put the ball in the back of the net? Did you come in from behind in extra time? I got along with the bog-boys better than he did; pretty soon every-one was calling him Scorcher, not always in a nice way. He wasn't pleased, but he hid it well. Like I said, I could have done a lot worse, and he knew it. I had been considering "Michelle."

We didn't make much effort to stay in touch, once we got back out into the big bad world, but when we ran into each other we went for drinks, mainly so we could keep tabs on who was winning. He made detective five months before I did, I beat him out of the floater pool and onto a squad by a year and a half; he got married first, but then he also got di-vorced first. All in all, the score was about even. The blond kid didn't sur-prise me. Where most Murder detectives have a partner, Scorch would naturally prefer a minion.

Scorcher is close on six foot, an inch or so taller than me, but he holds himself like a little guy: chest out, shoulders back, neck very straight. He has darkish hair, a narrow build, a serious set of jaw muscles and a knack for attracting the kind of women who want to be status symbols when they grow up and don't have the legs to bag a rugby player. I know, without being told, that his parents have serviettes instead of napkins and would rather go without food than without lace curtains. Scorch's accent is carefully upper-middle, but something in the way he wears a suit gives him away.

On the steps of Number 16, he turned and took a second to look around the Place, taking the temperature of what he was dealing with here. He spotted me, all right, but his eyes went over me like he'd never seen me before. One of the many joys of Undercover is that other squads can never quite figure out when you're on the job and when you're, say, on a genuine night out with the lads, so they tend to leave you alone, just in case. If they called it wrong and blew your cover, the bollocking in work would be nothing compared to the lifetime's worth of slagging waiting in the pub.

When Scorch and his little bum-chum had vanished into that dark doorway, I said, "Wait here."

Shay asked, "Do I look like your bitch?"

"Only around the mouth. I'll be back in a while."

"Leave it," Kevin said to Shay, without looking up. "He's working."

"He's talking like a fucking cop."

"Well, *duh*," Kevin said, finally running out of patience; he had had a long day, brotherwise. "Well spotted. For fuck's *sake*." He swung himself off the steps and shouldered his way through a bunch of Hearnes, towards the top of the road and out. Shay shrugged. I left him to it and headed off to retrieve the suitcase.

Kevin was nowhere in sight, my car was still intact, and when I got back Shay had sloped off too, gone wherever Shay goes. Ma was on her tiptoes outside our door, flapping a hand at me and squawking something that sounded urgent, but then Ma always does. I pretended I didn't see her.

Scorcher was on the steps of Number 16, having what looked like a deeply unrewarding conversation with my favorite guard bogger. I tucked the suitcase under my arm and strolled in between them. "Scorch," I said, slapping him on the back. "Good to see you."

"Frank!" He caught me in a macho two-handed shake. "Well well well. Long time no see. I hear you got in here ahead of me, yeah?"

"My bad," I said, throwing the uniform a big grin. "I just wanted a quick look. I might have a bit of an inside track here."

"Jesus, don't tease me. This one's ice cold. If you've got anything to point us in the right direction, I'll owe you big-time."

"That's the way I like it," I said, shunting him away from the bog-monster, who was earwigging with his mouth open. "I've got a possible ID for you. My information says it could be a girl called Rose Daly who went missing from Number Three, a while back."

Scorcher whistled, eyebrows going up. "Sweet. Got a description?"

"Nineteen years old, five foot seven, curvy build—maybe ten stone—long curly red hair, green eyes. I can't tell you for sure what she was last seen wearing, but it probably included a denim jacket and fourteen-hole ox-blood Doc boots." Rosie lived in those boots. "Does that match what you found?"

Scorch said, carefully, "It doesn't exclude what we found."

"Come on, Scorch. You can do better than that."

Scorcher sighed, ran a hand through his hair and then patted it back into place. "According to Cooper, it's a young adult female, been there somewhere between five years and fifty. That's all he'll say till he gets her on the table. Techs found a bunch of unidentified crap, a jeans button and a handful of metal rings that could be the eyelets from those Docs. The hair might've been red; it's hard to tell."

That dark mess soaked with God knew what. I said, "Any idea what killed her?"

"If only. Bloody Cooper—do you know him? He's a prick if he doesn't like you, and for some reason he's never liked me. He won't confirm anything except that, no shit Sherlock, she's dead. To me it looks a lot like someone whacked her in the head a few times with a brick—the skull's smashed open—but what do I know, I'm only a detective. Cooper was droning on about post-mortem damage and pressure fractures . . ." Suddenly Scorcher stopped glancing around the road and looked hard at me. "Why all the interest? This isn't some informant who got herself in the shit for you, is it?"

It always amazes me that Scorcher doesn't get punched more often. I said, "My informants don't get whacked in the head with bricks, Scorcher. Ever. They lead long, happy, fulfilling lives and die of old age."

"Whoa," Scorch said, putting his hands up. "Excuse me for living. If she's not one of yours, then why do you care what happened to her—and, not to look a gift horse in the mouth, but how did you happen to wander in on this one?"

I gave him everything that he would have got somewhere else anyway: young love, midnight rendezvous, jilted hero galloping off into the cold cruel world, suitcase, trail of brilliant deductions. When I finished, he was giving me a wide-eyed look, awe tinged with something like pity, that I didn't like at all.

"Holy shit," he said, which did in fact sum things up fairly well.

"Breathe, Scorch. It's been twenty-two years. That torch burned out a long time back. I'm only here because my favorite sister sounded like she was about to have a heart attack, and that could have ruined my whole weekend."

"Still. Sooner you than me, mate."

"I'll call you if I need a shoulder to cry on."

He shrugged. "I'm just saying. I don't know how things work round your way, but I wouldn't enjoy explaining this one to my super."

"My super's a very understanding guy. Be nice to me, Scorch. I've got Christmas pressies for you."

I handed over the suitcase and my Fingerprint Fifi envelopes—he would get the job done faster than I could and with less hassle, and anyway Mr. Daly no longer felt like quite so much of a personal priority. Scorcher examined them like they had cooties. "What were you planning on doing with these?" he inquired. "If you don't mind me asking."

"Running them past a few friends in low places. Just to get an idea what we might be dealing with."

Scorcher raised an eyebrow, but he didn't comment. He flipped through the envelopes, reading the labels: Matthew Daly, Theresa Daly, Nora Daly. "You're thinking the family?"

I shrugged. "Nearest and dearest. As good a starting place as any."

Scorcher glanced up at the sky. The air had turned dark as evening, and the first big drops of rain were splattering down like they meant it; the crowd was starting to dissolve, people filtering back to whatever they were supposed to be doing, only the hard core of hoodies and head scarves sticking it out. He said, "I've got a couple of things to finish up here, and I'll want a quick preliminary chat with this girl's family. Then we should go for a pint, you and me, yeah? Do some catching up. The kid can keep an eye on the scene for a while; the practice'll do him good."

The sounds behind him changed, deep down in the house: a long grinding scrape, a grunt, boots thudding on hollow boards. Vague white shapes moved, mixed in with the thick layers of shadows and the hellfire glow coming up from the basement. The morgue boys were bringing out their catch.

The old ones gasped and blessed themselves, licking up every second. The morgue boys passed by me and Scorcher with their heads down against the building rain, one of them already bitching over his shoulder about traffic. They came close enough that I could have reached out and touched the body bag. It was just a shapeless crumple on their stretcher, so near flat that it could have been empty, so light that they carried it like it was nothing at all.

Scorch watched them sliding it into the back of the van. "I'll only be a few minutes," he said. "Stick around."

We went to the Blackbird, a few corners away, far enough and exclusively male enough that the news hadn't made it in yet. The Blackbird was the first pub I ever got served in, when I was fifteen and coming from my first day's casual work hauling bricks on a building site. As far as Joe the barman was concerned, if you did a grown man's job, you had earned a grown man's pint afterwards. Joe had been replaced by some guy with an equivalent toupee, and the fog of cigarette smoke had been improved into an aura of stale booze and BO so thick you could see it heaving, but apart from that nothing much had changed: same cracked black-and-white photos of unidentified sports teams on the walls, same fly-spotted mirrors behind the bar, same fake-leather seats with their guts spilling out, a handful of old

fellas on personal bar stools and a clump of guys in work boots, half of
them Polish and several of them definitely underage.

I planted Scorcher, who wears his job on his sleeve, at a discreet corner
table, and went up to the bar myself. When I brought back our pints,
Scorcher had his notebook out and was jotting away with a sleek designer
pen—apparently the Murder boys were above cheapo ballpoints. "So," he
said, snapping the notebook shut one-handed and accepting his glass with
the other, "this is your home turf. Who knew?"

I gave him a grin with just a touch of warning thrown in. "You figured
I grew up in a mansion in Foxrock, yeah?"

Scorch laughed. "Hardly. You always made it clear you were, well, salt
of the earth. You were so secretive about details, though, I figured you had
to come from some shit hole tower block. I never pictured somewhere
this—what'll we call it?—colorful."

"That's one word for it."

"According to Matthew and Theresa Daly, you haven't been seen in the
area since the night you and Rose flew the coop."

I shrugged. "There's only so much local color one man can take."

Scorch drew a neat smiley face in the head of his pint. "So. Nice to be
back home, yeah? Even if this isn't the way you pictured it?"

"If there's a silver lining here," I said, "which I doubt, that's not it."

He gave me a pained look, like I'd farted in church. "What you need to
do," he explained to me, "is see this as a positive."

I stared at him.

"I'm serious. Take the negative, turn it around into a positive." He held
up a beer mat and flipped it over, to demonstrate the concept of turning
something around.

Normally I would have communicated to him exactly what I thought
of this bat-shit crazy advice, but I wanted something from him, so I kept a
lid on it. "Enlighten me," I said.

Scorcher demolished the smiley face in one long gulp and wagged a
finger at me. "Perception," he said, when he came up for air, "is everything.
If you believe that this can work to your advantage, then it will. Do you
follow me?"

"Not really, no," I said. Scorcher gets meaningful on adrenaline, the way some guys get maudlin on gin. I wished I had ordered a short on the side.

"It's all about *belief*. This country's entire success is built on belief. Is Dublin property really worth a grand per square foot? Is it fuck. But that's what it goes for, because people *believe* it is. You and me, Frank, we were ahead of the curve there. Back in the eighties, this whole country was in the shit, it hadn't a hope in hell, but we believed in ourselves, you and me. That's how we got where we are today."

I said, "I got where I am today by being good at my job. And I'm hoping to Christ you did too, mate, because I'd like to see this one solved."

Scorcher gave me a stare that was halfway to an arm wrestle. "I am very fucking good at my job," he told me. "Very, very fucking good. Do you know the overall solve rate for the Murder Squad? Seventy-two percent. And do you know my personal solve rate?"

He left a gap for me to shake my head. "Eighty-six percent, sonny. Eighty-read-it-and-weep-six. You got lucky when you got me today."

I gave him a reluctantly impressed grin and a nod, letting him win. "I probably did, yeah."

"Damn right you did." Point made, Scorch relaxed back on his bench, winced and shot an irritable glare at a busted spring.

"Maybe," I said, holding my pint up to the light and squinting thoughtfully at it, "maybe this was both of our lucky day."

"How's that?" Scorcher demanded, suspiciously. Scorch knows me well enough to be suspicious on principle.

I said, "Think about this. When you start work on a case, what's the one thing you want most?"

"A full confession backed by eyewitnesses and forensics."

"No, no, no. Stay with me here, Scorcher. You're thinking specific. I need you to think universal. In one word, what's your biggest asset, as a detective? What's your favorite thing in all the whole wide world?"

"Stupidity. Give me five minutes with a thicko—"

"*Information.* Any type, any quality, any quantity, it's all good. Info is ammo, Scorch. Info is fuel. Without stupid, we can always find a way; without info, we're nowhere."

Scorcher considered this. "So?" he asked cautiously.

I spread out my arms and grinned at him. "The answer to your prayers, man."

"Kylie in a thong?"

"Your professional prayers. All the info you could ever want, all the info that you'll never get on your own because no one from around here is ever going to tell you, all neatly wrapped up in your very favorite trained observer. Me."

Scorcher said, "Do me a favor and come down to my level for a second, Frank. Get specific. What do you want?"

I shook my head. "This isn't about me. It's about a win-win situation. The best way for us to turn this into a positive is together."

"You want to be on the case."

"Forget what I want. Think about what's good for you and me both—not to mention for the case. We both want a solve here, am I right? Isn't that everyone's top priority?"

Scorcher pretended to think that over for a minute. Then he shook his head, slowly and regretfully. "No can do. Sorry, mate."

Who the hell says *No can do*? I gave him a grin like a dare. "Are you worried? You'll still be the lead detective, Scorch. It'll still be your name on the result. We don't do solve rates, over in Undercover."

"Well, good for you," Scorch said smoothly, not taking the bait. He'd got better at managing his ego, over the years. "You know I'd love to have you onboard, Frank, but my super would never go for it."

The Murder Squad super is in fact not my biggest fan, but I doubted Scorcher knew that. I raised an eyebrow and did amused. "Your super doesn't trust you to pick your own team?"

"Not unless I can back up my choices. Give me something solid to show him, Frank. Share some of this famous info. Did Rose Daly have any enemies?"

We both knew I wasn't in a position to point out that I had already shared plenty. "None that I know of. That's one reason why it never occurred to me that she could be dead."

He looked disbelieving. "What, was she an idiot?"

I said, on a pleasant note that let him figure out whether I was joking, "She was a lot smarter than you'll ever be."

"Boring?"

"A long way from."

"A dog?"

"The neighborhood babe. What the hell kind of taste do you think I have?"

"Then I guarantee you she had enemies. A bore or an uggo might manage not to get up anyone's nose, but if a girl's got brains and looks and personality, she's going to piss someone off, somewhere along the way." He gave me a curious look, over his pint. "The rose-colored glasses aren't your style, Frank. You must have been really crazy about this one, were you?"

Dangerous waters. "First love," I said, shrugging. "Long time ago. I probably idealized her, all right, but she was a genuinely nice girl. I don't know of anyone who had a problem with her."

"No exes with grudges? No catfights?"

"Rosie and I had been going out for years, Scorch. Since we were sixteen. I think she had a couple of boyfriends before me, but we're talking kid stuff: hold hands in the cinema, write each other's name on your desk in school, break up after three weeks because the commitment's getting to be too intense."

"Names?"

He had his shiny detective pen all ready. Some poor fuckers were going to be getting unwelcome visits. "Martin Hearne, aka Zippy at the time, although he might not answer to that nowadays. Lived at Number Seven, called himself Rosie's boyfriend very briefly when we were about fifteen. Before that there was some kid called Colm, who was in school with us till his parents moved back to bogland, and when we were about eight she kissed Larry Sweeney from Smith's Road on a dare. I seriously doubt any of them was still carrying a torch for her."

"No jealous girlies?"

"Jealous of what? Rosie wasn't the femme fatale type; she didn't flirt with other girls' fellas. And I may be a ride, but even if anyone had known we were going out together, which they didn't, I doubt some girl would have bumped Rosie off just to get her hands on my hot body."

Scorcher snorted. "I'm with you on that one. But Jesus, Frank, help me out here. You're giving me nothing I couldn't have got from any gossipy old one within a mile. If I'm going to wangle you past my super, I need something special. Give me a couple of motives, or the victim's juicy secrets, or— Ah, here we go." He snapped his fingers, pointed at me. "Talk me through the night you were supposed to meet her. Eyewitness stuff. Then we'll see what we can do."

In other words, where were you on the evening of the fifteenth, sonny boy. I wasn't clear on whether he genuinely thought I was stupid enough to miss that. "Fair enough," I said. "Sunday into Monday, December fifteenth to sixteenth, 1985. At approximately half past eleven, I left my home at Eight Faithful Place and proceeded to the top of the road, where I had arranged to meet Rose Daly around twelve o'clock, depending on when our families went to sleep and we found opportunities to exit our homes without being seen. I remained there until somewhere between five and six in the morning—I couldn't swear to the exact time. I left the spot only once, for maybe five minutes just after two o'clock, when I entered Number Sixteen to check whether there had been some confusion about the rendezvous point and Rose was waiting for me there instead."

"Any reason why Number Sixteen would have been an alternative meeting point?" Scorch was taking notes, in some kind of personal shorthand.

"We'd talked about it, before we decided on the end of the road. It was the local hangout spot; kids met there all the time. If you wanted to try drinking or smoking or snogging or anything your parents wouldn't approve of, and you weren't old enough to do it anywhere else, Number Sixteen was the place to go."

Scorch nodded. "So that's where you looked for Rose. Which rooms did you go into?"

"I checked every room on the first floor—I wasn't about to make any noise, so I couldn't call her. No one was there, I didn't see the suitcase, and I didn't see or hear anything unusual. I then moved on to the top floor, where I found a note signed by Rose Daly on the floor of the front right-hand room. The note implied that she had decided to make her way to England on her own. I left it there."

"I've seen it. It's not addressed to anyone. Why would you assume it was for you?"

The thought of him salivating over that note and dropping it delicately into an evidence bag made me want to deck him all over again, and that was before we got to the not-so-subtle hint that Rosie had been having doubts. I wondered what, exactly, the Dalys had chosen to tell him about me. "It seemed like a logical assumption to make," I said. "I was the one she was supposed to be meeting. If she left a note, it seemed like it would probably be for me."

"She hadn't dropped any hints that she was having second thoughts?"

"Not a one," I said, giving him a big smile. "And we don't know that she was, Scorch, now do we?"

"Maybe not," said Scorcher. He scribbled something on his pad and narrowed his eyes at it. "You didn't go down to the basement?"

"No. No one ever did: it was dark, it was rickety, it had rats and damp and it stank like hell, we left it alone. I had no reason to think Rosie would be there."

Scorcher bounced his pen off his teeth and examined his notes. I sank a third of my pint and thought, as briefly as I could, about the possibility that Rosie had in fact been in that basement while I was busy being love-lorn upstairs, a few yards away.

"So instead," Scorcher said, "in spite of the fact that you'd taken Rose's note as a Dear John, you went back to the end of the road and kept waiting. Why?"

His voice was mild, casual, but I caught the power rush in his eye. The little shitehawk was loving this. "Hope springs eternal," I said, shrugging. "And women change their minds. I figured I'd give her a chance to change hers back."

Scorch gave a manly little snort. "Women, eh? So you gave her three or four hours, and then cut your losses. Where did you go?"

I gave him the rundown on the squat and the smelly rockers and the generous sister, forgetting surnames, just in case he decided to give anyone hassle. Scorcher took notes. When I had finished he asked, "Why didn't you just go home?"

"Momentum, and pride. I wanted to move out anyway; what Rosie decided didn't change that. England didn't sound like as much fun all by myself, but neither did slinking back home like a gobshite with my tail between my legs. I was all geared up to leave, so I kept walking."

"Mmm," Scorcher said. "Let's go back to the approximately six hours— now that's love, specially in December—the six hours you spent waiting at the top of the road. Do you remember anyone passing by, entering or exiting any of the houses, anything like that?"

I said, "One or two things stick out. Somewhere around midnight, I can't give you an exact time, I heard what I thought was a couple doing the business nearby. Looking back, though, the noises could have gone either way: a shag or a struggle. And later, maybe between quarter past one and half past, someone went down the back gardens on the even-numbered side of the road. I don't know how much good it'll do you, after all this time, but take it for what it's worth."

"Anything could come in useful," Scorcher said neutrally, scribbling. "You know how it goes. And that was it for human contact? All night long, in a neighborhood like this one? Let's face it, it's not exactly the leafy suburbs."

He was starting to piss me off, which presumably was just what he was aiming for, so I kept my shoulders easy and took my time with my pint. "It was a Sunday night. By the time I got out there, everything was closed and just about everyone was in bed, or I'd have held off till later. There was no activity on Faithful Place; some people were still awake and talking, but no one went up or down the road, or in or out of any of the houses. I heard people passing around the corner, up towards New Street, and a couple of times someone got close enough that I moved out of the light so they wouldn't spot me, but I didn't recognize anyone."

Scorch twiddled his pen meditatively, watching the light move on the surface. "So no one would spot you," he repeated. "Because no one knew the two of you were an item. Isn't that what you said?"

"That's right."

"All this cloak-and-dagger stuff. Any particular reason for it?"

"Rosie's father didn't like me. He hit the roof when he first found out we were going out—that's why we'd been keeping the relationship under wraps ever since. If we'd told him I wanted to take his little girl off to

London, there would've been holy war. I figured it'd be easier to get forgiveness than permission."

"Some things never change," Scorch said, a little sourly. "Why didn't he like you?"

"Because he's got no taste," I said, grinning. "How could anyone not love this face?"

He didn't grin back. "Seriously."

"You'd have to ask him. He didn't share his thought process with me."

"I will. Anyone else know what the two of you were planning?"

"I didn't tell anyone. As far as I know, Rosie didn't either." Mandy was all mine. Scorcher could talk to her himself, and good luck to him; I would have enjoyed watching that one.

Scorcher looked over his notes, taking his time and sipping his pint. "Right," he said eventually, clicking his fancy pen shut. "That should just about do it, for now."

"See what your super thinks," I said. There wasn't a chance in hell he would talk to his super, but if I backed off too easily he would start wondering what kind of Plan B I had up my sleeve. "That lot might give him the warm fuzzies about a bit of collaboration."

Scorch met my eyes, and for just half a second too long he didn't blink. He was thinking what I had realized the instant I heard about that suitcase. The obvious suspect was the guy on the spot with motive and opportunity and not a sliver of an alibi, the guy waiting to meet Rosie Daly, the guy she had quite possibly been going to dump that night; the guy claiming, swear to God, Officer, that she never showed up.

Neither of us was about to be the first to put that on the table. "I'll do my best," Scorcher said. He tucked his notebook into his suit pocket. He wasn't looking at me. "Thanks for that, Frank. I might need you to go over it with me again, at some stage."

"No problem," I said. "You know where to find me."

He finished his pint in a long swallow. "And remember what I said to you. Think positive. Turn it around."

"Scorch," I said. "That mess your mates just hauled off used to be my girl. I thought she was across the water, living it up, happy as Larry. Forgive me if I'm having a hard time seeing the upside here."

Scorcher sighed. "OK," he said. "Fair enough. You want me to paint you a picture?"

"I can't think of anything I'd love more."

"You've got a good rep on the job, Frank, a great rep, except for one little thing: the word on the street is that you've got a tendency to fly solo. To—how will I put this?—to prioritize the rule book a tiny bit less than you should. That suitcase is exactly the kind of thing I'm talking about. And the brass like team players a whole lot better than flying aces. Mavericks are only cute when they're Mel Gibson. If you handle yourself right during an investigation like this one, where you're obviously under a lot of strain, if you show everyone that you can take a seat on the bench for the good of the team, then your stock could go up big-time. Think long term. Do you follow me?"

I gave him a big wide smile, so I wouldn't punch him. "That's one serious plate of mixed cliché salad, Scorcher. You'll have to give me a while to digest it all."

He eyed me for a moment; when he couldn't read anything off my face, he shrugged. "Whatever. Just a word to the wise." He stood up and settled the lapels of his jacket. "I'll be in touch," he said, making it sound just the subtlest shade like a warning, and then he picked up his poncified briefcase and strode out.

I had no intention of moving anytime soon. I already knew I was taking the rest of the weekend off. One reason was Scorcher. He and his Murder mates were going to spend the next couple of days bouncing around Faithful Place like a pack of Jack Russells on speed, snuffling in corners and poking their noses into people's delicate zones and generally pissing everyone off. I needed to make it clear to the Place that I was nothing to do with them.

The second reason was Scorch again, just from a different angle. He appeared to be a teensy bit wary where I was concerned, and keeping out of his hair for twenty-four hours would go a long way towards keeping him out of mine. When you look at someone you knew when you were young, you always see the person you first met, and Scorch was still seeing a hair-trigger kid who did things fast or not at all. It wouldn't occur to him that, while he was getting better at wrangling his ego, I might have been getting better at patience. If you want to hunt like a good little panting puppy dog, shooting off on the trail the second you're let off the leash, you work Murder. If you want Undercover, and I always did, you learn to hunt the way big cats do: set up your ambush, stay low to the ground and move closer by hidden inches, for as long as it takes.

The third reason was presumably fuming in Dalkey, in a full-on strop with me. Sometime very soon I needed to deal with both her and, God help us all, Olivia, but a man has his limits. I don't get drunk, but after the day I'd had, I felt I had every right to spend the evening discovering just how paralytic I could get before I fell over. I caught the barman's eye and said, "I'll have another."

The pub had emptied out, probably in response to Scorcher. The barman wiped glasses and examined me across the counter, taking his time. After a while he nodded towards the door. "Friend of yours?"

I said, "That's not the word I'd use."

"Haven't seen you in before."

"Probably not."

"You anything to the Mackeys up on Faithful Place?"

The eyes. "Long story," I said.

"Ah," the barman said, like he understood everything there was to know about me, "we've all got one of those," and he slid a glass under the tap with a neat flourish.

The last time Rosie Daly and I touched was on a Friday, nine days before Zero Hour. Town was crisp and cold and packed that evening, all the Christmas lights on and the shoppers hurrying and the street hawkers selling wrapping paper five for a pound. I wasn't a huge fan of Christmas in general—my ma's crazy always hit its impressive annual peak at Christmas dinner, so did my da's drinking, something always wound up broken and at least one person always wound up in tears—but that year it all felt unreal and glassy, right on the edge between enchanting and sinister: the shiny-haired private-school girls singing "Joy to the World" for charity were just a little too clean and blank-faced, the kids pressing their noses up against

Switzer's windows to stare at the fairy-tale scenes looked just a little too drugged on all that color and rhythm. I kept a hand in the pocket of my army parka as I headed through the crowds; that day of all days, the last thing I wanted was to get robbed.

Rosie and I always met in O'Neill's on Pearse Street—it was a Trinity student pub, which meant the wanker count was a little high, but we didn't stick out and there was no chance of running into anyone we knew. The Dalys thought Rosie was out with the girls; my family didn't give a damn where I was. O'Neill's is big, it was filling up fast and billowing with warmth and smoke and laughter, but I picked out Rosie right away by that burst of copper hair: leaning on the bar, saying something to make the barman grin. By the time she paid for our pints I had found us a table in a nice private corner.

"Little tosser," she said, putting the pints on the table and nodding backwards at a clump of snickering students up at the bar. "Tried to look down my top when I leaned over."

"Which one?"

I was already getting up, but Rosie threw me a look and pushed my pint towards me. "Sit down there, you, and drink that. I'll sort him myself." She slid onto the bench next to me, close enough that our thighs touched. "That fella there, lookit."

Rugby jersey, no neck, turning away from the bar with his precarious double handful of pints. Rosie gave him a wave to get his attention back; then she batted her lashes, leaned forward and swirled the tip of her tongue in little circles in the head of her pint. Rugby Boy's eyes popped, his mouth fell open, he got his ankles tangled in a stool and half his pints went down someone's back. "Now," Rosie said, giving him the finger and forgetting about him. "Did you get them?"

I put a hand into my coat, slung over the arm of the seat where I could keep an eye on it, and found the envelope. "There," I said, "all ours," and I fanned out two tickets and laid them on the banged-up wooden table between us. DUN LAOGHAIRE–HOLYHEAD, DEPARTING 06:30AM, MONDAY 16 DECEMBER. PLEASE ARRIVE AT LEAST 30 MINUTES BEFORE DEPARTURE.

The sight of them made my adrenaline spike all over again. The breath went out of Rosie in an amazed little laugh.

I said, "I thought the early boat was better. We could've had the overnight one, but it'd be harder to get our stuff and get away in the evening. This way we can head out to the harbor on Sunday night, whenever we get a chance, and then wait there till it's time. Yeah?"

"God," Rosie said after a moment, still breathless. "My God. I feel like we should be—" Her arm curved round the tickets, shielding them from the people at the next tables. "You know?"

I wove my fingers through hers. "We're all right here. We've never seen anyone we know, have we?"

"It's still Dublin. I won't feel safe till that ferry's out of Dun Laoghaire. Put them away, will you?"

"Will you look after them? My ma goes through our stuff."

Rosie grinned. "Not surprised. I wouldn't be surprised if my da goes through mine, as well, but he won't touch the knicker drawer. Give us those." She picked up the tickets like they were made of fine lace, slid them carefully into the envelope and tucked it into the top pocket of her jeans jacket. Her fingers stayed there for a moment, over her breast. "Wow. Nine days, and then . . ."

"And then," I said, lifting my pint, "here's to you and me and our new life."

We clinked glasses and took a drink, and I kissed her. The pint was top-notch, the warmth of the pub was starting to thaw out my feet after the walk through town, there was tinsel draped over the picture frames on the walls, and the bunch of students at the next table burst into loud tipsy laughter. I should have been the happiest camper in the whole pub, but the evening still had that precarious feel to it, like a brilliant sparkly dream that could turn nasty in a blink. I let Rosie go because I was afraid I was going to kiss her hard enough to hurt.

"We'll have to meet late," she said, hooking one knee over mine. "Midnight, or after. My da doesn't go to bed till eleven, and I'll have to give him a while to go asleep."

"My lot are conked out by half past ten, on a Sunday. Sometimes Shay stays out late, but as long as I don't run into him on his way in, no problem. Even if I do, he won't stop us; he'll be delighted to see the back of me."

Rosie flicked an eyebrow and took another swig of her pint. I said, "I'll head out by midnight. If it takes you a little longer, no bother."

She nodded. "Shouldn't be much later. The last bus'll be gone, though. Are you up for walking to Dun Laoghaire?"

"Not carrying all our stuff. By the time we got to the boat, we'd be dead on our feet. It'll have to be a taxi."

She gave me an impressed look that was only half put on. "La-di-da!"

I grinned and wound one of her curls around my finger. "I've a couple more nixers coming up this week; I'll have the cash. Nothing but the best for my girl. I'd get you a limo if I could, but that'll have to wait. Maybe for your birthday, yeah?"

She smiled back, but it was an absent smile; she wasn't in the mood for messing. "Meet in Number Sixteen?"

I shook my head. "The Shaughnessys have been hanging out there a lot, the last while. I don't fancy running into them." The Shaughnessy brothers were harmless, but they were also loud and thick and mostly stoned, and it would take way too long to get it through their heads why they needed to shut up and pretend they hadn't seen us. "Top of the road?"

"We'll get seen."

"Not after midnight on a Sunday. Who'll be out, except us and the Shaughnessy eejits?"

"All it'd take is one person. And anyway, what if it's raining?"

This wasn't like Rosie, this kind of edginess; mostly she didn't know what nerves were. I said, "We don't have to settle it now. We'll see how the weather's shaping up next week, decide then."

Rosie shook her head. "We shouldn't meet up again, not till we go. I don't want my da getting suspicious."

"If he hasn't by now . . ."

"I know. I know. I just—God, Francis, those tickets . . ." Her hand went back to her pocket. "It's this close to real. I don't want us relaxing, even for a second, in case something goes wrong."

"Like what?"

"I don't *know*. Someone stopping us."

"No one's going to stop us."

"Yeah," Rosie said. She bit down on her fingernail, and for a second her eyes slipped away from mine. "I know. We'll be grand."

I said, "What's up?"

"Nothing. Let's meet up at the top of the road, like you said, unless it's lashing rain. Then we'll go for Number Sixteen; the lads won't be out if the weather's awful. Yeah?"

"Yeah," I said. "Rosie. Look at me. Are you feeling guilty about this?"

One corner of her mouth twisted wryly. "I am in my arse. It's not like we're doing it just for the laugh; if my da hadn't acted like such a bleeding muppet about the whole thing, we'd never have thought of this. Why? Are you?"

"Not a chance. Kevin and Jackie are the only ones who'll miss me, I'll send them something nice out of my first wages, they'll be delighted. Are you going to miss your family, is that it? Or the girls?"

She thought about that for a moment. "The girls, yeah, I am. And my family, a bit. But, sure . . . I've known for ages that I'd be moving out soon enough. Before we even left school me and Imelda were talking about maybe heading to London ourselves, up until . . ." A fleeting, sideways grin to me. "Up until you and me came up with a better plan. Whatever happened, I'd say sooner or later I'd have been gone. Wouldn't you?"

She knew better than to ask whether I'd miss my family. "Yeah," I said—I wasn't sure whether it was true or not, but it was what both of us needed to hear. "I'd have been out of here, one way or another. I like this way a lot, though."

That flicker of smile again, still not a whole one. "Same here."

I asked, "Then what's up? Ever since you sat down, you've been acting like that seat's itching the arse off you."

That got Rosie's full attention. "Look who's talking. You're a laugh a minute tonight, so you are, it's like going out with Oscar the bleedin' Grouch—"

"I'm up to ninety because *you're* up to ninety. I thought you'd be over the moon about the tickets, and instead—"

"Bollix. You got here like that. You were only dying for a chance to punch the head off that pathetic eejit—"

"And so did you. Are you having second thoughts? Is that what this is about?"

"If you're trying to break it off with me, Francis Mackey, you act like a man and do it yourself. Don't you try to make me do your dirty work."

We glared at each other for a second, balanced on the edge of a flat-out row. Then Rosie let out her breath, slumped back on the bench and pushed her hands through her hair. She said, "I'll tell you what it is, Francis. The pair of us are nervous because we're after getting above ourselves."

I said, "Speak for yourself."

"I am doing. Here's us wanting to head off to London and take on the music industry, no less. No more factories for us, thanks very much, not our style, we're gonna be working for rock bands. What would your mammy say to you, if she knew?"

"She'd want to know who the bloody hell do I think I am. Then she'd give me a clatter round the ear, call me a fecking simpleton and tell me to get a hold of myself. It'd be loud."

"And that," Rosie said, raising her pint to me, "*that's* why we're up to ninety, Francis. Just about everyone we've ever known in our whole lives would say the same thing: they'd say we're getting above ourselves. If we fall for that shite, we'll only end up giving out to each other and making each other miserable. So we need to cop on to ourselves, rapid. Yeah?"

Secretly, I still get proud of the ways Rosie and I loved each other. We had no one else to learn from—none of our parents were shining examples of relationship success—so we learned this from each other: when someone you love needs you to, you can get a hold of your five-alarm temper, get a hold of the shapeless things that scare you senseless, act like an adult instead of the Cro-Magnon teenager you are, you can do a million things you never saw coming. I said, "Come here." I slid my hands up Rosie's arms and cupped her cheeks, and she leaned forward and tipped her forehead against mine so that the rest of the world vanished behind the bright heavy tangle of her hair. "You're dead right. I'm sorry I was a bollix."

"We might make an arse of this, but there's no reason we shouldn't give it our best shot."

I said, "You're a smart woman, d'you know that?"

Rosie watched me, close enough that I could see the gold flecks in the green of her eyes, the tiny crinkles at the corners where she was starting to smile. "Nothing but the best for my fella," she said.

This time I kissed her properly. I could feel the tickets pressed between my wild heartbeat and hers, and I felt like they were fizzing and crackling, ready to explode any second into a ceiling-high shower of gold sparks. That was when the evening fell into place and stopped smelling of danger; that was the moment when that riptide started rising inside me, like a shiver deep in my bones. From that second on, all I could do was go with its pull and believe it would lead us right, draw our feet through the tricky currents and over the wicked drops to all the safe stepping-stones.

When we separated, a little later, Rosie said, "You're not the only one that's been busy. I went into Eason's and looked through all the ads in the English newspapers."

"Any jobs?"

"Some. Mostly stuff we can't do, forklift drivers and substitute teachers, but there's a few for waitresses and bar staff—we can say we've got experience, they'll never check. No one wanting people to do lighting, or roadies, but we knew that; we'll have to go looking once we get there. And there's *loads* of flats, Francis. Hundreds."

"Can we afford any of them?"

"Yeah, we can. It won't even matter if we can't get jobs straight away; what we've got saved would be enough for the deposit, and we can manage a shite place just on the dole. It'd be pretty shite, now—just a bedsit, and we might have to share a bath with a few others—but at least we wouldn't be wasting our money on a hostel any longer than we have to."

I said, "I'll share a jacks and a kitchen and everything else, no probs. I just want us out of the hostel as fast as we can. It's stupid to live in bloody separate dorms, when—"

Rosie was smiling back at me, and the glow in her eyes nearly stopped my heart. She said, "When we could have a place of our own."

"Yeah," I said. "A place of our own."

That was what I wanted: a bed where Rosie and I could sleep through the night in each other's arms, wake up in the morning wrapped together. I would have given anything, anything at all, just for that. Everything else the world had to offer was gravy. I listen to the things people want out of love these days and they blow my mind. I go to the pub with the boys from the squad and listen while they explain, with minute precision, exactly what shape a woman should be, what bits she should shave how, what acts she should perform on which date and what she should always or never do or say or want; I eavesdrop on women in cafés while they reel off lists of which jobs a man is allowed, which cars, which labels, which flowers and restaurants and gemstones get the stamp of approval, and I want to shout, *Are you people out of your tiny minds?* I never once bought Rosie flowers—too hard for her to explain at home—and I never once wondered whether her ankles looked exactly the way they were supposed to. I wanted her, all mine, and I believed she wanted me. Till the day Holly was born, nothing in my life has ever been so simple.

Rosie said, "Some of the flats won't want Irish."

I said, "Fuck 'em." That tide was building, getting stronger; I knew that the first flat we walked into would be the perfect one, that this magnet pull would draw us straight to our home. "We'll tell them we're from Outer Mongolia. How's your Mongolian accent?"

She grinned. "Who needs an accent? We'll speak Irish and say it's Outer Mongolian. You think they'll know the difference?"

I did a fancy bow and said, "*Póg mo thóin*"— kiss my arse: about ninety percent of my Irish. "Ancient Mongolian greeting."

Rosie said, "Seriously, but. I'm only saying it because I know what you're like for patience. If we don't get a flat the first day, it's not a big deal, right? We've got loads of time."

I said, "I know. Some of them won't want us because they'll think we're drunks or terrorists. And some of them . . ." I took her hands off her pint and ran my thumbs across her fingers: strong, callused from the sewing, cheap street-stall silver rings shaped like Celtic swirls and cats' heads. "Some of them won't want us because we'll be living in sin."

Rosie shrugged. "Fuck them too."

"If you wanted," I said, "we could pretend. Get goldy-looking rings, call ourselves Mr. and Mrs. Just until—"

She shook her head, instantly and hard. "No. No way."

"It'd only be for a little while, till we've the money to do it for real. It'd make our lives a whole lot easier."

"Doesn't matter. I'm not faking that. Either you're married or you're not; it's not about what people think."

"Rosie," I said, and tightened my hold on her hands. "You know we'll do it, don't you? You know I want to marry you. There's nothing I want more."

That got the beginnings of a grin. "You'd better. Back when you and me started going out, I was a good girl, like the nuns taught me, and now here's me all ready to be your fancy woman—"

"I'm serious. Listen to me. There's plenty of people who, if they knew, they'd say you were crazy. They'd say the Mackeys are a shower of scumbags, and I'm going to take what I want off you and then leave you high and dry with a baby on your hands and your life flushed down the jacks."

"Not a chance. It's England; they've got johnnies."

I said, "I just want to you to know you won't regret this. Not if I can help it. I swear to God."

Rosie said gently, "I know that, Francis."

"I'm not my da."

"If I thought you were, I wouldn't be here. Now go up and get us a packet of crisps. I'm starving."

We stayed in O'Neill's that night till all the students had gone home and the barman started hoovering our feet. We stretched every pint as long as we could, we talked about safe easy everyday stuff, we made each other laugh. Before we walked home—separately, in case anyone spotted us, me keeping an eye on Rosie from a safe distance behind—we kissed good night for a long time, up against the back wall of Trinity. Then we stood still, wrapped around each other, pressed together from cheeks to toes. The air was so cold that it made a high fine ringing sound somewhere miles above us, like breaking crystal; her breath was hoarse and warm on my throat, her hair smelled like lemon drops and I could feel the fast shake of her heart trembling against my ribs. Then I let go of her and watched her walk away, one last time.

Of course I looked for her. The first time I was left alone with a police computer, I ran her name and birth date through it: she had never been arrested in the Republic of Ireland. This was hardly a revelation—I hadn't expected her to turn into Ma Barker—but I spent the rest of the day on a hard edgy high, just from inching that first step along her trail. As my contacts got better, so did my searches: she hadn't been arrested in the North, hadn't been arrested in England or Scotland or Wales or the USA, hadn't signed on the dole anywhere, hadn't applied for a passport, hadn't died, hadn't got married. I repeated all the searches every couple of years, sticking to contacts who owed me favors. They never asked.

Mostly, these days—I got mellower after Holly came along—I hoped Rosie would turn up under the radar somewhere, living one of those straightforward, contented lives that never hit the system, remembering me every now and then with a piercing little tug as the one who might have been. Sometimes I pictured her finding me: the phone ringing in the middle of the night, the tap at my office door. I pictured us side by side on a bench in some green park, watching in a bittersweet silence while Holly swung on a climbing frame with two little redheaded boys. I pictured an endless evening in some dim pub, our heads bending closer and closer under the talk and laughter as the night got later, our fingers sliding towards each other on the battered wood of the table. I pictured every inch of what she would look like now: the crow's-feet from smiles I hadn't seen, the softness of her belly from kids who weren't mine, all her life that I had missed written on her body in Braille for my hands to read. I pictured her giving me answers I had never thought of, the ones that would make sense of everything, send every jagged edge sliding smoothly into place. I pictured, believe it or not, a second chance.

Other nights, even after all this time, I still wanted what I wanted when I was twenty: to see her show up as some Domestic Violence Squad's frequent flier, in someone's hooker file flagged for HIV, as an overdose in a morgue in a ruthless part of London. I had read the descriptions of hundreds of Jane Does, over the years.

All my signposts had gone up in one blinding, dizzying explosion: my second chances, my revenge, my nice thick anti-family Maginot line. Rosie Daly dumping my sorry ass had been my landmark, huge and solid as a mountain. Now it was flickering like a mirage and the landscape kept shifting around it, turning itself inside out and backwards; none of the scenery looked familiar any more.

I ordered another pint, with a double Jameson's on the side, which as far as I could see was my only chance of making it to the morning. I couldn't think of a single other thing that would wipe my mind clean of that image, the nightmare made of slimy brown bones curled in its burrow, trickles of earth falling onto it with a sound like tiny scurrying feet.

7

They gave me a couple of hours on my own, with a kind of delicacy I hadn't expected, before they came looking for me. Kevin showed up first: sticking his head around the door like a kid on a hide-and-seek mission, sending a quick sly text while the barman pulled his pint, hovering and shuffling beside my table till I put him out of his misery and gestured for him to sit down. We didn't talk. It took the girls about three minutes to join us, shaking rain off their coats and giggling and shooting sideways glances around the pub—"Jaysus," Jackie said in what she thought was a whisper, pulling off her scarf, "I remember when we used to be dying to come in here, only because it was no girls allowed. We were better off, weren't we?"

Carmel gave the seat a suspicious look and a quick swipe with a tissue before she sat down. "Thank God Mammy didn't come after all. This place'd put the heart crossways in her."

"Christ," Kevin said, his head jerking up. "*Ma* was going to come?"

"She's worried about Francis."

"Dying to pick his brains, more like. She's not going to *follow* you or anything, is she?"

"Wouldn't put it past her," Jackie said. "Secret Agent Ma."

"She won't. I told her you were gone home," Carmel said to me, fingertips over her mouth, between guilty and mischievous. "God forgive me."

"You're a genius," Kevin said, heartfelt, slumping back into his seat.

"He's right. She'd only have wrecked all our heads." Jackie craned her neck, trying to catch the barman's eye. "Will I get served in here these days, will I?"

"I'll go up," Kevin said. "What'll you have?"

"Get us a gin and tonic."

Carmel pulled her stool up to the table. "Would they have a Babycham, d'you think?"

"Ah, Jesus, Carmel."

"I can't drink the strong stuff. You know I can't."

"I'm not going up there and asking for a poxy Babycham. I'll get the crap kicked out of me."

"You'll be grand," I said. "It's 1980 in here anyway; they've probably got a whole crate of Babycham behind the bar."

"And a baseball bat waiting for any guy who asks for it."

"I'll go."

"There's Shay now." Jackie half stood up and flapped a hand to get his attention. "He can go, sure; he's up already."

Kevin said, "Who invited him?"

"I did," Carmel told him. "And the pair of yous can act your age and be civil to each other, for once. This evening's about Francis, not about you."

"I'll drink to that," I said. I was pleasantly pissed, just heading into the stage where everything looked colorful and soft-edged and nothing, not even the sight of Shay, could grate on me. Normally the first hint of the warm fuzzies makes me switch to coffee, fast. That night I intended to enjoy every second of them.

Shay lounged over to our corner, running a hand through his hair to get rid of the raindrops. "I'd never have guessed this place was up to your standards," he said to me. "You brought your cop mate in here?"

"It was heartwarming. Everyone welcomed him like a brother."

"I'd have paid to watch that. What're you drinking?"

"Are you buying?"

"Why not."

"Sweet," I said. "Guinness for me and Kevin, Jackie'll have a G and T, and Carmel wants a Babycham."

Jackie said, "We just want to see you go up and order it."

"No problem to me. Watch and learn." Shay headed up to the bar, got the barman's attention with an ease that said this was his local, and waved the bottle of Babycham at us triumphantly. Jackie said, "Bleeding show-off."

Shay came back balancing all the glasses at once, with a precision that goes with plenty of practice. "So," he said, putting them down on the table. "Tell us, Francis: was that your mot, that all this fuss is about?" and, when everyone froze, "Cop on, will yous; you're all gagging to ask him the same thing. Was it, Francis?"

Carmel said in her best mammy-voice, "Leave Francis alone. I told Kevin and I'm telling you: you've to behave yourselves tonight."

Shay laughed and pulled up a stool. I had had plenty of time during the last couple of hours, while my brain was still mainly unpickled, to consider exactly how much I wanted to share with the Place, or anyway with my family, which amounted to pretty much the same thing. "It's all right, Melly," I said. "Nothing's definite yet, but yeah, it's looking like that was probably Rosie."

A quick suck of breath from Jackie, and then silence. Shay let out a long, low whistle.

"God rest," Carmel said softly. She and Jackie crossed themselves.

"That's what your man told the Dalys," Jackie said. "The fella you were talking to. But, sure, no one knew whether to believe him or not . . . Cops, you know? They'll say anything—not you, like, but the rest of them. He could've just wanted us to think that was her."

"How do they know?" Kevin asked. He looked faintly sick.

I said, "They don't, yet. They'll run tests."

"Like DNA stuff?"

"I wouldn't know, Kev. Not my field."

"Your field," Shay said, turning his glass between his fingers. "I've been wondering: what is your field, exactly?"

I said, "This and that." For obvious reasons, undercovers tend to tell civilians that we work in Intellectual Property Rights, or whatever else sounds dull enough to nip the conversation in the bud. Jackie thinks I implement strategic personnel utilization solutions.

Kevin asked, "Can they tell . . . you know. What happened to her?"

I opened my mouth, shut it again, shrugged and took a long swig of my pint. "Did Kennedy not talk to the Dalys about that?"

Carmel said, with her mouth pursing up, "Not a word. They *begged* him to tell them what happened to her, so they did, and he wouldn't say one word. Walked out and left them there to wonder."

Jackie was bolt upright with outrage; even her hair looked like it had got taller. "Their own daughter, and he told them it was none of their business if she was murdered or not. I don't care if he's your mate, Francis, that's just dirty, that is."

Scorcher was making an even better first impression than I had expected. I said, "Kennedy's no mate of mine. He's just a little poxbottle I have to work with every now and then."

Shay said, "I bet you're good enough mates that he told you what happened to Rosie."

I glanced around the pub. The conversations had cranked up a notch— not louder, but faster and more focused: the news had made it in at last. Nobody was looking at us, partly out of courtesy to Shay and partly because this was the kind of pub where most people had had problems of their own and understood the value of privacy. I said, leaning forward on my elbows and keeping my voice down, "OK. This could get me fired, but the Dalys deserve to know whatever we know. I need you to promise me it won't get back to Kennedy."

Shay was wearing a thousand-watt skeptical stare, but the other three were right with me, nodding away, proud as Punch: our Francis, after all these years still a Liberties boy first and a cop second, sure aren't we all great to be such a close-knit bunch. That was what the girls would pass on to the rest of the neighborhood, as the sauce to go with my little nuggets of tasty info: Francis is on our side.

I said, "It looks a lot like someone killed her."

Carmel gasped and crossed herself again. From Jackie: "God bless us and save us!"

Kevin was still looking pale. He asked, "How?"

"No news on that yet."

"But they'll find out, right?"

"Probably. After all this time, it could be tough, but the lab team knows what they're doing."

"Like *CSI?*" Carmel was round-eyed.

"Yep," I said, which would have given the useless tech an aneurysm— the Bureau all loathe *CSI* to the point of sputtering incoherence—but which would make the old ones' day. "Just like that."

"Except not magic," Shay said dryly, to his pint.

"You'd be surprised. Those boys can find just about anything they set their sights on—old blood spatter, tiny amounts of DNA, a hundred different kinds of injury, you name it. And while they're figuring out what happened to her, Kennedy and his crew are going to be figuring out who happened it. They'll be talking to everyone who lived around here, back then. They'll want to know who she was close to, who she argued with, who liked her and who didn't and why, what she did every moment of the last few days of her life, if anyone noticed anything odd that night she went missing, if anyone noticed anyone else acting funny around then or just after . . . They're going to be very bloody thorough, and they're going to take all the time they need. Anything, any tiny thing, could be crucial."

"Holy Mother," Carmel breathed. "It's just like the telly, isn't it? That's mad."

In pubs and kitchens and front rooms all around us, people were already talking: thinking back, dredging up old memories, comparing and contrasting, pooling them to come up with a million theories. In my neighborhood, gossip is a competitive sport that's been raised to Olympic standard, and I never diss gossip; I revere it with all my heart. Like I told Scorch, info is ammo, and there was bound to be plenty of live ammo being tossed around, in with the dud stuff. I wanted all that good gossip to be focused on dredging up the live rounds, and I wanted to make very sure they would get back to me, one way or another—if Scorcher had snubbed the Dalys, he was going to have a hard time extracting any kind of info from anyone in a half-mile radius. And I wanted to know that, if someone out there had something to worry about, he was going to be worrying hard.

I said, "If I hear anything else that the Dalys should know, I won't let them get left out of the loop."

Jackie put out a hand and touched my wrist. She said, "I'm so sorry, Francis. I was hoping it'd turn out to be something else—some kind of mix-up, I don't know, anything . . ."

"That poor young one," Carmel said softly. "What age was she? Eighteen?"

I said, "Nineteen and a bit."

"Ah, God; that's barely older than my Darren. And left on her own in that awful house all these years. Her parents going mad wondering where she was, and all the time . . ."

Jackie said, "I never thought I'd say this, but thank God for your man PJ Lavery."

"Let's hope," Kevin said. He drained his pint. "Who's ready for another?"

"Might as well," said Jackie. "What d'you mean, let's hope?"

Kevin shrugged. "Let's hope it turns out OK, is all I'm saying."

"Janey Mac, Kevin, how's it going to turn out OK? The poor girl's dead! Sorry, Francis."

Shay said, "He means let's hope the cops don't turn up anything that makes us all wish Lavery's boys had dumped that suitcase in a skip and let sleeping dogs lie."

"Like what?" Jackie demanded. "Kev?"

Kevin shoved back his stool and said, with a sudden burst of authority, "I've had this conversation right up to my tits, and Frank probably has too. I'm going up to the bar. If you're still talking about this crap when I get back, I'm leaving you the drinks and I'm going home."

"Will you look at that," Shay said, one corner of his mouth lifting. "The mouse that roared. Fair play to you, Kev; you're dead right. We'll talk about *Survivor*. Now get us a pint."

We got another round in, and then another. Hard rain gusted up against the windows, but the barman had the heating up high, and all the weather we got was the cold draft when the door opened. Carmel plucked up the courage to go to the bar and order half a dozen toasted sandwiches, and I realized that the last food I'd had was half of Ma's fry-up and that I was starving, the ferocious kind of hunger where you could spear something and eat it warm. Shay and I took turns telling jokes that made G&T go down Jackie's nose and made Carmel squeak and smack our wrists, once she got the punch lines; Kevin did a viciously accurate impression of Ma at Christmas dinner that sent us all into convulsions of hard, helpless, painful laughter. "Stop," Jackie gasped desperately, flapping a hand at him. "I swear to God, my bladder won't take it, if you don't stop I'll wet myself."

"She'll do it," I said, trying to get my breath back. "And you'll be the one that has to get a J-cloth and clean up."

"I don't know what you're laughing about," Shay told me. "This Christmas, you'll be right there suffering with the rest of us."

"My bollix. I'll be safe at home, drinking single malt and laughing every time I think about yous poor suckers."

"Just you wait, pal. Now that Ma's got her claws back into you, you think she'll let go with Christmas just around the corner? Miss her chance to make all of us miserable at once? Just you wait."

"Want to bet?"

Shay held out a hand. "Fifty quid. You'll be sat across the table from me for Christmas dinner."

"You're on," I said. We shook on it. His hand was dry and strong and callused, and the grip flicked a spark of static between us. Neither of us flinched.

Carmel said, "D'you know something, Francis, we said we wouldn't ask you, but I can't help it—Jackie, would you ever stop that, don't be pinching me!"

Jackie had got her bladder back under control and was giving Carmel the evil stare of doom. Carmel said, with dignity, "If he doesn't want to talk about it, he can tell me himself, so he can, Francis, why did you never come back before this?"

I said, "I was too scared that Ma would get the wooden spoon and beat the living shite out of me. Do you blame me?"

Shay snorted. Carmel said, "Ah, seriously, but, Francis. Why?"

She and Kevin and even Jackie—who had asked this question a bunch of times and never got an answer—were gazing at me, tipsy and perplexed and even a little hurt. Shay was picking a fleck of something out of his pint.

I said, "Let me ask you something. What would you die for?"

"Jaysus," Kevin said. "You're a barrel of laughs, aren't you?"

"Ah, leave him," Jackie said. "The day that's in it."

I said, "Da once told me he'd die for Ireland. Would you do that?"

Kevin rolled his eyes. "Da's stuck in the seventies. No one thinks like that any more."

"Try it for a second. Just for the crack. Would you?"

He gave me a bemused look. "Like why?"

"Say England invaded all over again."

"They couldn't be arsed."

"*If*, Kev. Stay with me here."

"I dunno. I never thought about it."

"That," Shay said, not too aggressively, aiming his pint at Kevin, "that right there, that's what has this country ruined."

"Me? What'd I do?"

"You and the rest like you. Your whole bloody generation. What do you care about, only Rolexes and Hugo Boss? What else do you think about, even? Francis is right, for once in his life. You'd want to get yourself something you'd die for, pal."

"For fuck's sake," Kevin said. "What would you die for? Guinness? A good ride?"

Shay shrugged. "Family."

"What are you on about?" Jackie demanded. "You hate Ma and Da's guts."

All five of us burst out laughing; Carmel had to tip her head back and knuckle tears out of her eyes. "I do," Shay acknowledged, "yeah. But that's not the point."

"Would *you* die for Ireland, yeah?" Kevin asked me. He still sounded a little miffed.

"I would in me hole," I said, which set everyone off again. "I was posted in Mayo for a while. Have yous ever been to Mayo, have yous? It's boggers, sheep and scenery. I'm not dying for that."

"What, then?"

"Like my man Shay says," I told Kev, waving my glass at Shay, "that's not the point. The point is that I *know*."

"I'd die for the kids," Carmel said. "God forbid."

Jackie said, "I'd say I'd die for Gav. Only if he really needed it, mind. Is this not terrible morbid, Francis? Would you not rather talk about something else?"

I said, "Back in the day, I would've died for Rosie Daly. That's what I'm trying to tell yous."

There was a silence. Then Shay raised his glass. "Here's to everything we'd die for," he said. "Cheers."

We clinked our glasses, took deep drinks and relaxed back into our seats. I knew this might well be because I was about nine tenths hammered, but I was fucking delighted that they had come in, even Shay. More than that: I was grateful. They might be a spectacularly messed-up bunch and what they felt about me was anyone's guess, but the four of them had dropped whatever they could have been doing this evening, put down their lives at a moment's notice and come in here to walk me through this night. We fit together like pieces of a jigsaw, and that felt like a warm gold glow wrapped all around me; like I had stumbled, by some perfect accident, into the right place. I was just sober enough not to try and put this into words.

Carmel leaned in to me and said, almost shyly, "When Donna was a baba, there was something went wrong with her kidneys; they thought she might need a transplant. I told them straight off, not a bother on me, they could take the both of mine. I didn't think twice. She was grand in the end, sure, and they'd only have needed the one anyway, but I never forgot that. D'you know what I mean?"

"Yep," I said, smiling at her. "I do."

Jackie said, "Ah, she's lovely, Donna is. She's a wee dote; always laughing. You'll have to meet her now, Francis."

Carmel told me, "I see you in Darren. D'you know that? I always did, from when he was a little young fella."

"God help him," Jackie and I said, together.

"Ah, now; in a good way. Going to college, like. He didn't get that off me or Trevor, we'd have been happy enough to see him go into the plumbing with his daddy. No, Darren came up with that all by himself, never said a word to us: just got all the course forms, decided what one he wanted, and worked like mad to get himself into the right Leaving Cert classes. Went after it bullheaded, all on his own. Like yourself. I always used to wish I was like that."

For a second there, I thought I saw a wave of sadness rise up across her face. "I remember you doing just fine when you wanted something," I said. "How about Trevor?"

The sadness vanished, and I got a quick mischievous snippet of giggle that made her look like a girl again. "I did, didn't I? That dance, the first time I saw him: I took one look and I said to Louise Lacey, I said, 'That one's mine.' He was wearing them flares that were all the rage—"

Jackie started to laugh.

"Don't be making fun, you," Carmel told her. "Your Gavin does be always in them raggedy old jeans; I like a fella that makes a bit of an effort. Trevor had a lovely little arse on him in the flares, so he did. And he smelled only gorgeous. What are yous two laughing at?"

"You brazen hussy, you," I said.

Carmel took a prim sip of her Babycham. "I was not. Things were different back then. If you were mad about a fella, you'd sooner die than let him know. You had to make him do the chasing."

Jackie said, "Jaysus, *Pride and* bleeding *Prejudice*. I asked Gavin out, so I did."

"I'm telling yous, it worked; better than all this rubbish nowadays, girls going to the clubs with no knickers on them. I got my fella, didn't I? Engaged on my twenty-first. Were you still here for that, Francis?"

"Just," I said. "I left about three weeks after." I remembered the engagement party: the two families squeezed into our front room, the mammies eyeing each other up like a pair of overweight pit bulls, Shay doing his bigbrother act and shooting Trevor the filthies, Trevor all Adam's apple and terrified bug-eyes, Carmel flushed and triumphant and squeezed into a pink pleated horror that made her look like an inside-out fish. Back then I was even more of an arrogant prick; I sat on the windowsill next to Trevor's piggy little brother, ignoring him and congratulating myself fervently on the fact that I was getting the hell out of Dodge and would never have an engagement party involving egg sandwiches. Careful what you wish for. Looking at the four of them around the pub table, I felt like I had missed something in that night; like an engagement party might have been, at least in the long run, something worth having.

"I wore my pink," Carmel said, with satisfaction. "Everyone said I looked only smashing."

"You did, all right," I said, winking at her. "If only you weren't my sister, I'd have fancied you myself."

She and Jackie squealed—"Yeuch, stop!"—but I wasn't paying attention any more. Down at their end of the table, Shay and Kevin had been having a chat of their own, and the defensive note in Kevin's voice had ratcheted up enough to make me tune in. "It's a *job*. What's wrong with it?"

"A job where you work your guts out licking yuppie arse, yes sir, no sir, three bags full sir, and all for the good of some fat corporation that'll throw you to the wolves as soon as the going gets tough. You make thousands a week for them, and what do you get out of it?"

"I get *paid*. Next summer I'm going to Australia, I'm going to snorkel around the Great Barrier Reef and eat Skippyburgers and get pissed at barbecues on Bondi Beach with gorgeous Aussie babes, because of that job. What's not to love?"

Shay laughed, a short scrape. "Better save your money."

Kevin shrugged. "Plenty more where that came from."

"There is in me arse. That's what they want you to believe."

"Who? What are you on about?"

"Times are changing, pal. Why do you think PJ Lavery—"

"Fucking bogger," said all of us in unison, except Carmel, who now that she was a mammy said, "Fecking bogger."

"Why do you think he's gutting those houses?"

"Who cares?" Kev was getting irritated.

"*You* should bloody well care. He's a cute hoor, Lavery; he knows what way the wind's blowing. He buys those three houses last year for top whack, sends out all those pretty brochures about quaint luxury apartments, and now all of a sudden he's dropping the whole idea and stripping them for parts?"

"So what? Maybe he's getting a divorce or having tax hassle or something. How is that my problem?"

Shay stared Kevin out of it for another moment, leaning forward, elbows on the table. Then he laughed again and shook his head. "You don't get it, do you?" he said, reaching for his pint. "You don't have a fucking clue. You swallow every bit of shite you're fed; you think it'll be all sunshine and roses forever. I can't wait to see your face."

Jackie said, "You're pissed."

Kevin and Shay never did like each other very much, but there were whole layers here that I was missing. It was like listening to the radio through stiff static: I could pick up just enough to catch the tone, not enough to know what was going on. I couldn't tell whether the interference came from twenty-two years or eight pints. I kept my mouth shut and my eyes open.

Shay brought his glass down with a flat crack. "I'll tell you why Lavery's not wasting his cash on fancy apartments. By the time he'd have them built, no one will have the money to buy them off him. This country's about to go down the tubes. It's at the top of the cliff, and it's about to go over at a hundred an hour."

"So no apartments," Kev said, shrugging. "Big deal. They'd only have given Ma more yuppies to bitch about."

"Yuppies are your bread and butter, pal. When they become extinct, so do you. Who's going to buy big-dick tellys once they're all on the dole? How well does a rent boy live if the johns go broke?"

Jackie smacked Shay's arm. "Ah, here, you. That's disgusting, that is." Carmel put up a hand to screen her face and mouthed *Drunk* at me, extravagantly and apologetically, but she had had three Babychams herself and she used the wrong hand. Shay ignored both of them.

"This country's built on nothing but bullshit and good PR. One kick and it'll fall apart, and the kick's coming."

"I don't know what you're so pleased about," Kevin said sulkily. He was a little the worse for wear, too, but instead of making him aggressive it had turned him inwards; he was slouched over the table, staring moodily into his glass. "If there's a crash, you're going down with all the rest of us."

Shay shook his head, grinning. "Ah, no, no, no. Sorry, man; no such luck. I've got a plan."

"You always do. And how far have any of them ever got you?"

Jackie sighed noisily. "Lovely weather we're having," she said to me.

Shay told Kevin, "This time's different."

"Sure it is."

"You watch, pal. Just you watch."

"That sounds lovely," Carmel said firmly, like a hostess hauling her dinner party back under control. She had pulled her stool up to the table and was sitting very straight, a ladylike pinky lifted off her glass. "Would you not tell us about it?"

After a moment Shay's eyes moved to her, and he leaned back in his seat and started to laugh. "Ah, Melly," he said. "You always were the only one could put manners on me. Do yous lot know, when I was a great lump of a teenager, our Carmel slapped me round the back of the legs till I ran, because I called Tracy Long a slut?"

"You deserved it," Carmel said primly. "That's no way to talk about a girl."

"I did. The rest of this shower don't appreciate you, Melly, but I do. Stick with me, girl. We'll go places."

"Where?" said Kevin. "The dole office?"

Shay shifted his focus back to Kevin, with an effort. "Here's what they don't tell you," he said. "In boom times, all the big chances go to the big fish. The workingman can make a living, but it's only the rich who can get richer."

Jackie asked, "Could the workingman not enjoy his pint and have a nice chat with his brothers and sisters, no?"

"When things start going bust, that's when anyone with a brain and a plan can pick up a big old handful of the pieces. And I've got those."

Hot date tonight, Shay used to say, crouching to slick back his hair in the mirror, but he'd never let on with who; or *Made a few extra shekels, Melly, get yourself and Jackie an ice cream,* but you never knew where the money had come from. I said, "So you keep telling us. Are you going to put out, or are you just going to keep cock-teasing all night long?"

Shay stared at me; I gave him a big innocent smile. "Francis," he said. "Our man on the inside. Our man in the system. Why would you care what a renegade like me does with himself?"

"Brotherly love."

"More like you think it'll be crap, and you want that nice warm feeling that you've beaten me again. Try this on for size. I'm buying the bike shop."

Just saying it brought a faint red flush onto his cheekbones. Kevin snorted; Jackie's high-up eyebrows shot up even farther. "Fair play to you," she said. "Our Shay, the entrepreneur, wha'?"

"Nice one," I said. "When you're the Donald Trump of the bike world, I'll come to you for my BMXs."

"Conaghy's retiring next year, and his son wants nothing to do with the business; he sells flash cars, bikes aren't good enough for him. So Conaghy gave me first refusal."

Kevin had surfaced from his sulk enough to look up from his pint. He asked, "Where're you going to get the dosh?"

The hot glitter in Shay's eyes made me see what girls saw in him. "I've got half of it already. I've been saving for this for a long time. The bank's giving me the rest. They're tightening up on the loans—they know there's trouble ahead, same as Lavery does—but I got in there just in time. This time next year, lads, I'll be a man of independent means."

Carmel said, "Well done," but there was something in her voice that caught my ear; something like reserve. "Ah, that's great altogether. Well done."

Shay took a swig of his pint and tried to play it cool, but there was a grin pressing at the corners of his mouth. "Like I told Kev, there's no point spending your life working to fill someone else's pockets. The only way to get anywhere is to be your own boss man. I'm just putting my money where my mouth is."

"So?" Kevin asked. "If you're actually right and the country's going down the tubes or whatever, you're still going with it."

"That's where you're wrong, mate. When this week's rich pricks find out they're in the shit, that's when I get my chance. Back in the eighties, when no one we knew had the money for a car, how did we get around? On bikes. As soon as the bubble bursts, Daddy's not going to be able to buy his little darlings BMWs to drive the half mile to school any more. That's when they show up at my door. I can't wait to see the faces on the little cunts."

"Whatever," Kevin said. "That's lovely, that is. Really." He went back to staring into his pint.

Carmel said, "Will it not mean living above the shop?"

Shay's eyes went to her, and something complicated passed between them. "It will. Yeah."

"And working full-time. Your hours won't be flexible any more."

"Melly," Shay said, much more gently, "it'll be all right. Conaghy's not retiring for a few months yet. By that time . . ."

Carmel took a tiny breath and nodded, like she was bracing for something. "Right," she said, almost to herself, and lifted her glass to her lips.

"I'm telling you. Don't be worrying."

"Ah, no, you're grand. God knows you deserve your chance. The way you've been the last while, sure, I knew you'd something up your sleeve; I just didn't . . . I'm delighted for you. Congratulations."

"Carmel," Shay said. "Look at me. Would I do that to you?"

"Here," Jackie said. "What's the story?"

Shay put a finger on Carmel's glass and moved it down so he could see her face. I'd never seen him tender before, and I found it even less soothing than Carmel did. "Listen to me. All the doctors said there's only a few months in it. Six, max. By the time I buy, he'll be in a home or in a chair, or anyway too weak to do any damage."

"God forgive us," Carmel said softly. "Hoping for . . ."

I said, "What's going on?"

They turned to stare at me, two identical pairs of expressionless blue eyes. It was the first time I'd seen them look alike. I said, "Are you telling me Da still hits Ma?"

A fast twitch like an electric shock went round the table, a tiny hiss of indrawn breath. "You mind your business," Shay said, "and we'll mind ours."

"Who elected you spokesgobshite?"

Carmel said, "We'd rather there was someone around, is all. In case Da has a fall."

I said, "Jackie told me that had stopped. Years back."

Shay said, "Like I told you. Jackie hasn't a clue. None of yous lot ever did. So fuck off out of it."

I said, "Do you know something? I'm getting just a tiny bit sick of you acting like you're the only one who ever had to take Da's shit."

Nobody was breathing. Shay laughed, a low ugly sound. He said, "You think you took shit from him?"

"I've got the scars to prove it. You and me lived in the same house, mate, remember? The only difference is that me, now I'm a big boy, I can go an entire conversation without whingeing about it."

"You took fuck-all, pal. Sweet fuck-all. And we didn't live in the same house, not for a single day. You lived in the lap of luxury, you and Jackie and Kevin, compared to what me and Carmel got."

I said, "Don't you ever tell me I got off easy."

Carmel was trying to look daggers at Shay, but he didn't notice; his eyes were fixed on me. "Spoilt rotten, the whole bloody three of yous. You think you had it bad? That's because we made sure you never found out what bad was like."

"If you want to go ask the barman for a tape measure," I said, "we can compare scar sizes, or dick sizes, or whatever the hell has your knickers in a knot. Otherwise, we'll have a much nicer night if you keep the martyr complex on your own side of the table and don't try to tell me what my life's been like."

"Cute. You always did think you were smarter than the rest of us, didn't you?"

"Only than you, sunshine. I just go with the evidence."

"What makes you any smarter? Just because me and Carmel were out of school the second we turned sixteen? Did you think that was because we were too thick to stay?" Shay was leaning forward, hands clenched on the edge of the table, and there was a patchy fever-red flush coming up on his cheekbones. "It was so we'd be putting our wages on the table when Da wasn't. So you could eat. So the three of you could buy your schoolbooks and your little uniforms and get your Leaving Certs."

"Christ," Kevin muttered, to his pint. "And he's off."

"Without me, you wouldn't be a cop today. You'd be nothing. You thought I was just mouthing off when I said I'd die for family? I damn near did it. I lost my education. I gave up every chance I had."

I raised one eyebrow. "Because otherwise you'd have been a college professor? Don't give me the giggles. You lost bugger-all."

"*I'll never know* what I lost. What did you ever give up? What did this family ever take off you? Name me one thing. One."

I said, "*This fucking family lost me Rosie Daly.*"

Absolute, frozen silence. The others were all staring at me; Jackie had her glass raised and her mouth half open, caught in midsip. I realized, slowly, that I was on my feet, swaying a little, and that my voice had been right on the edge of a roar. I said, "Leaving school is nothing; a few slaps are nothing. I'd have taken all that, begged for it, sooner than lose Rosie. And she's gone."

Carmel said, in a flat stunned voice, "You think she left you because of *us?*"

I knew there was something wrong with what I had said, something that had shifted, but I couldn't put my finger on it. As soon as I stood up, the booze had hit me right in the backs of the knees. I said, "What the hell do you think happened, Carmel? One day we were mad about each other, true love forever and ever, amen. We were going to get married. We had the tickets bought. I swear to God we would have done anything, Melly, any-thing, anything in this wide world to be together. The next day, the *next bloody day*, she ran off on me."

The regulars were starting to glance over, conversations falling away, but I couldn't get my voice back down. I always have the coolest head in any fight and the lowest blood-alcohol level in any pub. This evening was way off course, and it was much too late to salvage it. "What's the *only* thing that changed in between? Da went on a bender and tried to break into the Dalys' gaff at two in the morning, and then the whole classy bunch of yous had a screaming knock-down-drag-out row in the middle of the street. You remember that night, Melly. The whole Place remembers that night. Why *wouldn't* Rosie back out, after that? Who wants that for in-laws? Who wants that kind of blood in her children?"

Carmel said, very quietly and still with no expression at all, "Is that why you never came home? Because you've thought that all this time?"

"If Da had been decent," I said. "If he hadn't been a drunk, or even if he'd just bothered to be discreet about it. If Ma hadn't been Ma. If Shay hadn't been in and out of trouble every day of the week. If we'd been different."

Kevin said, bewildered, "But if Rosie didn't *go* anywhere—"

I couldn't make sense of what he was saying. The whole day had hit me, all of a sudden, and I was so exhausted that I felt like my legs were melting into the ratty carpet. I said, "Rosie dumped me because my family was a bunch of animals. And I don't blame her."

Jackie said, and I heard the hurt in her voice, "Ah, that's not on, Francis. That's not fair."

Shay said, "Rosie Daly had no problems with me, pal. Trust me on that."

He had himself back under control; he had eased back in his chair, and the red had faded off his cheekbones. It was the way he said it: that arrogant spark in his eyes, that lazy little smirk curving around the corners of his mouth. I said, "What are you talking about?"

"She was a lovely girl, was Rosie. Very friendly; very sociable, is that the word I'm after?"

I wasn't tired any more. I said, "If you're going to talk dirt about a girl who's not here to fight her own corner, at least do it straight out, like a man. If you don't have the guts to do that, then shut your gob."

The barman brought down a glass on the bar with a bang. "Hey! Yous lot! That'll do. Settle down *now* or you're all barred."

Shay said, "I'm only complimenting your taste. Great tits, great arse and a great attitude. She was a right little goer, wasn't she? Zero to sixty in no time flat."

A sharp voice somewhere at the back of my brain was warning me to walk away, but it reached me fuzzy and vague through all those layers of booze. I said, "Rosie wouldn't have touched you with someone else's."

"Think again, pal. She did a lot more than touch. Did you never smell me off her, once you got her stripped down?"

I had him hauled up off his chair by his shirtfront and I had my fist pulled back for the punch when the others swung into action, with that instant, clenched efficiency that only drunks' kids have. Carmel got between us, Kevin grabbed my punching arm and Jackie whipped drinks out of harm's way. Shay wrenched my other hand off his shirt—I heard something rip—and we both went stumbling backwards. Carmel got Shay by the shoulders, sat him neatly back down and held him there, blocking his view of me and talking soothing crap into his face. Kevin and Jackie caught me under the arms and had me turned around and halfway to the door before I got my balance back and figured out what was happening.

I said, "Get off. Get off me," but they kept moving. I tried to shake them away, but Jackie had made sure she was stuck to me tightly enough that I couldn't get rid of her without hurting her, and I was still a lot of drink away from that. Shay shouted something vicious over Carmel's shoulder, she upped the shushing noises, and then Kevin and Jackie had maneuvered me expertly around the tables and stools and the blank-faced regulars and we were outside, in the rush of cold sharp air on the street corner, with the door slamming behind us.

I said, "What the *fuck*?"

Jackie said peacefully, like she was talking to a child, "Ah, Francis. Sure, you know yous can't be fighting in there."

"That arsehole was asking for a punch in the gob, Jackie. *Begging* for it. You heard him. Tell me he doesn't deserve everything I can dish out."

"He does, of course, but you can't be wrecking the place. Will we go for a walk?"

"So what are you dragging *me* out for? Shay's the one who—"

They linked my arms and started walking. "You'll feel better out here in the fresh air," Jackie told me reassuringly.

"No. No. I was having a quiet pint on my own, doing no harm to anyone, till that prick walked in and started causing hassle. Did you hear what he said?"

Kevin said, "He's locked, and he was being a total dickhead. What are you, surprised?"

"So why the hell am I the one out on my ear?" I knew I sounded like a kid whining *He started it,* but I couldn't stop myself.

Kevin said, "It's Shay's local. He's there every other night."

"He doesn't own this whole bloody neighborhood. I've got as much right as he has—" I tried to reef myself away from them and head back to the pub, but the effort almost overbalanced me. The cold air wasn't sobering me up; instead it was slapping at me from all angles, baffling me, making my ears buzz.

"You do, of course," Jackie said, keeping me pointed firmly in the other direction. "But if you stay there, he'll only be annoying you. There's no point hanging around for that, sure there's not. We'll go somewhere else, will we?"

This is where some cold needle of sense managed to pierce through the Guinness fog. I stopped in my tracks and shook my head till the buzz faded a notch or two. "No," I said. "No, Jackie, I don't think we will."

Jackie twisted her head around to peer anxiously into my face. "Are you all right? You're not going to be sick, now?"

"No, I'm not going to bleeding well be sick. But it'll be a long, long time before I go anywhere on your say-so again."

"Ah, Francis, don't be—"

I said, "Do you remember where this whole thing started, Jackie, do you? You rang me up and convinced me that I wanted to get my arse over to this godforsaken dump. I swear to God I must've slammed my head in a car door somewhere along the way, or I'd have told you just where to shove that genius idea. Because look how it's turned out, Jackie. Look. Are you pleased with yourself, yeah? Are you getting that lovely glow of a job well done? Are you happy now?"

I was swaying. Kevin tried to get a shoulder under mine, but I shook them both off, let my weight fall back against the wall and put my hands over my face. A million little flecks of light were heaving behind my eyelids. "I knew better," I said. "I bloody well knew better."

Nobody said anything for a while. I could feel Kevin and Jackie glancing at each other, trying to make plans by eyebrow semaphore. Finally Jackie said, "Here, I don't know about yous two, but I'm freezing my tits off. If I go back in and get my coat, will yous hang on here for me?"

Kevin said, "Get mine as well."

"Grand. Don't be going anywhere, yeah? Francis?"

She gave my elbow a tentative little squeeze. I ignored her. After a moment I heard her sigh, and then the perky clip-clop of her heels heading back the way we had come.

I said, "This poxy fucking bastarding day."

Kevin leaned against the wall beside me. I could hear his breath, puffing a little against the cold air. He said, "It's not like it's exactly Jackie's fault."

"And I should care about that, Kev. I really should. But you're going to have to forgive me if, right this minute, I don't give a damn."

The laneway smelled of grease and piss. Somewhere a street or two away a couple of guys had started shouting at each other, no words, just hoarse mindless noise. Kevin shifted his weight against the wall. "For what it's worth," he said, "I'm glad you came back. It's been good, hanging out. I mean, like, obviously not all the Rosie stuff and . . . you know. But I'm really glad we got to see each other again."

"Like I said. I should care, but things don't always pan out the way they should."

Kevin said, "Because, I mean, family does matter to me. It always did. I didn't say I *wouldn't* die for them—you know, like Shay was going on about? I just didn't like him trying to tell me what to think."

I said, "And who would." I took my hands off my face and raised my head an inch or two away from the wall, to see if the world had stabilized any. Nothing tilted too badly.

"It used to be simpler," Kevin said. "Back when we were kids."

"That's definitely not how I remember it."

"Well, I mean, God, it wasn't *simple*, but . . . you know? At least we knew what we were *supposed* to do, even if doing it sometimes sucked. At least we *knew*. I think I miss that. You know what I mean?"

I said, "Kevin, my friend, I have to tell you, I really, truly do not."

Kevin turned his head against the wall to look at me. The cold air and the booze had left him rosy-cheeked and dreamy; shivering a little, with his snappy haircut all bedraggled, he looked like a kid on an old-fashioned Christmas card. "Yeah," he said, on a sigh. "OK. Probably not. It doesn't matter."

I detached myself carefully from the wall, keeping a hand on it just in case, but my knees held. I said, "Jackie shouldn't be wandering around on her own. Go find her."

He blinked at me. "Are you going to . . . I mean, will you wait here for us, yeah? I'll be back in a sec."

"No."

"Oh." He looked undecided. "What about, like, tomorrow?"

"What about it?"

"Are you gonna be around?"

"I doubt it."

"How about . . . you know. Like, ever?"

He looked so fucking young and lost, it killed me. I said, "Go find Jackie."

I got my balance solid and started walking. After a few seconds I heard Kevin's footsteps start up behind me, slowly, going the other way.

8

I got a few hours' kip in my car—I was way too polluted for any taxi driver to touch me, but nowhere near polluted enough to think that knocking on my ma's door would be a good idea. I woke up with my mouth tasting like something had died nastily in there, to the kind of chilly, heavy morning where the damp soaks straight through your bones. It took me about twenty minutes to disentangle the crick in my neck.

The streets were shining wet and empty, bells ringing for early Mass and nobody much paying attention. I found a depressing café full of depressed Eastern Europeans and got myself a nutritious breakfast: soggy muffins, a handful of aspirin and a bucket of coffee. When I figured I was probably under the limit, I drove home, threw the clothes I'd been wearing since Friday morning into the washing machine, threw myself into a very hot shower and considered my next move.

This case was, as far as I was concerned, over with an O the size of O'Connell Statue. Scorcher could have it all to himself and welcome. He might be an annoying little gobshite at the best of times, but for once his obsession with winning was on my side: sooner or later he would get Rosie justice, if it was there to be got. He would even update me on any major developments—not necessarily for altruistic reasons, but I didn't give a damn. In less than a day and a half, I had had enough of my family to last me another twenty-two years. That morning in the shower, I would have bet my soul to Satan that nothing in this world could drag me back into Faithful Place.

I had just a few loose ends to tidy up, before I could throw this mess back into whichever circle of hell it had come from. I believe that "closure"

is a steaming load of middle-class horseshite invented to pay for shrinks'
Jags, but all the same: I needed to know for sure if that had in fact been
Rosie in that basement, I needed to know how she had died, and I needed
to know if Scorcher and his boys had picked up any hint about where she
had been going, that night, before someone stopped her. I had spent my
whole adult life growing around a scar shaped like Rosie Daly's absence.
The thought of that lump of scar tissue vanishing had sent me so light-
headed and off balance that I ended up doing gobsmackingly moronic
things like getting hammered with my siblings, a concept that just two days
earlier would have sent me running screaming for the hills. I felt it would
be a good idea to get my bearings back before I did something dumb
enough to end in amputation.

I found clean clothes, went out to the balcony, lit a smoke and rang
Scorcher. "Frank," he said, with a level of politeness that was carefully cali-
brated to let me know he wasn't happy to hear from me. "What can I do
for you?"

I put a sheepish grin in my voice. "I know you're a busy man, Scorcher,
but I was hoping you might do me a favor here."

"I'd love to, old son, but I'm a little—"

Old son? "So I'll cut to the chase," I said. "My lovely squad buddy
Yeates—you know him?"

"We've met."

"Fun, right? We had a few last night, I told him the story here, and he's
giving me flak about my girlfriend walking out on me. Long story short,
and leaving aside how deeply wounded I am that my own colleague could
doubt my sexual magnetism, I've put down a hundred quid that says Rosie
didn't dump my sorry ass after all. If you've got anything that'll settle this
for me, we can go halves on the winnings." Yeates looks like he uses kittens
as Pop Tarts, and he's not the chummy type; Scorch wouldn't follow up.

Scorch said stuffily, "All information relating to the investigation is
confidential."

"I wasn't planning on selling it to the *Daily Star*. Last I checked, Yeates
was a cop, just like you and me, only bigger and uglier."

"A cop who's not part of my team. Just like you."

"Come on, Scorch. At least tell me whether that was Rosie in that basement. If it's some Victorian body dump, I can pay Yeates his money and move on."

"Frank, Frank, Frank," Scorcher said, layering on the sympathy. "I know this isn't easy on you, OK, mate? But do you remember what we talked about?"

"Vividly. What it boiled down to was that you wanted me out of your hair. So I'm offering you this one-time-only deal, Scorchie. Answer my tiny little question, and the next time you'll hear from me will be when I take you out for a nice feed of pints to congratulate you on solving this case."

Scorch let that lie for a second. "Frank," he said, when he felt I had grasped just how deeply he disapproved, "this isn't the Iveagh Market. I'm not about to make deals with you, or settle squad *bets*. This is a *murder* case, and my team and I need to work it without interference. I would have thought that would be enough to keep you out of my hair. Frankly, I'm a little disappointed in you."

I had a sudden mental image of one evening, back in Templemore, when Scorch got smashed off his face and challenged me to see who could piss the highest up a wall on our way home. I wondered when he had turned into a pompous middle-aged twat, or whether he had always been one at heart and the adolescent testosterone rush had just masked it for a while. "You're right," I said, all penitent. "It just goes against the grain to have that big lump Yeates thinking he's got one up on me, you know what I mean?"

"Mmm," Scorcher said. "You know, Frank, the impulse to win is a valuable thing, right up until you let it make you into a loser."

I was pretty sure this meant nothing at all, but his tone said he was sharing a profound insight. "A little over my head, mate," I said, "but I'll be sure and have a think about it. See you around." I hung up.

I had another smoke and watched the Sunday shopping brigade jostling up and down the quays. I love immigration; the range of babehood on display these days is several continents wider than it was twenty years ago, and while Irish women are busy turning themselves into scary orange lollipops, the lovely ladies from the rest of the world are busy making up for it. There were one or two who made me want to marry them on the spot and give Holly a dozen siblings who my mother would call half-castes.

The Bureau tech was no good to me: he wouldn't give me the steam off his piss, after the way I'd ruined his lovely afternoon of cyberporn. Cooper, on the other hand, likes me, he works weekends, and unless he had a massive backlog he would have done the post-mortem by now. There was a good chance that those bones had told him at least some of what I needed to know.

Another hour wasn't going to get Holly and Olivia any more pissed off than they already were. I threw my smoke away and got moving.

Cooper hates most people, and most people think he hates them at random. What they haven't figured out is this: Cooper doesn't like being bored, and he has a low threshold. Bore him once—and Scorch had obviously managed to do that, somewhere along the way—and you're out forever. Keep him interested, and he's all yours. I've been called many things, but I've never been called boring.

The City Morgue is a quick walk down the quays from my apartment, round the back of the bus station, in a beautiful piece of redbrick more than a hundred years old. I don't often have occasion to go in there, but usually the thought of the place makes me happy, the same way it makes me happy that Murder works out of Dublin Castle: what we all do runs through the heart of this city like the river, we deserve the good parts of its history and its architecture. That day, though, not so much. Somewhere in there, with Cooper weighing and measuring and examining every remaining bit of her, was a girl who might be Rosie.

Cooper came to the reception desk when I asked for him, but, like most people that weekend, he wasn't over the moon to see me. "Detective Kennedy," he informed me, pronouncing the name delicately as if it tasted bad, "specifically informed me that you were not a part of his investigative team, and had no need for any information about the case."

And after I'd bought him a pint, too. The ungrateful little bollix. "Detective Kennedy needs to take himself a tad less seriously," I said. "I don't have to be on his little *team* to be interested. It's an interesting case. And . . . well, I'd rather this didn't get around, but if the victim's who we think it is, I grew up with her."

That put a sparkle in Cooper's beady little eye, just like I'd known it would. "Indeed?"

I looked down and played reluctant, to tickle his curiosity. "Actually," I said, examining my thumbnail, "for a while, when we were teenagers, I went out with her."

That hooked him: his eyebrows hit his hairline, and the sparkle got brighter. If he hadn't so obviously found himself the perfect job, I'd have been worried about what this guy got up to in his spare time. "So," I said, "you can see how I'd really like to know what happened to her—that's if you're not too busy to talk me through it. What Kennedy doesn't know won't hurt him."

The corners of Cooper's mouth tucked in, which is as close as he gets to a smile. He said, "Do come in."

Long corridors, elegant stairwells, not-bad old watercolors on the walls—someone had draped fake-pine-needle garlands between them, for that discreet balance of festive and somber. Even the actual morgue, a long room with ceiling moldings and high windows, would be beautiful if it weren't for the little details: the thick chilly air, the smell, the stark tiles on the floor, the rows of steel drawers lining one wall. A plaque between drawers said, in neat engraved letters, FEET FIRST. NAME TAG ON HEAD.

Cooper pursed his lips thoughtfully at the drawers and ran a finger along the line, one eye half closed. "Our new Jane Doe," he said. "Ah, yes," and he stepped forward and pulled a drawer open in one long flourish.

There's a switch you learn to flick, very early on in Undercover. It gets easier, maybe too easy, with time: one click, somewhere in a corner of your mind, and the whole scene unfolds at a distance on a pretty little screen, in living color, while you watch and plan your strategies and give the characters a nudge now and then, alert and absorbed and safe as a general. The ones who don't find the switch fast wind up in new squads, or in the ground. I flicked that switch and looked.

The bones were arranged perfectly, on their slab of metal; almost artistically, like the ultimate jigsaw puzzle. Cooper and his crew had cleaned them up somehow, but they were still brownish and greasy-looking, except for the two neat rows of teeth, Colgate white. The thing looked a million times too small and fragile to be Rosie. For a split second, a part of me even hoped.

Somewhere out on the street a bunch of girls were laughing, high help-less shrieks, faint through the thick glass. The room felt too bright; Cooper was just an inch too close, watching me just a hair too intently. He said, "The remains are those of a young adult white female, between five feet six inches and five feet nine inches tall, of medium to strong build. The development of the wisdom teeth and the incomplete fusion of the epiphyses place her age between eighteen and twenty-two."

He stopped there. He waited till he made me ask, "Can you tell for sure if it's Rose Daly?"

"No dental X-rays are available, but records show that Rose Daly had one filling, in a rear right lower molar. The decedent also has one filling, in the same tooth."

He took the jawbone between his thumb and finger, levered it downwards and pointed into the mouth.

I said, "So do other people."

Cooper shrugged. "Improbable coincidences do, as we know, happen. Fortunately, we are not purely dependent on the filling for identification." He flicked through a neat stack of files on a long table and pulled out two transparencies, which he slapped up on a light board, one on top of the other. "There," he said, and switched the light on.

And there was Rosie, illuminated and laughing against red brick and gray sky, with her chin up and her hair lifting in the wind. For a second she was all I could see. Then I saw the tiny white Xs dotting her face, and then I saw the empty skull staring out from behind it.

"As you can see from the points I have marked," Cooper said, "the anatomical landmarks of the found skull—the size, angles and spacing of the eye sockets, nose, teeth, jaw, and so on—correspond precisely with Rose Daly's features. While this does not constitute conclusive identification, it does constitute a reasonable degree of certainty, particularly when combined with the filling and with the circumstances. I have informed Detective Kennedy that he is at liberty to notify the family: I would have no difficulty in stating under oath that I believe this to be Rose Daly."

I asked, "How did she die?"

"What you see, Detective Mackey," Cooper said, sweeping an arm at the bones, "is what I have. In skeletonized remains, the cause of death can rarely be determined with certainty. She was clearly assaulted, but I have no way of positively eliminating, for example, the possibility that she suffered a fatal heart attack during the course of the assault."

I said, "Detective Kennedy mentioned something about skull fractures."

Cooper gave me a high-level snotty glare. "Unless I am gravely mistaken," he said, "Detective Kennedy is not a qualified pathologist."

I managed to grin at him. "He's not a qualified bore, either, but he does the job just fine."

The corner of Cooper's mouth twitched. "Indeed," he said. "Detective Kennedy is, albeit accidentally, correct that the skull has been fractured."

He reached out one finger and rolled Rosie's skull to the side. "There," he said.

The thin white glove made his hand look wet and dead, sloughing away in layers. The back of Rosie's head looked like a windscreen that had been bashed, more than once, with a golf club: it was thick with crazy spiderwebs of cracks radiating out in all directions, crisscrossing and ricocheting. Most of her hair had come away, it had been dumped beside her in a matted heap, but a few thin strands were still curling from the wrecked bone.

"If you look closely," Cooper said, stroking the cracks delicately with a fingertip, "you will observe that the edges of the fractures are splintered, rather than snapped cleanly. This implies that, at the time of the injuries, the bone was flexible and moist, not dry and brittle. In other words, the fractures are not a post-mortem artifact; they were inflicted at or around the time of death. They were caused by several forceful blows—I would estimate at least three—from a flat surface, four inches wide or more, with no sharp edges or corners."

I beat the urge to swallow; he would see it if I did. "Well," I said. "I'm no pathologist either, but that looks to me like it could kill someone."

"Ah," Cooper said, smirking. "It could, but in this case, we cannot state with certainty that it did. Look here."

He groped around at Rosie's throat and fished out two fragile slips of bone. "This," he said, fitting them neatly together into a horseshoe, "is the hyoid bone. It lies at the top of the throat, just beneath the jaw, supporting the tongue and protecting the airway. As you see, one of the greater horns has been completely severed. A fractured hyoid bone is associated, so near exclusively as to be diagnostic, with either motor vehicle accidents or manual strangulation."

I said, "So, unless she was hit by an invisible car that somehow drove into a basement, someone choked the living shite out of her."

"This," Cooper informed me, waving Rosie's hyoid bone in my direction, "is in many ways the most fascinating aspect of the case. As we noted previously, it appears that our victim was aged nineteen. In adolescents, it is rare to find the hyoid broken, due to the flexibility of the bone—and yet this fracture, like the others, is clearly perimortem. The only possible explanation is that she was strangled with extreme force, by an assailant with some physical strength."

I said, "A man."

"A man is a more likely candidate, but a strong woman in a state of intense emotion certainly cannot be ruled out. One theory seems most consistent with the full constellation of injuries: the attacker caught her by the throat and slammed her head repeatedly against a wall. The two opposing forces, from the wall's impact and the attacker's momentum, combined to fracture the hyoid and compress the airway."

"And she suffocated."

"Asphyxiated," Cooper said, giving me a look. "So I believe. Detective Kennedy is in fact correct that the injuries to the head would have resulted in death in any case, due to intracranial hemorrhage and damage to the brain, but the process could have taken anything up to a few hours. Before that could occur, she was quite probably dead of hypoxia caused either by manual strangulation itself, by vagal inhibition due to manual strangulation, or by obstruction of the airway due to the fractured hyoid bone."

I kept hitting the mental switch, hard. For a second I saw the line of Rosie's throat when she laughed.

Cooper told me, just to ensure he fucked up my head as thoroughly as was humanly possible, "The skeleton shows no other perimortem injuries, but the level of decomposition makes it impossible to determine whether there were any injuries to the soft tissues. Whether, for instance, the victim was sexually assaulted."

I said, "I thought Detective Kennedy implied she had clothes on. For whatever that's worth."

He pursed up his lips. "Very little fabric remains. The Technical Bureau team did in fact discover a number of clothing-related artifacts on or near the skeleton—a zipper, metal buttons, hooks consistent with those used in a brassiere, and so forth—which implies that she was buried with a full or near-full complement of clothing. This does not, however, tell us that this clothing was in place at the time of burial. Both the natural course of decomposition and the considerable rodent activity have shifted these items enough to make it impossible for anyone to say whether they were buried *on* her or merely *with* her."

I asked, "Was the zipper open or closed?"

"It was closed. As were the brassiere hooks. Not that this is probative—she could have re-dressed herself after an assault—but it is, I suppose, indicative to some degree."

"The fingernails," I said. "Were they broken?" Rosie would have put up a fight; a hell of a fight.

Cooper sighed. I was starting to bore him, all these standard-issue questions that Scorcher had already asked; I needed to get interesting or get out. "Fingernails," he said, giving a dismissive little nod at a few brownish shavings beside Rosie's hand bones, "decompose. In this case, they, like the hair, were partially preserved by the alkalinity of the environment, but in a severely deteriorated form. And, as I am not a magician, I am incapable of guessing their condition prior to that deterioration."

I said, "Just one or two more things, if you've got the time, and then I'll be out of your way. Do you know if the Bureau found anything else with her, apart from the clothing artifacts? Keys, maybe?"

"It seems probable," Cooper said austerely, "that the Bureau would have more knowledge of that than would I."

His hand was on the drawer, ready to slide it shut. If Rosie had had her keys, either because her da had given them back or because she had nicked them, then she had had the option of coming out the front door that night, and she hadn't taken it. I could only think of one reason for that. She had been dodging me, after all.

I said, "They would, of course—it's hardly your job, Doctor—but half of them are one step up from trained monkeys; I wouldn't trust them to know what case I was talking about, never mind give me the correct info. You can see why I wouldn't want to play the monkey lottery on this one."

Cooper raised his eyebrows a wry fraction, like he knew what I was doing and didn't care. He said, "Their preliminary report lists two silver rings and three silver stud earrings, all tentatively identified by the Dalys as consistent with jewelry owned by their daughter, and one small key, compatible with a low-quality mass-produced lock, that apparently matches the locks of a suitcase found earlier at the scene. The report lists no other keys, accessories or other possessions."

And there I was, right back where I had been when I first set eyes on that suitcase: clueless, catapulted into zero-gravity dark without one solid thing to grab hold of. It hit me, for the first time, that I might never know; that that could actually happen.

Cooper inquired, "Was that all?"

The morgue was very quiet, just the temperature control humming to itself somewhere. I don't do regrets any more than I do drunk, but this weekend was special. I looked at the brown bones spread out naked under Cooper's fluorescents, and I wished from the bottom of my heart that I had backed off and let sleeping girls lie. Not for my own sake; for hers. She was everyone's, now: Cooper's, Scorcher's, the Place's, to pick at and finger and use for their own purposes. The Place would already have started the leisurely, enjoyable process of digesting her into just one more piece of local gore-lore, half ghost story and half morality play, half urban myth and half just the way life goes. It would eat her memory whole, the same way its ground had eaten her body. She had been better off in that basement. At least the only people running their hands over her memory had been the ones who loved her.

"Yeah," I said. "That was all."

Cooper slid the drawer shut, one long shush of steel on steel, and the bones were gone, honeycombed in tight among all the rest of his question-marked dead. The last thing I saw before I walked out of the morgue was Rosie's face still shining on the light board, luminous and transparent, those bright eyes and that unbeatable smile layered paper-thin over rotting bone.

Cooper walked me out. I did my most charming arse-licking thank-yous, I promised him a bottle of his favorite wine for Christmas, he waved bye-bye to me at the door and went back to doing whatever disturbing things Cooper does when he's left alone in the morgue. Then I went around the corner and punched the wall. I turned my knuckles into hamburger, but the pain was brilliant enough that just for a few seconds, while I was doubled over clutching my hand, it seared my mind white and empty.

9

I picked up my car, which smelled attractively of sweaty drunk sleeping in his clothes, and headed for Dalkey. When I rang Olivia's doorbell I heard muffled voices, a chair scraping back hard, footsteps thumping up the stairs—Holly in a bad mood weighs about two hundred pounds—and then a nuclear-level slam.

Olivia came to the door with her face closed over. "I sincerely hope you've got a good explanation. She's upset, she's angry and she's disappointed, and I think she has every right to be all three. I'm not particularly delighted with the ruins of my weekend either, just in case that matters to you."

There are days when even I have better sense than to waltz in and raid Olivia's refrigerator. I stayed where I was, letting leftover rain drip off the eaves into my hair. "I'm sorry," I said. "I really am, Liv. None of this was my choice, believe me. It was an emergency."

A tiny, cynical flick of the eyebrows. "Oh, really? Do tell: who died?"

"Someone I used to know, a long time ago. Before I left home."

She hadn't expected that, but it only took her a split second to recover. "In other words, someone you hadn't bothered to contact for twenty-odd years, and yet all of a sudden he was more important than your daughter. Should I even bother to reschedule with Dermot, or is there a chance that something, somewhere, might happen to someone you once met?"

"It's not like that. This girl and I were close. She was murdered the night I left home. Her body was found this weekend."

That got Olivia's full attention. "This girl," she said, after a long intent look. "When you say 'close,' you mean a girlfriend, don't you? A first love."

"Yeah. Something like that."

Liv took that in; her face didn't change, but I saw her withdraw, somewhere behind her eyes, to turn this over. She said, "I'm sorry to hear that. I think you should explain this to Holly—the gist of it, at least. She's in her room."

When I knocked on Holly's door, she yelled, "Go away!" Holly's bedroom is the only place in that house where you can still see that I exist: in among the pink and frillies are stuffed toys I bought her, bad cartoons I drew for her, funny postcards I sent her for no special occasion. She was facedown on the bed, with a pillow pulled over her head.

I said, "Hi, baby."

A furious wriggle, and she pulled the pillow tighter over her ears, but that was it. I said, "I owe you an apology."

After a moment, a muffled voice said, "*Three* apologies."

"How's that?"

"You brought me back to Mum, and you said you'd pick me up later but you didn't, and you said you'd come get me yesterday but you didn't."

Straight for the jugular. "You're right, of course," I said. "And if you come out here to me, I'll apologize three times to your face. But I'm not saying sorry to a pillow."

I could feel her deciding whether to keep punishing me, but Holly isn't a sulker; five minutes is about her max. "I owe you an explanation, too," I added, just for good measure.

Curiosity did it; after a second the pillow slid back a few inches and a suspicious little face poked out. I said, "I apologize. I apologize double. And I apologize triple, from the heart, with a cherry on top."

Holly sighed and sat up, pushing bits of hair off her face. She still wasn't looking at me. "What happened?"

"You remember I told you your auntie Jackie had a problem?"

"Yeah."

"Someone died, baby. Someone we used to know, a long time ago."

"Who?"

"A girl called Rosie."

"Why did she die?"

"We don't know. She died way back before you were born, but we just found out about it Friday night. Everyone was pretty upset. Do you see why I needed to go find Auntie Jackie?"

A small, one-shouldered shrug. "I guess."

"And does that mean we can go have a nice time with what's left of the weekend?"

Holly said, "I was going to go over to Sarah's house. Instead."

"Chickadee," I said. "I'm asking you a favor here. It would mean an awful lot to me if we could start this weekend over again. Go back to where we left off, on Friday evening, and fit in as much good stuff as we can before I have to bring you home tonight. Pretend everything in between never happened." I saw her eyelashes flick as she snatched a quick sideways glance at me, but she didn't say anything. "I know it's a lot to ask, and I know I might not deserve it, but every now and then people have to cut each other a little slack. That's the only way we all make it through the day. Could you do that for me?"

She thought it over. "Are you going to have to go back if something else happens?"

"No, sweetheart. We've got a couple of other detectives looking after all that now. No matter what happens, they're the ones who'll get called in to deal with it. It's not my problem any more. OK?"

After a moment Holly rubbed her head quickly up against my arm, like a cat. "Daddy," she said. "I'm sorry your friend died."

I ran a hand over her hair. "Thanks, baby. I'm not going to lie to you: it's been a pretty crap weekend. It's starting to look up, though."

Downstairs, the doorbell rang. I asked, "Expecting someone?"

Holly shrugged, and I rearranged my face ready to give Dermo a scare, but it was a woman's voice. Jackie: "Ah, howya, Olivia, isn't it terrible cold out?" A low, hurried interruption from Liv; a pause, and then the kitchen door shutting quietly, and then a tumble of undertones as they filled each other in on all the news.

"Auntie Jackie! Can she come with us?"

"Sure," I said. I went to lift Holly off the bed, but she ducked under my elbow and made a dive for her wardrobe, where she started rooting through layers of pastel fuzz on a hunt for the exact cardigan she had in mind.

Jackie and Holly get on like a house on fire. Unexpectedly, and a little disturbingly, so do Jackie and Liv—no man wants the women in his life to be too close, in case they start swapping notes. It took me a long time after I met Liv to introduce them; I'm not sure which one I was ashamed of, or afraid of, but it did occur to me that I would feel a lot safer if Jackie took against my new middle-class associations and flounced right back out of my life. Jackie is one of my favorite people, but I've always had a knack for spotting Achilles' heels, and that includes my own.

For eight years after I left home, I stayed well clear of the fallout zone, thought about my family maybe once a year when an old one on the street looked enough like Ma to make me dive for cover, and somehow managed to survive just fine. In a town this size, that was too good to last. I owe my reunion with Jackie to an underqualified flasher who picked the wrong girl with whom to share a moment. When Wee Willy leaped out of his alleyway, whipped out his skippy and started giving it his all, Jackie deflated both his egos by bursting out laughing and then kicking him in the bollix. She was seventeen and had just moved out of home; I was working my way up through Sex Crime on my way to Undercover, and since there had been a couple of rapes in the area, my super wanted someone to take Jackie's statement.

It didn't need to be me. In fact, it shouldn't have been: you stay out of cases that involve your family, and I knew as soon as I saw "Jacinta Mackey" on the complaint form. Half of Dublin is named one or the other, but I doubt anyone except my parents had the flair to combine them and call a kid Jackie Mackey. I could have said so to the super, let someone else take down her description of Wee Willy's inferiority complex, and gone through the rest of my life without ever having to think about my family, or Faithful Place, or the Mysterious Case of the Mysterious Case. But I was curious. Jackie had been nine when I left home, none of it had been her fault; and she had been a good kid, back then. I wanted to see how she had turned out. At the time my main thought was, basically: hey, how much harm can it do? Where I went wrong was taking that as a rhetorical question.

"Come on," I said to Holly, finding her other shoe and tossing it to her. "Let's go bring your auntie Jackie for a walk, and then we can get that pizza I promised you Friday night."

———

One of the many joys of divorce is that I no longer have to go for bracing Sunday walks in Dalkey, swapping polite nods with beige couples who feel that my accent brings down the property values. Holly likes the swings in Herbert Park—as far as I can gather from the intense low-level monologue once she gets her momentum on, they count as horses and have something to do with Robin Hood—so we took her there. The day had turned cold and bright, just the right side of frosty, and lots of divorced dads had had the same idea. Some of them had brought the trophy girlfriend along for the ride. What with Jackie and her fake-leopard jacket, I fit right in.

Holly launched herself at the swings, and Jackie and I found a bench where we could keep an eye on her. Watching Holly swing is one of the best therapies I know. The kid is strong, for such a little snip of a thing; she can keep going for hours without getting tired, and I can keep watching, happily getting hypnotized by the rhythm of it. When I felt my shoulders start to drop, I realized just how tight they had been. I took deep breaths and wondered how I was going to keep my blood pressure under control once Holly outgrew playgrounds.

Jackie said, "God, she's after growing a foot just since I saw her last, isn't she? She'll be taller than me in no time."

"Any day now, I'm going to lock her in her room till her eighteenth birthday. I'm only waiting till the first time she mentions a boy's name without making gagging noises." I stretched out my legs in front of me, clasped my hands behind my head, angled my face to the weak sun and thought about spending the rest of the afternoon exactly like this. My shoulders went down another notch.

"Brace yourself. They start awful early, these days."

"Not Holly. I've told her boys don't get potty-trained till they're twenty."

Jackie laughed. "That just means she'll go for the older fellas."

"Old enough to understand that Daddy has a revolver."

Jackie said, "Tell me something, Francis. Are you all right?"

"I will be once the hangover wears off. Got any aspirin?"

She rummaged in her bag. "I've nothing. A bit of a headache'll do you good: you'll mind your booze better the next time. That's not what I meant, anyway. I meant . . . you know. Are you all right, after yesterday? And last night?"

"I'm a man of leisure in the park with two lovely ladies. How could I be anything but happy?"

"You were right: Shay was being a prick. He should've never said that about Rosie."

"Won't do her much harm now."

"I wouldn't say he ever got next nor near her, sure. Not that way. He was only trying to annoy you."

"No shit, Sherlock. You can't keep a man from doing what he loves."

"He's not usually like that. I'm not saying he's a saint these days, but he's after chilling out loads since you knew him. He's just . . . he's not sure what to make of you coming back, know what I mean?"

I said, "Don't worry about it, babe. Seriously. Do me a favor: let it go, enjoy the sunshine and watch my kid being gorgeous. OK?"

Jackie laughed. "Grand," she said. "We'll do that."

Holly did her share by being every bit as beautiful as I could ask for: wisps of hair had come loose from her ponytails and the sun was setting them on fire, and she was singing away to herself in a happy undertone. The neat sweep of her spine and the effortless bend and stretch of her legs worked their way gradually through my muscles, loosening them sweetly like a first-rate spliff. "She's done all her homework," I said, after a while. "Want to go to the pictures, after we eat?"

"I'm calling in at home, sure."

All four of the others still put themselves through the weekly nightmare: Sunday evening with Mammy and Daddy, roast beef and tricolored ice cream and it's all fun and games until somebody loses their mind. I said, "So get there late. Be a rebel."

"I said I'd meet Gav in town first, for a pint before he goes off with the lads. If I don't spend a bit of time with him, he'll think I'm after getting myself a toy boy. I only called round to see were you all right."

"Tell him to come too."

"To some cartoon yoke?"

"Right at his level."

"Shut up, you," Jackie said peacefully. "You don't appreciate Gavin."

"Definitely not the way you do. But then, I doubt he'd want me appreciating him the way you do."

"You're bleeding disgusting, so you are. I was meaning to ask, what happened to your hand?"

"I was saving a screaming virgin from Satanist Nazi bikers."

"Ah, no, seriously. You didn't have a fall, did you? After you left us? You were a bit—now, I'm not saying you were *langered*, but—"

That was when my phone rang, the one my boys and girls in the field use. "Keep an eye on Holly," I said, fishing it out of my pocket: no name, and I didn't recognize the number. "I have to take this. Hello?"

I was getting up from the bench when Kevin said awkwardly, "Um, Frank?"

I said, "Sorry, Kev. Not a good time." I hung up, stashed the phone and sat back down.

Jackie asked, "Was that Kevin?"

"Yep."

"Are you not in the humor to talk to him, no?"

"No. I'm not."

She gave me a big-eyed sympathetic look. "It'll get better, Francis. It will, now."

I let that one slide. "I'll tell you what," Jackie said, inspiration striking. "Come over to Ma and Da's with me, after you leave Holly back. Shay'll have sobered up by then, sure, he'll want to apologize to you, and Carmel's bringing the kiddies—"

I said, "I don't think so."

"Ah, Francis. Why not?"

"Daddydaddydaddy!" Holly always has had beautiful timing: she launched herself off the swing and galloped over to us, knees going up in front, horse-style. She was rosy-cheeked and out of breath. "I just remembered, in case I forget again, can I have white boots? Ones that have fur round the edge and two zips and they're all soft and they come up to here?"

"You've got shoes. Last time I counted, you had three thousand and twelve pairs of shoes."

"Nooo, not like that! For a special thing."

I said, "It depends. Why?" If Holly wants something that doesn't involve either necessity or a major celebration, I make her explain her reasons; I want her learning the difference between *need, want,* and *sort of fancy.* I like the fact that, in spite of this, most of the time she asks me instead of Liv.

"Celia Bailey has them."

"Who's Celia again? Does she do the dance classes with you?"

Holly gave me a *Duh* look. "Celia *Bailey.* She's *famous.*"

"Fair play to her. What for?"

The look got blanker. "She's a celebrity."

"I'm sure she is. She an actress?"

"No."

"Singer?"

"No!" I was clearly getting dumber by the second. Jackie was watching this unfold with a little grin at the corners of her mouth.

"Astronaut? Pole-vaulter? Heroine of the French Resistance?"

"Daddy, *stop*! She's on the *telly*!"

"So are astronauts and singers and people who can make animal noises with their armpits. What's this lady *for*?"

Holly had her hands on her hips and was working up to a full on huff. "Celia Bailey's a model," Jackie told me, deciding to put the pair of us out of our misery. "You know her; you do. Blondie one, went out with that fella who owns the nightclubs a couple of years back, and then when he cheated on her she found his e-mails to the bit on the side and sold them to the *Star*. Now she's famous."

I said, "Oh. *Her*." Jackie was right, I did know her: a local bobblehead whose major life achievements were banging a trust-fund brat and regularly going on daytime TV to explain, with heartrending sincerity and pupils the size of pinheads, how she had won her battle with cocaine. This is what passes for a superstar in Ireland these days. "Holly, sweetie, that's not a celebrity. That's a slice of empty space in an undersized frock. What's she ever done that was worth doing?"

Shrug.

"What's she good at?"

Extravagant pissed-off shrug.

"Then what the hell is she *for*? Why would you want to be anything like her?"

Eye roll. "She's pretty."

"Good Jaysus," I said, genuinely appalled. "Not one bit of that girl is the same color it started out, never mind the same shape. She doesn't even look human."

Holly practically had smoke coming out of her ears from sheer bafflement and frustration. "She's a model! Auntie Jackie said!"

"She isn't even that. The girl was on a bloody poster for some yogurt drink. There's a difference."

"She's a *star*!"

"No she's not. Katharine Hepburn was a star. Bruce Springsteen is a star. This Celia chick is a great big zero. Just because she kept on telling people she was a star till she found a handful of small-town morons who believed her, that doesn't make it true. And it doesn't mean you have to be one of the morons."

Holly had gone red in the face and her chin was sticking out ready for a fight, but she kept a hold on her temper. "I don't even care. I just want white *boots*. Can I?"

I knew I was getting way more pissed off than the situation warranted, but I couldn't dial it down. "No. You start admiring someone who's famous for actually *doing* something—imagine that—and I swear to you I will buy you every item in her entire wardrobe. But over my own dead body will I spend time and money turning you into a clone of some brain-dead waste of skin who thinks the pinnacle of achievement is selling her wedding shots to a magazine."

"I hate you!" Holly yelled. "You're stupid and you don't understand anything and I *hate* you!" She gave the bench by my leg a huge kick and then flung herself full-tilt back towards the swings, too furious to notice if her foot hurt. Some kid had taken her swing. She thumped down on the ground cross-legged, to fume.

After a moment Jackie said, "Jaysus, Francis. I'm not telling you how to raise your child, God knows I haven't the first clue, but was there any need for that?"

"Obviously, yeah, there was. Unless you think I go around wrecking my kid's afternoons for kicks."

"She only wanted a pair of boots. What difference does it make where she saw them? That Celia Bailey one is a bit of an eejit, God bless her, but she's harmless."

"No she's not. Celia Bailey is the living embodiment of everything that's wrong with the world. She's about as harmless as a cyanide sandwich."

"Ah, cop on, will you. What's the big deal? In a month's time Holly'll have forgotten all about her, she'll be mad into some girl band—"

"This is not trivial shit, Jackie. I want Holly to be aware that there is a difference between truth and meaningless gibberish bullshit. She's completely surrounded, from every angle, by people telling her that reality is one hundred percent subjective: if you really *believe* you're a star then you deserve a record contract whether or not you can sing for shit, and if you really *believe* in weapons of mass destruction then it doesn't actually matter whether they exist or not, and fame is the be-all and end-all because *you* don't exist unless enough people are paying attention to you. I want my daughter to learn that not everything in this world is determined by how often she hears it or how much she wants it to be true or how many other people are looking. Somewhere in there, for a thing to count as real, there has got to be some actual bloody *reality.* God knows she's not going to learn that anywhere else. So I'm going to have to teach her all by myself. If she occasionally gets a little stroppy along the way, so be it."

Jackie raised her eyebrows and primmed up her lips. "I'm sure you're right," she said. "I'll just keep my mouth shut, will I?"

Both of us did that for a while. Holly had got herself a new swing and was painstakingly turning in circles to wind the chains into a snarl.

"Shay was right about one thing," I said. "Any country that worships Celia Bailey is just about ready to go down the tubes."

Jackie clicked her tongue. "Don't be calling down trouble."

"I'm not. If you ask me, a crash might not be a bad thing."

"Jaysus, Francis!"

"I'm trying to bring up a kid, Jackie. That alone is enough to scare the living daylights out of any sane human being. Throw in the fact that I'm trying to bring her up in a setting where she's constantly being told to think about nothing except fashion, fame and body fat, ignore the man behind the curtain and go buy yourself something pretty . . . I'm *petrified*, all the time. I could just about stay on top of it when she was a little kid, but every day she's getting older and I'm getting scareder. Call me crazy, but I kind of like the thought of her growing up in a country where people occasionally have no choice but to focus on something more crucial than dick-replacement cars and Paris Hilton."

Jackie said, with a wicked little grin pulling at the corner of her mouth, "D'you know who you sound like? Shay."

"Sweet jumping *Jesus*. If I thought that was true, I'd blow my brains out."

She gave me a long-suffering look. "I know what's wrong with you," she informed me. "You got a bad pint last night, and your bowels are in tatters. That does always put fellas in a mood. Am I right?"

My phone rang again: Kevin. I said, "For fuck's *sake*," more viciously than I meant to. Giving him the number had made sense at the time, but give my family an inch and they'll move into your house and start redecorating. I couldn't even turn the thing off, not with people out there who could need me anytime. "If bloody Kev is always this bad at taking hints, no wonder he doesn't have a girlfriend."

Jackie gave my arm a soothing pat. "Don't mind him. You just let it ring there. I'll ask him tonight was it anything important."

"No, thanks."

"I'd say he just wants to know when can yous meet up again."

"I don't know how to get this through to you, Jackie: I do not give a tinker's damn what Kevin wants. Although if it turns out you're right and he wants to know when we'll meet up, you can tell him this from me, with love and kisses: never. OK?"

"Ah, Francis, stop. You know you don't mean that."

"I do. Believe me, Jackie, I do."

"He's your brother."

"And as far as I can tell, he's a very nice guy who I'm sure is loved by all his wide circle of friends and acquaintances. But I'm not one of them. My only connection to Kevin was an accident of nature that tossed us into the same house for a few years. Now that we don't live there any more, he's nothing to do with me, any more than that guy on the bench over there. The same goes for Carmel, the same goes for Shay, and the same very definitely goes for Ma and Da. We don't know each other, we have exactly fuck-all in common, and I can't see any reason on God's green earth why we would want to meet for tea and cookies."

Jackie said, "Cop on to yourself, would you ever. You know well it's not that simple."

The phone rang again. "Yeah," I said. "It is."

She poked at leftover leaves with a toe and waited for the phone to shriek itself into silence. Then she said, "Yesterday you said you blamed us for Rosie walking out on you."

I took a long breath and lightened my voice. "I'm hardly going to blame you, chicken. You were barely out of diapers."

"Is that why you don't mind seeing me?"

I said, "I didn't think you'd even remember that night."

"I asked Carmel about it yesterday, after . . . I remember bits, only. All the times get mixed up together, you know yourself."

I said, "Not that time. That one's clear as crystal."

It was coming up to three in the morning by the time my mate Wiggy finished moonlighting at the nightclub and showed up at the car park to give me my few bob and take over the rest of his shift. I walked home through the last raucous, staggering dregs of Saturday night, whistling softly to myself and dreaming about tomorrow and pitying every man who wasn't me. When I turned the corner into Faithful Place, I was walking on air.

I knew straightaway, in my armpits, that something had happened. Half the windows on the street, including ours, were blazing with light. If you stood still at the top of the road and listened you could hear the voices buzzing away behind them, wound tight and giddy with excitement.

The door of our flat was scored with brand-new dents and scuff marks. In the front room there was a kitchen chair upside down against the wall, legs splayed and splintered. Carmel was on her knees on the floor, wearing her coat over a faded flowery nightie, sweeping up broken china with a dustpan and brush; her hands were shaking so hard that she kept dropping bits. Ma was planted in one corner of the sofa, breathing in heaves and dabbing at a split lip with a wet facecloth; Jackie was curled up in the other, with her thumb in her mouth and her blankie wrapped around her. Kevin was in the armchair, biting his nails and staring at nothing. Shay was leaning against the wall, shifting from foot to foot, with his hands dug deep into his pockets; his eyes had wild white rings around them, like a cornered animal's, and his nostrils flared when he breathed. He was getting a beauty of a black eye. From the kitchen I could hear the sound of my da getting sick, in great rasping shouts, into the sink.

I said, "What happened?"

They all jumped a mile. Five pairs of eyes turned towards me, enormous and unblinking, with no expression at all. Carmel had been crying.

Shay said, "You've got great timing." Nobody else said a word. After a while I took the dustpan and brush out of Carmel's hands, guided her gently onto the sofa between Ma and Jackie, and started sweeping up. A long time after that, the noises from the kitchen changed to snores. Shay went in, quietly, and came out with the sharp knives. None of us went to bed that night.

Someone had thrown my da a nixer of his own that week: four days' plastering work, no need to tell the dole. He had taken the extra to the pub and treated himself to all the gin he could hold. Gin makes my da sorry for himself; feeling sorry for himself makes my da mean. He had staggered back to the Place and done his little number in front of the Dalys' house, roaring for Matt Daly to come out and fight, only this time he had taken it that step further. He had started hurling himself against the door; when that got him nowhere except into a heap on the steps, he had pulled off a shoe and started throwing it at the Dalys' window. This was where Ma and Shay had got there and started trying to drag him inside.

Usually Da coped relatively well with the news that his evening was over, but that night he had plenty of fuel left in the tank. The rest of the road, including Kevin and Jackie, had watched from their windows while he called Ma a dried-up old cunt and Shay a worthless little faggot and Carmel, when she went out to help, a dirty whore. Ma had called him a waster and an animal and prayed he would die roaring and rot in hell. Da had told all three of them to get their hands off him or when they went to sleep that night he would slit their throats. In the meantime, he had done his level best to beat seven shades of shite out of them.

None of this was new. The difference was that, before, he had always kept it indoors. Losing that boundary felt like losing your brakes doing eighty. Carmel said, in a small flat final voice, "He's getting worse." No one looked at her.

Kevin and Jackie had screamed out of the window for Da to stop, Shay had screamed at them to get back inside, Ma had screamed at them that this was all their fault for driving their da to drink, Da had screamed at them to just wait till he got up there. Finally, someone—and the Harrison sisters were the only ones on the road who had a phone—had called the Guards. That was a no-no right up there with giving heroin to small children or swearing in front of the priest. My family had managed to push the Harrison sisters all the way out to the other side of that taboo.

Ma and Carmel had begged the uniforms not to take Da—the disgrace of it—and they had been sweet enough to oblige. For plenty of cops, back then, domestic violence was like vandalizing your own property: a dumb idea, but probably not a crime. They had dragged Da up the stairs, dumped him on the kitchen floor and left.

Jackie said, "It was a bad one, all right."

I said, "I figured that was what did it for Rosie. All her life, her da's been warning her about what a shower of filthy savages the Mackeys are. She's ignored him, she's fallen in love with me, she's told herself I'm different. And then, right when she's a few hours away from putting her whole life into my hands, right when every minuscule doubt in her mind has to be a thousand times its normal size, here come the Mackeys to demonstrate Daddy's point in living color: putting on a holy show for the entire neighborhood, howling and brawling and biting and throwing shite like a troop of baboons on PCP. She had to wonder what I was like behind closed doors. She had to wonder if, deep down, I was one of them. She had to wonder just how long that would take to surface."

"So you left. Even without her."

I said, "I figured I'd paid my way out."

"I wondered about that. Why you didn't just come home."

"If I'd had the money, I'd have hopped straight on a plane to Australia. The farther the better."

Jackie asked, "Do you still blame them? Or was that just the drink talking, last night?"

"Yeah," I said, "I do. The whole lot of them. That's probably unfair, but sometimes life can just be a big old bitch."

My phone beeped: text message. *Hi frank, kev here, not meanin 2 hassle u cos i no u r a busy man but when u get a chance give us a bell ok? Could do w a chat. Thx.* I deleted it.

Jackie said, "But what if she wasn't walking out on you after all? If that never happened?"

I didn't have an answer for that one—a big part of my head didn't even understand the question—and it felt decades too late to go looking for one. I ignored Jackie till she shrugged and started refurbishing her lipstick. I watched Holly spin in great crazy circles as the swing chains untwisted, and I very carefully thought about exactly nothing except whether she needed to put on her scarf, how long it would be before she simmered down enough to be hungry, and what I wanted on my pizza.

10

We had our pizza, Jackie headed off to show Gavin some love, and Holly begged me into taking her to the Christmas ice rink in Ballsbridge. Holly skates like a fairy and I skate like a gorilla with neurological issues, which of course is a bonus for her because she gets to laugh at me when I smack into walls. By the time I dropped her back at Olivia's, both of us were happily exhausted and a little high on all those tinned Christmas carols, and both of us were in a much better mood. The sight of us on the doorstep, sweaty and messy and grinning, even wrung a reluctant smile out of Liv. I headed into town and had a couple of pints with the lads, I went home—Twin Peaks had never looked prettier—and took out a few nests of zombies on the Xbox, and I went to sleep loving the thought of a nice ordinary day's work so much that I thought I just might start off the next morning by snogging my office door.

I was right to enjoy the normal world while I had it. Deep down, even while I was shaking my fist at the sky and vowing never to darken the cobbles of that hellhole again, I must have known the Place was going to take that as a challenge. It hadn't given me permission to leave the building, and it was going to come looking for me.

It was coming up to lunchtime on Monday, and I had just finished introducing my boy with the drug-dealer situation to his brand-new granny, when my office phone rang.

"Mackey," I said.

Brian, our squad admin, said, "Personal call for you. Do you want to take it? I wouldn't have hassled you, only it sounds . . . well. Urgent. To say the *least*."

Kevin again; it had to be. Still a clingy little bastard, after all this time: one day of tagging along after me and he thought he was my new bestest buddy, or my sidekick, or God only knew what. The sooner that got nipped in the bud, the better. "What the hell," I said, rubbing the spot between my eyebrows that had suddenly started to throb. "Put him through."

"Her," Brian said, "and she's not a happy camper. I just thought I'd warn you."

It was Jackie and she was crying hard. "Francis, thank God, please, you've got to come—I don't *understand*, I don't know what happened, *please* . . ."

Her voice dissolved into a wail, a high thin sound way beyond anything like embarrassment or control. Something cold tightened at the back of my neck. "Jackie!" I snapped. "Talk to me. What's going on?"

I could barely understand the answer: something about the Hearnes, and the Guards, and a garden. "Jackie, I know you're upset, but I need you to pull it together for me, just for a second. Take a deep breath and tell me what's happened."

She gasped for breath. "Kevin. Francis . . . Francis . . . God . . . it's Kevin."

That icy clamp again, tighter. I said, "Is he hurt?"

"He's—Francis, oh God . . . He's *dead*. He's—"

"Where are you?"

"Ma's. Outside Ma's."

"Is that where Kevin is?"

"Yeah—no—not here, the back, the garden, he, he . . ."

Her voice disintegrated again. She was sobbing and hyperventilating at the same time. I said, "Jackie, listen to me. You need to sit down, drink something and make sure there's someone looking after you. I'm on my way."

I already had my jacket half on. In Undercover, nobody asks where you were this morning. I hung up and started running.

And there I was again, back in Faithful Place, just like I'd never been away. The first time I got out, it had let me run for twenty-two years before it jerked the leash tight. The second time, it had given me thirty-six hours.

The neighborhood was out again, like it had been on Saturday afternoon, but this time was different. The kids were in school and the adults were at work, so it was old people and stay-at-home mas and dole rats, wrapped tight against the slicing cold, and no one was milling around having a great day out. All the steps and all the windows were crammed with blank, watchful faces, but the street was empty except for my old friend the bogmonster, marching up and down like he was guarding the Vatican. The uniforms had been a step ahead this time, herded everyone back before that dangerous buzz could start to build. Somewhere a baby was wailing, but apart from that there was a killer silence, nothing but the far-off hum of traffic and the rap of the bogmonster's shoe lifts, and the slow drip of the morning's rain coming off the gutters.

No Bureau van this time, no Cooper, but in between the uniforms' marked car and the morgue van was Scorcher's pretty silver Beemer. The crime-scene tape was back up around Number 16, and a big guy in plain clothes—one of Scorch's boys, by the suit—was keeping an eye on it. Whatever had got Kevin, it wasn't a heart attack.

The bogmonster ignored me, which was a good choice. On the steps of Number 8 were Jackie, my ma and my da. Ma and Jackie were holding each other up; they looked like if either of them moved an inch they would both crumple. Da was ferociously laying into a cigarette.

Slowly, as I got close, their eyes focused on me, but without a flicker of recognition. They looked like they'd never seen me before. I said, "Jackie. What happened?"

Da said, "You came back. That's what happened."

Jackie grabbed the front of my jacket in a vice grip and pressed her face, hard, against my arm. I fought down the urge to shove her off me. "Jackie, pet," I said gently, "I need you to keep it together for me just a little longer. Talk to me."

She had started to shake. "Oh, Francis," she said, in a tiny amazed voice. "Oh, Francis. How . . . ?"

"I know, pet. Where is he?"

Ma said grimly, "He's out the back of Number Sixteen. In the garden. Out in that rain, all morning." She was leaning heavily on the railing and her voice sounded thick and pinched, like she had been sobbing for hours, but her eyes were sharp and dry.

"Do we have any idea what happened?"

Nobody said anything. Ma's mouth worked.

"OK," I said. "But we're a hundred percent positive it's Kevin?"

"Yeah, we are, you fecking simpleton," Ma snapped. She looked like she was seconds from hitting me across the face. "D'you think I can't recognize my own child that I carried? Are you gooky in the head, are you?"

I thought about pushing her down the steps. "Right," I said. "Well done. Is Carmel on her way?"

"Carmel's coming," Jackie said. "And Shay's coming. He just has to, he has to, he has to . . ."

Her words dried up. Da said, "He's waiting for the boss to come mind the shop." He dropped his cigarette butt over the railing and watched it fizzle out by the basement window.

"Good," I said. There was no way I was leaving Jackie on her own with these two, but she and Carmel could look after each other. "There's no reason for you to wait out here in the cold. Get inside, get something hot into you, and I'll go see what I can find out."

No one moved. I pried Jackie's fingers off my jacket, as gently as I could, and left the three of them there. Dozens of unblinking pairs of eyes followed me back up the road to Number 16.

The big guy at the tape took one look at my ID and said, "Detective Kennedy's out the back. Straight down the stairs and out the door." He had been warned to expect me.

The back door was propped open, letting an eerie gray slant of light into the basement and up the stairs. The four men in the garden looked like a tableau out of a painting or a morphine dream. The heavyset morgue boys in their pristine whites, leaning patiently on their stretcher among the tall weeds and the broken bottles and the nettles as thick as cables; Scorcher, sharp-edged and hyperreal with his slick head bent and his black overcoat flapping against the worn brick of the wall, crouching to stretch out a gloved hand; and Kevin. He was on his back, with his head towards the house and his legs splayed out at the wrong angles. One arm was across his chest; the other was doubled underneath him, like someone had him in an armlock. His head was thrown back wildly and turned away from me, and there were big uneven clots of something black matted in the dirt around it. Scorcher's white fingers were probing delicately in his jeans pocket. The wind whistled, a high crazy sound, over the wall.

Scorcher heard me first, or sensed me: he glanced up, whipped his hand away from Kevin and straightened. "Frank," he said, coming towards me. "I'm so sorry for your loss."

He was peeling his glove off, ready to shake my hand. I said, "I want a look at him."

Scorcher nodded and stepped back, out of my way. I knelt down in the dirt and the weeds, next to Kevin's body.

Dying had caved his face in, under the cheekbones and around the mouth; he looked forty years older than he would ever be. The upturned side of his face was ice white; the lower side, where the blood had settled, was mottled purple. There was a crusty thread of blood coming from his nose, and where his jaw had dropped I could see that his front teeth were broken. His hair was limp and dark with rain. One eyelid drooped a little over a cloudy eye, like a sly stupid wink.

It was like I had been shoved under an enormous battering waterfall, like the force of it was ripping my breath away. I said, "Cooper. We need Cooper."

"He's been here."

"And?"

A tiny silence. I saw the morgue boys glance at each other. Then Scorcher said, "According to him, your brother died either from a fractured skull or from a broken neck."

"How?"

Scorcher said, gently, "Frank, the lads need to take him away now. Come inside; we'll talk there. They'll take good care of him."

He reached out a hand towards my elbow, but he had better sense than to touch me. I took one last look at Kevin's face, that vacant wink and the black trickle of blood, and the little twist to his eyebrow that used to be the first thing I saw every morning, next to me on the pillow, when I was six years old. Then I said, "Right." As I turned to leave, I heard the heavy ripping noise of the boys unzipping their body bag.

I don't remember getting back into the house, or Scorcher guiding me up the stairs, out of the morgue boys' way. Juvenile shite like punching walls wouldn't touch this; I was so angry that for a minute I thought I had gone blind. When my eyes cleared we were on the top floor, in one of the back rooms that Kevin and I had checked out on Saturday. The room was brighter and colder than I remembered: someone had pushed up the bottom half of the filthy sash window, letting in a stream of icy light. Scorcher said, "Are you OK?"

I needed, like a drowning man needs air, to hear him talk to me cop-to-cop, box in this howling mess with neat flat preliminary-report words. I said, and my voice came out strange and tinny and distant, "What've we got?"

Regardless of all the many things that may be wrong with him, Scorcher is one of ours. I saw him get it. He nodded and leaned back against the wall, settling in for this. "Your brother was last seen at around twenty past eleven last night. He, your sister Jacinta, your brother Seamus, your sister Carmel and her family had had dinner at your parents' place, as per routine—stop me if I'm telling you anything you already know."

I shook my head. "Keep going."

"Carmel and her husband took their children home around eight. The others stayed put for a while longer, watching television and talking. Everyone except your mother had a few cans over the course of the evening; general consensus is that the men were a little drunk but definitely not blotto, and Jacinta only had the two. Kevin, Seamus and Jacinta left your parents' place together, just after eleven. Seamus went upstairs to his flat, and Kevin walked Jacinta down Smith's Road as far as the corner of New Street, where her car was parked. She offered Kevin a lift, but he said he wanted to walk off the gargle. She assumed his plan was to head back the way they'd come, along Smith's Road past the entrance to Faithful Place, then cut through the Liberties and along the canal to his flat in Portobello, but obviously she can't verify that. He watched her into her car, they waved goodbye, and she drove off. The last she saw of him, he was turning back down Smith's Road. That's our last confirmed sighting of him alive."

By seven he had given up and stopped ringing me. I had ignored him thoroughly enough that he hadn't thought it was worthwhile giving me one more try, before he tried to deal with whatever it was all by his great gormless self. "Only he didn't go home," I said.

"Doesn't look like it. The builders are next door today, so no one came in here till late this morning, when two kids called Jason and Logan Hearne headed in to have a look at the basement, glanced out the landing window and got more than they bargained for. They're thirteen and twelve, and why they weren't in school—"

"Personally," I said, "I'm delighted they weren't." With Number 14 and Number 12 empty, nobody would have spotted Kevin from a back window. He could have stayed there for weeks. I've seen bodies after that long.

Scorch gave me a quick, apologetic sideways glance; he'd got carried away. "Yeah," he said. "There is that. Anyway, they legged it out of there and called their mother, who called us and apparently half the neighborhood. Ms. Hearne also recognized the deceased as your brother, so she notified your mother, who made the definitive ID. I'm sorry she had to see that."

I said, "My ma's tough." Behind me, somewhere downstairs, there was a thump, a grunt and a scraping sound as the morgue boys maneuvered their stretcher through the narrow corridors. I didn't turn around.

"Cooper puts time of death somewhere in the region of midnight, plus or minus a couple of hours either way. Add in your family's statements, and the fact that your brother was found in the same clothes that they describe him wearing yesterday evening, and I think we can take it that after walking Jacinta to her car, he headed directly back to Faithful Place."

"And then what? How the *fuck* did he wind up with his neck broken?"

Scorch took a breath. "For whatever reason," he said, "your brother came into this house and upstairs to this room. Then, one way or another, he went out the window. If it's any comfort, Cooper says death was probably pretty near instantaneous."

Stars were exploding in front of my eyes, like I'd been bashed over the head. I raked a hand through my hair. "No. That doesn't make sense. Maybe he fell off the garden wall, one of the walls—" For a confused second I was seeing Kev sixteen and limber, vaulting his way across dark gardens in pursuit of Linda Dwyer's blouse bunnies. "Out of here makes no sense."

Scorcher shook his head. "The walls on both sides are, what, six feet high—seven, tops? According to Cooper, the injuries say he fell around twenty. And the trajectory was straight down. He went out this window."

"No. Kevin didn't like this place. On Saturday I practically had to drag him in by the scruff of his neck, he spent the whole time moaning about rats and heebie-jeebies and the ceilings falling in, and that was in broad daylight, with two of us there. What the hell would he be doing here on his own, in the middle of the night?"

"We'd like to know the same thing. I wondered if he needed a piss before he headed home and came in for a bit of privacy, but then why come all the way up here? He could've hung his mickey out the hall-floor window just as easily, if he was aiming to water the garden. I don't know about you, but when I'm a bit the worse for wear, I don't take on stairs without a reason."

That was when I realized that the smudges on the window frame weren't grime, they were print dust, and that was when it hit me why the sight of Scorcher had given me that nasty feeling. I said, "What are you doing here?"

Scorch's eyelids flickered. He said, picking his words, "At first we were thinking in terms of an accident. Your brother comes up here, for whatever reason, and then something makes him stick his head out the window—maybe he hears a noise in the back garden, maybe the booze isn't sitting well and he thinks he's going to get sick. He leans out, overbalances, doesn't catch himself in time . . ."

Something cold hit the back of my throat. I clamped my teeth on it.

"But I did a bit of experimenting, just to see for myself. Hamill, downstairs, the guy at the tape? He's very near your brother's height and build. I've spent most of the morning making him hang out that window. It doesn't work, Frank."

"What are you talking about?"

"On Hamill, that sash comes up to about here." Scorch put the side of his hand to his ribs. "To get his head under it, he has to bend his knees, and that brings his backside down and keeps his center of gravity well inside the room. We tried it a dozen different ways: same result. It'd be almost impossible for someone Kevin's size to fall out that window by accident."

The inside of my mouth felt icy. I said, "Somebody pushed him."

Scorch hiked up his jacket to shove his hands in his pockets. He said carefully, "We've got no signs of a struggle, Frank."

"What are you saying?"

"If he'd been forced out that window, I'd expect to see scuffle marks on the floor, the window sash smashed away where he went through it, breakage to his fingernails from grabbing at the attacker or the window frame, maybe cuts and bruises where they fought. We haven't found any of that."

I said, "You're trying to tell me Kevin killed himself."

That made Scorcher look away. He said, "I'm trying to tell you it wasn't an accident, and there's nothing that says he was pushed. According to Cooper, every one of his injuries is consistent with the fall. He was a big guy, and from what I've gathered, he may have been drunk last night, but he wasn't legless. He wouldn't have gone down without a fight."

I took a breath. "Right," I said. "Fair enough. You've got a point. Come here for a second, though. There's something I should probably show you."

I guided him towards the window; he gave me a suspicious look. "What've you got?"

"Take a good look at the garden from this angle. Where it meets the base of the house, specifically. You'll see what I mean."

He leaned on the sill and craned his neck out under the window sash. "Where?"

I shoved him harder than I meant to. For a split second I thought I wasn't going to be able to pull him back inside. Deep down, a sliver of me was fucking delighted.

"Jesus Christ!" Scorch leaped back from the window and stared at me, wide-eyed. "Have you lost your fucking mind?"

"No scuffle marks, Scorch. No broken window sash, no broken fingernails, no cuts and bruises. You're a big guy, you're stone-cold sober, and you'd have been gone without a squeak. Bye-bye, thank you for playing, Scorcher has left the building."

"Bloody *hell* . . ." He tugged his jacket straight and slapped dust off it, hard. "Not funny, Frank. You scared the shit out of me."

"Good. Kevin was not the suicidal type, Scorch. You're going to have to trust me on this one. There's no way he'd have taken himself out."

"Fine. Then tell me this: who was out to get him?"

"Nobody that I know of, but that doesn't mean anything. He could have had the entire Sicilian Mafia on his arse for all I know."

Scorcher kept his mouth shut and let that speak for itself.

I said, "So we weren't bosom buddies. I didn't have to live in his pocket to know he was a healthy young guy, no mental illness, no love-life troubles, no money troubles, happy as Larry. And then one night, out of nowhere, he decides to wander into a derelict house and take a header out the window?"

"It happens."

"Show me one piece of evidence that says it happened here. One."

Scorch patted his hair back into place and sighed. "OK," he said. "But I'm sharing this with you as a fellow cop, Frank. Not as a family member of the vic. You don't breathe a word about it outside this room. Are you OK with that?"

"I'm just ducky," I said. I already knew this was going to be bad.

Scorcher leaned over his poofy briefcase, fiddled around inside and came up holding a clear plastic evidence bag. "Don't open it," he said.

It was one small sheet of lined paper, yellowish and quartered by deep creases where it had spent a long time folded. It looked blank till I flipped it over and saw the faded ballpoint, and then before my brain worked out what was happening the handwriting came roaring up out of every dark corner and slammed into me like a runaway train.

> *Dear Mam and Dad and Nora,*
>
> *By the time you read this I'll be on my way to England with Francis. We're going to get married, we're going to get good jobs not in factories and we're going to have a brilliant life together. The only thing I wish is that I wouldn't have had to lie to you, every single day I wanted to look yous all in the eye and say I'm going to marry him but Dad I didn't know what else to do. I knew you would go mental but Frank is NOT a waster and he is NOT going to hurt me. He makes me happy. This is the happiest day of my life.*

"The lads at Documents will need to run some tests," Scorcher said, "but I'd say we've both seen the other half of that before."

Outside the window the sky was gray-white, turning icy. A cold swipe of air whipped in through the window and a tiny swirl of dust specks rose from the floorboards, sparkled for a second in the weak light, then fell and vanished. Somewhere I heard the hiss and rattle of plaster disintegrating, trickling away. Scorcher was watching me with something that I hoped, for the sake of his health, wasn't sympathy.

I said, "Where did you get this?"

"It was in your brother's inside jacket pocket."

Which rounded off this morning's set of one-two-three punches beautifully. When I got some air into my lungs I said, "That doesn't tell you where he got it. It doesn't even tell you he was the one who put it there."

"No," Scorcher agreed, too mildly. "It doesn't."

There was a silence. Scorch waited a tactful amount of time before he held out his hand for the evidence bag.

I said, "You're thinking this means Kevin killed Rosie."

"I'm not thinking anything. At this stage I'm just collecting the evidence."

He reached for the bag; I whipped it away. "You keep collecting. Do you hear me?"

"I'm going to need that back."

"Innocent until proven guilty, Kennedy. This is a long, long way from proof. Remember that."

"Mmm," Scorch said, neutrally. "The other thing I'm going to need is you keeping out of my way, Frank. I'm very serious."

"There's a coincidence. So am I."

"Before was bad enough. But now . . . It doesn't get much more emotionally involved than this. I realize you're upset, but any interference from you could compromise my whole investigation, and I won't allow that."

I said, "Kevin didn't kill anyone. Not himself, not Rosie, not anyone. You just keep collecting that evidence."

Scorcher's eyes flickered, away from mine. After a moment I gave him his precious Ziploc and left.

As I went through the door Scorcher said, "Hey, Frank? At least now we know for a fact she wasn't planning on leaving you."

I didn't turn around. I could still feel the heat of her writing, reaching right through Scorcher's prissy little label to wrap round my hand, searing me to the bones. *This is the happiest day of my life.*

She had been coming to me, and she had almost made it. There had been about ten yards between us and our hand-in-hand brave new world. It felt like freefalling, like being shoved out of a plane with the ground rushing up hard towards me and no parachute cord to pull.

11

I opened the front door a crack and closed it loudly, for Scorcher's benefit; then I went down the back stairs, out to the garden and over the wall. I didn't have time to deal with my family. Word spreads fast on the job, specially when the gossip is this juicy. I switched my mobiles off and headed for the squad, fast, to tell my super I was taking some time off before he could tell me the same thing.

George is a big guy, pushing retirement, with a droopy, exhausted face like a toy basset hound's. We love him; suspects make the mistake of thinking they can love him too. "Ah," he said, heaving himself out of his chair, when he saw me at the door. "Frank." He held out his hand, across the desk. "I'm sorry for your loss."

"We weren't close," I said, giving him a good firm grip, "but it's a shock, all right."

"They're saying it looks like he might have done it himself."

"Yep," I agreed, watching the sharp assessing flash in his eye as he sank back into his chair. "They are. It's a head wrecker, all round. Boss, I've got a lot of holiday time saved up. If it's all right with you, I'd like to cash it in, effective immediately."

George passed a hand over his bald spot and examined it mournfully, pretending to consider that. "Can your investigations afford it?"

"Not a problem," I said. Which he already knew: reading upside down is one of life's more useful skills, and the file in front of him was one of mine. "Nothing's at a crucial stage. They just need watching. An hour or two to get my paperwork in shape, and I can be ready to hand over."

"Right," George said, on a sigh. "Why not. Hand over to Yeates. He's having to ease off on the southside coke op for a while; he's got time."

Yeates is good; we don't have duds in Undercover. "I'll bring him up to speed," I said. "Thanks, boss."

"Take a few weeks. Clear the head. What'll you do? Spend time with the family?"

In other words, are you planning to hang around the scene, asking awkward questions. I said, "I was thinking about getting out of town. Wexford, maybe. I hear the coastline's lovely this time of year."

George massaged his forehead folds like they hurt. "Some gobshite from Murder was onto me bright and early this morning, giving out about you. Kennedy, Kenny, whatever. Says you've been interfering with his investigation."

The squealing little arse-gerbil. "He's PMSing," I said. "I'll bring him some pretty flowers and he'll be grand."

"Bring him whatever you want. Just don't be bringing him any excuse to ring me again. I don't like gobshites annoying me before I've had my cup of tea; banjaxes my bowels."

"I'll be in Wexford, boss, remember? I won't have the opportunity to get Little Miss Murder's frillies in a twist, even if I wanted to. I'll just tidy up a few things"—I jerked a thumb in the direction of my office—"and I'll be on my way, out of everyone's hair."

George inspected me, under heavy lids. Eventually he flapped a big weary hand and said, "Tidy away. Take your time."

"Cheers, boss," I said. This is why we love George. One of the things that makes a great super is knowing when he doesn't want to know. "I'll see you in a few weeks."

I was halfway out the door when he called, "Frank."

"Boss?"

"Anywhere the squad can make a donation, in your brother's name? Charity? Sports club?"

And it hit me all over again, like a rabbit punch straight to the gullet. For a second nothing came out of my mouth. I didn't even know if Kev had been in a sports club, although I doubted it. I thought there should be a charity created specially with fucked-up situations like this one in mind, a fund to send young guys snorkeling round the Great Barrier Reef and paragliding down the Grand Canyon, just in case that day turned out to be their last chance.

"Give it to the Victims of Homicide crowd," I said. "And thank you, boss. I appreciate it. Tell the lads thanks."

Deep down in his heart, every Undercover believes that, by and large, Murder are a bunch of big pussy boys. There are exceptions, but the fact is that the Murder lads are our pro boxers: they fight hard, but when you come right down to it they have gloves and gumshields and a referee ringing his little bell when everyone needs to take a breather and wipe off the blood. Undercovers fight bare-knuckle, we fight backstreet and we fight till someone goes down. If Scorch wants into a suspect's house, he fills in a square mile of paperwork and waits for the rubber stamps and assembles the appropriate entry team so no one gets hurt; me, I bat the baby-blues, spin a good story and waltz right in, and if the suspect should decide he wants to kick the shit out of me, I'm on my own.

This was about to work for me. Scorch was used to fighting by the rules. He took it for granted that, with the odd minor bad-little-boy breach, I fought the same way. It would take a while to occur to him that my rules had sweet fuck-all in common with his.

I spread out a bunch of files on my desk, in case anyone happened to stop by and needed to see me busyworking towards a handover. Then I phoned my mate in Records and asked him to e-mail me the personnel file of every floater working on the Rose Daly murder. He did a little fussing about confidentiality, but a couple of years back his daughter had got off on possession charges when someone was sloppy enough to misfile three wraps of coke and her statement sheet, so I figured he owed me at least two major or four minor favors. Underneath the fussing, he saw it the same way. His voice sounded like his ulcer was growing by the moment, but the files came through almost before we got off the phone.

Scorcher had himself five floaters, more than I would have expected for a stone-cold case; apparently he and his eighty-whatever percent really did get props with the Murder boys. The fourth floater was the one I needed.

Stephen Moran, twenty-six years old, home address in the North Wall, good Leaving Cert results, straight from school into Templemore, string of glowing evaluations, out of uniform just three months. The photo showed a skinny kid with scruffy red hair and alert gray eyes. A working-class Dublin boy, smart and determined and on the fast track, and—thank heaven for little newbies—way too green and too eager to question anything a squad detective might happen to tell him. Young Stephen and I were going to get along just fine.

I tucked Stephen's details into my pocket, deleted the e-mail very thoroughly, and spent a couple of hours getting my cases good and ready for Yeates; the last thing I wanted was him ringing me at the wrong moment to clarify something or other. We did a nice quick handover—Yeates had too much sense to give me any sympathy, beyond a slap on the shoulder and a promise that he'd take care of everything. Then I packed up my stuff, closed my office door and headed over to Dublin Castle, where the Murder Squad works, to annex Stephen Moran.

If someone else had been running the investigation, Stephen might have been harder to find; he could have finished up at six or seven or eight, and if he was out in the field, he might not have bothered to check back in at the squad and hand in his paperwork before he headed home. But I know Scorcher. Overtime gives the brass palpitations and paper gives them orgasms, so Scorchie's boys and girls would clock out at five on the dot, and they would fill out all their forms before they did it. I found myself a bench in the Castle gardens with a good view of the door and a nice anti-Scorch screen of bushes, lit a smoke and waited. It wasn't even raining. This was my lucky day all over.

One thing in particular was slapped straight across the front of my mind: Kevin hadn't had a torch on him. If he had, Scorcher would have mentioned it, to back up his little suicide theory. And Kevin never did dangerous shit unless he had a damn good reason; he left the because-it's-there stuff to me and Shay. There wasn't enough tinned Guinness in all of Dublin to make him think it would be fun to go wandering around Number 16 on his own, in pitch-darkness, just for kicks and giggles. Either he had seen or heard something, on his way past, that made him think he had no choice except to go and investigate—something too urgent to let him go get backup, but discreet enough that no one else on the road had noticed a thing—or someone had called him in there, someone who had magically known that he would be passing the top of Faithful Place right about then; or he had been bullshitting Jackie. He had been heading to that house all along, to meet someone who would come prepared.

It was dark and I had built up a nice little pile of cigarette butts by my feet before, sure enough, at five on the dot Scorcher and his sidekick came out of that door and headed for the car park. Scorcher had his head up and a spring in his step, and he was swinging his briefcase and telling some story that made the ferret-faced kid laugh dutifully. Almost before they were gone, out came my boy Stephen, trying to wrangle a mobile and a knapsack and a bicycle helmet and a long scarf. He was taller than I had expected, and his voice was deeper, with a rough edge that made him sound younger than he was. He was wearing a gray overcoat that was very good quality and very, very new: he had blown his savings to make sure he would fit in with the Murder boys.

The nice thing was that I had a free hand here. Stephen might have his doubts about getting chatty with a victim's brother, but I was willing to bet that he hadn't actually been warned off me; Cooper was one thing, but Scorch would never in a million years have told an itty-bitty floater that he was feeling threatened by little old me. Scorcher's overdeveloped sense of hierarchy was, in fact, about to come in useful all round. In his personal world, uniforms are scut-monkeys, floaters are droids, only squad detectives and up get any respect. That attitude is always a very bad idea, not only because of how much you might be wasting, but because of how many weak spots you're creating for yourself. Like I said before, I've always had a lovely eye for a weak spot.

Stephen hung up and stashed his mobile in a pocket, and I threw my smoke away and stepped out of the gardens into his path. "Stephen."

"Yeah?"

"Frank Mackey," I said, putting out a hand. "Undercover."

I saw his eyes widen, just a touch, with what could have been awe or fear or anything in between. Over the years I've planted and watered a number of interesting legends about myself, some of them true, some of them not, all of them useful, so I get that a lot. Stephen at least made a decent stab at keeping it under wraps, which I approved of. "Stephen Moran, General Unit," he said, shaking my hand just a little too firmly and holding the eye contact just a little too long; the kid was working hard to impress me. "It's good to meet you, sir."

"Call me Frank. We don't 'sir' in Undercover. I've been keeping an eye on you for a while now, Stephen. We've been hearing a lot of very nice things."

He managed to hold back both the blush and the curiosity. "That's always good to know." I was starting to like this kid.

I said, "Walk with me," and headed back into the gardens—there were going to be more floaters and more Murder boys coming out of that building. "Tell me something, Stephen. You made detective three months ago, am I right?"

He walked like a teenager, that long springy stride when you have too much energy to fit in your body. "That's right."

"Well done. Correct me if I'm wrong, but I don't see you as the type to spend the rest of your career in the General Unit, tagging along after whatever squad detective snaps his fingers this week. You've got too much potential for that. You'll want to run investigations of your own, eventually. Am I right?"

"That's the plan."

"Which squad are you aiming for?"

This time a little bit of the blush made it through. "Murder or Undercover."

"You've got good taste," I said, grinning. "So working a murder case must be a dream come true, yeah? Having fun?"

Stephen said, cautiously, "I'm learning a lot."

I laughed out loud. "You are in your arse. That means Scorcher Kennedy's been treating you like his very own trained chimpanzee. What's he got you doing, making coffee? Picking up his dry cleaning? Mending his socks?"

One corner of Stephen's mouth twitched reluctantly. "Typing up witness statements."

"Oh, lovely. How many words per minute can you do?"

"I don't mind. I mean, I'm the newest, you know? All the others have a few years under their belts. And someone has to do the—"

He was struggling valiantly to get it right. "Stephen," I said. "Breathe. This isn't a test. You're wasted on secretarial work. You know that, I know that, and if Scorch had bothered to take ten minutes to read your file, he'd know it too." I pointed to a bench, under a lamppost so I could watch his face and out of view of any of the main exits. "Have a seat."

Stephen slung his knapsack and helmet on the ground and sat down. In spite of the flattery, his eyes were wary, which was good. "We're both busy men," I said, joining him on the bench, "so I'll cut to the chase. I'd be interested in hearing how you get on in this investigation. From your perspective, not from Detective Kennedy's, since we both know just how much use his would be. No need to be diplomatic: we're talking strictly confidential, just between the two of us."

I could see his mind moving fast, but he had a decent poker face and I couldn't pick out which way it was taking him. He said, "Hearing how I get on. What d'you mean by that, exactly?"

"We meet up now and then. Maybe I buy you a nice pint or two. You tell me what you've been at the last few days, what you think about it, how you'd be handling the case differently if you were the boss man. I see what I think of how you work. How does that strike you?"

Stephen picked a stray dead leaf off the bench and started folding it carefully along the veins. "Can I talk to you straight? Like we were off duty. Man to man."

I spread my hands. "We are off duty, Stephen my friend. Hadn't you noticed?"

"I mean—"

"I know what you mean. At ease, mate. Say whatever springs to mind. No repercussions."

His eyes came up from the leaf to meet mine, level and gray and intelligent. "Word is you've got a personal interest in this case. A double interest, now."

"That's hardly a state secret. And?"

"What it sounds like to me," Stephen said, "is you want me to spy on this murder investigation and report back to you."

I said cheerfully, "If that's how you want to look at it."

"I'm not mad about the sound of that."

"Interesting." I found my cigarettes. "Smoke?"

"No, thanks."

Not as green as he had looked on paper. No matter how badly the kid wanted to be in my good books, he was nobody's bitch. Normally I would have approved of this, but right that minute I wasn't in the mood for doing dainty footwork around his stubborn side. I lit up and blew smoke rings up into the smudgy yellow light of the lamp. "Stephen," I said. "You need to think this through. I presume you're worried about three aspects of this: the level of commitment involved, the ethics, and the potential consequences, not necessarily in that order. Am I right?"

"More or less, yeah."

"Let's start with the commitment. I won't be asking you for in-depth daily reports on everything that goes on in that squad room. I'll be asking you very specific questions that you'll be able to answer with a minimum expenditure of time and effort. We're talking two or three meetings a week, none of which need to last more than fifteen minutes if you've got something better to do, plus maybe another half hour's worth of research before each meeting. Does that sound like something you could manage, just hypothetically speaking?"

After a moment Stephen nodded. "It's not about having better things to do—"

"Good man. Next, possible consequences. Yes, Detective Kennedy would quite probably have the mother of all hissy fits if he found out you and I were talking, but there's no reason why he should. It ought to be obvious to you that I'm very, very good at keeping my mouth shut. How about you?"

"I'm not a squealer."

"I didn't think so. In other words, the risk of Detective Kennedy catching you and sending you to the naughty corner is minimal. And, Stephen? Keep in mind that's not the only possible consequence here. Plenty of other things could come out of this."

I waited till he asked, "Like what?"

"When I said you had potential, I wasn't just blowing smoke up your arse. Remember, this case won't last forever, and as soon as it ends, you go back to the floater pool. Looking forward to that?"

He shrugged. "It's the only way onto a squad. It needs doing."

"Following up on stolen cars and broken windows, and waiting for someone like Scorcher Kennedy to whistle for you so you can fetch his sandwiches for a few weeks. Sure, it needs doing, but some people do it for a year and some people do it for twenty. Given the choice, when would you, personally, want to get out of there for good?"

"The sooner the better. Obviously."

"That's what I thought. I guarantee you, I will in fact be noticing exactly how you work, just like I said I would. And every time a place opens up on my squad, I remember people who've done good work for me. I can't guarantee the same for my friend Scorcher. Tell me something, just between the two of us: does he even know your first name?"

Stephen didn't answer. "So," I said, "I think that takes care of potential consequences, don't you? Which leaves us with the ethics of the situation. Am I asking you to do anything that might compromise your work on the murder case?"

"Not so far."

"And I don't plan to. If at any point you feel that our association is jeopardizing your ability to give your full attention to your official assignment, just let me know and you won't hear from me again. You've got my word on that." Always, always give them a free out that they'll never have a chance to use. "Fair enough?"

He didn't look reassured. "Yeah."

"Am I asking you to disobey anyone else's orders?"

"That's splitting hairs. OK, Detective Kennedy hasn't told me not to talk to you, but that's only because it hasn't even occurred to him that I might."

"So? It should've occurred to him. If it hasn't, that's his problem, not yours or mine. You don't owe him anything."

Stephen ran a hand through his hair. "I do, though," he said. "He's the one that brought me onto this case. Right now, he's my boss. The rule is, I take orders from him. No one else."

My jaw dropped. "The *rule*? What the . . . ? I thought you said you had your eye on Undercover. Were you just hand-jobbing me there? Because I don't like being hand-jobbed by boys, Stephen. I really don't."

He shot upright. "No! Of course I— What are you— I *do* want Undercover!"

"And you think we can afford to sit around all day reading the *rule* book? You think I made it through three years in deep cover in a *drug* ring by sticking to the *rules*? Tell me you're having a laugh, kid. Please. Tell me I haven't been flushing my time down the jacks whenever I picked up your file."

"I never asked you to read my file. For all I know, anyway, you never saw it till this week. Till you wanted someone inside this case."

Fair play to the kid. "Stephen. I'm offering you an opportunity that every floater on the force, every guy you trained with, every guy you'll see in work tomorrow morning would sell his granny for. You're going to throw it away because I can't prove I've been paying enough *attention* to you?"

He was red all over his freckles, but he held his ground. "*No.* I'm trying to do the right *thing*."

Sweet Jesus, he was young. "If you don't know this by now, mate, you'd better write it down and learn it by heart: the right thing is not always the same as what's in your pretty little rule book. To all intents and purposes, this right here is an undercover assignment that I'm offering you. A bit of moral ambiguity comes with the job. If you can't cope with it, now would be just a perfect time to figure that out."

"This is different. It's undercover against our own."

"Sunshine, you would be amazed at how often that happens. Amazed. Like I said, if you can't handle it, not only do you need to know that, but so do I. Both of us might have to do some rethinking about your career goals."

The corners of Stephen's mouth tightened. "If I don't do this," he said, "I can forget about a place in Undercover."

"Not out of spite, kid. Don't fool yourself. A guy could bang both my sisters at once, stick the video on YouTube, and I'd happily work with him, as long as I thought he'd get the job done. But if you make it clear to me that you're fundamentally unsuited to undercover work, then no, I'm not going to recommend you. Call me crazy."

"Can I have a few hours to think about it?"

"Nope," I said, flicking my cigarette away. "If you can't make this call fast, I don't need you to make it at all. I've got places to go and people to see, and I'm sure you have too. Here's what it comes down to, Stephen. For the next few weeks, you can be Scorcher Kennedy's typist, or you can be my detective. Which one of those sounds more like what you signed up for?"

Stephen bit his lip and wrapped the end of his scarf around his hand. "If we did this," he said. "If. What kind of thing would you be wanting to know? Just for example."

"Just for example, when the fingerprint results come back, I'd be fascinated to hear whose prints, if any, were on that suitcase, on the contents of that suitcase, on the two halves of that note, and on the window Kevin went out of. I'd also be interested in a full description of his injuries, preferably with the diagrams and the post-mortem report. That might well be enough info to keep me going for a while; who knows, it might even turn out to be all I ever need. And that should be back within the next couple of days, no?"

After a moment Stephen let out a long breath, a trail of white in the cold air, and lifted his head. "No offense," he said, "but before I go spilling inside info on a murder case to a total stranger, I'd like to see some ID."

I burst out laughing. "Stephen," I said, finding my ID, "you're a man after my own heart. We're going to be good for each other, you and me."

"Yeah," Stephen said, a little dryly, "I'm hoping." I watched his disorganized red head bent over the ID, and just for a second, under the hard throb of triumph—*Up yours, Scorchie baby, he's my boy now*—I felt a little pulse of affection towards the kid. It felt good to have someone on my side.

12

And that was about as long as I could put off going home. I tried fortifying myself for it at Burdock's—the thought of Burdock's was the only thing that had ever tempted me to go back to the Liberties—but even the finest smoked cod and chips have their limits. Like most undercovers, I don't have much of a knack for fear. I've walked into meetings with men who had every intention of chopping me into convenient sections and arranging me artistically under the nearest patch of concrete, and never broken a sweat. This, though, had me shitting an entire brickworks. I told myself what I had told young Stephen: count this as an undercover op, Frankie the Intrepid Detective on his most daring mission yet, into the jaws of doom.

The flat was a different place. The house was unlocked, and as soon as I stepped into the hall the wave came rolling down the stairs and hit me: warmth and voices and the smell of hot whiskey and cloves, all pouring out of our open door. The heating was on full blast and the sitting room was packed with people, crying, hugging, clumping up to put their heads together and enjoy the horror of it all, carrying six-packs or babies or plates of EasiSingle sandwiches covered in plastic wrap. Even the Dalys were there; Mr. Daly looked tense as hell and Mrs. Daly looked like she was on some pretty high-powered happy peanuts, but death trumps everything. I clocked Da instantly and automatically, but he and Shay and a few other lads had staked out a man-zone in the kitchen, with smokes and cans and monosyllabic conversation, and so far he looked fine. On a table under the Sacred Heart, propped up between flowers and Mass cards and electric candles, were photos of Kevin: Kevin as a fat red sausage of a baby, in a spiffy white *Miami Vice* suit at his confirmation, on a beach with a gang of shouting, sun-broiled lads waving lurid cocktails.

"There you are," Ma snapped, elbowing someone out of her way. She had changed into an eye-popping lavender getup that was clearly her top-level finery, and she had done some fairly serious crying since that afternoon. "You took your time, didn't you?"

"I came back as fast as I could. Are you holding up all right?"

She got the soft part of my arm in that lobster pinch I remembered so well. "Come here, you. That fella from your work, the one with the jaw on him, he's been saying Kevin fell out a window."

She had apparently decided to take this as a personal insult. With Ma, you never know what's going to fit that bill. I said, "That's what it looks like, yeah."

"I never heard such a load of rubbish. Your friend's talking out his hole. You get on to him and you tell him our Kevin wasn't a bleeding spastic and he never fell out a window in his life."

And here Scorcher thought he was doing a favor for a mate, smoothing a suicide into an accident. I said, "I'll be sure and pass that on."

"I'm not having people think I raised a thicko who couldn't put one foot in front of the other. You ring him up and tell him. Where's your phone?"

"Ma, it's out of office hours. If I hassle him now, I'll only put his back up. I'll do it in the morning, how's that?"

"You will not. You're only saying that to keep me quiet. I know you, Francis Mackey: you always were a liar, and you always did think you were smarter than everyone else. Well, I'm telling you now, I'm the mammy and you're not smarter than me. You ring that fella right now, while I can see you do it."

I tried to detach my arm, but that made her clamp down harder. "Are you afraid of your man, is that it? Give us that phone and I'll tell him meself, if you haven't got the guts. Go on, give it here."

I asked, "Tell him what?" Which was a mistake: the crazy level was rising fast enough without any encouragement from me. "Just out of interest. If Kevin didn't fall out that window, what the hell do you think happened to him?"

"Don't you be cursing at me," Ma snapped. "He was hit by a car, of course. Some fella was driving home drunk from his Christmas party and he hit our Kevin, and then—are you listening to me?—instead of facing the music like a man, he put our poor young fella in that garden and hoped no one would find him."

Sixty seconds with her, and my head was already spinning. It didn't help that, when you got down to the basics of the situation, I more or less agreed with her. "Ma. That didn't happen. None of his injuries were consistent with a car crash."

"Then get your arse out there and find out what happened to him! It's your job, yours and your la-di-da friend's, not mine. How would I know what happened? Do I look like a detective to you?"

I spotted Jackie coming out of the kitchen with a tray of sandwiches, caught her eye and sent her the superurgent sibling distress signal. She shoved the tray at the nearest teenager and zipped over to us. Ma was still going strong ("*Not consistent*, will you listen to him, who do you think you are at all . . .") but Jackie hooked an arm through mine and told us both, in a rushed undertone, "Come here, I said to Auntie Concepta I'd bring Francis over to her the second he got here, she'll go *mental* if we wait any longer. We'd better go."

Which was a nice move: Auntie Concepta is actually Ma's aunt, and the only person around who can beat her in a psychological cage fight. Ma sniffed and delobstered my arm, with a glare to warn me this wasn't over, and Jackie and I took deep breaths and plunged into the crowd.

It was, no competition, the most bizarre evening of my life. Jackie steered me around the flat introducing me to my nephew and nieces, to Kevin's old girlfriends—I got a burst of tears and a double-D hug off Linda Dwyer—to my old friends' new families, to the four phenomenally bewildered Chinese students who lived in the basement flat and who were clustered against a wall politely holding untouched cans of Guinness and trying to look at this as a cultural learning experience. Some guy called Waxer shook my hand for five solid minutes while he reminisced fondly about the time he and Kevin got caught shoplifting comics. Jackie's Gavin punched me clumsily on the arm and muttered something heartfelt. Carmel's kids gave me a quadruple blue-eyed stare, until the second youngest—Donna, the one who according to everyone was a great laugh—dissolved into big hiccuppy sobs.

They were the easy part. Just about every face from once upon a time was in that room: kids I had scrapped with and walked to school with, women who had smacked me round the back of the legs when I got muck on their clean floors, men who had given me money to run to the shop and buy them their two cigarettes; people who looked at me and saw young Francis Mackey, running wild in the streets and getting suspended from school for the mouth on him, just you watch he'll end up like his da. None of them looked like themselves. They all looked like some makeup artist's shot at the Oscar, hanging jowls and extra bellies and receding hairlines superimposed obscenely over the real faces I knew. Jackie aimed me at them and murmured names in my ear. I let her think I didn't remember.

Zippy Hearne slapped me on the back and told him I owed him a fiver: he had finally managed to get his leg over Maura Kelly, even though he had had to marry her to do it. Linda Dwyer's ma made sure I got some of her special egg sandwiches. I caught the occasional funny look across the room, but on the whole, the Place had decided to welcome me back with open arms: I had apparently played enough of my cards right over the weekend, and a good slice of bereavement always helps, especially with a scandal-flavored topping. One of the Harrison sisters—shrunk to the size of Holly, but miraculously still alive—clutched my sleeve and stood on tiptoe to tell me at the top of her frail lungs that I had grown up very handsome.

By the time I managed to unhook myself from everyone and find myself a nice cold can and an inconspicuous corner, I felt like I had run some kind of surreal psych-ops gauntlet carefully designed to disorient me beyond any chance of recovery. I leaned back against the wall, pressed the can to my neck and tried not to catch anyone's eye.

The mood of the room had swung upwards, the way wakes do: people had worn themselves out on pain, they needed to catch their breath before they could go back there. The volume was rising, more people were piling into the flat and there was a burst of laughter from a gang of lads near me: "And just when the bus starts pulling away, right, Kev leans out the top window with the traffic cone up like this and he's yelling at the cops through it, 'KNEEL BEFORE ZOD!' . . ." Someone had pushed back the coffee table to clear a space in front of the fireplace, and someone else was pulling Sallie Hearne up to start the singing. She did the compulsory bit of protesting, but sure enough, once someone had got her a drop of whiskey to wet her throat, there it was: "There were three lovely lassies from Kimmage," and half the room joining in on the echo, "From Kimmage . . ." Every party in my childhood had kicked off the sing-along the same way, right back to me and Rosie and Mandy and Ger hiding under tables to dodge being sent to the group kiddie bed in whoever's back bedroom. These days Ger was bald enough that I could check my shave in his head.

I looked around at the room and I thought, *Someone here.* He would never have missed this. It would have stuck out a mile, and my guy was very, very good at keeping his nerve and blending in. Someone in this room, drinking our booze and ladling out the maudlin memories and singing along with Sallie.

Kev's mates were still cracking up; a couple of them could hardly breathe. ". . . Only it's around ten minutes before we stop pissing ourselves laughing, right? And *then* we remember that we were legging it so hard we just jumped on the first bus we saw, we don't have a fucking *clue* where we're going . . ."

"And whenever there's a bit of a scrimmage, sure I was the toughest of all . . ." Even Ma, on the sofa sandwiched protectively between Auntie Concepta and her nightmare friend Assumpta, was singing along: red-eyed, dabbing at her nose, but raising her glass and sticking out all her chins like a fighter. There was a gaggle of little kids running around at knee level, wearing their good clothes and clutching chocolate biscuits and keeping a wary eye out for anyone who might decide they were up too late. Any minute now they would be hiding under the table.

"So we get off the bus and we think we're somewhere in Rathmines, and the party's in *Crumlin*, not a chance we're gonna make it. And Kevin says, 'Lads, it's Friday night, it's all students round here, there's *got* to be a party somewhere . . .'"

The room was heating up. It smelled rich, reckless and familiar: hot whiskey, smoke, special-occasion perfume and sweat. Sallie pulled up her skirt and did a little dance step on the hearth, between verses. She still had the moves. "When he's had a few jars he goes frantic . . ." The lads hit their punch line—" . . . And by the end of the night, Kev's gone home with the fittest girl in the place!"—and doubled over, shouting with laughter and clinking their cans to Kevin's long-ago score.

Every undercover knows the dumbest thing you can ever do is start thinking you belong, but this party had been built into me a long time before that lesson. I joined in on the singing—"Goes frantic . . ."—and when Sallie glanced my way I gave her an approving wink and a little lift of my can.

She blinked. Then her eyes slid away from mine and she kept singing, half a beat faster: "But he's tall and he's dark and romantic, and I love him in spite of it all . . ."

As far as I knew, I had always got on just fine with all the Hearnes. Before I could make sense of this one, Carmel materialized at my shoulder. "D'you know something?" she said. "This is lovely, so it is. When I die, I'd love a send-off like this."

She was holding a glass of wine cooler or something equally horrific, and her face had that mixture of dreamy and decisive that goes with just the right amount of drink. "All these people," she said, gesturing with the glass, "all these people cared about our Kev. And I'll tell you something: I don't blame them. He was a dote, our Kevin. A little dote."

I said, "He was always a sweet kid."

"And he grew up lovely, Francis. I wish you'd had a chance to get to know him properly, like. My lot were mad about him."

She shot me a quick glance and for a second I thought she was going to say something else, but she checked herself. I said, "That doesn't surprise me."

"Darren ran away once—only the once, now, he was fourteen—and, sure, I wasn't even worried; I knew straightaway he'd gone to Kevin. He's only devastated, Darren is. He says Kevin was the only one of the lot of us that wasn't mental, and now there's no point to being in this family."

Darren was mooching around the edges of the room, picking at the sleeves of his big black jumper and doing a professional emo sulk. He looked miserable enough that he had even forgotten to be embarrassed about being there. I said, "He's eighteen and his head's wrecked. He's not firing on all cylinders right now. Don't let him get to you."

"Ah, I know, he's only upset, but . . ." Carmel sighed. "D'you know something? There's ways I think he's right."

"So? Mental is a family tradition, babe. He'll appreciate it when he's older."

I was trying to get a smile off her, but she was rubbing at her nose and giving Darren a troubled stare. "D'you think I'm a bad person, Francis?"

I laughed out loud. "You? Jesus, Melly, no. It's been a while since I checked, but unless you've been running a whorehouse out of that lovely semi-d, I'd say you're fine. I've met a few bad people along the way, and take it from me: you wouldn't fit in."

"This'll sound terrible," Carmel said. She squinted dubiously at the glass in her hand, like she wasn't sure how it had got there. "I shouldn't say this, now; I know I shouldn't. But you're my brother, aren't you? And isn't that what brothers and sisters are for, sure?"

"It is, of course. What have you done? Am I going to have to arrest you?"

"Ah, go 'way with you. I've done nothing. It's what I was thinking, only. Don't be laughing at me, will you?"

"Wouldn't dream of it. Swear to God."

Carmel gave me a suspicious look in case I was taking the piss, but then she sighed and took a careful sip of her drink—it smelled of fake peaches. "I was jealous of him," she said. "Of Kevin. Always."

This I hadn't seen coming. I waited.

"I am of Jackie, as well. I used to be of you, even."

I said, "I got the impression you were pretty happy, these days. Am I wrong?"

"No; ah, God, no. I'm happy, all right. I've a great life."

"Then what's to be jealous about?"

"It's not that. It's . . . Do you remember Lenny Walker, Francis? I went out with him when I was only a young one, before Trevor?"

"Vaguely. Great big crater-face on him?"

"Ah, stop; the poor boy had acne. It went away after. I wasn't bothered about his skin, anyway; I was just delighted I had my first fella. I was dying to bring him home and show him off to all of yous, but, sure, you know yourself."

I said, "I do, yeah." None of us had ever brought anyone home, even on those special occasions when Da was supposed to be at work. We knew better than to take anything for granted.

Carmel glanced round, quickly, to make sure no one was listening. "But then," she said, "one night myself and Lenny were having a bit of a kiss and a cuddle up on Smith's Road, and didn't Da come past on his way home from the pub and catch us. He was only *livid*. He gave Lenny a clatter and told him to get out of it, and then he got me by the arm and started slapping me round the face. And he was calling me names—the language out of him, I wouldn't repeat it . . . He dragged me all the way home like that. Then he told me one more dirty slapper stunt and he'd put me in a home for bad girls. God help me, Francis, we'd never done more than kiss, myself and Lenny. I wouldn't have known how."

All this time later, the memory still turned her face a raw, mottled red. "That was the end of the pair of us, anyway. After that, when we seen each other about, Lenny wouldn't even look at me; too embarrassed. I didn't blame him, sure."

Da's attitude to Shay's and my girlfriends had been a lot more appreciative, if not more helpful. Back when Rosie and I were out in the open, before Matt Daly found out and came down on her like a ton of bricks: *The Daly young one, yeah? Fair play to you, son. She's a little daisy.* A too-hard slap on the back and a savage grin at the clench in my jaw. *The kegs on her, my Jaysus. Tell us, have you had a go of those yet?* I said, "That's shitty, Melly. That really is. Five-star shitty."

Carmel took a deep breath and flapped a hand at her face, and the red started to subside. "God, look at the state of me, people'll think I'm getting the hot flushes . . . It's not that I was head over heels about Lenny; I'd probably have broken it off with him soon enough anyway, he was an awful bad kisser. It's that I never felt the same, after. You wouldn't remember, but I was a cheeky little wagon, before that—I used to give Ma and Da dreadful back talk, so I did. After that, though, I was afraid of my own shadow. Sure, me and Trevor were talking about getting engaged for a year before we did it; he'd the money saved up for the ring and all, but I wouldn't do it, because I knew I'd have to have an engagement do. The two families in the one room. I was only petrified."

"I don't blame you," I said. For a second I wished I had been nicer to Trevor's piggy little brother.

"And Shay's the same. Not that he went frightened, like, and not that Da ever got in his way with the girls, but . . ." Her eyes went to Shay, leaning in the kitchen doorway with a can in his hand and his head bent close to Linda Dwyer's. "Do you remember that time—you would've been about thirteen—he went unconscious?"

I said, "I try my very best not to." That had been a fun one. Da had aimed a punch at Ma, for reasons that now escape me, and Shay had got hold of his wrist. Da didn't take well to challenges to his authority; he communicated that concept by grabbing Shay round the throat and giving his head a good smack off the wall. Shay blacked out, for what was probably a minute but seemed like an hour, and spent the rest of the evening cross-eyed. Ma wouldn't let us bring him to hospital—it wasn't clear whether she was worried about the doctors, the neighbors or both, but the thought sent her into a full-on conniption. I spent that night watching Shay sleep, assuring Kevin that he wouldn't die and wondering what the fuck I would do if he did.

Carmel said, "He wasn't the same, after. He turned hard."

"He wasn't exactly a big fluffy marshmallow before."

"I know yous never got on, but I swear to God, Shay was all right. Himself and myself used to have great chats sometimes, and he used to do grand in school . . . After that was when he started keeping to himself."

Sallie hit her big finish—"In the meantime we'll live with me ma!"—and there was a burst of cheers and applause. Carmel and I clapped automatically. Shay lifted his head and glanced around the room. For a second he looked like something out of a cancer ward: grayish and exhausted, with deep hollows under his eyes. Then he went back to smiling at whatever story Linda Dwyer was telling him.

I said, "What's this got to do with Kevin?"

Carmel sighed deeply and took another dainty sip of fake peaches. The droop to her shoulders said she was heading for the melancholy stage.

"Because," she said, "that's why I was jealous of him. Kevin and Jackie . . . they had a bad time, I know they did. But nothing like that ever happened to them; nothing where they weren't the same after. Me and Shay made sure of that."

"And me."

She considered that. "Yeah," she acknowledged. "And you. But we tried to look after you, as well—ah, we *did*, Francis. I always thought you were all right too. You'd the guts to leave, anyway. And then Jackie always told us you were in great form . . . I thought that meant you got out before your head was wrecked altogether."

I said, "I got pretty close. No cigar, though."

"I didn't know that till the other night, in the pub, when you said. We did our best for you, Francis."

I smiled down at her. Her forehead was a maze of little anxious grooves, from a lifetime of worrying about whether everyone within range was OK. "I know you did, sweetheart. No one could've done better."

"And can you see why I was jealous of Kevin, can you? Him and Jackie, they're still great at being happy. The way I was when I was a little young one. It wasn't that I wished anything worse would happen to him—God forbid. I just looked at him and I wanted to be like that too."

I said gently, "I don't think that makes you a bad person, Melly. It's not like you took it out on Kevin. You never in your life did anything to hurt him; you always did your best to make sure he was OK. You were a good sister to him."

"It's still a sin," Carmel said. She was gazing mournfully out at the room and swaying, just a tiny bit, on her good heels. "Envy. You've only to think it for it to be a sin; sure, you know that. 'Bless me, Father, for I have sinned, in my thoughts and in my words, in what I have done and in what I have failed to do . . .' How'll I ever say it in confession, now that he's dead? I'd be ashamed of my life."

I put an arm around her and gave her shoulder a quick squeeze. She felt squashy and comforting. "Listen here, babe. I absolutely guarantee you that you're not going to hell for a bit of sibling jealousy. If anything, it'll be the other way round: you'll get extra God points for working so hard to get over it. Yeah?"

Carmel said, "I'm sure you're right," automatically—years of humoring Trevor—but she didn't sound convinced. For a second I got the sense that, in some undefined way, I had let her down. Then she snapped upright and forgot all about me: "Merciful Jaysus, is that a can Louise has? Louise! Come here to me!"

Louise's eyes popped and she vanished into the crowd at lightning speed. Carmel charged after her.

I leaned back into my corner and stayed put. The room was shifting again. Holy Tommy Murphy was striking up "The Rare Old Times," in a voice that used to be flavored like peat smoke and honey. Old age had roughed up the smooth edges, but he could still stop a conversation mid-sentence. Women lifted their glasses and swayed shoulder to shoulder, kids leaned against their parents' legs and tucked their thumbs in their mouths to listen; even Kevin's mates brought the story-swapping down to a murmur. Holy Tommy had his eyes closed and his head tipped back to the ceiling. "Raised on songs and stories, heroes of renown, the passing tales and glories that once was Dublin town . . ." Nora, leaning in the window frame listening, almost stopped my heart: she looked so much like a shadow Rosie, dark and sad-eyed and still, just too far away to reach.

I got my eyes off her fast, and that was when I spotted Mrs. Cullen, Mandy's ma, over by the Jesus-and-Kevin shrine having an in-depth conversation with Veronica Crotty, who still looked like she had a year-round cough. Mrs. Cullen and I got on, back when I was a teenager; she liked laughing, and I could always make her laugh. This time, though, when I caught her eye and smiled, she jumped like something had bitten her, grabbed Veronica's elbow and started whispering double-time in her ear, throwing furtive glances my way. The Cullens never did subtle very well. Somewhere right around there, I started wondering why Jackie hadn't brought me over to say hello to them when I first arrived.

I went looking for Des Nolan, Julie's brother, who had also been a buddy of mine and whom we had also somehow managed to miss on the Jackie whistle-stop tour. The look on Des's face when he saw me would have been priceless, if I had been in a laughing mood. He muttered something incoherent, pointed at a can that didn't look empty to me, and made a dive for the kitchen.

I found Jackie backed into a corner, getting her ear bent by our uncle Bertie. I put on an agonized about-to-break-down face, detached her from his sweaty clutches, steered her into the bedroom and shut the door behind us. These days the room was peach-colored and every available surface was covered with little porcelain widgets, which argued a certain lack of foresight on Ma's part. It smelled of cough syrup and something else, medical and stronger.

Jackie collapsed onto the bed. "God," she said, fanning herself and blowing out air. "Thanks a million. Jaysus, I know it's bad to pass remarks, but has he not had a wash since the midwife?"

"Jackie," I said. "What's going on?"

"What d'you mean, like?"

"Half the people here won't say a word to me, they won't even look me in the eye, but they've got plenty to say when they think I'm not looking. What's the story?"

Jackie managed to look innocent and shifty at the same time, like a kid neck-deep in denials and chocolate. "You've been away, sure. They haven't seen you in twenty years. They're only feeling a bit awkward."

"Bollix. Is this because I'm a cop now?"

"Ah, no. Maybe a little bit, like, but . . . Would you not just leave it, Francis? Do you not think maybe you're only being paranoid?"

I said, "I need to know what's going on, Jackie. I'm serious. Do not fuck with me on this."

"Jaysus, relax the kacks; I'm not one of your bleeding suspects." She shook the cider can in her hand. "Do you know are there any more of these left, are there?"

I shoved my Guinness at her—I had barely touched it. "Now," I said.

Jackie sighed, turning the can between her hands. She said, "You know the Place, sure. Any chance of a scandal . . ."

"And they're on it like vultures. How did I turn into today's Happy Meal?"

She shrugged uncomfortably. "Rosie got killed the night you left. Kevin died two nights after you came back. And you were on at the Dalys not to go to the cops. Some people . . ."

She let it trail off. I said, "Tell me you're shitting me, Jackie. Tell me the Place is not saying I killed Rosie and Kevin."

"Not the whole Place. Some people, only. I don't think—Francis, listen to me—I don't think they even believe it themselves. They're saying it because it makes a better story—what with you having been away, and being a cop, and all. Don't mind them. They're only looking for more drama, so they are."

I realized that I still had Jackie's empty in my hand, and that I had crushed it into a mangled mess. I had expected this from Scorcher, from the rest of the Murder stud-muffins, maybe even from a few guys in Undercover. I had not expected it from my own street.

Jackie was gazing at me anxiously. "D'you know what I mean? And, as well, everyone else who could've hurt Rosie is from round here. People don't want to be thinking—"

I said, "*I'm from round here.*"

There was a silence. Jackie reached out a hand, tentatively, and tried to touch my arm; I whipped it away. The room felt underlit and threatening, shadows piled up too thick in the corners. Outside in the sitting room people were joining in, raggedly, with Holy Tommy: "The years have made me bitter, the gargle dims my brain, and Dublin keeps on changing; nothing seems the same . . ."

I said, "People accused me of that, to your face, and you let them into this house?"

"Don't be thicker than you can help," Jackie snapped. "Nobody's said a word to me, d'you think they'd have the nerve? I'd bleeding splatter them. It's hints, only. Mrs. Nolan said to Carmel that you're always around for the action, Sallie Hearne said to Ma that you always had a temper on you and did she remember that time you punched Zippy's nose in—"

"Because *he was hassling Kevin.* That's why I punched Zippy, for fuck's sake. When we were about *ten.*"

"I know that. Ignore them, Francis. Don't give them the satisfaction. They're only eejits. You'd think they'd have enough drama on their plates as it is, but that lot always have room for a bit more. The Place, sure."

"Yeah," I said. "The Place." Outside the singing was rising, getting stronger as more people joined in and someone threw in a harmony: "Ring-a-ring-a-rosy as the light declines, I remember Dublin city in the rare oul' times . . ."

I leaned back against the wall and ran my hands over my face. Jackie watched me sideways and drank my Guinness. Eventually she asked, tentatively, "Will we go back out, will we?"

I said, "Did you ever ask Kevin what he wanted to talk to me about?"

Her face fell. "Ah, Francis, I'm sorry—I would've, only you said . . ."

"I know what I said."

"Did he not get a hold of you, in the end?"

"No," I said. "He didn't."

Another small silence. Jackie said, again, "I'm so sorry, Francis."

"It's not your fault."

"People'll be looking for us."

"I know. Give me one more minute and we'll go back out."

Jackie held out the can. I said, "Fuck that. I need something serious." Under the windowsill was a loose floorboard where Shay and I used to hide our smokes from Kevin, and sure enough, Da had found it too. I flipped out a half-full naggin of vodka, took a swig and offered it to Jackie.

"Jaysus," she said. She actually looked startled. "Why not, I suppose." She took the bottle off me, had a ladylike sip and dabbed at her lipstick.

"Right," I said. I took another good mouthful and stuck the bottle back in its little hidey-hole. "Now let's go face the lynch mob."

That was when the sounds from outside changed. The singing trailed off, fast; a second later the buzz of conversation died. A man snapped something low and angry, a chair clattered against a wall, and then Ma went off like something between a banshee and a car alarm.

Da and Matt Daly were squared off, chin to chin, in the middle of the sitting room. Ma's lavender getup was splattered with something wet, all down the top, and she was still going ("I knew it, you bollix, I knew it, just the one evening, that's all I asked you for . . ."). Everyone else had fallen back so as not to get in the way of the drama. I caught Shay's eye across the room, with an instant click like magnets, and we started elbowing between the gawkers.

Matt Daly said, "Sit down."

"Da," I said, touching him on the shoulder.

He didn't even know I was there. He told Matt Daly, "Don't you give me orders in my own home."

Shay, on his other side, said, "Da."

"Sit down," Matt Daly said again, low and cold. "You're after causing a scene."

Da lunged. The really useful skills never fade: I was on him just as fast as Shay was, my hands still knew the grip, and my back was all braced and ready when he stopped fighting and let his knees go limp. I was scarlet, right to my hairline, with pure scorching shame.

"Get him out of here," Ma spat. A bunch of clucking women had clumped up around her and someone was swiping at her top with a tissue, but she was too furious to notice. "Go on, you, get out, get back to the gutter where you belong, I should've never pulled you out of it—your own son's wake, you bastard, have you no respect—"

"Bitch!" Da roared over his shoulder, as we danced him neatly out the door. "Poxy hoor's melt!"

"Out the back," Shay said brusquely. "Let the Dalys go out the front."

"Fuck Matt Daly," Da told us, on our way down the stairs, "and fuck Tessie Daly. And fuck the pair of yous. Kevin was the only one of the three of yous that was worth a shite."

Shay let out a harsh, bitten-off clip of a laugh. He looked dangerously exhausted. "You're probably right there."

"The best of the lot," Da said. "My blue-eyed boy." He started to cry.

"You wanted to know how he's getting on?" Shay asked me. His eyes, meeting mine across the back of Da's neck, looked like the flames on Bunsen burners. "Here's your chance to find out. Enjoy." He hooked the back door deftly open with one foot, dumped Da on the step, and headed back upstairs.

Da stayed where we had dropped him, sobbing luxuriously and throwing out the odd comment about the cruelty of life and enjoying himself no end. I leaned against the wall and lit a smoke. The dim orange glow coming from nowhere in particular gave the garden a spiky Tim Burton look. The shed where the toilet used to be was still there, missing a few boards now and leaning at an impossible angle. Behind me, the hall door slammed: the Dalys going home.

After a while Da's attention span ran out, or his arse got cold. He dialed down the opera, wiped his nose on his sleeve and rearranged himself more comfortably on the step, wincing. "Give us a smoke."

"Say please."

"I'm your father and I said to give us a smoke."

"What the hell," I said, holding one out. "I'll always give to a good cause. You getting lung cancer definitely qualifies."

"You always were an arrogant little prick," Da said, taking the smoke. "I should've kicked your ma down the stairs when she told me she was on the bubble."

"And you probably did."

"Bollix. I never laid a hand on any of yous unless you deserved it."

He was too shaky to light up. I sat down next to him on the steps, took the lighter and did it for him. He stank of stale nicotine and stale Guinness, with a saucy little top-note of gin. All the nerves in my spine were still stone-cold petrified of him. The flow of conversation coming out the window above us was starting to pick up again, awkwardly, in patches.

I asked, "What's wrong with your back?"

Da let out a huge lungful of smoke. "None of your business."

"Just making small talk."

"You were never into the small talk. I'm not thick. Don't treat me like it."

"I never thought you were," I said, and meant it. If he had spent a little more time getting an education and a little less getting an alcohol habit, my da could have been a contender. When I was twelve or so, we did World War II in school. The teacher was a bitchy, closeted little bogger who felt that these inner-city kids were too stupid to understand anything that complex, so he didn't bother trying. My da, who happened to be sober that week, was the one who sat down with me and drew pencil diagrams on the kitchen tablecloth and got out Kevin's lead soldiers for armies and talked me through the whole thing, so clearly and so vividly that I still remember every detail like I saw the movie. One of my da's tragedies was always the fact that he was bright enough to understand just how comprehensively he had shat all over his life. He would have been a lot better off thick as a plank.

"What do you care about my back?"

"Curiosity. And if someone's going to come after me for part of the cost of a nursing home, it'd be fun to know in advance."

"I've asked you for nothing. And I'm not going into any nursing home. Shoot myself in the head first."

"Good for you. Don't leave it too late."

"I wouldn't give yous the satisfaction."

He took another massive drag on the cigarette and watched the smoke ribbons curl out of his mouth. I asked, "What was that all about, upstairs?"

"This and that. Man's business."

"Which means what? Matt Daly rustled your cattle?"

"He shouldn't have come in my house. Tonight of all nights."

Wind nosed through the gardens, shouldered at the walls of the shed. For a split second I saw Kevin, just the night before, lying purple and white and battered in the dark, four gardens away. Instead of making me angry, it just made me feel like I weighed twenty stone; like I was going to have to sit there all night long, because my chances of ever being able to get up from that step by myself were nil.

After a while Da said, "D'you remember that thunderstorm? You'd've been, I don't know, five, six. I brought you and your brother outside. Your ma had a fit."

I said, "Yeah. I remember." It had been the kind of pressure-cooker summer evening where no one can breathe and vicious fights erupt out of nowhere. When the first bang of thunder went off, Da let out a great laughing roar of relief. He scooped Shay up in one arm and me in the other and legged it down the stairs, with Ma yelping furiously behind us. He held us up to see the lightning flickering above the chimney pots and told us not to be scared of the thunder, because it was just the lightning heating up air as fast as an explosion, and not to be scared of Ma, who was leaning out the window getting shriller by the second. When a sheet of rain finally swept over us he threw his head back to the purple-gray sky and whirled us round and round in the empty street, Shay and me screaming with laughter like wild things, huge warm drops of rain splattering our faces and electricity crackling in our hair, thunder shaking the ground and rumbling up through Da's bones into ours.

"That was a good storm," Da said. "A good night."

I said, "I remember the smell of it. The taste."

"Yeah." He got one last minuscule puff off his smoke and threw the butt into a puddle. "Tell you what I wanted to do, that night. I'd've only loved to take the pair of yous and leave. Up into the mountains, live there. Rob a tent and a gun somewhere, live off what we could kill. No women nagging us, no one telling us we weren't good enough, no one keeping the workingman down. You were good young fellas, you and Kevin; good strong young fellas, able for anything. I'd say we'd have done grand."

I said, "That night was me and Shay."

"You and Kevin."

"Nope. I was still small enough that you could pick me up. That means Kevin would've been a baby. If he was even born."

Da thought that over for a while. "And fuck you, anyway," he told me. "Do you know what that was? That there was one of my finest memories of my dead son. Why would you be a little bollix and take it away?"

I said, "The reason you've got no actual memories of Kevin is that, by the time he came along, your brain was basically mashed potato. If you feel like explaining how that was my fault, exactly, I'm all ears."

He took a breath, gearing up to hit me with his best shot, but it sent him into a fit of coughing that almost jolted him right off the back step. All of a sudden both of us made me sick. I had spent the last ten minutes angling for a punch in the face; it had taken me that long to figure out that I wasn't picking on someone my own size. It struck me that I had about three more minutes within range of that house before I lost my mind.

"Here," I said, and held out another cigarette. Da still couldn't talk, but he took it in a shaky hand. I said, "Enjoy," and left him to it.

Upstairs, Holy Tommy had picked up the singing again. The night had got to the stage where people had switched from Guinness to spirits and we were fighting the British. "No pipe did hum nor battle drum did sound its loud tattoo, but the Angelus bell o'er the Liffey's swell rang out through the foggy dew . . ."

Shay had vanished, and so had Linda Dwyer. Carmel was leaning on the side of the sofa, humming along, with one arm around half-asleep Donna and the other hand on Ma's shoulder. I said softly, in her ear, "Da's out the back. Someone should check on him, sooner or later. I've got to head." Carmel whipped her head round, startled, but I put a finger over my lips and nodded at Ma. "Shh. I'll see you soon. Promise."

I left before anyone else could find anything to say to me. The street was dark, just one light at the Dalys' and one in the hairy students' flat; everyone else was asleep or over at our place. Holy Tommy's voice came out our bright sitting-room window, faint and ageless through the glass: "As back through the glen I rode again, my heart with grief was sore, for I parted then with valiant men whom I never shall see more . . ." It followed me all the way up the Place. Even when I turned down Smith's Road I thought I could hear him, under the buzz of passing cars, singing his heart out.

13

I got in my car and drove to Dalkey. It was late enough that the street was dark and creepily silent, everyone neatly tucked up in their high thread counts. I parked under a decorous tree and sat there for a while, looking up at Holly's bedroom window and thinking about nights when I had come home late from work to that house, parked in the drive like I belonged and turned my key in the lock without making a sound. Olivia used to leave me stuff on the breakfast bar: imaginative sandwiches and little notes, and whatever Holly had drawn that day. I would eat the sandwiches sitting at the bar, looking at the drawings by the light through the kitchen window and listening for the sounds of the house under the thick layer of silence: the hum of the refrigerator, the wind in the eaves, the soft tides of my girls' breathing. Then I would write Holly a note to help her with her reading ("HELLO HOLLY, THAT IS A VERY VERY GOOD TIGER! WILL YOU DRAW ME A BEAR TODAY? LOTS OF LOVE, DADDY") and kiss her good night on my way to bed. Holly sleeps sprawled on her back, taking up the maximum possible surface area. Back then, at least, Liv slept curled up, leaving my place ready. When I got into bed she would murmur something and press back against me, fumbling for my hand to wrap my arm around her.

I started by phoning Olivia's mobile, so as not to wake Holly. When she let it ring out to voice mail three times running, I switched to the landline.

Olivia snatched it up on the first ring. "*What*, Frank."

I said, "My brother died."

Silence.

"My brother Kevin. He was found dead this morning."

After a moment, her bedside lamp went on. "My God, Frank. I'm so sorry. What on earth . . . ? How did he . . . ?"

"I'm outside," I said. "Could you let me in?"

More silence.

"I didn't know where else to go, Liv."

A breath, not quite a sigh. "Give me a moment." She hung up. Her shadow moved behind her bedroom curtains, arms going into sleeves, hands running through her hair.

She came to the door in a worn white dressing gown with a blue jersey nightdress peeking out from underneath, which presumably meant that at least I hadn't dragged her away from hot Dermo love. She put a finger to her lips and managed to draw me into the kitchen without touching me.

"What happened?"

"There's a derelict house, at the end of our road. Same house where we found Rosie." Olivia was pulling up a stool and folding her hands on the bar, ready to listen, but I couldn't sit down. I kept moving fast, up and down the kitchen; I didn't know how to stop. "They found Kevin there this morning, in the back garden. He went out a top-floor window. His neck was broken."

I saw Olivia's throat move as she swallowed. It had been four years since I'd seen her hair loose—it only comes down for bed—and it gave my grip on reality another swift, painful kick in the knuckles. "Thirty-seven years old, Liv. He had half a dozen girls on the go because he wasn't ready to settle down yet. He wanted to see the Great Barrier Reef."

"Sweet Lord, Frank. Was it . . . how . . . ?"

"He fell, he jumped, someone pushed him, take your pick. I don't know what the hell he was doing in that house to start with, never mind how he fell out of it. I don't know what to do, Liv. I don't know what to do."

"Do you need to do anything? Is there not an investigation?"

I laughed. "Oh, yeah. Is there ever. The Murder Squad got it—not that there's anything to say it's a murder, but because of the link to Rosie: same location, the time frame. It's Scorcher Kennedy's baby now."

Olivia's face closed over another notch. She knows Scorcher and doesn't particularly like him, or else doesn't particularly like me when I'm around him. She inquired politely, "Are you pleased?"

"No. I don't know. At first I thought, yeah, fine, we could do a whole lot worse. I know Scorch is a royal pain in the hole, Liv, but he doesn't give up, and we needed that here. This whole Rosie thing was cold as a witch's tit; nine Murder guys out of ten would have turfed it down to the basement so fast it would make your head spin, so they could move on to something where they had a hope in hell. Scorch wasn't about to do that. I thought that was a good thing."

"But now . . . ?"

"Now . . . The guy's a bloody pit bull, Liv. He's nowhere near as bright as he thinks he is, and once he gets hold of something he won't let go, even if what he's got is the wrong end of the stick. And now . . ."

I had stopped moving. I leaned back against the sink and ran my hands over my face, took a deep open-mouthed breath through my fingers. The eco-righteous bulbs were kicking in, turning the kitchen white-edged and humming and dangerous. "They're going to say Kevin killed Rosie, Liv. I saw the face on Scorcher. He didn't say it, but that's the way he's thinking. They're going to say Kev killed Rosie and then took himself out when he thought we were getting close."

Olivia had her fingertips to her mouth. "My God. Why? Do they . . . What makes them think . . . Why?"

"Rosie left a note—half a note. The other half turned up on Kevin's body. Anyone who shoved him out that window could have put it there, but that's not the way Scorcher thinks. He's thinking he's got an obvious explanation and a nice neat double solve, case closed, no need for interrogations or warrants or a trial or any of that fancy stuff. Why make life complicated?" I shoved myself off the sink and started pacing again. "He's Murder. Murder are a shower of fucking cretins. All they can see is what's laid out in a straight line in front of their noses; ask them to look just an inch off that line, just for once in their bloody lives, and they're lost. Half a day in Undercover and they'd all be dead."

Olivia smoothed a long lock of ash-gold hair and watched it tighten. She said, "I suppose, much of the time, the straightforward explanation is the right one."

"Yeah. Right. Great. I'm sure it is. But this time, Liv, this time it's all wrong. This time, the straightforward explanation is a fucking travesty."

For a second Olivia said nothing, and I wondered if she had twigged who the straightforward explanation must have been, right up until Kev took his swan dive. Then she said, very carefully, "It's been a long time since you last saw Kevin. Can you be absolutely sure . . . ?"

"Yes. Yes. Yes. I'm positive. I spent the last few days with him. He was the same guy I knew when we were kids. Better hair, a few more inches each way, but he was the same guy. You can't mistake that. I know everything important there was to know about him, and he wasn't a killer and he wasn't a suicide."

"Have you tried saying this to Scorcher?"

"Of course I have. I might as well have been talking to the wall. It wasn't what he wanted to hear, so he didn't hear it."

"What about talking to his superintendent? Would he listen?"

"No. Jesus, no. That's the worst thing I could do. Scorcher already warned me off his patch, and he's going to be keeping an eye on me to make sure I stay off. If I go over his head and try to shove my oar in, specially in ways that could banjax his precious solve rate, he'll just dig his heels in harder. So what do I do, Liv? What? What do I do?"

Olivia watched me, thoughtful gray eyes full of hidden corners. She said gently, "Maybe the best thing you can do is leave it, Frank. Just for a little while. Whatever they say, it can't hurt Kevin now. Once the dust settles—"

"*No.* Not a chance in hell. I'm not going to stand by and watch them make him into their fall guy just because he's dead. He may not be able to fight back, but I can bloody well do it for him."

A small voice said, "Daddy?"

We both jumped about six feet. Holly was in the doorway, wearing a too-big Hannah Montana nightie, one hand on the door handle and her toes curled up on the cold tiles. Olivia said swiftly, "Go to bed, love. Mummy and Daddy are just having a chat."

"You said somebody died. Who died?"

Oh, Jesus. "It's all right, love," I said. "Just someone I know."

Olivia went to her. "It's the middle of the night. Go to sleep. We'll all talk about it in the morning."

She tried to turn Holly back towards the stairs, but Holly clung on to the door handle and dug her feet in. "No! Daddy, who *died*?"

"Bed. Now. Tomorrow we can—"

"No! I want to *know*!"

Sooner or later I would have to explain. Thank God she already knew about death: goldfish, a hamster, Sarah's granddad. I couldn't have handled that conversation, on top of everything else. "Your auntie Jackie and I have a brother," I said—one long-lost relative at a time. "Had. He died this morning."

Holly stared at me. "Your brother?" she said, with a high little shake in her voice. "Like my uncle?"

"Yes, baby. Your uncle."

"Which one?"

"Not one of the ones you know. Those are your mammy's brothers. This was your uncle Kevin. You never met him, but I think you two would have liked each other."

For a second those butane eyes went huge; then Holly's face crumpled, her head went back and she let out a wild shriek of pure anguish. "*Noooo! No, Mummy, no, Mummy, no . . .*"

The scream dissolved into big gut-wrenching sobs, and she buried her face in Olivia's stomach. Olivia knelt down on the floor and wrapped her arms around Holly, murmuring soothing wordless things.

I asked, "Why is she crying?"

I was genuinely perplexed. After the last few days, my mind had slowed down to a crawl. It wasn't until I saw Olivia's quick up-glance, furtive and guilty, that I realized something was going on.

"Liv," I said. "Why is she crying?"

"Not now. Shh, darling, shh, it's all right—"

"*Nooo!* It's *not* all right!"

The kid had a point. "Yes, now. Why the *fuck* is she *crying*?"

Holly lifted her wet red face from Olivia's shoulder. "Uncle *Kevin*!" she screamed. "He showed me Super Mario Brothers and he was going to bring me and Auntie Jackie to the *panto*!"

She tried to keep talking, but it got swamped by another tsunami of crying. I sat down hard on a bar stool. Olivia kept her eyes away from mine and rocked Holly back and forth, stroking her head. I could have done with someone to give me the same treatment, preferably someone with very large bosoms and a massive cloud of enveloping hair.

Eventually Holly wore herself out and moved into the shuddery-gasp stage, and Liv steered her gently upstairs to bed. Her eyes were already closing. While they were up there I found a nice bottle of Chianti in the wine rack—Olivia doesn't stock beer, now that I'm gone—and cracked it open. Then I sat on the bar stool with my eyes shut, leaning my head back against the kitchen wall and listening to Olivia making soothing noises above me, and tried to work out whether I had ever been this angry before.

"So," I said pleasantly, when Olivia came back downstairs. She had taken the opportunity to put on her yummy-mummy armor, crisp jeans and caramel cashmere and a self-righteous expression. "I think I'm owed an explanation, don't you?"

She glanced at my glass, eyebrows going up delicately. "And a drink, apparently."

"Oh, no, no. Several drinks. I'm only getting started."

"I assume you don't think you can sleep here if you get too drunk to drive."

"Liv," I said, "normally I would be more than happy to fight you up and down as many sidetracks as you choose, but tonight, I think I should warn you, I'm going to be sticking fairly closely to the point. How the sweet shining fuck does Holly know Kevin?"

Olivia started pulling back her hair, winding an elastic around it in crisp deft flicks. She had obviously decided to play this cool, calm and collected. "I decided Jackie could introduce them."

"Oh, believe me, I'll be having a chat with Jackie. I can see how you might just be naïve enough to think this was a cute idea, but Jackie's got no excuse. Just Kevin, or the whole bloody Addams Family? Tell me it was just Kevin, Liv. Please."

Olivia folded her arms and set her back flat against the kitchen wall. Her battle stance: I'd seen it so many times. "Her grandparents, her uncles and aunt, and her cousins."

Shay. My mother. My father. I've never hit a woman. I didn't realize I was thinking about it till I felt my hand squeezing the edge of the poofy little bar stool, hard.

"Jackie brought her over for tea on the odd evening, after school. She met her family, Frank. It's not the end of the world."

"You don't *meet* my family, you open hostilities. You bring a flame-thrower and a full set of body armor. How many odd evenings, exactly, has Holly spent *meeting my family?*"

A little shrug. "I haven't kept a tally. Twelve, fifteen? Maybe twenty?"

"Over how long?"

That one got a guilty flicker of her lashes. "About a year."

I said, "You've been getting my daughter to lie to me for a year."

"We told her—"

"A year. Every weekend for a year, I've been asking Holly what she did this week, and she's been giving me a big steaming heap of crap."

"We told her it would need to be a secret for a little while, because you'd had a fight with your family. That's all. We were going to—"

"You can call it keeping secrets, you can call it lying, you can call it whatever the fuck you want. It's what my family does best. It's a natural born, God given talent. My plan was to keep Holly as far from it as possible and hope she would somehow beat the genetic odds and grow up into an honest, healthy, nontwisted human being. Does that sound excessive to you, Olivia? Does that really sound like too much to ask?"

"Frank, you're going to wake her up again if—"

"Instead of which, you dumped her right smack into the middle of it. And hey presto, surprise surprise, the next thing you know, she's acting exactly like a fucking Mackey. She's taken to lying like a duck to water. And you're egging her on every step of the way. That's low, Liv. It really is. That's just about the lowest, dirtiest, shittiest thing I've ever heard."

She had at least the grace to redden. "We were going to tell you, Frank. We thought, once you saw how well it was working out—"

I laughed loud enough that Olivia flinched. "Suffering Jesus Christ, Liv! You call this working *out?* Correct me if I'm missing something here, but as far as I can see, this whole wretched cluster fuck is very, very far from working out."

"For heaven's sake, Frank, it's not as if we knew that Kevin was going to—"

"You knew I didn't want her anywhere near them. That should have been more than enough. What the hell else did you need to know?"

Olivia had her head down and a stubborn set to her chin that was exactly like Holly's. I reached for the bottle again and caught the flash of her eyes, but she managed to say nothing, so I gave myself a great big refill, letting a good dollop slosh onto the lovely slate bar. "Or is that why you did it—because you knew I was dead set against it? Are you really that pissed off with me? Come on, Liv. I can take it. Let's get it all out in the open. Did you enjoy making a fool of me? Did you get a good laugh out of it? Did you really throw Holly into the middle of a shower of raving lunatics just to spite me?"

That one snapped her back straight. "Don't you *dare*. I would *never* do anything to hurt Holly, and you know that. Never."

"Then why, Liv? Why? What on God's green earth could have made this seem like a good idea?"

Olivia took a quick breath through her nose and got her control back; she's had practice. She said coolly, "They're her family too, Frank. She kept asking. Why she doesn't have two grannies like all her friends, whether you and Jackie have any more brothers and sisters, why she couldn't go see them—"

"Bull*shit*. I think she's asked me about my side *once*, in her entire life."

"Yes, and your reaction showed her not to ask you again. She asked me instead, Frank. She asked Jackie. She wanted to know."

"Who gives a fuck what she wants? She's nine years old. She also wants a lion cub and a diet made up of pizza and red M&Ms. Are you going to give her those too? We're her parents, Liv. We're supposed to give her what's good for her, not whatever the hell she wants."

"Frank, *shhh*. Why on earth should this have been bad for her? The only thing you've ever said about your family was that you didn't want to get back in touch. It's not as if you'd told me they were a shower of *ax* murderers. Jackie is lovely, she's never been anything but good to Holly, and she said the rest of them were perfectly nice people—"

"And you took her word for it? Jackie lives in her happy place, Liv. She thinks Jeffrey Dahmer just needed to meet a nice girl. Since when does she make our child-rearing decisions?"

Liv started to say something, but I punched the words in harder till she gave up and shut her face. "I feel sick here, Liv, physically sick. This is the *one* place where I thought I could rely on you to back me up. You always thought my family wasn't good enough for you. What the hell makes them good enough for Holly?"

Olivia finally lost the rag. "When did I *ever* say that, Frank? *When?*"

I stared. She was white with anger, hands pressed back against the door, breathing hard. "If you think your family isn't good enough, if you're ashamed of them, then that's your problem, not mine. Don't you put it on me. I never once said that. I never *thought* it. Never."

She whipped around and grabbed the door open. It shut behind her with a click that, if it hadn't been for Holly, would have been a house-shaking slam.

I sat there for a while, gawping at the door like a cretin and feeling my brain cells whiz-bang like dodgem cars. Then I picked up the wine bottle, found another glass and went after Olivia.

She was in the conservatory, on the wicker sofa, with her legs curled under her and her hands tucked deep into her sleeves. She didn't look up, but when I held out a glass to her she disentangled a hand and took it. I poured us each a quantity of wine that could have drowned a small animal and sat down next to her.

It was still raining, patient relentless drops pattering off the glass, and a cold draft was filtering in at some crack and spreading like smoke through the room—I caught myself making a mental note, even after all this time, to find the crack and caulk it over. Olivia sipped her wine and I watched her reflection in the glass, shadowed eyes concentrating on something only she could see. After a while I asked, "Why didn't you ever say anything?"

Her head didn't turn. "About what?"

"All of it. But let's start with why you never told me my family didn't bother you."

She shrugged. "You never seemed particularly anxious to discuss them. And I didn't think it needed saying. Why would I have a problem with people I've never met?"

"Liv," I said. "Do me a favor: don't play dumb. I'm too tired for that. We're in *Desperate Housewives* country, here—in a *conservatory*, for fuck's sake. It's far from conservatories I was reared. My family is more along the *Angela's Ashes* lines. While your lot sit in the conservatory sipping Chianti, my lot are off in their tenement deciding which greyhound to blow the dole money on."

That got the faintest twitch of her lips. "Frank, I knew you were working-class the first time you opened your mouth. You never made a secret of that. I still went out with you."

"Yeah. Lady Chatterley likes her bit of rough."

The bitter edge took us both by surprise. Olivia turned to look at me; in the faint light trickling through from the kitchen her face was long and sad and lovely, like something off a holy card. She said, "You never thought that."

"No," I acknowledged, after a moment. "Maybe not."

"I wanted you. It was as simple as that."

"It was simple as long as my family was out of the picture. You may have wanted me, but you never wanted my uncle Bertie who starts fart-volume competitions, or my great-aunt Concepta who will explain to you how she was sitting behind a black on the bus and you should have seen the lips on him, or my cousin Natalie who put her seven-year-old on the sun beds for First Communion. I can see how I, personally, wouldn't give the neighbors full-on heart attacks, maybe just a few mild palpitations, but we both know how the rest of the clan would go down with Daddy's golf cronies or Mummy's brunch club. Instant YouTube classic."

Olivia said, "I'm not going to pretend that's not true. Or that it never occurred to me." She was quiet for a while, turning her glass in her hands. "At first, yes, I thought the fact that you weren't in touch with them probably made things easier. Not that they weren't good enough; just . . . easier. But once Holly came along . . . She changed the way I thought about everything, Frank, everything. I wanted her to have them. They're her family. That takes priority over their sun-bed habits."

I sat back on the sofa, got more wine into me and tried to rearrange my head to make room for this information. It shouldn't have stunned the bejasus out of me, at least not to this extent. Olivia has always been a vast mystery to me, at every moment of our relationship and especially in the moments when I thought I understood her best.

When we met, she was a lawyer in the Office of Public Prosecutions. She wanted to prosecute a D-list smack dealer called Pippy who had been picked up in a Drug Squad sweep, while I wanted to let him skip along his merry way, on the grounds that I had spent the last six weeks becoming Pippy's new BFF and I didn't feel we had exhausted his many interesting possibilities. I called round to Olivia's office, to convince her in person. We argued for an hour, I sat on her desk and wasted her time and made her laugh, and then when it got late I took her to dinner so we could keep arguing in comfort. Pippy got a few extra months of freedom, and I got a second date.

She was something else: sleek suits and subtle eye shadow and impeccable manners, a mind like a razor, legs that just kept on keeping on, a backbone like steel and an aura of up-and-coming that you could almost taste. Marriage and babies were the last things on her mind, which as far as I was concerned was one of the fundamentals of any good relationship. I was just disentangling myself from another one—the seventh or maybe the eighth, I don't know—that had started cheerfully and then descended into stagnation and bitchery after about a year, when my lack of intentions became clear to both of us. If the pill were infallible, Liv and I would have gone the same way. Instead we got a church wedding with all the trimmings, a reception in a country-house hotel, a house in Dalkey, and Holly.

"I've never regretted it for a second," I said. "Have you?"

It took her a moment, either to decide what I meant or to decide on the answer. Then she said, "No. Neither have I."

I put out a hand and covered hers, where it lay on her lap. The cashmere jumper was soft and worn and I still knew the shape of her hand like I knew my own. After a while I went back into the sitting room, got a throw off the sofa and wrapped it around her shoulders.

Olivia said, without looking at me, "She wanted to know about them so badly. And they're her family, Frank. Family *matters*. She had a right."

"And I had a right to have a say about it. I'm still her father."

"I know. I should have told you. Or respected what you wanted.

But . . ." She shook her head, against the back of the sofa; her eyes were closed, and the semidarkness rubbed shadows like great bruises underneath them. "I knew if I brought it up it would turn into an enormous argument. And I didn't have the energy. So . . ."

"My family is terminally fucked up, Liv," I said. "In far too many ways to go into. I don't want Holly to turn out like them."

"Holly's a happy, well-adjusted, healthy little girl. You know she is. It wasn't doing her any harm; she loved seeing them. This is . . . Nobody could have predicted this."

I wondered, wearily, if that was even true. Personally, I would in fact have bet on at least one member of my family coming to a sticky and complicated end, although my money wouldn't have been on Kevin. I said, "I keep thinking about all those times I asked what she'd been up to, and she went on about going Rollerblading with Sarah or making a volcano in science class. Chirpy as a little chickadee, not a bother on her. I never once suspected she was hiding anything. It kills me, Liv. It just kills me."

Olivia's head turned towards me. "It wasn't as bad as it sounds, Frank. Truly. She didn't think of it as lying to you. I told her that we might have to wait a while before we talked to you about it, because you'd had a big argument with your family, and she said, 'Like that time I had that fight with Chloe, and all week I didn't even want to think about her or I cried.' She understands more than you think."

"I don't want her protecting me. Ever. I want it to be the other way round."

Something moved across Olivia's face, something a little wry and a little sad. She said, "She's growing up, you know. In a few years she'll be a teenager. Things change."

"I know," I said. "I know." I thought about Holly sprawled in her bed upstairs, tearstained and dreaming, and about the night we made her: the low triumphant laugh in Liv's throat, her hair wrapped round my fingers, the taste of clean summer sweat on her shoulder.

After a few minutes Olivia said, "She'll need to talk about all this, in the morning. It would help her if we were both there. If you want to stay in the spare room . . ."

"Thanks," I said. "That'd be good."

She stood up, shook out the throw and folded it over her arm. "The bed's made up."

I tilted my glass. "I'll finish this first. Thanks for the drink."

"Several drinks." Her voice had the sad ghost of a smile in it.

"Those too."

Behind the sofa she stopped and her fingertips came down, so tentatively I barely felt them, on my shoulder. She said, "I'm so sorry about Kevin."

I said, and I heard the rough edge on my voice, "That was my baby brother. It doesn't matter how he went out that window, I should have caught him."

Liv caught her breath like she was about to say something urgent, but after a moment she let it out in a sigh. She said very softly, maybe to herself, "Oh, Frank." Her fingers slipped off my shoulder, leaving small cold spots where they had been warm, and I heard the door click quietly behind her.

14

When Olivia tapped lightly on the spare-room door, I went from dead asleep to awake and depressed in under a second, even before any of the context came back to me. I had spent way too many nights in that spare room, back when Liv and I were in the process of discovering that she no longer felt like being married to me. Even the smell of it, emptiness and a dainty spritz of fake jasmine, makes me feel sore and tired and about a hundred, like all my joints are worn down to the quick.

"Frank, it's half past seven," Liv said quietly, through the door. "I thought you might want to talk to Holly, before she goes to school."

I swung my legs out of bed and rubbed my hands over my face. "Thanks, Liv. I'll be there in a minute." I wanted to ask if she had any suggestions, but before I could come up with the words I heard her heels going down the stairs. She wouldn't have come into the spare room anyway, possibly in case I met her in my birthday suit and tried to lure her into a quickie.

I've always loved strong women, which is lucky for me because once you're over about twenty-five there is no other kind. Women blow my mind. The stuff that routinely gets done to them would make most men curl up and die, but women turn to steel and keep on coming. Any man who claims he's not into strong women is fooling himself mindless: he's into strong women who know how to pout prettily and put on baby voices, and who will end up keeping his balls in their makeup bags.

I want Holly to be the one in millions. I want her to be everything that bores me stupid in a woman, soft as dandelions and fragile as spun glass. No one is turning my kid to steel. When she was born I wanted to go out and kill someone for her, so she would know for sure, all her life, that I was ready to do it if it needed doing. Instead, I landed her with a family that had already, within a year of first laying eyes on her, taught her to lie and broken her heart.

Holly was cross-legged on her bedroom floor in front of her dollhouse, with her back to me. "Hello, sweetheart," I said. "How're you doing?"

Shrug. She had her school uniform on. In the navy-blue blazer her shoulders looked so slight I could have spanned them one-handed.

"Can I come in for a bit?"

Another shrug. I shut the door behind me and sat down on the floor next to her. Holly's dollhouse is a work of art, a perfect replica of a big Victorian house, complete with tiny overcomplicated furniture and tiny hunting scenes on the walls and tiny servants being socially oppressed. It was a present from Olivia's parents. Holly had the dining-room table out and was polishing it furiously with a chewed-looking piece of kitchen roll.

"Sweetheart," I said, "it's OK that you're really upset about your uncle Kevin. So am I."

Her head bent down farther. She had done her own plaits; there were wisps of pale hair sprouting out of them at odd angles.

"Got any questions you want to ask me?"

The polishing slowed down, just a fraction. "Mum said he fell out a window." Her nose was still stuffed up from all the crying.

"That's right."

I could see her picturing it. I wanted to cover her head with my hands and block the image out. "Did it hurt?"

"No, sweetie. It was very fast. He never even knew what was happening."

"Why did he fall?"

Olivia had probably told her it was an accident, but Holly has a two-home kid's passion for cross-checking. I have no scruples about lying to most people, but I have a whole separate conscience just for Holly. "Nobody's sure yet, love."

Her eyes finally swung up to meet mine, swollen and red-rimmed and intense as a punch. "But you're going to find out. Right?"

"Yeah," I said. "I am."

She stared at me for another second; then she nodded and ducked her head back down over the little table. "Is he in heaven?"

"Yes," I said. Even my special Holly conscience has its limits. Privately I consider religion to be a load of bollix, but when you have a sobbing five-year-old wanting to know what happened to her hamster, you develop an instant belief in anything that dissolves some of the heartbreak off her face. "Definitely. He's up there right now, sitting on a beach a million miles long, drinking a Guinness the size of a bathtub and flirting with a beautiful girl."

She made a noise somewhere between a giggle, a sniffle and a sob. "Daddy, *no*, I'm not messing!"

"Neither am I. And I bet he's waving down at you right now, telling you not to cry."

Her voice wobbled harder. "I don't *want* him to be dead."

"I know, baby. Me neither."

"Conor Mulvey kept taking my scissors in school, before, and Uncle Kevin told me next time he did it I should say to him, 'You only did that because you fancy me,' and he'd go all red and stop annoying me, so I did and it worked."

"Good for your uncle Kevin. Did you tell him?"

"Yeah. He laughed. Daddy, it's not *fair*."

She was on the verge of another huge dam-burst of tears. I said, "It's massively unfair, love. I wish there was something I could say to make it better, but there isn't. Sometimes things are just really, really bad, and there's nothing anyone can do about it."

"Mum says if I wait a while I'll be able to think about him and it won't make me sad any more."

"Your mammy's usually right," I said. "Let's hope she's right this time."

"One time Uncle Kevin said I was his favorite niece because you used to be his favorite brother."

Oh, God. I reached to put an arm around her shoulders, but she shifted away and rubbed harder at the table, pushing the paper into tiny wooden curlicues with a fingernail. "Are you mad because I went to Nana and Granddad's?"

"No, chickadee. Not at you."

"At Mum?"

"Just a little bit. We'll sort it out."

Holly's eyes flicked sideways to me, just for an instant. "Are you going to yell at each other some more?"

I grew up with a mother who has a black belt in guilt-tripping, but her finest work is nothing compared to what Holly can do without even trying. "No yelling," I said. "Mostly I'm just upset that nobody told me what was going on."

Silence.

"Remember how we talked about secrets?"

"Yeah."

"Remember we said it's fine for you and your friends to have good secrets together, but if anything ever bothers you, that's the bad kind of secret? The kind you need to talk about to me or your mammy?"

"It wasn't *bad*. It's my *grandparents*."

"I know, sweetie. What I'm trying to tell you is that there's another kind of secret as well. The kind where, even if there's nothing bad about it, someone else has a right to know it too." Her head was still down, and her chin was starting to get its stubborn look. "Say your mammy and I decide to move to Australia. Should we tell you we're going? Or should we just put you on a plane in the middle of the night?"

Shrug. "Tell me."

"Because that would be your business. You'd have a right to know it."

"Yeah."

"When you started hanging out with my family, that was my business. Keeping it secret from me was the wrong thing to do."

She didn't look convinced. "If I'd told you, you'd just have got all upset."

"I'm a whole lot more upset this way than I would've been if someone had told me straightaway. Holly, sweetie, it's always better to tell me things early on. Always. OK? Even if they're things I don't like. Keeping them secret is only going to make it worse."

Holly slid the table carefully back into the dollhouse dining room, adjusted it with a fingertip. I said, "I try to tell you the truth, even when it hurts a little bit. You know that. You need to do the same for me. Is that fair?"

Holly said to the dollhouse, in a small muffled voice, "Sorry, Daddy."

I said, "I know you are, love. It's going to be OK. Just remember this, next time you're thinking about keeping a secret from me, all right?"

Nod. "There you go," I said. "Now you can tell me how you got on with our family. Did your nana make you trifle for your tea?"

A shaky little sigh of relief. "Yeah. And she says I've got lovely hair."

Holy shit: a compliment. I'd been all geared up to contradict criticisms of everything from Holly's accent through her attitude through the color of her socks, but apparently my ma was getting soft in her old age. "Which you do. What are your cousins like?"

Holly shrugged and pulled a tiny grand piano out of the dollhouse living room. "Nice."

"What kind of nice?"

"Darren and Louise don't talk to me that much because they're too big, but me and Donna do imitations of our teachers. One time we laughed till Nana told us to shhh or the police would come get us."

Which sounded a little more like the Ma I knew and avoided. "How about your aunt Carmel and uncle Shay?"

"They're OK. Aunt Carmel's sort of boring, but when Uncle Shay's home he helps me with my maths homework, because I told him Mrs. O'Donnell yells if you get stuff wrong."

And here I had been delighted that she was finally getting a handle on division. "That's nice of him," I said.

"Why don't you go see them?"

"That's a long story, chicken. Too long for one morning."

"Can I still go even if you don't?"

I said, "We'll see." It all sounded perfectly idyllic, but Holly still wasn't looking at me. Something was bugging her, apart from the obvious. If she had seen my da in his preferred state of mind, there was going to be holy war and possibly a brand-new custody hearing. I asked, "So what's on your mind? Did one of them annoy you?"

Holly ran a fingernail up and down the piano keyboard. After a moment she said, "Nana and Granddad don't have a car."

This wasn't what I'd been expecting. "Nope."

"Why?"

"They don't need one."

Blank look. It struck me that Holly had never before in her life met anyone who didn't have a car, whether they needed one or not. "How do they get places?"

"They walk, or they take buses. Most of their friends live just a minute or two away, and the shops are right round the corner. What would they do with a car?"

She thought about that for a minute. "Why don't they live in a whole house?"

"They've always lived where they do. Your nana was born in that flat. I pity anyone who tries to get her to move."

"How come they don't have a computer, or a dishwasher even?"

"Not everyone does."

"Everyone has a *computer*."

I loathed admitting this even to myself, but somewhere at the back of my mind I was gradually getting an inkling of why Olivia and Jackie might have wanted Holly to see where I come from. "Nope," I said. "Most people in the world don't have the money for that kind of stuff. Even a lot of people right here in Dublin."

"Daddy. Are Nana and Granddad *poor*?"

There was a faint pink stain on her cheeks, like she had said a bad word. "Well," I said. "It depends who you ask. They'd say no. They're a lot better off than they were when I was little."

"Then were they poor?"

"Yeah, sweetie. We weren't starving or anything, but we were pretty poor."

"Like what?"

"Like we didn't go on holidays, and we had to save up if we wanted to go to the cinema. Like I wore your uncle Shay's old clothes and your uncle Kevin wore mine, instead of getting new ones. Like your nana and granddad had to sleep in the sitting room because we didn't have enough bedrooms."

She was wide-eyed, like it was a fairy tale. "Seriously?"

"Yep. Plenty of people lived like that. It wasn't the end of the world."

Holly said, "But." The pink stain had turned into a full-on blush. "Chloe says poor people are skangers."

This came as absolutely no surprise. Chloe is a simpering, bitchy, humorless little object with an anorexic, bitchy, humorless mother who talks to me loudly and slowly, using small words, because her family crawled out of the gutter a generation before mine and because her fat, bitchy, humorless husband drives a Tahoe. I always thought we should ban the whole vile bunch of them from the house; Liv said Holly would outgrow Chloe in her own good time. This lovely moment, as far as I was concerned, settled the argument once and for all.

"Right," I said. "What does Chloe mean by that, exactly?"

I kept my voice level, but Holly is good at me and her eyes slid sideways quickly, checking my face. "It's not a swear word."

"It's definitely not a nice word. What do you think it means?"

Wriggly shrug. "*You* know."

"If you're going to use a word, chick, you've got to have some idea what you're saying. Come on."

"Like stupid people. People who wear tracksuits and they don't have jobs because they're lazy, and they can't even talk properly. *Poor* people."

I said, "What about me? Do you think I'm stupid and lazy?"

"Not *you!*"

"Even though my whole family was poor as dirt."

She was getting flustered. "That's *different.*"

"Exactly. You can be a rich scumbag just as easily as a poor scumbag, or you can be a decent human being either way. Money's got nothing to do with it. It's nice to have, but it's not what makes you who you are."

"Chloe says her mum says it's superimportant to make sure people know straightaway you've got plenty of money. Otherwise you don't get any respect in this world."

"Chloe and her family," I said, hitting the end of my patience, "are vulgar enough to make your average blinged-up skanger blush."

"What's vulgar?"

Holly had stopped messing with the piano and was looking up at me in pure bewilderment, eyebrows pulled together, waiting for me to illuminate everything and make perfect sense of it all. For maybe the first time in her life, I had no idea what to say to her. I had no clue how to explain the difference between working poor and scumbag poor to a kid who thought everyone had a computer, or how to explain vulgar to a kid who was growing up on Britney Spears, or how to explain to anyone at all how this situation had turned into such a terminal mess. I wanted to grab hold of Olivia and get her to show me the right way to do this, except that that wasn't Liv's job any more; my relationship with Holly was all my own problem now. In the end I took the miniature piano out of her hand, put it back in the dollhouse and pulled her onto my lap.

Holly said, leaning back to watch my face, "Chloe's stupid, isn't she?"

"My God, yes," I said. "If there was a worldwide shortage of stupid, Chloe and her family between them could fix it in a heartbeat."

She nodded and curled in against my chest, and I tucked her head under my chin. After a while she said, "Someday will you take me and show me where Uncle Kevin fell out of the window?"

"If you feel like you need to have a look," I said, "then sure. I'll show you."

"Not today, though."

"No," I said. "Let's all just get through today in one piece." We sat there on the floor in silence, me rocking Holly back and forth and her sucking pensively on the end of a plait, until Olivia came in to tell us it was time for school.

I picked up an extralarge coffee and an undefined organic-looking muffin in Dalkey—I get the sense Olivia thinks that feeding me might be taken as an invitation to move back in—and had breakfast sitting on a wall, watching overweight suits in tanks get outraged when the traffic waves didn't part specially for them. Then I dialed my voice mail.

"Yeah, um, Frank . . . Hi. It's Kev. Listen, I know you said this wasn't a good time, but . . . I mean, not now, like, but whenever you're free, can you give us a ring? Like tonight or whatever, even if it's late, that's OK. Um. Thanks. Bye."

The second time, he hung up, no message. Same thing the third time, while Holly and Jackie and I were stuffing our faces with pizza. The fourth call had come in just before seven, presumably when Kevin was on his way into Ma and Da's. "Frank, it's me again. Listen . . . I kind of need to talk to you. I know you probably don't want to think about any of this crap, right, but honest to God, I'm not trying to mess with your head, I just . . . Could you ring me? OK, um, I guess . . . bye."

Something had changed, between Saturday night when I sent him back to the pub and Sunday afternoon when the phone campaign kicked in. It could have been something that had happened along the way, maybe in the pub—for several of the Blackbird's regulars, the fact that they haven't killed anyone yet is down to pure chance—but I doubted it. Kevin had started getting edgy well before we ever hit that pub. Everything I knew about him—and I still thought that was worth something—told me he was a laid-back guy, but he had been acting squirrelly since right around the time we headed into Number 16. I had put it down to the fact that your average civilian does tend to get a little thrown by the idea of dead people—my mind had been on other things. It had been a lot more than that.

Whatever had been bothering Kevin, it wasn't something that had just happened this weekend. It had already been stashed at the bottom of his mind, maybe for twenty-two years, until something on Saturday jarred it loose. Slowly, over the rest of the day—our Kev was never the fastest little sprinter on the track—it had bobbed to the surface and started nudging at him, harder and harder. He had spent twenty-four hours trying to ignore it or figure it out or deal with the implications all by himself, and then he had gone to big brother Francis for help. When I told him to get lost, he had turned to the worst possible person.

He had a nice voice, on the phone. Even confused and worried, he was easy to listen to. He sounded like a good guy; someone you would want to get to know.

As far as next moves went, my options were limited. The thought of chummy chats with the neighbors had lost a lot of its sparkle now that I knew half of them thought I was a cold-blooded ninja brother-killer, and anyway I needed to stay well out of Scorcher's line of vision, if only for the sake of George's bowels. On the other hand, the idea of hanging around kicking my heels and watching my mobile for Stephen's number to come up, like a teenage girl after a snog, didn't particularly appeal to me either. When I do nothing, I like it to have a purpose.

Something was pinching at the back of my neck, like someone tugging out little hairs one by one. I pay attention to that tug; there have been plenty of times when ignoring it would have got me killed. There was something I was missing, something I had seen or heard and let slip by.

Undercovers don't get to video all the best parts, the way the Murder boys do, so we have very, very good memories. I got more comfortable on the wall, lit a smoke and went back over every bit of information I had picked up in the last few days.

One thing stuck out: I still wasn't clear on just how that suitcase had got up that chimney. According to Nora, it had been put there sometime between Thursday afternoon, when she bummed Rosie's Walkman, and Saturday night. But according to Mandy, Rosie hadn't had her keys for those two days, which more or less ruled out the possibility of sneaking the case out at night—there had been an awful lot of inconvenient garden walls between her and Number 16—and Matt Daly had been keeping an eagle eye on her, which would have made it pretty tough to smuggle out something sizable during the day. Also according to Nora, on Thursdays and Fridays Rosie walked to and from work with Imelda Tierney.

Friday evening, Nora had been out at the pictures with her little mates; Rosie and Imelda could have had the bedroom to themselves, to pack and plan. Nobody had been paying attention to Imelda's comings and goings. She could have waltzed out of that flat carrying just about anything she liked.

These days Imelda lived on Hallows Lane, just far enough from Faithful Place to be outside Scorch's perimeter. And going by the look in Mandy's eye, there was a decent chance that Imelda was at home in the middle of a workday, and that her relationship with the neighborhood was mixed enough to give her a soft spot for a prodigal son who was walking the fine line between in and out. I tossed back the last of my cold coffee and headed for my car.

My mate in the electric company pulled up an electricity bill for an Imelda Tierney at 10 Hallows Lane, Flat 3. The house was a kip: slates missing from the roof, paint flaking off the door, net curtains sagging behind grimy windows. You could tell the neighbors were praying the landlord would sell up to a nice respectable yuppie or two, or at least burn the place down for the insurance money.

I had been right: Imelda was home. "Francis," she said, somewhere between shocked and delighted and horrified, when she opened the flat door. "Jaysus."

Not one of those twenty-two years had been nice to Imelda. She had never been a stunner, but she had had height and good legs and a good walk, and those three can take you a long way. These days she was what the boys on the squad call a BOBFOC: body off *Baywatch*, face off *Crimewatch*. She had kept her figure, but there were pouches under her eyes and her face was covered in wrinkles like knife scars. She was wearing a white tracksuit with a coffee stain down the front, and her bleach job had about three inches of exhausted roots. The sight of me made her whip up a hand to fluff it into shape, like that was all it would take to snap us straight back to those glossy teenagers fizzing with Saturday night. That little gesture was the part that went straight to my heart.

I said, "Howya, 'Melda," and gave her my best grin, to remind her that we had been good pals, way back when. I always liked Imelda. She was a smart kid, restless, with a moody streak and sharp edges that she had earned the hard way: instead of one permanent father she had way too many temporary ones, several of them married to people who weren't her mother, and in those days that mattered. Imelda took a lot of flak about her ma, when we were all kids. Most of us lived in glass houses, one way or another, but an unemployed alco father was nowhere near as bad as a ma who had sex.

Imelda said, "I heard about Kevin, God rest him. I'm awful sorry for your trouble."

"God rest," I agreed. "While I'm back in the area, I thought I'd call in on a few old mates."

I stayed there, in the doorway, waiting. Imelda shot a fast glance over her shoulder, but I wasn't moving and she didn't have a choice. After a second she said, "The place is in bits—"

"You think I care about that? You should see my gaff. It's just good to see you again."

By the time I finished talking, I was past her and through the door. The place wasn't quite a shit hole, but I saw her point. One look at Mandy at home had said this woman was contented; not permanently ecstatic, maybe, but her life had turned out to be something she liked. Imelda, not so much. The sitting room felt even smaller than it was because there was stuff everywhere: used mugs and Chinese takeaway cartons on the floor around the sofa, women's clothes—various sizes—drying on the radiators, dusty piles of bootleg DVD cases toppling over in corners. The heat was up too high and the windows hadn't been opened in a long time; the place had a thick smell of ashtrays, food and women. Everything except the telly-on-steroids needed replacing.

"This is a great little place," I said.

Imelda said shortly, "It's shite."

"I grew up in a lot worse."

She shrugged. "So? Doesn't stop this being shite. Will you have tea?"

"Love some. How've you been?"

She headed into the kitchen. "You can see for yourself. Sit down there."

I found a noncrusty patch of sofa and settled in. "I hear you've got daughters these days, yeah?"

Through the half-open kitchen door I saw Imelda pause, with her hand on the kettle. She said, "And I heard you're a Guard now."

I was getting used to the illogical shot of anger when someone informed me I had turned into The Man's bum-boy; it was even starting to come in useful. "*Imelda*," I said, outraged and wounded to the bone, after a second of shocked silence. "Are you serious? You think I'm here to give you hassle about your kids?"

Shrug. "How do I know? They've done nothing, anyway."

"I don't even know their *names*. I was only *asking*, for fuck's sake. I don't give a rat's arse if you've raised the bleeding Sopranos; I only wanted to say howya, for old times' sake. If you're just going to throw freakers about what I do for a living, then tell me and I'll get out of your hair. Believe me."

After a moment I saw the corner of Imelda's mouth twitch reluctantly, and she flicked on the kettle. "Same old Francis; the bleeding temper on you. Yeah, I've three. Isabelle, Shania and Genevieve. Holy fucking terrors, the three of them; teenagers. What about you?"

No mention of a father, or fathers. "One," I said. "She's nine."

"It's all ahead of you. God help you. They say boys wreck your house and girls wreck your head, and it's the truth." She tossed tea bags into mugs. Just watching the way she moved made me feel old.

"Are you still doing the sewing?"

A sniff that could have been a laugh. "God, that's going back a while. I quit the factory twenty years back. I do bits and bobs, now. Cleaning, mostly." Her eyes flicked sideways to me, belligerent, checking whether I wanted to make something of that. "The Eastern Europeans'll do it cheaper, but there's still a few places want someone that speaks English. I do all right, so I do."

The kettle boiled. I said, "You heard about Rosie, yeah?"

"I did, yeah. That's only shocking. All this time . . ." Imelda poured the tea and gave her head a quick shake, like she was trying to get something out of it. "All this time I thought she was off in England. When I heard, I couldn't believe it. I couldn't. I swear, the rest of the day I was walking around like a zombie."

I said, "Same here. It hasn't been a great week all round."

Imelda brought out a carton of milk and a packet of sugar, made room for them on the coffee table. She said, "Kevin was always a lovely young fella. I was sorry to hear about him; really sorry, now. I would've called round to yours, the night it happened, only . . ."

She shrugged, let it trail off. Chloe and Chloe's mummy would never in a million years have understood the subtle, definite class gap that made Imelda think, probably correctly, that she might not be welcome in my mother's house. I said, "I was hoping I'd see you there. But hey, this way we get to have a proper chat, am I right?"

Another half grin, a little less reluctant this time. "And same old Francis again. You always were a smooth talker."

"I've got better hair now, though."

"Jaysus, yeah. The spikes, d'you remember?"

"It could've been worse. I could've had a mullet, like Zippy."

"Yeuch; stop. The head on him."

She headed back to the kitchen for the mugs. Even if I'd had all the time in the world, sitting around shooting the breeze wouldn't do me any good here: Imelda was a lot harder than Mandy, she already knew I had an agenda even if she couldn't put her finger on it. When she came out I said, "Can I ask you something? I'm being a nosy bollix, but I swear I've got a good reason for asking."

Imelda put a stained mug in my hand and sat down in an armchair, but she didn't lean back and her eyes were still wary. "Go on."

"When you put Rosie's suitcase in Number Sixteen for her, where'd you leave it exactly?"

The instant blank look, half mule and half moron, brought it home to me all over again just where I stood now. Nothing in the world quite canceled out the fact that Imelda was, against every instinct in her body, talking to a cop. She said, inevitably, "What suitcase?"

"Ah, c'mon, Imelda," I said, easy and grinning—one wrong note and this whole trip would sink into a waste of time. "Me and Rosie, we'd been planning this for months. You think she didn't tell me how she was getting stuff done?"

Slowly some of the blank look dissolved off Imelda's face; not all of it, but enough. She said, "I'm not getting in any hassle about this. If anyone else asks me, I never saw no suitcase."

"Not a problem, babe. I'm not about to drop you in the shite; you were doing us a favor, and I appreciate that. All I want to know is whether anyone messed with the case after you dropped it off. Do you remember where you left it? And when?"

She watched me sharply, under her thin lashes, figuring out what this meant. Finally she reached into a pocket for her smoke packet and said, "Rosie said it to me three days before yous were heading off. She never said nothing before that; me and Mandy guessed something was up, like, but we didn't know anything for definite. Have you seen Mandy, yeah?"

"Yep. She's looking in great form."

"Snobby cow," Imelda said, through the click of the lighter. "Smoke?"

"Yeah, thanks. I thought you and Mandy were mates."

A hard snort of laughter, as she held the lighter for me. "Not any more. She's too good for the likes of me. I don't know were we ever really mates to begin with; we just both used to hang out with Rosie, and after she left . . ."

I said, "You were always the one she was closest to."

Imelda gave me a look that said better men had tried to soft-soap her and failed. "If we'd been that close, she'd have told me from the start what yous had planned, wouldn't she? She only said anything because her da had his eye on her, so she couldn't get her gear out on her own. The two of us used to walk back and forth from the factory together some days, talk about whatever girls talk about, I don't remember. This one day she said to me she needed a favor."

I said, "How'd you get the suitcase out of their flat?"

"Easy. After work the next day—the Friday—I went over to the Dalys', we told her ma and da we were going to Rosie's room to listen to her new Eurythmics album, all they said was for us to keep it down. We had it just loud enough that they wouldn't hear Rosie packing." There was a tiny slip of a smile nudging at one corner of Imelda's mouth. Just for a second, leaning forward with her elbows on her knees, smiling to herself through cigarette smoke, she looked like the quick-moving smart-mouthed girl I used to know. "Should've seen her, Francis. She was dancing round that room, she was singing in her hairbrush, she had these new knickers she was after buying so you wouldn't see her manky old ones and she was waving them round her head . . . She had me dancing along and all; we must've looked like a right pair of eejits, laughing our arses off and trying to do it quiet enough that her ma wouldn't come in and see what we were at. I think it was being able to say it to someone, after keeping it under wraps all that time. She was over the moon with herself."

I slammed the door on that picture fast; it would keep for later. "Good," I said. "That's good to hear. So when she finished packing . . . ?"

The grin spread to both sides of Imelda's mouth. "I just picked up the case and walked out. Swear to God. I had my jacket over it, but that wouldn't have fooled anyone for a second, not if they'd been looking proper. I went out of the bedroom and Rosie said good-bye to me, nice and loud, and I shouted good-bye to Mr. Daly and Mrs. Daly—they were in the sitting room, watching the telly. He looked round when I went past the door, but he was only checking to make sure Rosie wasn't going with me; he never even noticed the case. I just let meself out."

"Fair play to the pair of yous," I said, grinning back. "And you took it straight across to Number Sixteen?"

"Yeah. It was winter: dark already, and cold, so everyone was indoors. No one saw me." Her eyes were hooded against the smoke, remembering. "I'm telling you, Francis, I was afraid for my life, going into that house. I'd never been in there in the dark before, not on my own anyway. The worst was the stairs; the rooms had a bit of light coming in through the windows, but the stairs were black. I'd to feel my way up. Cobwebs all over me, and half the steps rocking like the whole place was about to fall down around my ears, and little noises everywhere . . . I swear to God I thought there was someone else in there, or a ghost maybe, watching me. I was all ready to scream if someone grabbed me. I legged it out of there like my arse was on fire."

"Do you remember where you put the suitcase?"

"I do, yeah. Me and Rosie had that all arranged. It went up behind the fireplace in the top front room—the big room, you know the one. If it hadn't've fit there, I was going to put it under that heap of boards and metal and shite in the corner of the basement, but I didn't fancy going down there unless I had to. It fit grand, in the end."

"Thanks, Imelda," I said. "For giving us a hand. I should've thanked you a long time ago, but better late than never."

Imelda said, "Now can I ask you something, can I? Or does it only go the one way?"

"Like the Gestapo, ve ask ze questions? Nah, babe, fair's fair: it goes both ways. Ask away."

"People are saying Rosie and Kevin were killed, like. Murdered. The pair of them. Are they only saying that for the scandal, or is it true?"

I said, "Rosie was killed, yeah. No one's sure about Kevin yet."

"How was she killed?"

I shook my head. "No one's telling me."

"Yeah. Right."

"Imelda," I said. "You can keep thinking of me as a cop if you want, but I guarantee you, right now there's not one person on the force thinking that way. I'm not working this case; I'm not even supposed to be *near* this case. I've put my job on the line just by coming here. I'm not a cop this week. I'm the annoying fucker who won't go away because he loved Rosie Daly."

Imelda bit down on the side of her lip, hard. She said, "I loved her too, so I did. I loved that girl to bits."

"I know that. That's why I'm here. I haven't a clue what happened to her, and I don't trust the cops to bother their arses finding out. I need a hand here, 'Melda."

"She shouldn't've been kilt. That's dirty, that is. Rosie never did anything to anyone. She only wanted . . ." Imelda went silent, smoking and watching her fingers twist through a hole in the threadbare sofa cover, but I could feel her thinking and I didn't interrupt. After a while she said, "I thought she was the one that got away."

I raised an inquiring eyebrow. There was a faint flush on Imelda's worn cheeks, like she had said something that might turn out to be stupid, but she kept going. "Look at Mandy, right? The spitting image of her ma. Got married as fast as she could, quit working to look after the family, good little wife, good little mammy, lives in the same *house*, I swear to God she even wears the same clothes her ma used to wear. Everyone else we knew growing up is the same: image of their parents, no matter how loud they told themselves they'd be different."

She mashed out her smoke in a full ashtray. "And look at me. Where I've ended up." She jerked her chin at the flat around us. "Three kids, three das— Mandy probably told you that, did she? I was twenty having Isabelle. Straight onto the dole. Never had a decent job since, never got married, never kept a fella longer than a year—half of them are married already, sure. I'd a million plans, when I was a young one, and they came to fuck-all. Instead I turned into my ma, not a peep out of me. I just woke up one morning and here I am."

I flipped two more smokes out of my pack, lit Imelda's for her. "Thanks." She turned her head to blow smoke away from me. "Rosie was the only one of us that didn't turn into her ma. I liked thinking about her. When things weren't great, I liked knowing she was out there, in London or New York or Los Angeles, doing some mad job I'd never heard of. The one that got away."

I said, "I didn't turn into my ma. Or my da, come to that."

Imelda didn't laugh. She gave me a brief look I couldn't read—something to do with whether turning into a cop counted as an improvement, maybe.

After a moment she said, "Shania's pregnant. Seventeen. She's not sure who the da is."

Even Scorcher couldn't have turned that one into a positive. I said, "At least she's got a good mammy to see her through."

"Yeah," Imelda said. Her shoulders sagged a notch lower, like part of her had been hoping I would have the secret to fix this. "Whatever."

In one of the other flats, someone was blasting 50 Cent and someone else was screaming at him to turn it down. Imelda didn't seem to notice. I said, "I need to ask you one more thing."

Imelda had good antennae, and something in my voice had tweaked them: the blank look slid back onto her face. I said, "Who'd you tell that me and Rosie were heading off?"

"I didn't tell anyone. I'm not a bleeding squealer."

She was sitting up straighter, ready for a fight. I said, "Never thought you were. But there's all kinds of ways to get info out of someone, squealer or no. You were only, what—eighteen, nineteen? It's easy to get a teenager drunk enough that she lets something slip, maybe trick her into dropping a hint or two."

"And I'm not stupid, either."

"Neither am I. Listen to me, Imelda. Someone waited for Rosie in Number Sixteen, that night. Someone met her there, killed her stone dead and threw her body away. Only three people in the world knew Rosie was going to be there to pick up that suitcase: me, Rosie, and you. Nobody heard it from me. And like you just said yourself, Rosie had kept her mouth shut for months; you were probably the best mate she had, and she wouldn't even have told you if she'd had any choice. You want me to believe she went and spilled her guts to someone else as well, just for the crack? Bollix. That leaves you."

Before I finished the sentence, Imelda was up out of her chair and whipping the mug out of my hand. "The fucking cheek of you, calling me a mouth in my own house— I shouldn't've let you in the door. Giving it all that about calling in to see your old mate—mate, my arse, you just wanted to find out what I knew—"

She headed for the kitchen and slammed the mugs into the sink. Only guilt gets you that kind of all-guns-blazing attack. I went after her. "And you were giving it all that about loving Rosie. Wanting her to be the one who got away. Was that all a great big load of bollix too, Imelda? Was it?"

"You haven't a clue what you're talking about. It's easy for you, swanning in after all this time, Mr. Big Balls, you're able to walk away whenever you like— I've to *live* here. My kids have to *live* here."

"Does it look to you like I'm fucking walking away? I'm right here, Imelda, whether I like it or not. I'm not going anywhere."

"Yeah, you are. You get out of my home. Take your questions and shove them up your hole, and get out."

"Tell me who you talked to, and I'm gone."

I was too close. Imelda had her back pressed up against the cooker; her eyes flashed around the room, looking for escape routes. When they came back to me, I saw the mindless flare of fear.

"Imelda," I said, as gently as I could. "I'm not going to hit you. I'm only asking you a question."

She said, "Get out."

One of her hands was behind her back, clenched on something. That was when I realized the fear wasn't a reflex, wasn't a leftover from some arsehole who had smacked her around. Imelda was afraid of me.

I said, "What the fuck do you think I'm going to do to you?"

She said, low, "I was warned about you."

Before I knew it, I had taken a step forward. When I saw the bread knife rising and her mouth opening to scream, I left. I was at the bottom of the stairs before she pulled herself together to lean down the stairwell and shout after me, for the neighbors' benefit, "And don't you bleeding come back!" Then the door of her flat slammed.

15

I headed deeper into the Liberties, away from town; the whole city center was packed with Christmas-shopping lemmings elbowing each other out of the way in a frenzy to credit-card everything they laid eyes on, the more overpriced the better, and sooner or later one of them was going to give me an excuse for a fight. I know a nice man called Danny Matches who once offered to set fire to anything that I ever felt needed burning. I thought about Faithful Place, about the avid look on Mrs. Cullen's face and the uncertainty on Des Nolan's and the fear on Imelda's, and I considered giving Danny a call.

I kept going till I had walked off most of the urge to punch anyone who got too close to me. The lanes and alleys had the same look as the people at Kevin's wake, twisted versions of familiar, like a joke I wasn't in on: brand-new BMWs jammed together in front of what used to be tenements, teenage mas yelling into designer prams, dusty corner shops turned into shiny franchises. When I could stop moving, I was at Pat's Cathedral. I sat in the gardens for a while, resting my eyes on something that had stayed put for eight hundred years and listening to drivers work themselves into road rage as rush hour got closer and the traffic stopped moving.

I was still sitting there, smoking a lot more than Holly would have approved of, when my phone beeped. The text was from my boy Stephen, and I would have bet he had rewritten it four or five times to get it just right. *Hello Detective Mackey, just to let you know I have the information you requested. All the best, Stephen Moran (Det).*

The little beauty. It was coming up towards five. I texted him back, *Well done. Meet you in Cosmo's ASAP.*

Cosmo's is a shitty little sandwich joint tucked away in the tangle of lanes off Grafton Street. None of the Murder Squad would be caught dead there, which was one big plus. The other was that Cosmo's is one of the few places in town that still hire Irish staff, meaning none of them will lower themselves to look directly at you. There are occasions when this is a good thing. I meet my CIs there sometimes.

By the time I got there the kid was already at a table, nursing a mug of coffee and drawing patterns in a sugar spill with one fingertip. He didn't look up when I sat down. I said, "Good to see you again, Detective. Thanks for getting in touch."

Stephen shrugged. "Yeah. Well. I said I would."

"Ah. Are we having issues?"

"This feels sleazy."

"I promise I'll respect you in the morning."

He said, "Back in Templemore, they told us the force was our family now. I paid attention to that, you know? I took it seriously."

"And so you should. It is your family. This is what families do to each other, sunshine. Hadn't you noticed?"

"No. I hadn't."

"Well, lucky old you. A happy childhood is a beautiful thing. This is how the other half lives. What've you got for me?"

Stephen bit down on the inside of his cheek. I watched with interest and let him work through the conscience thing all by himself, and finally, of course, rather than grabbing his knapsack and legging it out of Cosmo's, he leaned over and pulled out a slim green folder. "The post-mortem," he said, and handed it over.

I flicked through the pages with a thumbnail. Diagrams of Kev's injuries jumped out at me, organ weights, cerebral contusions, not your ideal coffee-shop reading. "Nicely done," I said. "And much appreciated. Summarize it for me, thirty seconds or less."

That startled him. He had probably done family notification before, but not in full technical detail. When I didn't blink, he said, "Um . . . OK. He—I mean, the deceased; um, your brother . . . he fell from a window, head first. There were no defensive injuries or combat injuries, nothing that would point to another person being involved. The fall was approximately twenty feet, onto hard earth. He hit the ground just to one side of the top of his head, around here. The fall fractured his skull, which damaged his brain, and broke his neck, which would have paralyzed his breathing. One or the other killed him. Very quickly."

Which was exactly what I had asked for, but all the same I almost fell in love with the overgroomed waitress for showing up right at that moment. I ordered coffee and some kind of sandwich. She wrote down the wrong thing twice to prove that she was too good for this job, rolled her eyes at my stupidity and nearly knocked Stephen's mug into his lap whipping my menu away, but by the time she wiggled off, I had managed to unclench my jaw at least partway. I said, "No surprises there. Got the fingerprint reports?"

Stephen nodded and pulled out another file, thicker. Scorcher had put some serious pressure on the Bureau, to get results this fast. He wanted this case over and done with. I said, "Give me the good parts."

"The outside of the suitcase was a mess: all that time up the chimney rubbed off most of whatever was there before, and then we've got the builders and the family who—your family." He ducked his head, embarrassed. "There's still a few prints that match Rose Daly, plus one matching her sister Nora, plus three unknowns—probably from the same hand and made at the same time, going by the position. On the inside, we've got more or less the same: lots of Rose on everything that'll hold prints, lots of Nora all over the Walkman, a couple from Theresa Daly on the inside of the actual case—which makes sense, I mean, it used to be hers—and loads from all the Mackey family, mostly Josephine Mackey. Is that, um, your mother?"

"Yep," I said. Ma would definitely have been the one to unpack that suitcase. I could hear her: *Jim Mackey, you get your great dirty hands out of that yoke, that's knickers in there, are you some kind of pervert?* "Any unknowns?"

"Not inside. We've also got, um, a few of your prints on the envelope the tickets were in."

Even after the last few days, I had just enough room for that to hurt: my prints from that gobsmackingly innocent evening in O'Neill's, still fresh as yesterday after twenty years hidden in the dark, ready for the Bureau techs to play with. I said, "Yeah, you do. It didn't occur to me to wear gloves when I bought them. Anything else?"

"That's it for the suitcase. And it looks like the note was wiped clean. On the second page, the one that was found in 1985, we've got Matthew, Theresa and Nora Daly, the three lads who found it and brought it to them, and you. Not one print from Rose. On the first page, the one from Kevin's pocket, we've got nothing. Like, no prints at all. Clean as a whistle."

"And the window he went out of?"

"Opposite problem: too many prints. The Bureau's pretty sure we've got Kevin's on the top and bottom sashes, where you'd expect them if he opened the window, and his palm prints on the sill where he leaned out—but they won't swear to it. There's too many layers of other prints underneath; the details get lost."

"Anything else I might want to know about?"

He shook his head. "Nothing that sticks out. Kevin's prints showed up in a couple of other places—the hall door, the door of the room he fell from—but nowhere you wouldn't expect. The whole house is covered in unknowns; the Bureau's still running them. So far a few have popped up guys with minor records, but they're all local fellas who could have been in there just messing about. Years ago, for all we know."

"Nicely done," I said. I squared off the edges of the files and stashed them in my case. "I won't forget this. Now let's hear you summarize Detective Kennedy's theory of what happened."

Stephen's eyes followed my hands. "Tell me again how this is ethically OK."

I said, "It's ethically OK because it's done and dusted, kid. Summarize."

After a second his eyes came up to meet mine. He said, "I'm not sure how to talk to you about this case."

The waitress smacked down my coffee and our sandwiches and flounced off to get ready for her close-up. We both ignored her. I said, "You mean because I'm connected to just about everyone and everything involved."

"Yeah. That can't be easy. I don't want to go making it worse."

And bedside manner, too. Give the kid five years and he'd be running the force. I said, "I appreciate your concern, Stephen. But what I need from you right now isn't sensitivity, it's objectivity. You need to pretend this case has nothing to do with me. I'm just an outsider who happened to wander in and needs briefing. Can you do that?"

He nodded. "Yeah. Fair enough."

I settled back in my chair and pulled my plate towards me. "Wonderful. Hit me."

Stephen took his time, which was good: drowned his sandwich in ketchup and mayo, rearranged his crisps, made sure he had his thoughts in order. Then he said, "OK. Detective Kennedy's theory goes like this. Late on December fifteenth 1985, Francis Mackey and Rose Daly are planning to meet at the top of Faithful Place and elope together. Mackey's brother Kevin gets wind of it—"

"How?" I didn't see Imelda pouring her heart out to a fifteen-year-old kid.

"That's not clear, but obviously someone did, and Kevin adds up better than most people. That's one of the factors backing up Detective Kennedy's theory. According to everyone we've talked to, Francis and Rose had kept the elopement totally under wraps, no one had a clue what they were planning. Kevin, though: he was in a privileged position. He shared a room with Francis. He could have seen something."

My girl Mandy had kept her mouth shut. "Let's say that's out. There was nothing in that room to see."

Stephen shrugged. He said, "I'm from the North Wall. I'd say the Liberties work the same way, or anyway they did back then: people live on top of each other, people talk, there's no such thing as a secret. I've got to tell you, I'd be amazed if no one knew about that elopement. Amazed."

I said, "Fair enough. We can leave that part vague. What happens next?"

Concentrating on giving his report was relaxing him a little; we were back in his comfort zone. "Kevin decides to intercept Rose before she meets Francis. Maybe he arranges to meet her or maybe he knows she'll need to pick up her suitcase, but either way, they meet up, most likely somewhere in Number Sixteen Faithful Place. They get into an argument, he snaps, he grabs her by the throat and hits her head off the wall. From what Cooper says, that part would've taken no time; a few seconds, maybe. When Kevin gets his temper back, it's too late."

"Motive? Why would he intercept her to begin with, never mind argue with her?"

"Unknown. Everyone says Kevin was pretty attached to Francis, so it could be he didn't want Rose taking him away. Or it could be sexual jealousy—he was just at the age to cope really badly with that. She was gorgeous, by all accounts. Maybe she'd turned Kevin down, or maybe they'd had something on the side—" Stephen suddenly remembered who he was talking to. He blushed, shut up and shot me an apprehensive look.

I remember Rosie, Kevin had said. *That hair and that laugh, and the way she walked . . .* I said, "The age gap was a little wide for that—we're talking fifteen and nineteen, remember. But he could have fancied her, all right. Keep going."

"Well. The motive doesn't even have to be anything big; I mean, as far as we know, it's not like he was planning on killing her. It looks more like it just happened. When he realizes she's dead, he drags her body to the basement— unless they're down there already—and puts her under the concrete. He was strong for his age; he'd worked part-time on a building site, that summer, fetching and carrying. He would've been able for it." Another quick glance. I picked ham out of a back tooth and watched him blandly.

"At some stage in all this, Kevin finds the note Rose was going to leave for her family, and he realizes he can use it to his advantage. He stashes the first page and leaves the second where it is. The idea is, if Francis leaves anyway, everyone will basically tumble to the original plan: the two of them have gone off together, and the note's for her parents. If Francis ends up going home when Rose doesn't show up, or if he gets in touch with his family at some stage, everyone will think the note was for him and she's gone off on her own."

"And for twenty-two years," I said, "that's exactly what happens."

"Yeah. Then Rose's body turns up, we start investigating, and Kevin panics. According to everyone we've talked to, he was pretty stressed out the last couple of days, and getting worse. Finally he can't take the tension any more. He digs out the first page of the note from wherever he's been keeping it all this time, he spends one last evening with his family, and then he goes back to the place where he killed Rose and . . . Well."

"He says his prayers and takes a header out the top-floor window. And justice is served."

"More or less, I guess. Yeah." Stephen watched me covertly, over his coffee, to see if he had pissed me off.

I said, "Well done, Detective. Clear, concise and objective." Stephen let out a quick breath of relief, like he was coming out of an oral exam, and dove into his sandwich. "How long do you think we've got before that turns into the official Gospel according to Kennedy, and both cases get closed?"

He shook his head. "A few days, maybe? He hasn't sent the file upstairs yet; we're still gathering evidence. He's thorough, Detective Kennedy is. I mean, I know he has his theory, but it's not like he's just slapping it onto the case and throwing the whole thing away. He's talking like we—me and the other floaters—we'll be staying with Murder for the rest of the week, anyway."

Which meant that, basically, I had about three days. Nobody likes going backwards. Once this case was officially closed out, I would need to come up with notarized video footage of someone else committing both murders before anyone would reopen it. "I'm sure that'll be a blast," I said. "What do you, personally, think of Detective Kennedy's theory?"

That caught Stephen off guard. It took him a second to get his mouthful under control. "Me?"

"You, sunny Jim. I already know how Scorcher works. Like I told you before, I'm interested in what you've got to offer. Apart from your mad typing skills."

He shrugged. "It's not my job to—"

"Yeah, it is. I'm asking you; that makes it your job. Does his theory float your boat?"

Stephen shoved more sandwich in his mouth, to give himself time to think. He was watching his plate, keeping his eyes invisible. I said, "Yep, Stevie, you do indeed need to bear in mind that I could be biased as all hell, or crazed with grief, or just plain crazy to start with, and any or all of those could make me a very bad person to share your innermost thoughts with. But all the same, I'm betting this isn't the first time it's crossed your mind that Detective Kennedy might just be wrong."

He said, "It's occurred to me."

"Of course it has. If it hadn't, you'd be an idiot. Has it occurred to any-one else on your team?"

"Not that they've mentioned."

"And they won't. They've all thought about it, because they're not idiots either, but they're keeping their mouths shut because they're terrified of getting on Scorchie's bad side." I leaned in across the table, close enough that he had to look up. "That leaves you, Detective Moran. You and me. If the guy who killed Rose Daly is still out there, no one's going after him except the two of us. Are you starting to see just why our little game is *ethically OK*?"

After a moment Stephen said, "I guess."

"It's ethically just peachy all over, because your primary responsibility here isn't to Detective Kennedy—or to me, come to that. It's to Rose Daly and Kevin Mackey. We're all they've got. So quit faffing about like a virgin clutching her knickers, and tell me what you think of Detective Kennedy's theory."

Stephen said, simply, "I'm not mad about it."

"Why not?"

"I don't mind the holes—no known motive, not sure how Kevin found out about the elopement, all that stuff. You'd expect gaps like that, after this long. What's bothering me is the print results."

I had been wondering if he would spot that. "What about them?"

He licked mayo off his thumb and held it up. "First off, the unknowns on the outside of the suitcase. They could be nothing, but if this were my investigation, I'd want to identify them before I closed the case out."

I was pretty sure who had left those unknowns, but I didn't feel like sharing. I said, "So would I. Anything else?"

"Yeah. The other thing is, right"—a finger went up—"why no prints on the first page of the note? Wiping the second page makes sense: if anyone starts getting suspicious and reports Rose missing, Kevin doesn't want the cops finding his prints on her good-bye letter. But the first page? He takes it out from wherever he's been keeping it all this time, he's planning to use it as a suicide note and a *confession*, right, but he wipes it clean and uses *gloves* to stick it in his pocket? In case what, someone *connects* it to him?"

"And what does Detective Kennedy have to say about that?"

"He says minor anomaly, no biggie, every case has them. Kevin wipes both pages that first night, hides the first one away, when he takes it back out he doesn't leave prints—people don't always. Which is true enough, except . . . We're talking about someone who's about to *kill* himself. Someone who's basically confessing to *murder*. I don't care how cool you are, you're going to be sweating like a motherf— like mad. And when you sweat, you leave prints." Stephen shook his head. "That page should have prints," he said, "end of story," and he went back to demolishing his sandwich.

I said, "Just for fun, let's try something. Let's assume for a moment that my old friend Detective Kennedy is off base for once, and Kevin Mackey didn't kill Rose Daly. Then what've we got?"

Stephen watched me. He asked, "Are we assuming Kevin was murdered too?"

"You tell me."

"If he didn't wipe off that note and put it in his own pocket, someone else did it for him. I'm going with murder."

I felt that sudden, treacherous flood of affection rush through me again. I almost got the kid in a headlock and tousled his hair. "Works for me," I said. "And what do we know about the murderer?"

"We're thinking it's the one person?"

"I sincerely hope so. My neighborhood may be a little on the freaky side, but I'm hoping to God it's not freaky enough to have two separate killers doing their thing on the one road."

Somewhere in the last sixty seconds, since he started having opinions, Stephen had got a lot less scared of me. He was leaning forward, elbows on the table, so focused he had forgotten all about the rest of his sandwich. There was a new, hard flash in his eyes, harder than I would have expected from such a sweet little blushing newbie. "Then, going by Cooper, it's probably a man. Aged between, say, late thirties and fifty—so he'd have been between his midteens and thirty when Rose died—and pretty fit, then and now. This took a guy with some muscle on him."

I said, "Rose did. Kevin didn't. If you'd found a way to get him leaning out that window—and he wasn't the suspicious type—one little shove would have been all it took. No muscle needed."

"So, if our man was between fifteen and fifty when he got hold of Rose, that puts him anywhere between late thirties and seventy now."

"Unfortunately. Anything else we can say about him that might narrow it down?"

Stephen said, "He grew up somewhere very near Faithful Place. He knows Number Sixteen inside out: when he realized Rose was dead, he must have been big-time shocked, but he still remembered those slabs of concrete in the basement. And from what everyone's telling us, the people who know Number Sixteen are people who lived on or near Faithful Place when they were teenagers. He might not live there any more—there's dozens of ways he could've found out about Rose's body showing up—but he did."

For the first time in my career, I was getting an inkling of why Murder love their job the way they do. When undercovers go hunting, we'll take anything that wanders into our snares; half the skill is knowing what to use as bait, what to toss back where it came from and what to knock on the head and bring home. This was a whole different thing. These boys were the specialists called in to track down a rogue predator, and they focused on him like they were focusing on a lover. Anything else that wandered into their sights, while they were trawling the dark for that one shape, meant sweet fuck-all. This was specific and it was intimate, and it was powerful stuff: me and that one man, somewhere out there, listening hard for each other to put a foot wrong. That evening in the Very Sad Café, it felt like the most intimate connection I had.

I said, "The big question isn't how he found out Rose had shown up—like you say, probably everyone who's ever lived in the Liberties got a phone call about that. The big question is how he found out Kevin was a threat to him, after all this time. As far as I can see, there's only one person who could have made that clear to him, and that's Kevin. Either the two of them were still in contact, or they ran into each other during all the hoo-ha this weekend, or Kevin went out of his way to get in touch. When you get the chance, I'd like you to find out who Kevin phoned in his last forty-eight hours—mobile phone and landline, if he had one—who he texted, and who phoned or texted him. Please tell me I'm right in assuming Detective Kennedy's pulled his records."

"They're not in yet, but he has, yeah."

"If we find out who Kevin talked to this weekend, we find our man." I remembered Kevin losing the head and storming off, Saturday afternoon, while I went to get the suitcase for Scorcher. The next time I saw him had been in the pub. He could have gone to find just about anyone, in between.

Stephen said, "Here's the other thing: I think probably he's been violent. I mean, *obviously* he's been violent, but I mean more than just those two times. I think there's a good chance he has a record, or at least a reputation."

"Interesting theory. Why's that?"

"There's a difference between the two murders, right? The second one had to be planned, even if it was only a few minutes ahead of time, but the first one almost definitely wasn't."

"So? He's older now, he's more controlled, he thinks ahead. The first time, he just snapped."

"Yeah, but that's what I mean. That's how he snaps. That won't change, no matter how old he is."

I cocked one eyebrow—I knew what he meant, but I wanted to hear him explain it. Stephen rubbed clumsily at one ear, trying to find the words. "I've got a couple of sisters," he said. "One of them's eighteen, right, and if you annoy her, she yells loud enough that you can hear her right down the road. The other one, she's twenty, and when she loses the head she throws stuff at their bedroom wall—nothing breakable, like, just pens or whatever. That's the way they've always been, ever since we were kids. If the younger one threw something one day or the older one started yelling, or if either of them got violent with anyone, I'd be amazed. People snap the way they snap."

I dredged up an approving grin for him—the kid had earned a pat on the head—and I was starting to ask how he snapped, when it hit me. The sick dull crack of Shay's head off the wall, his mouth lolling open as he hung limp by the neck from Da's big hands. Ma screaming *Look what you've done now, you bastard, you're after killing him,* and Da's thick hoarse voice *Serve him right.* And Cooper: *The attacker caught her by the throat and slammed her head repeatedly against a wall.*

Something in my face worried Stephen; maybe I was staring. He said, "What?"

"Nothing," I said, swinging my jacket on. Matt Daly, flat and final: *People don't change.* "You're doing a good job, Detective. I mean that. Get in touch as soon as you've got those phone records."

"I will, yeah. Is everything—"

I found twenty quid and shoved it across the table at him. "Sort the bill. Let me know right away if the Bureau turns up a match to those unknowns on the suitcase, or if Detective Kennedy tells you when he's planning to close out this investigation. Remember, Detective: it's down to you and me. We're all there is."

I left. The last thing I saw was Stephen's face, watery through the glass of the café window. He was holding the twenty quid and watching me go, and he had his mouth open.

16

I kept walking for another few hours. Along the way I cut down Smith's Road past the entrance to the Place, the way Kevin had been meant to go after he dropped Jackie to her car Sunday night. For a good stretch of the way I had a clear view of the top back windows of Number 16, where Kevin had taken his header, and I got a quick over-the-wall glimpse of the first-floor ones; after I went past the house, if I turned around, I got a full view of the front while I passed the top of Faithful Place. The street lamps meant that anyone waiting inside would have seen me coming, but they also turned the windows a flat, smoky orange: if there had been a torch lit in the house, or some kind of action going on, I would never have spotted it. And if someone had wanted to lean out and call me, he would have had to do it loud enough to risk the rest of the Place hearing. Kevin hadn't wandered into that house because something shiny caught his eye. He had had an appointment.

When I got to Portobello I found a bench by the canal and sat down long enough to go through the post-mortem report. Young Stephen had a talent for summarizing: no surprises, unless you counted a couple of photos that in fairness I should have been ready for. Kevin had been healthy all over; as far as Cooper was concerned he could have lived forever, if he had just managed to stay away from tall buildings. The manner of death was listed as "undetermined." You know your life is deep in the shit when even Cooper goes tactful on you.

I headed back to the Liberties and swung by Copper Lane a couple of times, checking out footholds. As soon as it hit around half past eight and everyone was busy eating dinner or watching telly or putting the kiddies to bed, I went over the wall, through the Dwyers' back garden and into the Dalys'.

I needed to know, fast, just what had happened between my father and Matt Daly. The thought of knocking on random neighbors' doors wasn't particularly appealing, and besides, given the choice, I go to the source. I was pretty sure that Nora had always had a soft spot for me. Jackie had said she lived out in Blanchardstown or somewhere, but normal families, unlike mine, pull closer when bad things happen. After Saturday, I was willing to bet that Nora had left her husband and her kid to babysit each other and was spending a few days back under Mammy and Daddy Daly's roof.

Gravel crunched under my feet when I landed. I stood still in the shadows up against the wall, but no one came looking.

Gradually my eyes got used to the dark. I had never been in that garden before; like I had told Kevin, too scared of getting caught. It was what you'd expect from Matt Daly: a lot of decking, neatly trimmed shrubs, labeled poles stuck in flower beds ready for spring, the jacks had been turned into a sturdy little garden shed. I found a darling wrought-iron bench in a conveniently shadowy corner, wiped it more or less dry and settled in to wait.

There was a light on in a first-floor window, and I could see a neat row of pine cupboards on the wall: the kitchen. And sure enough, after about half an hour, in came Nora, wearing an oversized black jumper, with her hair pulled back in a rough bun. Even at that distance, she looked tired and pale. She ran herself a glass of tap water and leaned against the sink to drink it, staring blankly out of the window, her free hand going up to knead the back of her neck. After a moment her head snapped up; she called something over her shoulder, gave the glass a fast rinse and dumped it on the draining board, grabbed something from a cupboard and left.

So there I was, all dressed up and nowhere to go until Nora Daly decided it was bedtime. I couldn't even have a smoke, just in case someone spotted the glow: Matt Daly was the type to go after prowlers with a baseball bat, for the sake of the community. For the first time in what felt like months, all I could do was sit still.

The Place was winding down for the night. A telly threw stuttering flickers on the Dwyers' wall; music was seeping faintly from somewhere, a woman's sweet wistful voice aching out over the gardens. In Number 7 multicolored Christmas lights and pudgy Santas sparkled in the windows, and one of Sallie Hearne's current crop of teenagers screamed, "No! I hate you!" and slammed a door. On the top floor of Number 5, the epidural yuppies were putting their kid to bed: Daddy carrying him into his room fresh from the bath in a little white dressing gown, swinging him into the air and blowing raspberries on his tummy, Mummy laughing and bending to shake out blankets. Just across the road, my ma and my da were presumably staring catatonically at the telly, wrapped in their separate unimaginable thoughts, seeing if they could make it to bedtime without having to talk to each other.

The world felt lethal, that night. Normally I enjoy danger, there's nothing like it to focus the mind, but this was different. This was the earth rippling and flexing underneath me like a great muscle, sending us all flying, showing me all over again who was boss and who was a million miles out of his depth in this game. The tricky shiver in the air was a reminder: everything you believe is up for grabs, every ground rule can change on a moment's whim, and the dealer always, always wins. It wouldn't have startled me if Number 7 had crumbled inwards on top of the Hearnes and their Santas, or Number 5 had gone up in one great *whoof* of flames and pastel-toned yuppie dust. I thought about Holly, in what I had been so sure was her ivory tower, trying to work out how the world could exist without Uncle Kevin; about sweet little Stephen in his brand-new overcoat, trying not to believe what I was teaching him about his job; about my mother, who had taken my father's hand at the altar and carried his children and believed that was a good idea. I thought about me and Mandy and Imelda and the Dalys, sitting silent in our separate corners of this night, trying to see what shape these last twenty-two years fell into without Rosie, somewhere out there, pulling at their tides.

We were eighteen and in Galligan's, late on a Saturday night in spring, the first time Rosie said *England* to me. My whole generation has stories about Galligan's, and the ones who don't have their own borrow other people's. Every middle-aged suit in Dublin will tell you happily how he legged it out of there when the place was raided at three in the morning, or bought U2 a drink there before they were famous, or met his wife or got a tooth knocked out moshing or got so stoned he fell asleep in the jacks and nobody found him till after the weekend. The place was a rat hole and a firetrap: peeling black paint, no windows, spray-stenciled murals of Bob Marley and Che Guevara and whoever else the current staff happened to admire. But it had a late bar—more or less: no beer license, so you chose between two types of sticky German wine, both of which made you feel mildly poncy and severely ripped off—and it had the kind of live-music lottery where you never knew what you were going to get tonight. Kids nowadays wouldn't touch the place with someone else's. We loved it.

Rosie and I were there to see a new glam-rock band called Lipstick On Mars that she had heard was good, plus whoever else happened to be on. We were drinking the finest German white and dancing ourselves dizzy—I loved watching Rosie dance, the swing of her hips and the whip of her hair and the laugh curving her mouth: she never let her face go blank when she danced like other girls did, she always had an expression. It was shaping up to be a good night. The band was no Led Zeppelin, but they had smart lyrics, a great drummer and that reckless shine that bands did have, back then, when no one had anything to lose and the fact that you didn't have a snowball's chance in hell of making it big didn't matter, because throwing your whole heart into this band was the only thing that stopped you being just another futureless dole bunny moping in his bedsit. It gave them something: a drop of magic.

The bass player broke a string to prove he was serious, and while he was changing it Rosie and I went up to the bar for more wine. "That stuff's poxy," Rosie told the barman, fanning herself with her top.

"I know, yeah. I think they make it out of Benylin. Leave it in the airing cupboard for a few weeks and away you go." The barman liked us.

"Poxier than usual, even. You got a bad batch. Have you nothing decent, have you not?"

"This does the job, doesn't it? Otherwise, ditch the boyfriend, wait till we close up and I'll take you somewhere better."

I said, "Will I give you a smack myself, or will I just leave it to your mot?" The barman's girlfriend had a mohawk and sleeve tattoos. We got on with her, too.

"You do it. She's harder than you are." He winked at us and headed off to get my change.

Rosie said, "I've a bit of news."

She sounded serious. I forgot all about the barman and started frantically trying to add up dates in my head. "Yeah? What?"

"There's someone retiring off the line at Guinness's, next month. My da says he's been talking me up every chance he gets, and if I want the job, it's mine."

I got my breath back. "Ah, deadly," I said. I would have had a tough time getting delighted for anyone else, especially since Mr. Daly was involved, but Rosie was my girl. "That's brilliant. Fair play to you."

"I'm not taking it."

The barman slid my change down the bar; I caught it. "What? Why not?"

She shrugged. "I don't want anything my da gets for me, I want something I get myself. And anyway—"

The band started up again with a happy blast of drum overkill, and the rest of her sentence got lost. She laughed and pointed to the back of the room, where you could usually hear yourself think. I got her free hand and led the way, through a clump of bouncing girls with fingerless gloves and raccoon eyeliner, orbited by inarticulate guys hoping that if they just stayed close enough they would somehow end up getting a snog. "Here," Rosie said, pulling herself up onto the ledge of a bricked-up window. "They're all right, these fellas, aren't they?"

I said, "They're great." I had spent that week walking into random places in town, asking if they had any work going, and getting laughed out of just about every single one. The world's filthiest restaurant had had a kitchen-porter gig open and I had started getting my hopes up, on the grounds that no sane person would want it, but the manager had turned me down once he saw my address, with an unsubtle hint about inventory going missing. It had been months since Shay let a day go by without some line about how Mr. Leaving Cert and all his education couldn't put a wage on the table. The barman had just taken the guts of my last tenner. Any band that played loud and fast enough to blow my mind empty was in my good books.

"Ah, no; not great. They're all right, but half of it's that." Rosie motioned with her wineglass to the ceiling. Galligan's had a handful of lights, most of them lashed to beams with what looked like baling wire. A guy called Shane was in charge of them. If you got too near his lighting desk carrying a drink, he threatened to punch you.

"What? The lights?" Shane had managed to get some kind of fast-moving silvery effect that gave the band an edgy, sleazy almost-glamour. At least one of them was bound to get some action after their set.

"Yeah. Your man Shane, he's good. He's what's making them. This lot, they're all atmosphere; knock out the lights and the costumes, and they're just four lads making eejits of themselves."

I laughed. "So's every band, sure."

"Sort of, yeah. Probably." Rosie's eyes went sideways to me, almost shyly, over the rim of her glass. "Will I tell you something, Francis?"

"Go on." I loved Rosie's mind. If I could have got inside there, I would happily have spent the rest of my life wandering around, just looking.

"That's what I'd love to do."

"Lights? For bands?"

"Yeah. You know what I'm like for the music. I always wanted to work in the business, ever since I was a little young one." I knew that—everyone knew that, Rosie was the only kid in the Place who had spent her confirmation money on albums—but this was the first time she had said anything about lighting. "I can't sing for shite, but, and the arty stuff wouldn't be me anyway—writing songs or playing the guitar, nothing like that. This is what I like." She tilted her chin up at the crisscrossing beams of light.

"Yeah? Why?"

"Because. That fella's after making this band better. End of story. It doesn't matter if they're having a good night or a bad one, or if only half a dozen people show up, or if anyone else even notices what he's at: whatever happens, he'll come in and he'll make them better than they would've been. If he's honest-to-God brilliant at what he does, he can make them a *load* better, every time. I like that."

The glow in her eyes made me happy. Her hair was wild from dancing; I smoothed it down. "It's good stuff, all right."

"And I like that it makes a difference if he's brilliant at his job. I've never done anything like that. No one gives a toss if I'm brilliant at the sewing;

as long as I don't make a bollix of it, that's all that matters. And Guinness's would be exactly the same. I'd love to be good at something, really good, and have it *matter*."

I said, "I'll have to sneak you in backstage at the Gaiety and you can pull switches," but Rosie didn't laugh.

"God, yeah; imagine. This here is only a crap little rig; imagine what you could do with a real one, like in a big venue. If you were working for a good band that goes on tour, you'd get your hands on a different rig every couple of days . . ."

I said, "I'm not having you go off on tour with a bunch of rock stars. I don't know what else you'd be getting your hands on."

"You could come too. Be a roadie."

"I like that. I'll end up with enough muscles that even the Rolling Stones wouldn't mess with my mot." I flexed a bicep.

"Would you be into it?"

"Do I get to road test the groupies?"

"Dirtbird," Rosie said cheerfully. "You do not. Not unless I get to ride the rock stars. Seriously, but: would you do it? Roadie, something like that?"

She was really asking; she wanted to know. "Yeah, I would. I'd do it in a heartbeat. It sounds like great crack: get to travel, hear good music, never get bored . . . It's not like I'll ever get the chance, though."

"Why not?"

"Ah, come on. How many bands in Dublin can pay a roadie? You think these lads can?" I nodded at Lipstick On Mars, who didn't look like they could afford their bus fare home, never mind support staff. "I guarantee you, their roadie is someone's little brother shoving the drum kit into the back of someone's da's van."

Rosie nodded. "I'd say lighting's the same: only a few gigs going, and they're going to people who've already got experience. There's no course you can take, no apprenticeship, nothing like that—I checked."

"No surprise there."

"So say you were really into getting your foot in the door, right? No matter what it took. Where would you start?"

I shrugged. "Nowhere around here. London; maybe Liverpool. England, anyway. Find some band that could just about afford to feed you while you learned the trade, then work your way up."

"That's what I think, too." Rosie sipped her wine and leaned back in the alcove, watching the band. Then she said, matter-of-fact, "Let's go to England, so."

For a second I thought I had heard wrong. I stared at her. When she didn't blink I said, "Are you serious?"

"I am, yeah."

"Jaysus," I said. "Serious, now? No messing?"

"Serious as a heart attack. Why not?"

It felt like she had set light to a whole warehouse of fireworks inside me. The drummer's big finishing riff tumbled through my bones like a great beautiful chain of explosions and I could hardly see straight. I said—it was all that came out—"Your da'd go through the roof."

"Yeah, he would. So? He's going to go through the roof anyway, when he finds out we're still together. At least that way we wouldn't be here to hear it. Another good reason why England: the farther the better."

"Course," I said. "Right. Jaysus. How would we . . . ? We don't have the money. We'd need enough for tickets, and a gaff, and . . . Jaysus."

Rosie was swinging one leg and watching me steadily, but that made her grin. "I know that, you big sap. I'm not talking about leaving tonight. We'd have to save up."

"It'd take months."

"Have you got anything else to be doing?"

Maybe it was the wine; the room felt like it was cracking open around me, the walls flowering in colors I'd never seen before, the floor pounding with my heartbeat. The band finished up with a flourish, the singer whacked the mike off his forehead and the crowd went wild. I clapped automatically. When things quieted down and everyone including the band headed for the bar, I said, "You mean this, don't you?"

"That's what I've been telling you."

"Rosie," I said. I put down my glass and moved close to her, face-to-face, with her knees on either side of me. "Have you thought about this? Thought it all the way through, like?"

She took another swig of wine and nodded. "Course. I've been thinking about it for months."

"I never knew. You never said."

"Not till I was sure. I'm sure now."

"How?"

She said, "The Guinness's job. That's what's after making up my mind for me. As long as I'm here, my da's going to keep trying to get me in there, and sooner or later I'll give up and take the job—because he's right, you know, Francis, it's a great chance, there's people would kill for that. Once I go in there, I'll never get out."

I said, "And if we go over, we won't be coming back. No one does."

"I know that. That's the point. How else are we going to be together— properly, like? I don't know about you, but I don't want my da hanging over my shoulder giving out shite for the next ten years, wrecking our heads every chance he gets, till he *finally* figures out we're happy. I want you and me to get a proper start: doing what we want to do, together, without our families running our whole bleeding lives. Just the two of us."

The lights had changed to a deep underwater haze and behind me a girl started singing, low and throaty and strong. In the slow spinning beams of green and gold Rosie looked like a mermaid, like a mirage made out of color and light; for a second I wanted to grab her and crush her tight against me, before she could vanish between my hands. She took my breath away. We were still at the age when girls are years older than guys, and the guys grow up by doing their best when the girls need them to. I had known since I was a tiny kid that I wanted something more than what the teachers told us we were meant for, factories and dole queues, but it had never hit me that I might actually be able to go out and build that something more with my own hands. I had known for years that my family was fucked up beyond repair, and that every time I gritted my teeth and walked into that flat another little piece of my mind got strafed to rubble; but it had never once occurred to me, no matter how deep the crazy piled up, that I could walk away. I only saw it when Rosie needed me to catch up with her.

I said, "Let's do it."

"Jaysus, Francis, stall the ball! I didn't mean for you to decide tonight. Just have a think about it."

"I've thought."

"But," Rosie said, after a moment. "Your family. Would you be able to leave?"

We had never talked about my family. She had to have some idea—the whole Place had some idea—but she had never once mentioned them, and I appreciated that. Her eyes were steady on mine.

I had got out that night by swapping Shay, who drove a hard bargain, for all of next weekend. When I left, Ma had been screeching at Jackie for being such a bold girl that her da had to go to the pub because he couldn't stand to be around her. I said, "You're my family now."

The smile started somewhere far back, hidden behind Rosie's eyes. She said, "I'll be that anywhere, sure. Here, if you can't leave."

"No. You're dead right: that means we need to get out."

That slow, wide, beautiful smile spread right across Rosie's face. She said, "What are you doing for the rest of my life?"

I slid my hands up her thighs to her soft hips and pulled her closer to me on the ledge. She wrapped her legs around my waist and kissed me. She tasted sweet from the wine and salty from the dancing, and I could feel her still smiling, up against my mouth, until the music rose around us and the kiss got fiercer and the smile fell away.

The only one who didn't turn into her ma, Imelda's voice said in the dark beside my ear, rough with a million cigarettes and an infinite amount of sadness. *The one that got away.* Imelda and I were a pair of liars born and bred, but she hadn't been lying about loving Rosie, and I hadn't been lying about her being the one who had come closest. Imelda, God help her, had understood.

The yuppie baby had fallen asleep, in the safe glow of his night-light. His ma stood up, inch by inch, and slipped out of the room. One by one, the lights started to go out in the Place: Sallie Hearne's Santas, the Dwyers' telly, the Budweiser sign hanging crooked in the hairy students' gaff. Number 9 was dark, Mandy and Ger were snuggled up together early; probably he had to be in work at dawn, cooking businessmen their banana fry-ups. My feet started to freeze. The moon hung low over the roofs, blurred and dirty with cloud.

At eleven o'clock on the dot Matt Daly stuck his head into his kitchen, had a good look around, checked that the fridge was closed and switched off the light. A minute later, a lamp went on in a top back room and there was Nora, disentangling her hair elastic with one hand and covering a yawn with the other. She shook her curls free and reached up to draw the curtains.

Before she could start changing into her nightie, which might make her feel vulnerable enough to call Daddy to deal with an intruder, I tossed a piece of gravel at her window. I heard it hit with a sharp little crack, but nothing happened; Nora had put the sound down to birds, wind, the house settling. I threw another, harder.

Her lamp went out. The curtain twitched, just a cautious inch. I flicked on my torch, pointed it straight at my face and waved. When she had had time to recognize me, I put a finger to my lips and then beckoned.

After a moment Nora's lamp went on again. She pulled back a curtain and flapped a hand at me, but it could have meant anything, *Go away* or *Hang on*. I beckoned again, more urgently, grinning reassuringly and hoping the torchlight wouldn't turn it into a Jack Nicholson leer. She pushed at her hair, getting frustrated; then—resourceful, like her sister—she leaned forward on the windowsill, breathed on the pane and wrote with a finger: WAIT. She even did it backwards, fair play to her, to make it easy for me to read. I gave her the thumbs-up, switched off the torch and waited.

Whatever the Dalys' bedtime routine involved, it was nearly midnight before the back door opened and Nora came half running, half tiptoeing down the garden. She had thrown on a long wool coat over her skirt and jumper and she was breathless, one hand pressed to her chest. "God, that door—I had to haul on it to get it open and then it *slammed* back on me, sounded like a car crash, did you hear it? I nearly fainted—"

I grinned and moved over on the bench. "Didn't hear a sound. You're a born cat burglar. Have a seat."

She stayed where she was, catching her breath and watching me with quick-moving, wary eyes. "I can only stay a minute. I just came out to see . . . I don't know. How you're doing. If you're all right."

"I'm better for seeing you. You look like you nearly had a heart attack there, though."

That got a reluctant little smile. "I nearly did, yeah. I was sure my da'd be down any second . . . I feel like I'm sixteen and climbed down the drainpipe."

In the dark winter-blue garden, with her face washed clean for the night and her hair tumbling, she looked barely older. I said, "Is that how you spent your wild youth? You little rebel, you."

"Me? God, no, not a chance; not with my da. I was a good girl. I missed out on all that stuff; I only heard about it from my mates."

"In that case," I said, "you've got every right to all the catching up you can get. Try this, while you're at it." I pulled out my cigarettes, flipped the packet open and offered it to her with a flourish. "Cancer stick?"

Nora gave it a doubtful look. "I don't smoke."

"And there's no reason you should start. Tonight doesn't count. Tonight you're sixteen and a bold little rebel. I only wish I'd brought a bottle of cheap cider."

After a moment I saw the corner of her mouth slowly curve up again. "Why not," she said, and she dropped down beside me and took a smoke.

"Good woman yourself." I leaned over and lit it for her, smiling into her eyes. She pulled too hard on it and collapsed into a coughing fit, with me fanning her and both of us stifling giggles and pointing at the house and shushing each other and snickering even harder. "Oh, my Jaysus," Nora said, wiping her eyes, when she could breathe again. "I'm not cut out for this."

"Little puffs," I told her. "And don't bother inhaling. Remember, you're a teenager, so this isn't about the nicotine; this is all about looking cool. Watch the expert." I slouched down on the bench James Dean style, slid a cigarette into the corner of my lip, lit it and jutted my jaw to blow out smoke in a long stream. "There. See?"

She was giggling again. "You look like a gangster."

"That's the idea. If you want to go for the sophisticated starlet look, though, we can do that too. Sit up straight." She did. "Cross your legs. Now, chin down, look at me sideways, purse up your lips, and . . ." She took a puff, threw in an extravagant wrist flourish and blew smoke at the sky. "Beautiful," I said. "You are now officially the ice-coolest wild child on the block. Congratulations."

Nora laughed and did it again. "I am, amn't I?"

"Yep. Like a duck to water. I always knew there was a bad girl in there."

After a moment she said, "Did you and Rosie use to meet out here?"

"Nah. I was too scared of your da."

She nodded, examining the glowing tip of her smoke. "I was thinking about you, this evening."

"Yeah? Why?"

"Rosie. And Kevin. Is that not why you came here, as well?"

"Yeah," I said, carefully. "More or less. I figured, if anyone knows what the last few days have been like . . ."

"I miss her, Francis. A lot."

"I know you do, babe. I know. So do I."

"I wouldn't have expected . . . Before, I only missed her once in a blue moon: when I had the baby and she wasn't there to come see him, or when Ma or Da got on my nerves and I'd have loved to ring Rosie and give out about them. The rest of the time I barely thought about her, not any more. I'd other things to be thinking about. But when we found out she was dead, I couldn't stop crying."

"I'm not the crying type," I said, "but I know what you mean."

Nora tapped ash, aiming it into the gravel where Daddy might not spot it in the morning. She said, with painful jagged edges on her voice, "My husband doesn't. He can't understand what I'm upset about. Twenty years since I saw her, and I'm in bits . . . He said for me to pull myself together, before I upset the baba. My ma's on the Valium, and my da thinks I should be looking after her, she's the one lost a child . . . I kept thinking about you. I thought you were the only person who maybe wouldn't think I was being stupid."

I said, "I'd seen Kevin for a few hours out of the last twenty-two years, and it still hurts like hell. I don't think you're being stupid at all."

"I feel like I'm not the same person any more. Do you know what I mean? All my life, when people asked had I any brothers or sisters, I said, *Yeah; yeah, I've a big sister.* Now I'll be saying, *No, it's just me.* Like as if I was an only child."

"There's nothing to stop you telling people about her anyway."

Nora shook her head so hard that her hair whipped her face. "No. I'm not going to lie about that. That's the worst part: I was lying all along, and I didn't even know it. Whenever I told people I had a sister, it wasn't true. I was already an only child, all that time."

I thought of Rosie, in O'Neill's, digging in her heels at the thought of pretending we were married: *No way, I'm not faking that, it's not about what people think . . .* I said gently, "I don't mean lie. I just mean she doesn't have to vanish. *I had a big sister,* you can say. *Her name was Rosie. She died.*"

Nora shivered, suddenly and violently. I said, "Cold?"

She shook her head and ground out her cigarette on a stone. "I'm grand. Thanks."

"Here, give me that," I said, taking the butt off her and tucking it back into my packet. "No good rebel leaves behind evidence of her teenage kicks for her da to find."

"It doesn't matter. I don't know what I was getting all worked up about. It's not like he can ground me. I'm a grown woman; if I want to leave the house, I can."

She wasn't looking at me any more. I was losing her. Another minute and she would remember that she was in fact a respectable thirty-something, with a husband and a kid and a certain amount of good sense, and that none of the above were compatible with smoking in a back garden at midnight with a strange man. "It's parent voodoo," I said, putting a wry grin on it. "Two minutes with them and you're straight back to being a kid. My ma still puts the fear of God into me—although, mind you, she actually would give me a clatter of the wooden spoon, grown man or no. Not a bother on her."

After a second Nora laughed, a reluctant little breath. "I wouldn't put it past my da to try grounding me."

"And you'd yell at him to stop treating you like a child, same as you did when you were sixteen. Like I said, parent voodoo."

This time the laugh was a proper one, and she relaxed back onto the bench. "And someday we'll do the same to our own kids."

I didn't want her thinking about her kid. "Speaking of your father," I said. "I wanted to apologize for the way my da acted, the other night."

Nora shrugged. "There were the two of them in it."

"Did you see what started them off? I was chatting away with Jackie and missed all the good part. One second everything was grand, the next the two of them were setting up for the fight scene from *Rocky*."

Nora adjusted her coat, tucking the heavy collar tighter around her throat. She said, "I didn't see it either."

"But you've an idea what it was about. Don't you?"

"Men with a few drinks on them, you know yourself; and they were both after having a tough few days . . . Anything could have got them going."

I said, with a harsh sore scrape to it, "Nora, it took me half an hour just to get my da calmed down. Sooner or later, if this keeps going, it'll give him a heart attack. I don't know if the bad blood between them is my fault, if it's because I went out with Rosie and your da wasn't happy about it; but if that's the problem, I'd at least like to know, so I can do something about it before it kills my father."

"God, Francis, don't be saying that! No way is it your fault!" She was wide-eyed, fingers wrapped round my arm: I had hit the right mix of guilt-tripped and guilt-tripper. "Honest to God, it's not. The two of them never got on. Even back when I was a little young one, way before you ever went out with Rosie, my da never . . ."

She dropped the sentence like a hot coal, and her hand came off my arm. I said, "He never had a good word to say about Jimmy Mackey. Is that what you were going to say?"

Nora said, "The other night, that wasn't your fault. That's all I was saying."

"Then whose bloody fault was it? I'm lost here, Nora. I'm in the dark and I'm drowning and nobody will lift one finger to help me out. Rosie's gone. Kevin's gone. Half the Place thinks I'm a murderer. I feel like I'm losing my mind. I came to you because I thought you were the *one* person who would have some clue what I'm going through. I'm begging you, Nora. Tell me what the hell is going on."

I can multitask; the fact that I was aiming to push her buttons didn't stop me from meaning just about every word. Nora watched me; in the near dark her eyes were enormous and troubled. She said, "I didn't see what started the two of them off, Francis. If I had to guess, but, I'd say it was that your da was talking to my ma."

And there it was. Just that quickly, like gears interlocking and starting to move, dozens of little things going right back to my childhood spun and whirred and clicked neatly into place. I had thought up a hundred possible explanations, each one more involved and unlikely than the last—Matt Daly ratting out one of my da's less legal activities, some hereditary feud going back to who stole whose last potato during the Famine—but I had never thought of the one thing that starts practically every fight between two men, specially the truly vicious ones: a woman. I said, "The two of them had a thing together."

I saw her lashes flutter, quick and embarrassed. It was too dark to tell, but I would have bet she was blushing. "I think so, yeah. No one's ever said it to me straight out, but . . . I'm almost sure."

"When?"

"Ah, ages ago, before they were married—it wasn't an *affair*, nothing like that. Just kid stuff."

Which, as I knew better than most people, never stopped anything from mattering. "And then what happened?"

I waited for Nora to describe unspeakable acts of violence, probably involving strangulation, but she shook her head. "I don't know, Francis. I don't. Like I said, nobody ever talked to me about it; I just figured it out on my own, from bits and bobs."

I leaned over and jammed out my smoke on the gravel, shoved it back in the packet. "Now this," I said, "I didn't see coming. Color me stupid."

"Why . . . ? I wouldn't've thought you'd care."

"You mean, why do I care about anything that happened around here, when I couldn't be arsed coming back for twenty-odd years?"

She was still gazing at me, worried and bewildered. The moon had come out; in the cold half-light the garden looked pristine and unreal, like some symmetrical suburban limbo. I said, "Nora, tell me something. Do you think I'm a murderer?"

It scared me shitless, how badly I wanted her to say no. That was when I knew I should get up and leave—I already had everything she could give me, every extra second was a bad idea. Nora said, simply and matter-of-factly, "No. I never did."

Something twisted inside me. I said, "Apparently a lot of people do."

She shook her head. "Once, when I was just a wee little young one—five or six, maybe—I had one of Sallie Hearne's cat's kittens out in the street to play with, and a bunch of big fellas came along and took it away, to tease me. They were throwing it back and forth, and I was screaming . . . Then you came and made them stop: got the kitten for me, told me to take it back to Hearne's. You wouldn't remember."

"I do, yeah," I said. The wordless plea in her eyes: she needed the two of us to share that memory, and of all the things she needed that was the only tiny one I could give. "Of course I remember."

"Someone who'd do that, I can't see him hurting anyone; not on purpose. Maybe I'm just stupid."

That twist again, more painful. "Not stupid," I said. "Just sweet. The sweetest thing."

In that light she looked like a girl, like a ghost, she looked like a breathtaking black-and-white Rosie escaped for one thin slice of time from a flickering old film or a dream. I knew if I touched her she would vanish, turn back into Nora in the blink of an eye and be gone for good. The smile on her lips could have pulled my heart out of my chest.

I touched her hair, only, with the tips of my fingers. Her breath was quick and warm against the inside of my wrist. "Where have you been?" I said softly, close to her mouth "Where have you been all this time?"

We clutched at each other like wild lost kids, on fire and desperate. My hands knew the soft hot curves of her hips by heart, their shape rose up to meet me from some fathoms-deep place in my mind that I had thought was lost forever. I don't know who she was looking for; she kissed me hard enough that I tasted blood. She smelled like vanilla. Rosie used to smell of lemon drops and sun and the airy solvent they used in the factory to clean stains off the cloth. I dug my fingers deep into Nora's rich curls and felt her breasts heave against my chest, so that for a second I thought she was crying.

She was the one who broke away. She was crimson-cheeked and breathing hard, pulling down her jumper. She said, "I've to go in now."

I said, "Stay," and took hold of her again.

For a second I swear she thought about it. Then she shook her head and detached my hands from her waist. She said, "I'm glad you came tonight."

Rosie would have stayed. I almost said it; I would have, if I had thought there was a chance it would do me any good. Instead I leaned back on the bench, took a deep breath and felt my heart start to slow down. Then I turned Nora's hand over and kissed her palm. "So am I," I said. "Thank you for coming out to me. Now go inside, before you have me driven mad. Sweet dreams."

Her hair was tumbled and her lips were full and tender from kissing. She said, "Safe home, Francis." Then she stood up and walked back up the garden, pulling her coat around her.

She slipped into the house and closed the door behind her without once looking back. I sat there on the bench, watching her silhouette move in the lamplight behind her bedroom curtain, till my knees stopped shaking and I could climb over the walls and head for home.

17

The answering machine had a message from Jackie, asking me to give her a ring: "Nothing important, now. Just . . . ah, you know yourself. Bye." She sounded drained and older than I had ever heard her. I was wrecked enough myself that a part of me was actually scared to leave it overnight, given what had happened when I ignored Kevin's messages, but it was some ungodly hour of the morning; the phone would have given her and Gavin matching heart attacks. I went to bed. When I pulled off my jumper I could still smell Nora's hair on the collar.

Wednesday morning I woke up late, around ten, feeling several notches more exhausted than I had the night before. It had been a few years since I'd been in top-level pain, mental or physical. I had forgotten just how much it takes out of you. I stripped off a layer or two of brain fluff with cold water and black coffee, and phoned Jackie.

"Ah, howya, Francis."

Her voice still had that dulled note, even heavier. Even if I'd had the time or the energy to tackle her about Holly, I wouldn't have had the heart. "Howya, honeybunch. I just got your message."

"Oh . . . yeah. I thought afterwards, maybe I shouldn't have . . . I didn't want to give you a fright, like. Make you think anything else had happened. I just wanted . . . I don't know. To see how you were getting on."

I said, "I know I headed off early, Monday night. I should have stuck around."

"Maybe, yeah. Sure, it's done now. There was no more drama, anyway: everyone had more drink, everyone sang a while longer, everyone went home."

There was a thick layer of background noise going on: chitchat, Girls Aloud and a hair dryer. I said, "Are you at work?"

"Ah, sure. Why not. Gav couldn't take another day off, and I didn't fancy hanging about the flat on my own . . . Anyway, if you and Shay are right about the state of the country, I'd better keep my regulars happy, wha'?" It was meant as a joke, but she didn't have the energy to put a bounce on it.

"Don't push yourself, sweetheart. If you're wrecked, go home. I'd say your regulars wouldn't leave you for love or money."

"You never know, do you? Ah, no, I'm grand. Everyone's being lovely; they're bringing me cups of tea and letting me have a smoke break whenever I need one. I'm better off here. Where are you? Are you not in work?"

"Taking a few days off."

"That's good, Francis. You work too hard, sure. Do something nice for yourself. Bring Holly somewhere."

I said, "Actually, while I've got the free time, I'd love a chance to have a chat with Ma. On our own, without Da around. Is there a good time of day for that? Like, does he go out to the shops, or to the pub?"

"Most days he does, yeah. But . . ." I could hear the effort she was putting into trying to focus. "He was having a terrible time with his back, yesterday. Today as well, I'd say. He could hardly get out of the bed. When his back does be at him, he mostly just has a sleep." Translation: some doctor gave him the good pills, Da topped up with floorboard vodka, he was out for the foreseeable. "Mammy'll be there all day, till Shay gets home anyway, in case he needs anything. Call over to her; she'll be delighted to see you."

I said, "I'll do that. You tell that Gav to take good care of you, OK?"

"He's been brilliant, so he has, I don't know what I'd do without him . . . Come here, d'you want to call round to us this evening? Have a bit of dinner with us, maybe?"

Fish and chips with pity sauce: sounded tasty. "I've got plans," I said. "But thanks, hon. Maybe some other time. You'd better get back to work before someone's highlights turn green."

Jackie tried obligingly to laugh, but it fell flat. "Yeah, I probably had. Mind yourself, Francis. Say howya to Mammy for me." And she was gone, back into the fog of hair-dryer noise and chatter and cups of sweet tea.

Jackie was right: when I rang the buzzer, Ma came down to the hall door. She looked exhausted too, and she had lost weight since Saturday: at least one belly was missing. She eyed me for a moment, deciding which way to go. Then she snapped, "Your da's asleep. Come on into the kitchen and don't be making noise." She turned around and stumped painfully back up the stairs. Her hair needed setting.

The flat stank of spilled booze, air freshener and silver polish. The Kevin shrine was even more depressing by daylight; the flowers were half dead, the Mass cards had fallen over and the electric candles were starting to fade and flicker. Faint, satisfied snores were trickling through the bedroom door.

Ma had every bit of silver she owned spread out on the kitchen table: cutlery, brooches, photo frames, mysterious pseudo-ornamental tat that had clearly spent a long time on the regift merry-go-round before falling off here. I thought of Holly, puffy with tears and rubbing furiously away at her dollhouse furniture. "Here," I said, picking up the polishing cloth. "I'll give you a hand."

"You'll only make a bags of it. The great clumsy hands on you."

"Let me have a go. You can tell me where I'm going wrong."

Ma shot me a suspicious look, but that offer was too good to pass up. "Might as well make yourself useful, I suppose. You'll have a cup of tea."

It wasn't a question. I pulled up a chair and got started on the cutlery, while Ma bustled in cupboards. The conversation I wanted would have worked best as a confidential mother-and-daughter chat; since I didn't have the equipment for that, a little joint housework would at least steer us towards the right vibe. If she hadn't been doing the silver, I would have found something else to clean.

Ma said, by way of an opening salvo, "You went off very sudden, Monday night."

"I had to go. How've you been getting on?"

"How d'you expect? If you wanted to know, you'd have been here."

"I can't imagine what this has been like for you," I said, which may be part of the formula but was probably true. "Is there anything I can do?"

She threw tea bags into the pot. "We're grand, thanks very much. The neighbors've been great: brought us enough dinners for a fortnight, and Marie Dwyer's letting me keep them in her chest freezer. We've lived without your help this long, we'll survive a bit longer."

"I know, Mammy. If you think of anything, though, you just let me know. OK? Anything at all."

Ma spun round and pointed the teapot at me. "I'll tell you what you can do. You can get a hold of your friend, him, what's-his-name with the jaw, and you can tell him to send your brother home. I can't get onto the funeral home about the arrangements, I can't go to Father Vincent about the Mass, I can't tell anyone when I'll be burying my own son, because some young fella with a face like Popeye on him won't tell me when he'll be *releasing the body*—that's what he called it. The brass neck of him. Like our Kevin's his property."

"I know," I said. "And I promise you I'll do my best. But he's not trying to make your life any more difficult. He's just doing his job, as fast as he can."

"His job's his problem, not mine. If he keeps us waiting any longer it'll have to be a closed casket. Did you think of that?"

I could have told her the casket would probably have to be closed anyway, but we had already taken this line of conversation about as far as I felt like going. I said, "I hear you've met Holly."

A lesser woman would have looked guilty, even just a flicker, but not my ma. Her chins shot out. "And about time! That child would've been married and giving me great-grandchildren before you'd have lifted a finger to bring her here. Were you hoping if you waited long enough I'd die before you had to introduce us?"

The thought had crossed my mind. "She's pretty fond of you," I said. "What do you think of her?"

"The image of her mammy. Lovely girls, the pair of them. Better than you deserve."

"You've met Olivia?" I tipped my hat to Liv, mentally. She had skated around that one very prettily.

"Twice, only. She dropped Holly and Jackie down to us. Was a Liberties girl not good enough for you?"

"You know me, Ma. Always getting above myself."

"And look where that got you. Are the two of yous divorced now, or are yous only separated?"

"Divorced. A couple of years back."

"Hmf." Ma's mouth pursed up tight. "I never divorced your da."

Which was unanswerable on so many levels. "True enough," I said.

"Now you can't take Communion."

I knew better than to rise to that, but no one can get to you quite like family. "Ma. Even if I wanted to take Communion, and I don't, the divorce wouldn't be a problem. I can divorce myself into a coma for all the Church cares, as long as I don't shag anyone who's not Olivia. The problem would be the lovely ladies I've ridden since the divorce."

"Don't be dirty," Ma snapped. "I'm not a smart-arse like you, I don't know all the ins and outs, but I know this much: Father Vincent wouldn't give you Communion. In the church where you were baptized." She jabbed a triumphant finger at me. Apparently this counted as a win.

I reminded myself that I needed a chat more than I needed the last word. I said meekly, "You're probably right."

"I am, of course."

"At least I'm not raising Holly to be a heathen too. She goes to Mass."

I thought the mention of Holly would smooth Ma down again, but this time it just put her back up further; you never can tell. "She might as well be a heathen, for all the good it's done me. I missed her First Communion! My first granddaughter!"

"Ma, she's your third granddaughter. Carmel's got two girls older than her."

"The first one with our *name*. And the last, by the looks of it. I don't know what Shay's playing at, at all—he could have a dozen girls on the go and we'd never know, he's never brought one to meet us in his life, I swear to God I'm ready to give up on him altogether. Your da and meself thought Kevin would be the one who . . ."

She bit down on her lips and upped the volume on the tea-making clatter, bashing cups onto saucers and biscuits onto a plate. After a while she said, "And now I suppose that's the last we'll see of Holly."

"Here," I said, holding up a fork. "Is that clean enough?"

Ma threw it a half glance. "It is not. Get between the prongs." She brought the tea things over to the table, poured me a cup and pushed milk and sugar towards me. She said, "I'm after buying Holly her Christmas presents. Lovely little velvet dress, I got her."

"That's a couple of weeks away," I said. "Let's see how we go."

Ma gave me a sideways look that told me nothing, but she left it. She found another cloth, sat down opposite me and picked up something silver that could have been a bottle stopper. "Drink that tea," she said.

The tea was strong enough to reach out of the pot and give you a punch. Everyone was out at work and the street was very quiet, just the soft even pattering of the rain and the far-off rush of traffic. Ma worked her way through various undefined silver widgets; I finished the cutlery and moved on to a photo frame—it was covered in fancy flowers that I would never get clean to Ma's standards, but at least I knew what it was. When the room felt like it had settled enough, I said, "Tell me something. Is it true Da was doing a line with Theresa Daly, before you came on the scene?"

Ma's head snapped up and she stared at me. Her face didn't change, but an awful lot of things were zipping across her eyes. "Where'd you hear that?" she demanded.

"So he was with her."

"Your da's a fecking eejit. You knew that already, or you're as bad."

"I did, yeah. I just didn't know that was one of the specific ways he was a fecking eejit."

"She was always trouble, that one. Always drawing attention to herself, wiggling down the road, screaming and carrying on with her friends."

"And Da fell for it."

"They all fell for it! The fellas are stupid; they go mad for all that. Your da, and Matt Daly, and half the fellas in the Liberties, all hanging out of Tessie O'Byrne's arse. She lapped it up: kept three or four of them dangling at once, broke it off with them every other week when they weren't giving her enough attention. They just came crawling back for more."

"We don't know what's good for us," I said. "Specially when we're young. Da would've been only a young fella back then, wouldn't he?"

Ma sniffed. "Old enough to know better. I was three years younger, sure, and I could've told him it would end in tears."

I said, "You'd already spotted him, yeah?"

"I had, yeah. God, yeah. You wouldn't think . . ." Her fingers had slowed on the widget. "You wouldn't think it now, but he was only gorgeous, your da was, back then. A load of curly hair on him, and those blue eyes, and the laugh; he'd a great laugh."

We both glanced involuntarily out the kitchen door, towards the bedroom. Ma said, and you could still hear that the name used to taste like superfancy ice cream in her mouth, "Jimmy Mackey could've had his pick of any girl around."

I gave her a little smile. "And he didn't go straight for you?"

"I was a child, sure. I was fifteen when he started chasing after Tessie O'Byrne, and I wasn't like these young ones nowadays that look twenty before they're twelve; I'd no figure on me, no makeup, I hadn't a clue . . . I used to try and catch his eye when I'd see him on my way to work in the morning, but he'd never look twice. He was mad on Tessie. And she liked him best of the lot."

I had never heard any of this before, and I was willing to bet that Jackie hadn't either, or she would have passed it on. Ma isn't the let's-all-share-our-feelings type; if I had asked her about this story a week earlier or later, I would have got nowhere. Kevin had left her fractured and peeled raw. You use what you've got. "So why did they break up?" I asked.

Ma's mouth pursed up. "If you want to do that silver, do it properly. Get into the cracks. There's no point if I'll have to do the lot again after you."

I said, "Sorry," and upped the display of elbow grease. After a moment she said, "I'm not saying your da was a holy innocent. Tessie O'Byrne never had a bit of shame, but there was the pair of them in it."

I waited, rubbing away. Ma caught my wrist and pulled it towards her to check the shine on the frame; then she gave a grudging little nod and let go. "That's better. Things weren't the same, back then. We had a bit of decency about us; we weren't riding all round us just because that's what they did on the telly."

I inquired, "Da rode Tessie O'Byrne on the telly?"

That got me a clout on the arm. "No! Amn't I telling you, if you'll only listen to me? They were always wild, the pair of them. Made each other worse. One day in summer your da borrowed a car off a friend of his and drove Tessie down to Powerscourt on a Sunday afternoon, to see the water-fall. Only the car broke down, on the way back."

Or that had been Da's story. Ma was giving me a meaningful look. "And?" I asked.

"And they stayed there! Overnight! We'd no mobile phones back then; they couldn't ring for a mechanic, or even to let anyone know what was after happening. They tried walking for a bit, but they were out in a lane in the middle of Wicklow, sure, and it was getting dark. They stayed in the car, and the next morning they got a jump start off a farmer going past. By the time they got home, everyone thought they were after eloping."

She tilted the silver widget to the light, to check that the finish was per-fect and to stretch the pause—Ma always did have a taste for drama. "Well. Your da always said to me he slept in the front seat and Tessie slept in the back. I wouldn't know, sure. But that's not what the Place thought."

I said, "I bet it wasn't."

"Girls didn't stay out with fellas, back then. Only slappers did that. I'd never known a girl who did the bold thing before she was married."

"I'd have thought the two of them would've had to get married, after that. To preserve her reputation."

Ma's face closed over. She said, with a sniff in her voice, "I'd say your da would've done it, he was that mental about her, the fecking eejit. But he wasn't good enough for the O'Byrnes—they always did have notions of themselves. Tessie's da and her uncles bet the living shite out of him; I saw him the day after, I hardly recognized him. They told him not to be going near her again. Said he'd done enough damage."

I said, "And he did what he was told." I liked that, a lot. It felt reassur-ing. Matt Daly and his buddies could have beaten me to within an inch of my life, and the second I got out of the hospital I would have headed for Rosie as fast as I could limp.

Ma said, prim and satisfied, "He hadn't got much choice. Tessie's da had always let her away with murder, so he had—and look where that got him—but after that he'd hardly let her go out the door, only to go to work and he walked her there himself. I wouldn't blame him; everyone was talk-ing about it. The little gurriers were calling things after her on the street, all the aul' ones were waiting for her to turn up in trouble, half her friends weren't allowed speak to her in case she turned them into hoors as well; Father Hanratty gave a homily about loose women weakening the country, and that wasn't what the men died for in 1916. No names, mind you, but everyone knew who he meant. That put a stop to Tessie's gallop."

Straight across almost half a century, I could feel the feeding frenzy: the whirling hysteria of it, the double-speed pump of adrenaline as the Place smelled blood and went into attack mode. Those weeks had quite probably sown the crazy seeds in Tessie Daly's mind. "It'd do that, all right," I said.

"And serve her right! Taught her what was what. She liked messing about with the fellas, but she didn't want the name for it, did she?" Ma was sitting up straight, with her virtuous face on her. "She started going with Matt Daly straight after—he'd been making goo-goo eyes at her for years, but she'd never paid him any notice. Not till he came in useful. He was a decent fella, Matt was; Tessie's da didn't mind her going with him. It was the only way she was allowed out the door."

I said, "And that's what Da has against Matt Daly? He nicked his girl?"

"That was most of it. Sure, they never liked each other to start with." She lined up the silver gizmo with three more like it, flicked a minute speck of something off the side, picked out a twee little Christmas-tree ornament from the to-do pile. "Matt was always jealous of your da. Your da was a million miles better-looking than Matt, so he was, and he was popular— not just with the girls, the fellas thought he was great as well, a great laugh . . . Matt was a boring little bollix. No go in him."

Her voice was layered with old things, triumph and bitterness and spite twisted together. I said, "So when Matt was the one who got the girl, he rubbed it in?"

"That wasn't enough for him. Your da was after applying to Guinness's, as a driver. He'd been told the job was as good as his, as soon as the next driver retired. But Matt Daly'd been working there a few years, and his da before him; he knew people. After all that with Tessie, Matt went to his foreman and told him Jimmy Mackey wasn't the kind of fella they wanted at Guinness's. There were twenty lads applying for every job. They didn't need anyone that might bring trouble."

"So Da ended up doing the plastering." No humor intended.

"That was my uncle Joe got him the apprenticeship. We got engaged not long after that whole carry-on with Tessie. Your da needed a trade, if we were going to be having a family."

I said, "You were a fast worker."

"I saw my chance and I took it. I was seventeen by then; old enough to make the boys look. Your da was . . ." Ma's lips vanished, and she twisted her cloth tighter into the crannies of the ornament. "I knew he was still mad into Tessie," she said after a moment, and there was a defiant spark in her voice that gave me a hair's-breadth glimpse of a girl with her chin out, watching wild Jimmy Mackey from this kitchen window and thinking *Mine.* "But I didn't mind that. I thought I'd change that, once I got my hands on him. I never wanted a lot; I wasn't one of those ones that think they'll be film stars in Hollywood. I never had notions. All I wanted was a little house of my own and a few childer, and Jimmy Mackey."

"Well," I said. "You got the kids, and you got the man."

"I got him in the end, all right. What Tessie and Matt left of him. He'd started on the drink by then."

"But you wanted him anyway." I kept my voice nice and non-judgmental.

"I'd my heart set on him. My mammy, God rest her soul, she warned me: never go with a drinking man. But I hadn't a clue. My own da—you won't remember him, Francis, but he was a lovely man—he never touched a drop; I hadn't a notion what a drinker was like. I knew Jimmy'd have a few, but sure, all the fellas would. I thought it was no more than that—and it wasn't, not when I first spotted him. Not till Tessie O'Byrne wrecked his head for him."

I believed her. I know what the right woman, at the right moment, can do to a man—not that Tessie seemed to have got away scot-free herself. Some people should never meet. The fallout spreads too wide and gets into the ground for much too long.

Ma said, "Everyone had always said Jimmy Mackey'd be good for nothing. His ma and da were a pair of aul' alcos, never worked a day in their lives; ever since he was only a little chiseler he'd be going round to the neighbors asking could he stay for the dinner because there was nothing at home, he'd be out running the streets in the middle of the night . . . By the time I knew him, everyone said for definite he'd wind up a waster like his ma and da." Her eyes had strayed off the polishing, away towards the window and the falling rain. "I knew they were wrong, but. He wasn't bad, Jimmy wasn't; just wild. And he wasn't thick. He could've been something. He didn't need Guinness's, he could've had his own little business—there was no need for him to be answering to bosses every day, he hated that. He always loved the driving; he could've done deliveries, had his own van . . . If your woman hadn't got to him first."

And there was the motive, gift wrapped and tied with ribbon, to go ever so perfectly with that signature MO. One day Jimmy Mackey had had a top-flight girl on his arm and a top-flight job in the bag, he'd been all ready to paint the future in his colors and give the finger to the bastards who said he'd never do it. Then he made one slipup, just one, and prissy little Matt Daly waltzed in cool as a cucumber and pocketed Jimmy's whole life for himself. By the time Jimmy's head cleared, he was married to a girl he never wanted, scrambling for the odd day's work on a job with no prospects and drinking enough to kill Peter O'Toole. He spent twenty-odd years watching his lost life unfold right across the road, in another man's home. Then, all in one weekend, Matt Daly humiliated him in front of the whole street and almost got him arrested—in what passes for an alcoholic's brain, it's always someone else's doing—and he somehow found out that Rosie Daly was wrapping his son around her finger and dancing him off to wherever suited her.

And there could have been more to it than that, more and worse. Da grinning at me, winking, daring me to talk back: *The Daly young one, yeah? She's a little daisy. The kegs on her, my Jaysus* . . . My girl Rosie, the sweet spitting image of his Tessie O'Byrne.

He must have heard me after all, tiptoeing through the front room, sure I was untouchable. I'd seen him pretend to be asleep a hundred times. Maybe he had only meant to tell her to get her hands off his family; maybe he had wanted something more. But then there she was, in front of him, slapping him in the face with just how little it mattered what he wanted:

Tessie O'Byrne's daughter irresistible and untouchable all over again, Matt Daly's daughter taking away whatever Jimmy had that she fancied. Probably he was drunk, at least until he realized what had happened. He had been a strong man, back then.

We hadn't been the only ones awake that night. Somewhere in there, Kevin had got up, maybe to go out to the jacks, and found us both gone. At the time it had meant nothing to him: Da regularly vanished for days on end, Shay and I both had the occasional nighttime errand of one kind or another. But this weekend, when he realized that someone had been out killing Rosie that night, Kevin had remembered.

I felt like I had known every detail of this story, in some chasm in the deepest part of my brain, since the second I heard Jackie's voice on the answering machine. It felt like icy black water, filling up my lungs.

Ma said, "He should've waited for me to grow up. She was pretty enough, Tessie was, but by the time I got to sixteen there was plenty of fellas thought I was pretty as well. I know I was young, but I was growing. If he'd just taken his great stupid eyes off her long enough to notice me for one minute, none of this would have happened."

The solid weight of grief in her voice could have sunk ships. That was when I realized that she thought Kevin had been drunk out of his skull, just like he learned from Daddy, and that was what had sent him out of that window.

Before I could pull myself together enough to set her straight, Ma swiped her fingers across her mouth, looked at the clock on the windowsill and let out a screech. "Holy God, will you look at that, it's gone one o'clock! I've to eat something or I'll be getting a weakness." She shoved the ornament away from her and pushed back her chair. "You'll have a sandwich."

I said, "Will I bring one in to Da?"

For one more second Ma's face turned towards the bedroom door. Then she said, "Leave him," and went back to pulling things out of the fridge.

The sandwiches were soft butter and reconstituted ham on white sliced pan, cut into triangles. They took me straight back to when my feet didn't touch the floor at that same table. Ma made another pot of ferocious tea and ate her way methodically through her triangles. The way she chewed said she'd got better dentures, somewhere along the way. When we were kids she always told us her missing teeth were our fault: she had lost them having us, a tooth for every child. When the tears started coming, she put down her mug, pulled a faded blue handkerchief out of her cardigan pocket and waited for them to stop. Then she blew her nose and went back to her sandwich.

18

A part of me would have sat there with my ma forever, giving the teapot a reheat every hour or so and making the occasional batch of sandwiches. Ma wasn't bad company, as long as she kept her mouth shut, and for the first time her kitchen felt like shelter, at least compared to what was waiting for me outside. As soon as I stepped through that door, the only thing left for me to do was go after solid proof. That wasn't the hard part—I figured it should take about twenty-four hours, max. That was where the full-on nightmare kicked in. Once I had proof, I would have to figure out what to do with it.

Around two o'clock, noises started up in the bedroom: bedsprings creaking, a wordless throat-clearing shout, that endless retching full-body cough. I figured that was my cue to leave, which triggered a volley of complicated Christmas-dinner questions from Ma ("*If* yourself and Holly both came, I'm only saying *if*, would she eat white meat or dark meat, or would she have any at all, because she's said to me her mammy doesn't give her turkey unless it does be that free-range one . . ."). I kept my head down and kept moving. As I dived out the door, she called after me, "Lovely seeing you, come back soon!" Behind her Da shouted, through phlegm, "Josie!"

I even knew exactly how he could have found out where Rosie was going to be that night. The only way to that info had been through Imelda, and I could only think of one reason why my da would be anywhere near her. Here I had always taken it for granted that when he vanished for a day or three, it was booze he was hunting. Even after everything else he had done, it had never once occurred to me that he would cheat on my ma—if

I had thought about it, I would have figured he had an alcohol-related inability to do any such thing. My family is just chock-full of surprises.

Imelda could have told her ma outright what Rosie had told her—girly bonding, looking for attention, who knew—or she could have dropped a hint when my da was around, just a little one to make her feel smarter than the man who was fucking her mother. Like I said, my da is no eejit. He would have put two and two together.

This time, when I rang Imelda's buzzer, no one answered. I stepped back and watched her window: something moved, behind the net curtain. I leaned on the buzzer for a good three minutes before she snatched up the handset. "*What.*"

"Howya, Imelda. It's Francis. Surprise."

"Fuck off."

"Ah, now, 'Melda, be nice. We need to talk."

"I've got nothing to say to you."

"Tough. I've got nowhere else to be, so I'll be waiting across the road, in my car, for as long as this takes. It's the silver 1999 Merc. When you get bored of this game, come down to me, we'll have a quick chat and then I'll leave you alone for life. If I get bored first, I'm going to start asking your neighbors questions about you. Have you got that?"

"Fuck off."

She hung up. Imelda had plenty of stubborn in the tank; I figured it would take at least two hours, maybe three, before she cracked and came down to me. I headed back to my car, turned on Otis Redding and opened the window to share with the neighbors. It was a toss-up whether they would peg me as a cop, a drug dealer or a moneylender's goon. None of the above would go down well.

At that hour Hallows Lane was quiet. An old fella on a walker and an old one polishing her brasswork had a long disapproving conversation about me, and a couple of yummy mummies gave me sideways looks on their way back from shopping. A guy with a shiny tracksuit and a large number of problems spent a solid forty minutes outside Imelda's house, swaying back and forth and using all his remaining brain cells to shout "Deco!" up at the top window at ten-second intervals, but Deco had better things to do and eventually the guy staggered off. Around three o'clock, someone who was clearly Shania hauled herself up the steps of Number 10 and let herself in. Isabelle got home not long after. She was the living spit of Imelda in the eighties, right down to the defiant angle of her chin and the long-legged screw-you walk; I couldn't work out whether she made me sad or gave me hope. Every time the dirty lace curtains twitched, I waved.

A little after four, when it was getting dark and Genevieve had come home from school and I had moved on to James Brown, a knuckle tapped on my passenger window. It was Scorcher.

I'm not supposed to be near this case, I had told Imelda; *I've put my job on the line just by coming here.* I wasn't sure whether to despise her for squealing or admire her resourcefulness. I turned off the music and rolled down the window. "Detective. What can I do for you?"

"Open the door, Frank."

I raised my eyebrows, doing surprised at the grim tone, but I leaned over and unlocked the door. Scorcher got in and slammed it hard. "Now drive," he said.

"Are you on the run? You can hide in the boot if you want."

"I'm not in the mood for funnies. I'm getting you out of here before you intimidate those poor girls any more than you already have."

"I'm just a man in his car, Scorch. Sitting here having a nostalgic look at the old home turf. What's so intimidating about that?"

"*Drive.*"

"I'll drive if you'll take a few deep breaths for me. I'm not insured for third-party heart attacks. Deal?"

"Don't make me arrest you."

I burst out laughing. "Oh, Scorchie, you're a treasure. I always forget why I'm so fond of you. We can arrest each other, how's that?" I pulled out into the traffic and went with the flow. "Now tell me. Who've I been intimidating?"

"Imelda Tierney and her daughters. As you well know. Ms. Tierney says you tried to force your way into the flat yesterday, and she had to threaten you with a knife to get you to leave."

"Imelda? Is that who you're calling a girl? She's forty-odd, Scorcher. Show some respect. The polite term these days is *woman.*"

"And her daughters are girls. The youngest one's only eleven. They say you've been sitting back there all afternoon, making obscene gestures at them."

"I haven't had the pleasure of their acquaintance. Are they nice girls? Or do they take after their mammy?"

"What did I tell you, last time we saw each other? What was the *one* thing I told you to do?"

"Stay out of your way. I got that part, loud and clear. What I missed was the part where you turned into my boss. Last time I looked, my boss was a lot heavier than you, and not nearly as good-looking."

"I don't need to be your bloody boss to tell you to stay the hell out of my case. *My* investigation, Frank; *my* orders. You ignored them."

"So report me. Do you need my ID number for that?"

"Yeah, Frank, hilarious. I know the rules are one big bloody joke to you. I know you think you're immune. Hell, maybe you're right; I don't know how things work over in Undercover." Outrage didn't suit Scorcher; it swelled up his jaw to twice its normal size and gave him a forehead vein that looked dangerous. "But maybe you should keep in mind that I've been doing my best to do you a *favor* here, for Christ's sake. I've been going *miles* out of my way for you. And at this stage, I honestly can't remember why I'm bothering. If you keep on fucking me about, every single bloody chance you get, I might just change my mind."

I stopped myself from slamming on the brakes and smacking his head off the windscreen. "Favor? You mean putting it about that Kevin was an accident?"

"Not just putting it about. It'll go on the death cert."

"Oh, well, then: wow. I'm overwhelmed with gratitude, Scorch. Really, I am."

"This isn't just about you, Frank. You may not give a damn whether your brother goes down as accident or suicide, but I bet your family does."

"Oh, no, no, no. No. Don't even try to pull that one. When it comes to my family, pal, you don't have the tiniest clue what you're dealing with. For one thing, this may come as a shock, but you don't rule their universe: they'll all believe exactly what they want to believe, regardless of what you and Cooper put on the death cert—my mother, for example, would like me to inform you that it was, I shit you not, a traffic accident. For another, if most of my family were on fire, I wouldn't piss on them to put them out. I certainly don't give the world's smallest fuck what they think happened to Kevin."

"Can a suicide go into consecrated ground, these days? What does the priest say in a suicide's homily? What does the rest of the neighborhood say about him? What does it do to the people who get left behind? Don't fool yourself, Frank: you're not bloody immune to that."

My temper was starting to get a little ragged around the edges. I pulled into a narrow cul-de-sac between two blocks of flats—in reverse, so that I could make a quick getaway if I ended up shoving Scorcher out of the car—and switched off the ignition. Above us, some architect had got cute with blue-painted balconies, but the Mediterranean effect was undermined by the fact that they looked out on a brick wall and a clump of skips.

"So," I said. "Kevin gets filed away under 'accident,' all nice and pretty. Let me ask you this. What are you filing Rosie under?"

"Murder. Obviously."

"Obviously. Murder by who? Person or persons unknown?"

Scorcher left a silence. I said, "Or by Kevin."

"Well. It's a little more complicated than that."

"How complicated can it be?"

"If our suspect's dead too, we've got a certain amount of discretion. It's a fine line. On the one hand, it's not like there's going to be an arrest, so the brass aren't wild about the idea of pumping resources into the case. On the other hand . . ."

"On the other hand, there's the almighty solve rate."

"Mock all you want. These things matter. You think I'd have been able to give your girlfriend this much manpower if my solve rate had been in the toilet? It's a cycle: the more I get out of this case, the more I can put into the next one. Sorry, Frank, but I'm not going to jeopardize the next victim's shot at justice *and* my reputation, just to spare your feelings."

"Translate for me, Scorch. What exactly are you planning on doing about Rosie?"

"I'm planning on doing this right. We'll keep collecting and collating evidence and witness statements for the next couple of days. After that, assuming nothing unexpected turns up . . ." He shrugged. "I've worked a couple of these cases before. Normally, we try to handle the situation as compassionately as possible. The file goes to the DPP, but on the quiet; nothing's made publicly available, specially if we're not talking about a career criminal. We'd rather not wreck a man's name when he's not around to defend himself. If the DPP agrees that we'd have a good case, we have a chat with the victim's family—make it clear that nothing's definitive here, but we can at least give them a certain amount of closure—and that's the end of that. They get to move on, the killer's family get to keep their peace of mind, we get to mark the case solved. That'd be the normal procedure."

I said, "Why do I get the feeling you're trying to threaten me?"

"Oh, come on, Frank. That's a very dramatic way of putting it."

"How would you put it?"

"I'd say I'm trying to warn you. And you're not making it easy."

"Warn me *what*, exactly?"

Scorcher sighed. "If I need to go for an in-depth inquest to determine Kevin's cause of death," he said, "I'll do it. And I'd be willing to bet the media will be all over it like a rash. Regardless of how you feel about the suicide issue, we both know one or two journos who like nothing better than a dodgy cop. And I think you can see how, in the wrong hands, this story could make you look dodgy as all hell."

I said, "That sounds a lot like a threat to me."

"I think I've made it pretty obvious that I'd rather not go down that road. But if this is the only way to make you stop playing Boy Detective . . . I'm just trying to get your attention, Frank. I haven't had much luck any other way."

I said, "Think back, Scorcher. What was the one thing *I* told *you*, last time we saw each other?"

"That your brother wasn't a killer."

"That's right. And how much attention did you pay to that?"

Scorcher flipped down the sun visor and checked a shaving cut in the mirror, tilting his head back to run a thumb along his jaw. "In some ways," he said, "I suppose I owe you a thank-you. I've got to admit, I'm not sure I'd have found Imelda Tierney if you hadn't found her for me. And she's turning out very useful."

The cunning little bitch. "I bet she is. She's the obliging type. If you know what I mean."

"Oh, no. She's not just trying to make me happy. Her evidence'll hold up, if it comes to that."

He let it hang there. The tiny smirk he couldn't hide gave me the general idea, but I went along anyway. "Go on, then. Hit me. What's she come up with?"

Scorch pursed up his lips, pretending to think about it. "She may end up being a witness, Frank. All depending. I can't tell you her evidence if you're going to try and harass her into changing it. I think we both know just how badly that could end, don't we?"

I took my time. For a long, cold moment I stared him out of it; then I let my head fall back against the headrest and ran my hands over my face. "You know something, Scorch? This has been the longest week of my life."

"I know that, old son. I'm hearing you. But, for everyone's sake, you're going to have to find somewhere more productive to direct that energy."

"You're right. I shouldn't have gone looking for Imelda to begin with; that was well out of order. I just figured . . . she and Rosie were close, you know? I thought, if anyone knew anything . . ."

"You should have given me her name. I'd have talked to her for you. Same end result, none of this hassle."

"Yes. You're right again. It's just . . . It's hard to let go when there's nothing definite one way or the other, you know? I like knowing what's going on."

Scorch said dryly, "Last time we talked, you sounded pretty sure you knew exactly what was going on."

"I thought I did. I was positive."

"But now . . . ?"

I said, "I'm tired, Scorch. Over the past week I've dealt with dead exes, dead brothers and a hefty dose of my parents, and I'm a very wrecked little puppy. Maybe that's what's doing it. I'm not positive about anything any more. Nothing at all."

I could tell by the puffy look on Scorcher's face that he was about to enlighten me, which was bound to put him in a better mood. "Sooner or later, Frank," he told me, "we all end up getting a good kick in the certainties. That's what life is. The trick is to turn that kick into a stepping-stone towards the next level of certainty. Do you get me?"

This time I swallowed my helping of tossed metaphor salad like a good boy. "Yeah, I do. And I bloody hate admitting this, to you of all people, but I need a hand up to that next level. I really do, mate. Put me out of my misery: what's Imelda saying?"

"You're not going to give her grief about it?"

"As far as I'm concerned, my life will be complete if I never see Imelda Tierney again."

"I'm going to need your word on this, Frank. No dodging."

"I give you my word I will not go near Imelda. Not about Kevin, not about Rosie, not about anything ever."

"No matter what."

"No matter what."

"Believe me, I don't want to complicate your life. And I won't have to, as long as you don't complicate mine. Don't force my hand here."

"I won't."

Scorcher smoothed his hair into place and snapped the sun visor shut. "In a way," he said, "you were right to go after Imelda. Your technique may suck, my friend, but your instincts are spot-on."

"She knew something."

"She knew plenty. I've got a bit of a surprise for you, old son. I know you thought you and Rose Daly were keeping your relationship a big secret, but in my experience, when a woman says she won't tell a soul, what she means is she'll only tell her two very best friends. Imelda Tierney knew all along. The relationship, the plans to elope, everything."

"God," I said. I shook my head, did a shamefaced half laugh, let Scorcher inflate with satisfaction. "Right. She . . . wow. Now that I didn't see coming."

"You were only a kid. You didn't know the rules of the game."

"Still. Hard to believe I was ever that naïve."

"Here's something else you may have missed: Imelda says Kevin had a massive thing for Rose, way back when. You've got to admit, that fits with what you've told me: she was the neighborhood babe, all the boys fancied her."

"Well, sure. Yeah. But *Kevin?* He was only fifteen."

"That's old enough for the hormones to be going bananas. And old enough to wangle his way into clubs where he shouldn't have been going. One night Imelda was in Bruxelles, and Kevin came up to her and offered to buy her a drink. They got talking, and he asked her—begged her—to put in a good word for him with Rose. That cracked Imelda up, but Kevin looked genuinely hurt, so once she stopped laughing, she told him it wasn't personal: Rose was taken. That was as far as she was planning to go, but Kevin kept pestering her about who the guy was, and he kept buying her more drink . . ."

Scorch was managing to keep his face grave, but he was having a great old time. Right under the surface, he was still that deodorant-drenched teenager pumping his fist and hissing *Score!* "In the end, she spilled the whole thing. She didn't see any harm in it: she thought he was a lovely sweet kid, plus she figured he'd back off once he knew they were talking about his own brother, right? Wrong. He lost the plot: shouting, kicking walls, throwing glasses . . . The bouncers had to boot him out of the place."

Which would have been several miles out of character—when Kev lost his temper, the worst he ever did was flounce off in a huff—but apart from that, it all hung together just gorgeously. I was getting more impressed with Imelda by the minute. She was well up on the barter system: she had known before she ever called Scorcher that if she wanted him to get the nasty man off her street, she would have to give him something he wanted in exchange. Probably she had rung around a few old friends, to find out exactly what that might be. The Murder boys had obviously made it clear, while they were doing their door-to-door, that they were interested in any link between Kevin and Rosie; the Place would have had no trouble filling in the blanks. I supposed I should consider myself lucky that Imelda had been sharp enough to do her research, rather than just flying off the handle and dumping me in the firing line.

"Jesus," I said. I leaned my arms on the steering wheel and slumped forward, staring out through the windscreen at the traffic inching past the mouth of the laneway. "Sweet Jesus. And I never had a clue. When was this?"

Scorcher said, "A couple of weeks before Rose died. Imelda feels pretty guilty about the whole thing, now that she knows where it led. That's what made her come forward. She's going to give me an official statement as soon as we're finished here."

I just bet she was. "Well," I said. "I guess that's evidence, all right."

"I'm sorry, Frank."

"I know. Thanks."

"I know this isn't what you were hoping to hear—"

"That's for sure."

"—but, like you said, any kind of certainty helps. Even if that's not your perception right now. At least it means you've got some closure. When you're ready, you'll be able to start integrating all of this into your worldview."

"Scorcher," I said. "Let me ask you something. Do you go to a shrink?"

He managed to look embarrassed and self-righteous and belligerent all at once. "Yeah. Why? Do you want a recommendation?"

"No, thanks. I was just wondering."

"The guy's pretty good. He's helped me discover a lot of interesting things. How to bring my outer reality into sync with my inner reality, that kind of stuff."

"Sounds very motivational."

"It is. I think he could do a lot for you."

"I'm an old-fashioned kind of guy. I still think my inner reality should get in sync with the outer one. I'll keep the offer in mind, though."

"Yeah. Do that." Scorcher gave my dashboard a manly pat, like it was a horse that had learned its lesson. "It's been good talking with you, Frank. I should probably get back to the grindstone, but give me a ring anytime if you need a chat, yeah?"

"Will do. I reckon what I really need is some time by myself, though, to take all this in. It's a lot to absorb."

Scorch did a profound nod-and-eyebrows number that he had presumably picked up from his shrink. I said, "Do you want a lift back to the squad?"

"No, thanks. The walk'll do me good; got to keep an eye on the old waistline." He tapped his stomach. "Take care of yourself, Frank. We'll talk."

The laneway was narrow enough that he had to open the car door about six inches and wriggle his way out, which brought down the tone of his exit, but he got it back once he got into his Murder Squad stride. I watched him swing off through the tired scurrying crowds, a man with a briefcase and a purpose, and remembered the day a few years back when we had run into each other and discovered we had both joined the divorce club. The drinking session had lasted fourteen hours and had finished up in a UFO-themed joint in Bray where Scorch and I tried to convince two brain-dead lovelies that we were Russian millionaires over here to buy Dublin Castle, except we kept losing it and snickering helplessly into our pints like a pair of kids. It occurred to me that I had kind of liked Scorcher Kennedy for the last twenty years, and that I was actually going to miss him.

People routinely underestimate me and it's one of my favorite things, but all the same I was a little surprised at Imelda; she didn't seem like the type to overlook the less fluffy side of human nature. In her place I would at least have had a large ugly friend with some form of weapon spend a few days with me, but on Thursday morning the Tierney household appeared to be back to business as usual. Genevieve schlepped off to school sucking on a Kit Kat, Imelda headed for New Street and came back carrying two plastic bags, Isabelle stalked off somewhere that called for pulled-back hair and a sharp white shirt; there was no sign of any bodyguard, armed or otherwise. This time no one saw me watching.

Around noon, a couple of teenage girls with a couple of babies rang the buzzer, Shania came downstairs and they all wandered off to window-shop or shoplift or whatever. Once I was sure she wasn't going to come back for her smokes, I cracked the front-door lock and went up to Imelda's flat.

She had some talk show turned up loud, people howling at each other and the audience baying for blood. The door was crusted with locks, but when I put my eye to the crack, only one of them was actually on. It took me about ten seconds to pick. The telly covered the sound of the door creaking open.

Imelda was sitting on her sofa wrapping Christmas presents, which would have been more adorable if it hadn't been for the TV show and the fact that most of them were fake Burberry. I had the door closed and I was coming up behind her when something—my shadow, a floorboard—made her whip around. She caught her breath to scream, but before she could get started I had a hand over her mouth and the other forearm leaning across her wrists, pinning them down on her lap. I got comfortable on the arm of the sofa and said, close to her ear, "Imelda, Imelda, Imelda. And here you swore to me you weren't a squealer. I'm disappointed in you."

She aimed an elbow at my stomach; when I tightened my hold, she tried to bite my hand. I pressed it down harder, pulling her head back, till her neck arched and I could feel her teeth crushing against her lip. I said, "When I take my hand away, I want you to think about two things. The first one is that I'm a whole lot closer than anyone else. The second one is what Deco upstairs would think if he knew there was an informer living here, because it would be very, very easy for him to find out. Do you think he'd take it out on you, personally, or would he decide Isabelle's juicier? Or maybe Genevieve? You tell me, Imelda. I don't know what kind of taste he's got."

Her eyes were lit up with pure fury, like a trapped animal's. If she could have bitten my throat out, she would have done it. I said, "So what's the plan? Are you going to scream?"

After a moment, her muscles slowly loosened and she shook her head. I let go, tossed a bunch of Burberry off an armchair onto the floor and settled in. "There," I said. "Isn't this cozy?"

Imelda rubbed tenderly at her jaw. "Prick," she said.

"This wasn't my choice, babe, now was it? I gave you two separate chances to talk to me like a civilized person, but no: you wanted it this way."

"My fella'll be home any minute now. He does the security. You don't want to be messing with him."

"That's funny, because he wasn't home last night and there's nothing in this room that says he's ever existed." I kicked the Burberry out of the way so I could stretch out my legs. "Why would you lie about something like that, Imelda? Don't tell me you're afraid of me."

She was sulking in the corner of the sofa, arms and legs crossed tight, but that got a rise out of her. "You wish, Francis Mackey. I've bet the shite out of a lot tougher than you."

"Oh, I'm sure you have. And if you can't beat the shite out of them, you run and tell someone who might. You squelt on me to Scorcher Kennedy—*no*, shut your bloody great gob and don't be trying to lie your way out—and I'm not one bit happy about it. But it's easily fixed. All you have to do is tell me who you ran to about me and Rosie, and hey presto, all will be forgiven."

Imelda shrugged. In the background, the TV baboons were still belting each other with studio chairs; I leaned over, keeping a sharp eye on Imelda just in case, and yanked the plug out of the wall. Then I said, "I didn't hear you."

Another shrug. I said, "I think I've been more than patient. But this right here, what you're looking at? This is the last of my patience, sweetheart. Take a good long look. It's a whole lot prettier than what comes next."

"So?"

"So I thought you'd been warned about me."

I caught the flash of fear across her face. I said, "I know what they're saying around here. Which one do you think I killed, Imelda? Rosie or Kevin? Or is it both?"

"I never said—"

"See, I'm betting on Kevin. Am I right? I thought he killed Rosie, so I booted him out that window. Is that what you've figured out?"

Imelda had better sense than to answer. My voice was rising fast, but I didn't care if Deco and his drug buddies heard every word. I had been waiting all week for a chance to lose my temper like this. "Tell me this: how thick do you have to be, how incredibly *stupid*, to play games with someone who would do that to his own brother? I'm in no mood to be fucked with, Imelda, and you spent yesterday afternoon fucking with me. Do you think that was a good idea?"

"I just wanted—"

"And now here you are, doing it *again*. Are you deliberately trying to push me that extra inch? Do you *want* me to snap, is that it?"

"No—"

I was up out of the armchair, gripping the sofa back on either side of her head, shoving my face so close to hers I could smell cheese-and-onion crisps on her breath. "Let me explain something, Imelda. I'll use small words, so it'll get through your thick skull. Inside the next ten minutes, I swear to Christ, you're going to answer my question. I know you'd rather stick to the story you told Kennedy, but you don't have that option. Your only choice is whether you want to answer with a few slaps or without."

She tried to duck her head away from me, but I got one hand cupped around her jaw and forced her face up to mine. "And before you decide, think about this: how hard would it be for me to get carried away and wring your neck like a chicken's? Everyone around here already thinks I'm Hannibal Lecter. What the hell have I got to lose?" Maybe she was ready to talk by then, but I didn't give her the chance. "Your friend Detective Kennedy may not be my biggest fan, but he's a cop, just like me. If you turn up beaten to pulp, or God forbid dead as a doornail, don't you think he's going to look after his own? Or do you seriously think he'll care more about some bone-stupid skanger tramp whose life wasn't worth a fiver to anyone in this world? He'll throw you away in a heartbeat, Imelda. Like the piece of shite you are."

I knew the look on her face, the slack jaw, the blind black eyes stretched too wide to blink. I had seen it on my ma a hundred times, in the second when she knew she was about to get hit. I didn't care. The thought of the back of my hand cracking across Imelda's mouth almost choked me with how badly I wanted it. "You didn't mind opening your ugly yap for anyone else who asked. Now, by Jesus, you're going to open it for me. Who'd you tell about me and Rosie? Who, Imelda? Who was it? Was it your slut ma? Who the *fuck* did you—"

I could already hear her spitting it at me like great slimy gobs of poison, *Your alco da, your filthy dirty whoremaster da,* and I was all ready and braced for it to hit me when her mouth opened wide and red and she almost howled into my face, "I told your brother!"

"Bull*shit*, you lying bitch. That's the crap you fed Scorcher Kennedy and he lapped it up, but do I look as stupid as him? Do I?"

"Not Kevin, you thick bastard, what would I be doing with Kevin? Shay. I told Shay."

The room went soundless, a huge perfect silence like snowfall, as if there had never been a noise in all the world. After what might have been a long time I noticed that I was sitting in the armchair again and that I was numb all over, like my blood had stopped moving. After a while longer I noticed that someone upstairs had a washing machine on. Imelda had shrunk into the sofa cushions. The terror on her face told me what mine must look like.

I said, "What did you tell him?"

"Francis . . . I'm sorry, right. I didn't think—"

"What did you tell him, Imelda."

"Just . . . you and Rosie. That yous were heading off."

"When did you say it to him?"

"The Saturday night, in the pub. The night before yous were leaving. I thought, sure, what harm at that stage, it was too late for anyone to stop yous—"

Three girls leaning on the railings and tossing their hair, glossy and restless as wild fillies, fidgeting on the edge of their anything-can-happen evening. Apparently just about anything had. I said, "If you give me one more shitty excuse, I'm going to put my foot through that robbed telly."

Imelda shut up. I said, "Did you tell him when we were going?"

A quick jerk of a nod.

"And where you'd left the suitcase?"

"Yeah. Not what room, like; just . . . in Number Sixteen."

The dirty-white winter light through the lace curtains was vicious on her. Slumped in the corner of the sofa, in this overheated room that stank of grease and cigarettes and waste, she looked like an underfilled bag of bones wrapped in gray skin. I couldn't think of one thing this woman could have wanted that would have been worth what she had thrown away. I said, "Why, Imelda? Why the hell?"

She shrugged. It dawned on me in a slow wave, with the faint red stain mottling her cheeks. "You've got to be kidding me," I said. "You were into Shay?"

Another shrug, this one sharper and pricklier. Those bright-colored girls shrieking and play-fighting, *Mandy said to ask if your brother fancies going to the pictures* . . . I said, "I thought Mandy was the one who had a thing for him."

"Her too. We all did—not Rosie, but loads of us. He had his pick."

"And so you sold Rosie out to get his attention. Is that what you had in mind when you told me you loved her?"

"That's not bleeding fair. I never meant to—"

I fired the ashtray at the telly. It was heavy and I put my whole body behind it; it smashed through the screen with an impressive crashing noise and an explosion of ash and butts and splinters of glass. Imelda let out something between a gasp and a yelp and cringed away from me, one forearm thrown up to protect her face. Specks of ash filled up the air, whirled and settled on the carpet, the coffee table, her tracksuit bottoms.

"Now," I said. "What did I warn you?"

She shook her head, wild-eyed. She had a hand pressed over her mouth: someone had trained her not to scream.

I flicked away glittering speckles of glass and found Imelda's smokes on the coffee table, under a ball of green ribbon. "You're going to tell me what you said to him, word for word, as close as you can remember. Don't leave anything out. If you can't remember something for definite, say so; don't make shit up. Is that clear?"

Imelda nodded, hard, into her palm. I lit a smoke and leaned back in the armchair. "Good," I said. "So talk."

I could have told the story myself. The pub was some place off Wexford Street, Imelda didn't remember the name: "We were going dancing, me and Mandy and Julie, but Rosie had to be home early—her da was on the warpath—so she didn't want to pay in to the disco. So we said we'd go for a few pints first . . ." Imelda had been up at the bar, getting her round in, when she spotted Shay. She had got chatting to him—I could see her, tossing her hair, jutting one hip, slagging him off. Shay had flirted back automatically, but he liked them prettier and softer and a lot less mouthy, and when his pints arrived he had gathered them up and turned to head back to his mates in their corner.

She had just been trying to keep his attention. *What's wrong, Shay? Is Francis right, yeah, are you more into the fellas?*

Look who's talking, he'd said. *When was the last time that little prick had a girlfriend?* And he had started to move off.

Imelda had said, *That's all you know.*

That had stopped him. *Yeah?*

The lads are waiting on their pints. Go on, off you go.
I'll be back in a sec. You just hang on there.
I might. Or I might not.

Of course she had waited for him. Rosie laughed at her when she dropped the drinks down to them in a rush, and Mandy faked an outraged sniff (*Robbing my fella*), but Imelda gave them the finger and hurried back up to the bar in time to be lounging there, all casual and sipping her glass of lager and one button undone, when Shay got back. Her heart was going ninety. He had never looked twice at her before.

He bent his head close and gave her the intense blue gaze that never let him down, slouched on a bar stool and slid one of his knees in between hers, bought her the next drink and ran a finger over her knuckles when he passed it to her. She spun the story out as long as she could, to keep him with her, but in the end the whole plan was spread out on the bar between them: the suitcase, the meeting place, the boat, the London bedsit, the music-business jobs, the tiny wedding; every secret thing Rosie and I had spent months building up, fragment by fragment, and keeping safe and precious next to our skin. Imelda felt like shite about doing it; she couldn't even stand to look over at Rosie, cracking up laughing with Mandy and Julie over something or other. Twenty-two years later and the color still flamed up in her cheeks when she talked about it. She had done it anyway.

It was such a pathetic little story, a snip of nothing, the kind teenage girls fight over and forget every day. It had led us to this week and this room.

"Tell me," I said. "Did he at least throw you a quick fuck, after all that?"

Imelda wasn't looking at me, but the red patches deepened. "Oh, good. I'd hate to think you went to the hassle of selling me and Rosie down the river, all for nothing. This way, yeah, two people ended up dead and a big bunch of lives ended up getting blown to smithereens, but hey, at least you got the ride you were after."

She said, in a thin stretched voice, "You mean . . . ? Me saying it to Shay. Did that get Rosie killed?"

"You're a fucking genius."

"Francis. Did . . . ?" Imelda shuddered all over, like a spooked horse. "Did Shay . . . ?"

"Did I say that?"

She shook her head.

"Well spotted. Pay attention, Imelda: if you go spreading that shite around, if you say it to even one person, you will regret it for the rest of your life. You've done your best to wreck one of my brothers' name; I'm not having you wreck the other."

"I'll say nothing to anyone. I swear, Francis."

"That includes your daughters. Just in case squealing runs in the family." She flinched. "You never talked to Shay, and I was never here. Have you got me?"

"Yeah. Francis . . . I'm sorry. God, I'm so sorry. I never once thought . . ."

I said, "Look what you did." It was the only thing that would come out of my mouth. "Sweet Jesus, Imelda. Just look what you did." And I left her there, staring at ash and broken glass and nothing.

19

That night lasted a long time. I almost rang my lovely lady friend from the Tech Bureau, but I figured few things can put a damper on a cheerful shag quite like a partner who knows too many details about how your ex died. I thought about going to the pub, but there was no point unless I was planning to get moldy drunk, which struck me as a truly lousy idea. I even thought, a lot, about ringing Olivia and asking if I could come over, but I figured I had probably pushed my luck far enough that week. I ended up at Ned Kelly's on O'Connell Street, playing game after game of back-room pool with three Russian guys who didn't speak much English but who could spot the international signs of a man in need. When Ned's closed up, I went home and sat on my balcony, chain-smoking, till my arse started to freeze, at which point I went inside and watched delusional white boys make rapper hand signs at each other on some reality show until it got light enough that I could eat breakfast. Every few minutes I tried to hit that mental switch hard enough that I wouldn't see Rosie's face, or Kevin's, or Shay's.

It wasn't Kev all grown up I kept seeing; it was the sticky-faced kid who had shared a mattress with me for so long that I could still feel his feet tucked between my shins to keep warm in winter. He had been the prettiest of us by a mile, a chubby blond angel off a cereal ad; Carmel and her mates used to haul him around like a rag doll, changing his clothes and shoving sweets in his mouth and practicing to be mammies someday. He would lie back in their dolly prams with a big happy grin on his face, lapping up the attention. Even at that age, our Kev had loved the ladies. I hoped someone had told his multiple girlfriends, and been gentle about it, why he wouldn't be coming over any more.

And it wasn't Rosie shining with first love and big plans who kept sliding into my mind; it was Rosie angry. An autumn evening when we were seventeen, Carmel and Shay and me smoking on the steps—Carmel smoked back then, and she let me bum off her during school terms, when I wasn't working and couldn't afford my own. The air smelled of peat smoke, mist and Guinness's, and Shay was whistling "Take Me Up to Monto" softly to himself between his teeth. Then the shouting started.

It was Mr. Daly and he was going apeshit. The details got lost, but the gist of it was that he wouldn't be crossed under his own roof and that someone was going to get the back of his hand in a minute if she wasn't careful. My insides turned into one solid lump of ice.

Shay said, "A quid says he caught his missus riding some young fella."

Carmel clicked her tongue. "Don't be filthy."

I said, keeping my voice casual, "You're on." We had been going out for a little over a year, me and Rosie. Our mates knew, but we played it down, to keep the word from spreading too far: just having a laugh, just messing, nothing serious. That felt more like bollix to me every week, but Rosie said her da wouldn't be happy, and she said it like she meant it. Part of me had spent the last year waiting for this evening to kick me in the teeth.

"You haven't got a quid."

"Won't need it."

Windows were sliding open already—the Dalys fought less than just about anyone in the Place, so this was high-quality scandal. Rosie yelled, "You haven't a bleeding clue!"

I got one last drag out of my smoke, down to the filter. "Quid," I said to Shay.

"You'll get it when I get paid."

Rosie flung herself out of Number 3, slammed the door hard enough that the nosy biddies shot back into their lairs to enjoy being shocked in private, and headed our way. Against the gray autumn day, her hair looked like it was about to set the air on fire and blow the whole Place sky-high.

Shay said, "Howya, Rosie. Looking gorgeous as always."

"And you're looking like a bag of spanners, as always. Francis, can I have a word?"

Shay whistled; Carmel's mouth was open. I said, "Yeah, sure," and got up. "We'll go for a walk, will we?" The last thing I heard behind me, as we turned the corner onto Smith's Road, was Shay's dirtiest laugh.

Rosie had her hands jammed deep in the pockets of her jeans jacket and she was walking so fast I could hardly keep up. She said, biting off the words, "My da found out."

I had known that was coming, but my stomach hit my shoes anyway. "Ah, *shite*. I thought that, all right. How?"

"When we were in Neary's. I should've known it wasn't safe: my cousin Shirley and her mates drink there, and she's a mouth on her the size of a church door. The little cow saw us. She told her ma, her ma told my ma, and my ma bleeding well told my da."

"And he went ballistic."

Rosie exploded. "The *bastard*, the bloody bastard, next time I see Shirley I'm going to *splatter* her—he didn't listen to a word I said, might as well have been talking to the *wall—*"

"Rosie, slow *down—*"

"He said not to come crying to him when I wound up pregnant and dumped and covered in bruises, *Jesus*, Frank, I could've killed him, I swear to God—"

"Then what are you doing here? Does he know—?"

Rosie said, "Yeah, he does. He sent me round to break it off with you."

I didn't even realize I had stopped in the middle of the pavement till she turned back to see where I'd gone. "I'm not *doing* it, you big eejit! You seriously think I'd leave you 'cause my da told me to? Are you mental?"

"Christ," I said. My heart slowly slid back down to where it belonged. "Are you trying to give me a heart attack? I thought . . . Christ."

"Francis." She came back to me and laced her fingers through mine, hard enough to hurt. "I'm not. OK? I just don't know what to *do*."

I would have sold a kidney to be able to come out with the magic answer. I went for the most impressive dragon-slaying offer I could think of. "I'll call in and talk to your da. Man to man. I'll tell him there's no way I'd mess you around."

"I already *told* him that. A hundred times. He thinks you're after selling me a load of bollix so you can get into my knickers, and I'm after buying every word. You think he'll listen to you, when he won't to me?"

"So I'll show him. Once he sees I'm treating you right—"

"We don't have *time*! He says I'm to break it off with you tonight or he'll throw me out of the house, and he will, he'll do it. It'd break my mammy's heart, but he wouldn't care. He'll tell her she can't even *see* me again and, God help her, she'll do what she's told."

After seventeen years of my family, my default solution to everything was a tightly zipped lip. I said, "So tell him you did it. Dumped me. Nobody has to know we're still together."

Rosie went motionless, and I saw her mind start to move fast. After a moment she said, "For how long?"

"Till we come up with a better plan, till your da chills out, I don't know. If we just hang in there long enough, something's bound to change."

"Maybe." She was still thinking hard, head bent over our joined hands. "D'you think we could pull it off? The way people talk around here . . ."

I said, "I'm not saying it'd be easy. We'll have to tell everyone we're after breaking up, and make it sound good. We won't be able to go to our debs together. You'll be always worrying that your da'll find out and throw you out."

"I don't give a damn. What about you, though? You don't need to be sneaking around; your da isn't trying to make you into a nun. Is it worth it?"

I said, "What are you on about? I *love* you."

It stunned me. I had never said it before. I knew that I would never say it again, not really; that you only get one shot at it in a lifetime. I got mine out of nowhere on a misty autumn evening, under a street lamp shining yellow streaks on the wet pavement, with Rosie's strong pliable fingers woven through mine.

Rosie's mouth opened. She said, "Oh." It came out on something like a wonderful, helpless, breathless laugh.

"There you go," I said.

She said, "Well, then," in another burst of almost-laughter. "Then it's all OK, isn't it?"

"Is it?"

"Yeah. I love you, too. So we'll find a way. Am I right?"

I was out of words; I couldn't think of anything to do except pull her tight against me. An old fella walking his dog dodged around us and muttered something about shocking carry-on, but I couldn't have moved if I'd wanted to. Rosie pressed her face hard into the angle of my neck; I felt her eyelashes flicker against my skin, and then wetness where they had been. "We will," I said, into her warm hair, and I knew for certain it was true because we were holding the trump card, the wild joker that beat everything else in the pack. "We'll find a way."

We went home, once we had walked and talked ourselves exhausted, to start the careful, crucial process of convincing the Place we were history. Late that night, in spite of the long cunning wait we had planned, we met in Number 16. We were way beyond caring how dangerous the timing was. We lay down together on the creaking floorboards and Rosie wrapped us chest to chest in the soft blue blanket she always brought with her, and that night she never said *Stop*.

That evening was one of the reasons it had never occurred to me that Rosie could be dead. The blaze of her, when she was that angry: you could have lit a match by touching it to her skin, you could have lit up Christmas trees, you could have seen her from space. For all that to have vanished into nothing, gone for good, was unthinkable.

Danny Matches would burn down the bike shop and arrange all the evidence artistically to point straight to Shay, if I asked him nicely. Alternatively, I knew several guys who made Danny look like a cream puff and who would do a beautiful job, complete with whatever level of pain I required, of making sure none of Shay's component parts were ever seen again.

The problem was that I didn't want Danny Matches, or the bolt-gun brigade, or anyone else. Scorcher was right off the menu: if he needed Kevin for his bad guy that much, he could have him—Olivia was right, nothing anyone said could hurt Kev now, and justice had slid way down my Christmas wish list. All I wanted in the world was Shay. Every time I looked out over the Liffey I saw him at his window, somewhere in that tangle of lights, smoking and staring back across the river and waiting for me to come find him. I had never wanted any girl, not even Rosie, as badly as I wanted him.

Friday afternoon I texted Stephen: *Same time, same place.* It was raining, thick sleety rain that soaked through everything you were wearing and chilled you down to the bone; Cosmo's was packed with wet tired people counting shopping bags and hoping if they stayed put long enough they would get warm. This time I only ordered coffee. I already knew this wasn't going to take long.

Stephen looked a little unsure about what we were doing there, but he was too polite to ask. Instead he said, "Kevin's phone records haven't come in yet."

"I didn't think they had. Do you know when the investigation's winding up?"

"We've been told probably Tuesday. Detective Kennedy says . . . well. He figures we've got enough evidence to make a case. From now on, we're just tidying up the paperwork."

I said, "It sounds to me like you've heard about the lovely Imelda Tierney."

"Well. Yeah."

"Detective Kennedy thinks her story is the final piece of the puzzle, perfect fit, now he can wrap everything up in a pretty parcel and tie it with ribbons and present it to the DPP. Am I right?"

"More or less, yeah."

"And what do you think?"

Stephen rubbed at his hair, leaving it standing up in tufts. "I think," he said, "from what Detective Kennedy's said—and tell me if this is wrong—I think Imelda Tierney's well pissed off with you."

"I'm not her favorite person right now, no."

"You know her, even if it's from ages ago. If she was pissed off enough, would she make up something like this?"

"I'd say she'd do it in a heartbeat. Call me biased."

Stephen shook his head. "Maybe I would, only I've still got the same problem with the fingerprints as I had before. Unless Imelda Tierney can explain the note being wiped, it outweighs her story as far as I'm concerned. People lie; evidence doesn't."

The kid was worth ten of Scorcher, and probably of me. I said, "I like the way you think, Detective. Unfortunately, I'm pretty sure Scorcher Kennedy's not going to start thinking the same way anytime soon."

"Not unless we come up with an alternative theory that's too solid for him to ignore." He still put a shy little twist on the "we," like a teenager talking about his first girlfriend. Working with me had been a big deal to him. "So that's what I've been concentrating on. I've spent a lot of time going over this case in my head, looking for what we could've missed, and last night something hit me."

"Yeah? What would that be?"

"OK." Stephen took a deep breath: he had rehearsed this, ready to impress me. "So far, we've none of us paid any attention to the fact that Rose Daly's body was concealed, yeah? We've thought about the implications of *where* it was concealed, but not the fact that it was concealed to start with. And I think that should've told us something. Everyone's agreed that this looks like an unplanned crime, right? Our fella just snapped?"

"That's what it looks like."

"So his head must've been well wrecked once he saw what he'd done. Me, I'd have legged it out of that house as fast as I could go. Instead, our guy got up the willpower to stay put, find a hiding place, stash a heavy body under a heavy concrete slab . . . That took time and effort, loads of it. He *needed* that body hidden. Like, badly. Why? Why not just leave her for someone to find in the morning?"

He'd make a profiler yet. I said, "You tell me."

Stephen was leaning forward across the table, eyes fixed on mine, all wrapped up in the story. "Because he knew someone out there could link him either to Rose or to the house. Has to be. If her body had been found the next day, someone out there would've said, 'Hang on, I saw So-and-so going into Number Sixteen last night,' or 'I think So-and-so was planning on meeting Rose Daly.' He couldn't *afford* to let her be found."

"Sounds about right to me."

"So all we need to do is find that link. We're discounting Imelda's story, but someone out there has another story a lot like that one, only true.

Probably they've forgotten all about it, since they never realized it was important, but if we can just jog their memory . . . I'd start by talking to the people who were closest to Rose—her sister, her best friends—and the people who used to live on the even-numbered side of Faithful Place. Your statement says you heard someone going through those gardens; he could have been seen out a back window."

A few more days working along these lines and he was going to get somewhere. He looked so hopeful, I hated to smack the poor little bastard down—it was like kicking a half-grown retriever who had brought me his best chew toy—but it needed doing. I said, "Good thinking, Detective. That all hangs together very nicely. Now leave it."

Blank stare. "What . . . ? What d'you mean, like?"

"Stephen. Why do you think I texted you today? I knew you wouldn't have the phone records for me, I already knew about Imelda Tierney, I was pretty sure you would've been in touch if something momentous had happened. Why did you think I wanted to meet up?"

"I just figured . . . updates."

"You could call it that. Here's the update: from now on, we're leaving this case to its own devices. I'm back on my holidays, and you're back on typist duty. Enjoy."

Stephen's coffee cup went down with a flat bang. "What? *Why?*"

"Did your mother ever tell you, 'Because I said so'?"

"You're not my mother. What the *hell*—" Then he stopped in midsentence as the lightbulb went on. "You've found out something," he said, "haven't you? Last time, when you legged it out of here: something had hit you. You chased it for a couple of days, and now—"

I shook my head. "Another cute theory, but no. I'd have loved this case to solve itself in a blinding flash of inspiration, but I hate to break it to you: they just don't do that as often as you'd think."

"—and now that you've got it, you're keeping it to yourself. Bye-bye, Stephen, thanks for playing, now get back in your box. I suppose I should be flattered that you're worried about me catching up, should I?"

I sighed, leaned back in my chair and kneaded at the back of my neck. "Kid. If you don't mind hearing one little piece of advice from someone who's been doing this job a lot longer than you have, let me share this secret with you: with almost no exceptions, the simplest explanation is the right one. There's no cover-up, there's no big conspiracy, and the government has not planted a chip behind your ear. The only thing I found out, over the last couple of days, is that it's time for you and me to let this case go."

Stephen was staring at me like I had grown an extra head. "Hang on a minute here. What happened to us having a *responsibility* to the victims? What happened to 'It's just you and me, we're all they've got'?"

I said, "It got pointless, kid. That's what happened. Scorcher Kennedy's right: he's got a beauty of a case. If I were the DPP, I'd give him the go-ahead in a heartbeat. There's no way in hell he's going to ditch his whole theory and start from scratch even if the Angel Gabriel comes down from heaven to tell him he's got it wrong, never mind because something a little funny shows up on Kevin's phone records or because you and I think Imelda's story smells icky. It doesn't matter what happens between now and Tuesday: this case is over."

"And you're OK with that?"

"No, sunshine, I'm not. I'm not one little bit OK with it. But I'm a grown-up. If I'm going to throw myself in front of a bullet, it's going to be for something where that might possibly make a difference. I don't do lost causes, no matter how romantic, because they're a waste. Just like it would be a waste for you to get reverted to uniform and booted to a backwoods desk job for the rest of your career because you got caught leaking useless info to me."

The kid had a redhead's temper: one fist was clenched on the table, and he looked like he was just about ready to plant it in my face. "That's my decision. I'm a big boy; I'm well able to look after myself."

I laughed. "Don't fool yourself: I'm not trying to protect you. I would happily get you to keep putting your career on the line through 2012, never mind through next Tuesday, if I thought for one second it would do any good. But it wouldn't."

"*You* wanted me to get involved here, you practically *shoved* me into it, and now I'm involved and I'm staying that way. You don't get to keep changing your mind every few days: Fetch the stick, Stephen, drop the stick, Stephen, fetch the stick, Stephen . . . I'm not your bitch, any more than I'm Detective Kennedy's."

"Actually," I said, "you are. I'm going to be keeping an eye on you, Stevie my friend, and if I get just one hint that you're still poking your nose where it doesn't belong, I'm going to take that post-mortem report and that fingerprint report to Detective Kennedy and tell him where I got them. Then you'll be in his bad books, you'll be in my bad books, and more than likely you'll be at that desk in the arsehole of nowhere. So I'm telling you one more time: back off. Do you get that?"

Stephen was too stunned and too young to keep his face under control; he was staring at me with a naked, blazing mix of fury, amazement and disgust. This was exactly what I was aiming for—the snottier he got with me, the further he would be from the various forms of nasty that were coming up—but somehow it still stung. "Man," he said, shaking his head, "I don't get you. I really don't."

I said, "Ain't that the truth," and started fishing for my wallet.

"And I don't need you buying me coffee. I can pay my own way."

If I kicked him in the ego too hard, he might keep chasing the case just to prove to himself that he still had a pair. "Your choice," I said. "And, Stephen?" He kept his head down, rummaging in his pockets. "Detective. I'm going to need you to look at me." I waited till he cracked and reluctantly met my eyes before I said, "You've done some excellent work here. I know this isn't how either of us wanted it to end, but all I can tell you is that I'm not going to forget it. When there's something I can do for you—and there will be—I'm going to be all over it."

"Like I said. I can pay my own way."

"I know you can, but I like paying my debts too, and I owe you. It's been a pleasure working with you, Detective. I look forward to doing it again."

I didn't try to shake hands. Stephen shot me a dark look that gave away nothing, slapped a tenner onto the table—which counted as a serious gesture, from someone on newbie wages—and shrugged on his coat. I stayed where I was and let him be the one who walked away.

And there I was, back where I had been just a week before, parking in front of Liv's place to pick Holly up for the weekend. It felt like it had been years.

Olivia was wearing a discreet caramel-colored number instead of last week's discreet little black dress, but the message was the same: Dermo the Pseudo-Pedo was on his way, and he was in with a chance. This time, though, instead of barricading the door, she opened it wide and drew me quickly into the kitchen. Back when we were married, I used to dread Liv's "We need to talk" signals, but at this stage I actually welcomed them. They beat her "I've got nothing to say to you" routine, hands down.

I said, "Holly not ready, no?"

"She's in the bath. It was bring-a-friend day at Sarah's hip-hop class; she just got home, all sweaty. She'll be a few minutes."

"How's she doing?"

Olivia sighed, ran a hand lightly over her immaculate hairdo. "I think she's all right. As all right as we could expect, anyway. She had a nightmare last night, and she's been quiet, but she doesn't seem . . . I don't know. She loved the hip-hop class."

I said, "Is she eating?" When I moved out, Holly went on hunger strike for a while.

"Yes. But she's not five any more; she's not always as obvious about her feelings, these days. That doesn't mean they're not there. Would you try talking to her? Maybe you can get a better sense of how she's coping."

"So she's keeping stuff to herself," I said, nowhere near as nastily as I could have. "I wonder where she got that idea."

The corners of Olivia's lips tightened up. "I made a mistake. A bad one. I've admitted that, and apologized for it, and I'm doing my utmost to fix the damage. Believe me: there's nothing you can say that would make me feel any worse about hurting her."

I pulled out one of the bar stools and parked my arse heavily—not to piss Olivia off, this time, just because I was wrecked enough that even a two-minute sit-down in a room that smelled of toast and strawberry jam felt like a big treat. "People hurt each other. That's how it works. At least you were trying to do something good. Not everyone can say that much."

The tightness had spread down to Liv's shoulders. She said, "People don't necessarily hurt each other."

"Yes, Liv, they do. Parents, lovers, brothers and sisters, you name it. The closer you get, the more damage you do."

"Well, sometimes, yes. Of course. But talking like it's some unavoidable law of nature— That's a cop-out, Frank, and you know it."

"Let me pour you a nice cold refreshing glass of reality. Most people are only too delighted to wreck each other's heads. And for the tiny minority who do their pathetic best not to, this world is going to go right ahead and make sure they do it anyway."

"Sometimes," Olivia said coldly, "I really wish you could hear yourself. You sound like a teenager, do you realize that? A self-pitying teenager with too many Morrissey albums."

It was an exit line, her hand was on the door handle, and I didn't want her walking out. I wanted her to stay in the warm kitchen and bicker with me. I said, "I'm only speaking from experience here. Maybe there are people out there who never do anything more destructive than make each other cups of hot cocoa with marshmallows, but I've never personally encountered them. If you have, by all means enlighten me. I've got an open mind. Name one relationship you've seen, just one, that didn't do damage."

I may not be able to make Olivia do anything else I want, but I've always been wonderful at making her argue. She let go of the door handle, leaned back against the wall and folded her arms. "All right," she said. "Fine. This girl Rose. Tell me: how did she ever hurt you? Not the person who killed her. She herself. Rose."

And the other half of me and Liv is that, in the end, I always bite off more than I can chew. I said, "I think I've had more than enough talk about Rose Daly for one week, if that's OK with you."

Liv said, "She didn't leave you, Frank. It never happened. Sooner or later, you're going to have to come to terms with that."

"Let me guess. Jackie and her big mouth?"

"I didn't need Jackie to tell me that some woman had hurt you, or at least that you believed she had. I've known that practically ever since we met."

"I hate to burst your bubble here, Liv, but your telepathy skills aren't at their finest today. Better luck next time."

"And I didn't need telepathy, either. Ask any woman you've ever had a relationship with: I guarantee she knew she was second best. A placeholder, till the one you actually wanted came home."

She started to say something else, but then she bit it back. Her eyes were apprehensive, almost stunned, like she had just realized how deep the water was around here.

I said, "Go ahead and get it off your chest. You've started, you might as well finish."

After a moment Liv made a tiny movement like a shrug. "All right. That was one of the reasons why I asked you to move out."

I laughed out loud. "Oh. Right. OK, then. So all those endless bloody fights about work and me not being around enough, those were what, a diversion? Just to keep me guessing?"

"You know that's not what I said. And you know perfectly well that I had every reason to be sick to *death* of never being sure whether 'See you at eight' meant tonight or next Tuesday, or of asking you what you did today and being told 'Work,' or—"

"All I know is that I should've got it written into the settlement that I never needed to have this conversation again. And what Rose Daly has to do with anything—"

Olivia was keeping her voice even, but the undercurrent was powerful enough that it could have thrown me off my bar stool. "She had plenty to do with it. I always knew all the rest of it was tied up with the fact that I wasn't this other woman, whoever she was. If she had rung you at three in the morning to see why you weren't home, you would have picked up the bloody phone. Or, more likely, you would have *been* home to begin with."

"If Rosie had rung me at three in the morning, I'd have made millions from my hotline to the afterlife and moved to Barbados."

"You know exactly what I mean. You would never, *ever* have treated her the way you treated me. Sometimes, Frank, sometimes it felt like you were shutting me out specifically to punish me for whatever she had done, or just for not being her. *Trying* to make me leave you, so that when she came back, she wouldn't find someone else in her place. That's what it felt like."

I said, "I'm going to try this one more time: you dumped me because you wanted to. I'm not saying it came as a huge surprise, and I'm not even saying I didn't deserve it. But I *am* saying that Rose Daly, especially given the fact that you didn't know she had ever existed, had sweet fuck-all to do with it."

"Yes she did, Frank. Yes she did. You went into our marriage taking it for granted, beyond any doubt, that it wasn't going to last. It took me a long time to realize that. But once I worked it out, there didn't seem to be much point any more."

She looked so lovely, and so tired. Her skin was starting to turn worn and fragile, and the sickly kitchen light picked out crow's-feet around her eyes. I thought of Rosie, round and firm and bloomed like ripe peaches, and how she never got the chance to be any other kind of lovely except perfect. I hoped Dermot realized just how beautiful Olivia's wrinkles were.

All I had wanted was a cozy little spat with her. Somewhere on the horizon, building momentum, was a fight that would make the worst Olivia and I had ever done to each other vanish into a little puff of harmless fluffy nothing. Every particle of anger I could generate was being sucked away into that huge vortex; I couldn't take the thought of a full-on deep and meaningful fight with Liv. "Look," I said. "Let me go up and get Holly. If we stay here, I'm just going to keep being a narky bastard until this turns into a massive row and I put you in a bad mood and ruin your date. I already did that last week; I don't want to get predictable."

Olivia laughed, a startled, explosive breath. "Surprise," I said. "I'm not a complete prick."

"I know that. I never thought you were." I shot her a skeptical eyebrow and started hauling myself off the bar stool, but she stopped me. "I'll get her. She won't want you knocking while she's in the bath."

"What? Since when?"

A tiny smile, half rueful, moved across Olivia's lips. "She's growing up, Frank. She won't even let me into the bathroom till she has her clothes on; a few weeks ago I opened the door to get something, and she let out a yell like a banshee and then gave me a furious lecture on people needing privacy. If you go anywhere near her, I guarantee she'll read you the riot act."

"My God," I said. I remembered Holly two years old and leaping on me straight from her bath, naked as the day she was born, showering water everywhere and giggling like a mad thing when I tickled her delicate ribs. "Go up and get her quick, before she grows armpit hair or something."

Liv almost laughed again. I used to make her laugh all the time; these days, twice in one night would have been some kind of record. "I'll only be a moment."

"Take your time. I've got nowhere better to be."

On her way out of the kitchen she said, almost reluctantly, "The coffee machine's on, if you need a cup. You look tired."

And she pulled the door shut behind her, with a firm little click that told me to stay put, just in case Dermo arrived and I decided to meet him at the front door in my boxers. I detached myself from the stool and made myself a double espresso. I was well aware that Liv had all kinds of interesting points, several of them important and a couple of them deeply ironic. All of them could wait until I had figured out what in the dark vicious world to do about Shay, and then done it.

Upstairs I could hear bathtub water draining and Holly chattering away, with the occasional comment from Olivia. I wanted, so suddenly and hard it almost knocked me over, to run up there and wrap my arms around the pair of them, tumble the whole three of us into Liv's and my double bed the way I used to on Sunday afternoons, stay there shushing and laughing while Dermo rang the doorbell and worked himself into a chinless huff and Audi'd off into the sunset, order avalanches of takeaway food and stay there all weekend and deep into next week. For a second I almost lost my mind and gave it a try.

It took Holly a while to bring the conversation around to current events. Over dinner she told me about the hip-hop class, with full demonstrations and plenty of out-of-breath commentary; afterwards she got a start on her homework, with a lot less complaining than usual, and then curled up tight against me on the sofa to watch Hannah Montana. She was sucking on a strand of hair, which she hadn't done in a while, and I could feel her thinking.

I didn't push her. It wasn't until she was tucked up in bed, with my arm around her and her hot milk all drunk and her bedtime story read, that she said, "Daddy."

"What's on your mind?"

"Are you going to get married?"

What the hell? "No, sweetie. Not a chance. Being married to your mammy was plenty for me. What put that into your head?"

"Do you have a girlfriend?"

Ma, it had to be; probably something about divorce and no remarrying in the Church. "Nope. I told you that last week, remember?"

Holly thought that over. "That girl Rosie who died," she said. "The one you knew before I was born."

"What about her?"

"Was she your girlfriend?"

"Yep, she was. I hadn't met your mammy yet."

"Were you going to marry her?"

"That was the plan, yeah."

Blink. Her eyebrows, fine as brushstrokes, were pulled tight together; she was still concentrating hard. "Why didn't you?"

"Rosie died before we could get that far."

"But you said you didn't even know she died, till now."

"That's right. I thought she'd dumped me."

"Why didn't you know?"

I said, "One day she just disappeared. She left behind a note saying she was moving to England, and I found it and figured it meant she was dumping me. It turns out I had that wrong."

Holly said, "Daddy."

"Yep."

"Did somebody kill her?"

She was wearing her flowery pink-and-white pajamas that I had ironed for her earlier—Holly loves fresh-ironed clothes—and she had Clara perched on her pulled-up knees. In the soft golden halo from the bedside lamp she looked perfect and timeless as a little watercolor girl in a storybook. She terrified me. I would have given a limb to know that I was doing this conversation right, or even just that I wasn't doing it too horrifically wrong.

I said, "It looks like that could have been what happened. It was a long, long time ago, so it's hard to be sure about anything."

Holly gazed into Clara's eyes and thought about that. The strand of hair had found its way back into her mouth. "If I disappeared," she said. "Would you think I had run away?"

Olivia had mentioned a nightmare. I said, "It wouldn't matter what I thought. Even if I thought you'd hopped on a spaceship to another planet, I'd come looking for you, and I wouldn't stop till I found you."

Holly let out a deep sigh, and I felt her shoulder nudge in closer against me. For a second I thought I had accidentally managed to fix something. Then she said, "If you had married that girl Rosie. Would I never have been born?"

I detached the strand from her mouth and smoothed it into place. Her hair smelled of baby shampoo. "I don't know how that stuff works, chickadee. It's all very mysterious. All I know is that you're you, and personally I think you'd have found a way to be you no matter what I did."

Holly wriggled farther down in the bed. She said, in her ready-for-an-argument voice, "Sunday afternoon I want to go to Nana's."

And I could make chirpy chitchat with Shay across the good teacups. "Well," I said, carefully. "We can have a think about that, see if it'll fit with the rest of our plans. Any special reason?"

"Donna always gets to go over on Sundays, after her dad has his golf game. She says Nana makes a lovely dinner with apple tart and ice cream after, and sometimes Auntie Jackie does the girls' hair all fancy, or sometimes everyone watches a DVD—Donna and Darren and Ashley and Louise get to take turns picking, but Auntie Carmel said if I was ever there I could have first pick. I never got to go because you didn't know about me going over to Nana's, but now that you do, I want to."

I wondered if Ma and Da had signed some kind of treaty about Sunday afternoons, or if she just crushed a few happy pills into his lunch and then locked him in the bedroom with his floorboard naggin for company. "We'll see how we get on."

"One time Uncle Shay brought them all to the bike shop and let them try the bikes. And sometimes Uncle Kevin brings over his Wii and he has spare controllers, and Nana gives out because they jump around too much and she says they'll have the house down."

I tilted my head to get a proper look at Holly. She had Clara hugged a little too tight, but her face didn't tell me anything. "Sweetheart," I said. "You know Uncle Kevin won't be there this Sunday, right?"

Holly's head went down over Clara. "Yeah. Because he died."

"That's right, love."

A quick glance at me. "Sometimes I forget. Like Sarah told me a joke today and I was going to tell him, only then after a while I remembered."

"I know. That happens to me, too. It's just your head getting used to things. It'll stop in a while."

She nodded, combing Clara's mane with her fingers. I said, "And you know everyone over at Nana's is going to be pretty upset this weekend, right? It won't be fun, like the times Donna's told you about."

"I *know* that. I want to go because I just want to *be* there."

"OK, chickadee. We'll see what we can do."

Silence. Holly put a plait in Clara's mane and examined it carefully. Then: "Daddy."

"Yep."

"When I think about Uncle Kevin. Sometimes I don't cry."

"That's OK, sweetie. Nothing wrong with that. I don't either."

"If I cared about him, amn't I supposed to cry?"

I said, "I don't think there are any rules for how you're supposed to act when someone you care about dies, sweetheart. I think you just have to figure it out as you go along. Sometimes you'll feel like crying, sometimes you won't, sometimes you'll be raging at him for dying on you. You just have to remember that all of those are OK. So is whatever else your head comes up with."

"On *American Idol* they always cry when they talk about someone who died."

"Sure, but you've got to take that stuff with a grain of salt, sweetie. It's telly."

Holly shook her head hard, hair whipping her cheeks. "Daddy, *no*, it's not like films, it's real *people*. They tell you all their stories, like say if their granny was lovely and believed in them and then she died, and they always cry. Sometimes Paula cries too."

"I bet she does. That doesn't mean you're *supposed* to, though. Everyone's different. And I'll tell you a secret: a lot of the time those people are putting it on, so they'll get the votes."

Holly still looked unconvinced. I remembered the first time I saw death in action: I was seven, some fifth cousin up on New Street had had a heart attack, and Ma brought the bunch of us to the wake. It went along much the same lines as Kevin's: tears, laughs, stories, great towering piles of sandwiches, drinking and singing and dancing till all hours of the night—someone had brought an accordion, someone else had a full repertoire of Mario Lanza. As a beginner's guide to coping with bereavement, it had been a hell of a lot healthier than anything involving Paula Abdul. It occurred to me to wonder, even taking into account Da's contribution to the festivities, whether just possibly I should have brought Holly along to Kevin's wake.

The idea of being in a room with Shay and not being able to beat him to splintered bloody pulp made me light-headed. I thought about being a teenage ape-boy and growing up in great dizzying leaps because Rosie needed me to, and about Da telling me that a man should know what he would die for. You do what your woman or your kid needs, even when it feels a lot harder than dying.

"Tell you what," I said. "Sunday afternoon, we'll go along to your nana's, even if it's only for a little while. There'll be a fair bit of talk about your uncle Kevin, but I guarantee you everyone will deal with that their own way: they won't all spend the whole time in tears, and they won't think you're doing anything wrong if you don't do any crying at all. Think that might help you sort your head out?"

That perked Holly up. She was even looking at me, instead of at Clara. "Yeah. Probably."

"Well, then," I said. Something like ice water ran down my spine, but I was just going to have to put up with that like a big boy. "I guess that's a plan."

"Seriously? For definite?"

"Yeah. I'll go ring your auntie Jackie right now, tell her to let your nana know we'll be there."

Holly said, "Good," on another deep sigh. This time I felt her shoulders relax.

"And meanwhile, I bet everything would look brighter if you got a good night's sleep. Bedtime."

She wriggled down onto her back and stashed Clara under her chin. "Tuck me in."

I tucked the duvet around her, just tight enough. "And no nightmares tonight, OK, chickadee? Only sweet dreams allowed. That's an order."

"OK." Her eyes were already closing, and her fingers, curled in Clara's mane, were starting to loosen. "Night-night, Daddy."

"Night-night, sweetie."

Way before then, I should have spotted it. I had spent almost fifteen years keeping myself and my boys and girls alive by never, ever missing the signs: the sharp burnt-paper smell in the air when you walk into a room, the raw animal edge to a voice in a casual phone call. It was bad enough I had somehow missed them in Kevin; I should never, in a million years, have missed them in Holly. I should have seen it flickering like heat lightning around the stuffed toys, filling up that cozy little bedroom like poison gas: danger.

Instead I eased myself off the bed, switched off the lamp and moved Holly's bag so it wouldn't block the night-light. She lifted her face towards me and murmured something; I leaned over to kiss her forehead, and she snuggled deeper into the duvet and let out a contented little breath. I took a long look at her, pale hair swirled on the pillow and lashes throwing spiky shadows onto her cheeks, and then I moved softly out of the room and closed the door behind me.

20

Every cop who's been undercover knows there's nothing in the world quite like the day before you go into a job. I figure astronauts on countdown know the feeling, and parachute regiments lining up for the jump. The light turns dazzling and unbreakable as diamonds, every face you see is beautiful enough to take your breath away; your mind is crystal clear, every second spreads itself out in front of you in one great smooth landscape, things that have baffled you for months suddenly make perfect sense. You could drink all day and be stone-cold sober; cryptic crosswords are easy as kids' jigsaws. That day lasts a hundred years.

It had been a long time since I'd been under, but I recognized the feeling the second I woke up on Saturday morning. I spotted it in the sway of the shadows on my bedroom ceiling and tasted it at the bottom of my coffee. Slowly and surely, while Holly and I flew her kite in the Phoenix Park and while I helped her with her English homework and while we cooked ourselves too much macaroni with too much cheese, things clicked into place in my mind. By early Sunday afternoon, when the two of us got into my car and headed across the river, I knew what I was going to do.

Faithful Place looked tidy and innocent as something out of a dream, filled to the brim with a clear lemony light floating over the cracked cobbles. Holly's hand tightened around mine. "What's up, chickadee?" I asked. "Changed your mind?"

She shook her head. I said, "You can if you want, you know. Just say the word and we'll go find ourselves a nice DVD full of fairy princesses and a bucket of popcorn bigger than your head."

No giggle; she didn't even look up at me. Instead she hoisted her backpack more firmly onto her shoulders and tugged at my hand, and we stepped off the curb into that strange pale-gold light.

Ma went all out, trying to get that afternoon right. She had baked herself into a frenzy—every surface was piled with gingerbread squares and jam tarts—assembled the troops bright and early, and sent Shay and Trevor and Gavin out to buy a Christmas tree that was several feet too wide for the front room. When Holly and I arrived, Bing was on the radio, Carmel's kids were arranged prettily around the tree hanging ornaments, everyone had a steaming mug of cocoa and even Da had been installed on the sofa with a blanket over his knees, looking patriarchal and a lot like sober. It was like walking into an ad from the 1950s. The whole grotesque charade was obviously doomed—everyone looked wretched, and Darren was getting a wall-eyed stare that told me he was inches from exploding—but I understood what Ma was trying to do. It would have gone to my heart, if only she had been able to resist taking a quick sidestep into her usual MO and telling me that I was after getting awful wrinkly around the eyes and I'd have a face like tripe on me in no time.

The one I couldn't take my eyes off was Shay. He looked like he was running a low-grade fever: restless and high-colored, with new hollows under his cheekbones and a dangerous glitter in his eyes. What caught my attention, though, was what he was doing. He was sprawled in an armchair, jiggling one knee hard and having a fast-paced, in-depth conversation about golf with Trevor. People do change, but as far as I knew, Shay despised golf only marginally less than he despised Trevor. The only reason he would voluntarily get tangled up with both at once was out of desperation. Shay—and I felt this counted as useful information—was in bad shape.

We worked our way grimly through Ma's full ornament stash—never come between a mammy and her ornaments. I managed to ask Holly privately, under cover of "Santa Baby," "You having an OK time?"

She said, valiantly, "Amazing," and ducked back into the clump of cousins before I could ask any more questions. The kid picked up the native customs fast. I started mentally rehearsing the debriefing session.

Once Ma was satisfied that the tack alert level had reached Orange, Gavin and Trevor brought the kids down to Smithfield to see the Christmas Village. "Walk off that gingerbread," Gavin explained, patting his stomach.

"There was nothing wrong with that gingerbread," Ma snapped. "If you're after getting fat, Gavin Keogh, it's not my cooking that done it." Gav mumbled something and shot Jackie an agonized look. He was being tactful, in a large hairy way: trying to give us some family togetherness time, at this difficult moment. Carmel bundled the kids into coats and scarves and woolly hats—Holly went right into the lineup between Donna and Ashley, like she was one of Carmel's own—and off they went. I watched from the front-room window as the gaggle of them headed down the street. Holly, arm-linked with Donna so tight they looked like Siamese twins, didn't look up to wave.

Family time didn't work out quite the way Gav had planned: we all slumped in front of the telly, not talking, until Ma recovered from the ornament blitzkrieg and dragged Carmel into the kitchen to do things with baked goods and plastic wrap. I said quietly to Jackie, before she could get nabbed, "Come for a smoke."

She gave me a wary look, like a kid who knows she's earned a clatter when her ma gets her alone. I said, "Take it like a woman, babe. The sooner you get it over with . . ."

Outside it was cold and clear and still, the sky over the rooftops just deepening from thin blue-white to lilac. Jackie thumped down in her spot at the bottom of the steps, in a tangle of long legs and purple patent-leather boots, and held out a hand. "Give us a smoke, before you start giving out. Gav's after taking ours with him."

"So tell me," I said pleasantly, once I had lit her smoke and one for myself. "What the fuck were you and Olivia thinking?"

Jackie's chin was arranged all ready for an argument, and for a disturbing second she was the spitting image of Holly. "I thought it'd be great for Holly to get to know this lot. I'd say Olivia thought the same. And we weren't wrong there, were we? Did you see her with Donna?"

"Yeah, I did. They're cute together. I also saw her bleeding devastated over Kevin. Crying so hard she could barely breathe. That was less cute."

Jackie watched the curls of smoke from her cigarette spread out over the steps. She said, "So are all of us in bits. Ashley is as well, and she's only six. That's life, sure. You were worried Holly wasn't getting enough real stuff, were you not? I'd say this is as real as it gets."

Which was probably true, but being right is beside the point when it's Holly on the line. I said, "If my kid needs an extra dose of reality here and there, babe, I generally prefer to make that call myself. Or at least to be notified before someone else makes it for me. Does that sound unreasonable to you?"

Jackie said, "I should've told you. There's no excuse for that."

"Then why didn't you?"

"I was always meaning to, honest to God, but . . . At first I figured there was no point in getting you all bothered, when it mightn't even work out. I thought I'd just try bringing Holly the once, and then we could tell you after—"

"And I'd realize what a wonderful idea it was, I'd come running home with a big bunch of flowers for Ma in one hand and another one for you in the other, and we'd all throw a big party and live happily ever after. Was that the plan?"

She shrugged. Her shoulders were starting to ratchet up around her ears.

"Because God knows that would have been slimy enough, but it would've been a hell of a lot better than this. What changed your mind? For, and I have to pick up my jaw off the floor before I can say this, an entire *year*?"

Jackie still wouldn't look at me. She shifted on the step, like it was hurting her. "Don't be laughing at me, now."

"Believe me, Jackie. I'm not in a giggly mood."

She said, "I was frightened. All right? That's why I said nothing."

It took me a moment to be sure she wasn't yanking my chain. "Oh, come *on*. What the fuck did you think I was going to do? Beat the shite out of you?"

"I didn't say—"

"Then what? You can't drop a bleeding bombshell like that and then go all coy. When have I ever in my *life* given you *any* reason to be scared of me?"

"Look at you now, sure! The face on you, and talking like you hate my guts— I don't like people giving out and shouting and going ballistic. I never have. You know that."

I said, before I could stop myself, "You make me sound like Da."

"Ah, no. No, Francis. You know I didn't mean that."

"You'd better not. Don't go down that road, Jackie."

"I'm *not*. I just . . . I hadn't the nerve to tell you. And that's my own fault, not yours. I'm sorry. Really, really sorry, like."

Above us, a window slammed open and Ma's head popped out. "Jacinta Mackey! Are you going to sit there like the queen of Sheba waiting for me and your sister to put your supper in front of you on a gold plate, are you?"

I called up, "It's my fault, Ma. I dragged her out for a chat. We'll do the washing up after, how's that?"

"Hmf. Coming back here like he owns the place, giving orders all round him, with his silver polishing and his washing up and butter wouldn't melt in his mouth . . ." But she didn't want to give me too much hassle, in case I grabbed Holly and left. She pulled her head back in, even though I could hear her giving out steadily till the window banged down.

The Place was starting to switch on the lights for the evening. We weren't the only ones who had hit the Christmas decorations hard; the Hearnes' looked like someone had fired Santa's grotto at it out of a bazooka, tinsel and reindeer and flashing lights hanging off the ceiling, manic elves and gooey-eyed angels splattered across every visible inch of wall, "HAPPY XMAS" on the window in spray-on snow. Even the yuppies had put up a tasteful stylized tree in blond wood, complete with three Swedish-looking ornaments.

I thought about coming back to this same spot every Sunday evening, watching the Place move through the familiar rhythms of its year. Spring, and the First Communion kids running from house to house, showing off their outfits and comparing their hauls; summer wind, ice-cream vans jingling and all the girls letting their cleavage out to play; admiring the Hearnes' new reindeer this time next year, and the year after that. The thought made me mildly dizzy, like I was half drunk or fighting a heavy dose of the flu. Presumably Ma would find something new to give out about every week.

"Francis," Jackie said, tentatively. "Are we all right?"

I had had a first-class rant all planned out, but the thought of belonging here again had dissolved the momentum right out of me. First Olivia and now this: I was getting soft in my old age. "Yeah," I said. "We're OK. But when you have kids, I'm buying every one of them a drum kit and a St. Bernard puppy."

Jackie shot me a quick wary look—she hadn't been expecting to get off that easy—but she decided not to look a gift horse in the mouth. "Away you go. When I throw them out of the house, I'll give them your address."

Behind us, the hall door opened: Shay and Carmel. I had been placing mental bets with myself on how long Shay would be able to go without conversation, not to mention nicotine. "What were yous talking about?" he inquired, dropping into his spot at the top of the steps.

Jackie said, "Holly."

I said, "I was giving Jackie hassle for bringing her round here without telling me."

Carmel plumped down above me. "Oof! Janey, these are getting harder, only that I'm well padded I'd've done myself an injury there . . . Now, Francis, don't be giving out to Jackie. She was only going to bring Holly the once, just to meet us, like, but we were all so mad about her we made Jackie bring her back. That child's a little dote, so she is. You should be dead proud of her."

I got my back against the railings, so I could keep an eye on everyone at once, and stretched out my legs along the step. "I am."

Shay said, feeling for his smokes, "And our company hasn't even turned her into an animal. Mad, isn't it?"

I said sweetly, "I'm sure it's not for lack of trying."

Carmel said, with a tentative sideways look that made it into a question, "Donna's petrified she'll never see Holly again."

I said, "No reason why she shouldn't."

"Francis! Are you serious?"

"Course. I've got better sense than to come between nine-year-old girls."

"Ah, that's brilliant. The two of them are great mates, so they are; Donna would've been only heartbroken. Does that mean . . . ?" A clumsy little rub at her nose; I remembered the gesture, from a million years ago. "Will you be coming back as well, like? Or just letting Jackie bring Holly?"

I said, "I'm here, amn't I?"

"Ah, yeah. And it's lovely seeing you. But are you . . . ? You know. Are you home now?"

I smiled up at her. "Lovely seeing you too, Melly. Yeah, I'll be around."

"Jaysus, Mary and Joseph, and about bleedin' time," Jackie said, rolling her eyes. "Could you not have decided on that fifteen years ago, saved me a load of hassle?"

"Ah, deadly," Carmel said. "That's only deadly, Francis. I thought . . ." That embarrassed little swipe again. "Maybe I was being a drama queen, sure. I thought as soon as everything was sorted, you'd be gone again. For good, like."

I said, "That was the plan, yeah. But I've got to admit it: tearing myself away turned out harder than I expected. I guess, like you said, it's good to be home."

Shay's eyes were on me, that intent expressionless blue stare. I gave it right back and threw in a big old smile. I was just fine with Shay getting edgy. Not wildly edgy, not yet; just a shimmering extra thread of unease, running through what had to be a pretty uncomfortable evening already. All I wanted for now was to plant the tiny seed of realization, somewhere deep in his mind: this was just the beginning.

Stephen was out of my hair and Scorcher was getting there fast. Once they moved on to the next case on their list, it would be just me and Shay, forever and ever. I could spend a year bouncing him like a yo-yo before I let him be sure that I knew, another year hinting at my various interesting options. I had all the time in the world.

Shay, on the other hand, not so much. You don't have to like your family, you don't even have to spend time with them, to know them right down to the bone. Shay had started out high-strung, spent his whole life in a context that would have turned the Dalai Lama into a gibbering wreck, and done things that wrap years' worth of nightmares around your brain stem. There was no way he was more than a short stroll from a breakdown. Plenty of people have told me—and several of them even meant it as a compliment—that I have a God-given talent for fucking with people's minds; and what you can do to strangers is nothing compared to what you can do to your very own family. I was pretty near positive that, given time and dedication, I could make Shay put a noose around his neck, tie the other end to the banisters of Number 16, and go diving.

Shay had his head tilted back, eyes narrowed, watching the Hearnes move around Santa's workshop. He said, to me, "It sounds like you're settling back in already."

"Does it, yeah?"

"I heard you were round Imelda Tierney's the other day."

"I've got friends in high places. Just like you do, apparently."

"What were you looking for off Imelda? The chat or the ride?"

"Ah, now, Shay, give me some credit. Some of us have better taste than that, you know what I mean?" I threw Shay a wink and watched the sharp flash in his eye as he started to wonder.

"Stop that, you," Jackie told me. "Don't be passing remarks. You're not Brad Pitt yourself, in case no one's told you."

"Have you seen Imelda lately? She was no prize back in the day, but my Jaysus, the state of her now."

"A mate of mine did her once," Shay said. "A couple of years back. He told me he got the knickers off her and, honest to God, it was like looking at ZZ Top shot in the face."

I started to laugh and Jackie went off into a barrage of high-pitched outrage, but Carmel didn't join in. I didn't think she'd even heard the last part of the conversation. She was pleating her skirt between her fingers, staring down at it like she was in a trance. I said, "You all right, Melly?"

She looked up with a start. "Ah, yeah. I suppose. It just . . . Sure, yous know yourselves. It feels mad. Doesn't it?"

I said, "It does, all right."

"I keep thinking I'll look up and he'll be there; Kevin will. Just there, like, below Shay. Every time I don't see him, I almost ask where he is. Do yous not do the same?"

I reached up a hand and gave hers a squeeze. Shay said, with a sudden flick of savagery, "The thick bastard."

"What are you bleeding on about?" Jackie demanded. Shay shook his head and drew on his smoke.

I said, "I'd love to know the same thing."

Carmel said, "He didn't mean anything by it. Sure you didn't, Shay?"

"Figure it out for yourselves."

I said, "Why don't you pretend we're thick too, and spell it out for us."

"Who says I'd have to pretend?"

Carmel started to cry. Shay said—not unkindly, but like he'd said it a few hundred times this week—"Ah, now, Melly. Come on."

"I can't help it. Could we not be good to each other, just this once? After everything that's happened? Our poor little Kevin's *dead*. He's never coming back. Why are we sitting here wrecking each other's heads?"

Jackie said, "Ah, Carmel, love. We're only slagging. We don't mean it."

"Speak for yourself," Shay told her.

I said, "We're family, babe. This is what families do."

"The tosspot's right," Shay said. "For once."

Carmel was crying harder. "Thinking about us all sitting right here last Friday, the whole five of us . . . I was only over the moon, so I was. I never thought it'd be the last time, you know? I thought it was just the start."

Shay said, "I know you did. Will you try and keep it together, but? For me, yeah?"

She caught a tear with a knuckle, but they kept coming. "God forgive me, I knew something bad was probably after happening to Rosie, didn't we all? But I just tried not to think about that. D'yous think this is a comeuppance?"

All of us said, "Ah, *Carmel*," at once. Carmel tried to say something else, but it got tangled up in a pathetic cross between a gulp and a huge sniff.

Jackie's chin was starting to look a little wobbly around the edges, too. Any minute now, this was going to turn into one great big sob-fest. I said, "I'll tell yous what I feel like shit about. Not being here last Sunday evening. The night he . . ."

I shook my head quickly, against the railings, and let it trail off. "That was our last chance," I said, up to the dimming sky. "I should've been here."

The cynical glance I got off Shay told me he wasn't falling for it, but the girls were all big eyes and bitten lips and sympathy. Carmel fished out a hanky and put away the rest of her cry for later, now that a man needed attention. "Ah, Francis," Jackie said, reaching up to pat my knee. "How were you to know?"

"That's not the point. The point is, first I missed twenty-two years of him, and then I missed the last few hours anyone's ever going to get. I just wish . . ."

I shook my head, fumbled for another smoke and took a few tries to light it. "Never mind," I said, once I had taken a couple of hard drags to get my voice under control. "Come on: talk to me. Tell me about that evening. What'd I miss?"

Shay let out a snort, which got him matching glares from the girls. "Hang on till I think a minute," Jackie said. "It was just an evening, you know what I mean? Nothing special. Am I right, Carmel?"

The two of them gazed at each other, thinking hard. Carmel blew her nose. She said, "I thought Kevin was a bit out of sorts. Did yous not?"

Shay shook his head in disgust and turned his shoulder to them, distancing himself from the whole thing. Jackie said, "He looked grand to me. Himself and Gav were out here playing football with the kids."

"But he was smoking. After the dinner. Kevin doesn't smoke unless he's up to ninety, so he doesn't."

And there we were. Privacy for tête-à-têtes was in short supply around Ma's (*Kevin Mackey, what are the two of yous whispering about there, if it's that interesting then we all want to hear it . . .*). If Kevin had needed a word with Shay—and the poor thick bastard would have gone chasing after exactly that, once I blew him off; nothing more cunning would ever have entered his head—he would have followed him out to the steps for a smoke.

Kev would have made a bollix of it, messing about with his cigarette, fumbling and stammering over bringing out the jagged bits and pieces that were slicing into his mind. All that awkwardness would have given Shay plenty of time to recover and laugh out loud: *Holy Jaysus, man, are you seriously after convincing yourself I killed Rosie Daly? You've it all arseways. If you want to know what really happened . . .* Quick glance up at the window, stubbing out a smoke on the steps. *Not now, but; no time. Will we meet up later, yeah? Come back, after you leave. You can't call round to my gaff or Ma'll want to know what we're at, and the pubs'll be closed by then, but I'll meet you in Number Sixteen. It won't take long, sure.*

It was what I would have done, in Shay's place, and it would have been almost that easy. Kevin wouldn't have been happy about the idea of going back into Number 16, especially in the dark, but Shay was a lot smarter than he was and an awful lot more desperate, and Kevin had always been easy to bulldoze. It would never have occurred to him to be afraid of his own brother; not that kind of afraid. For someone who had grown up in our family, Kev had been so innocent it made my jaw ache.

Jackie said, "Honest to God, Francis, nothing happened. It was just like today. They all had a game of football, and then we had the dinner and watched a bit of telly . . . Kevin was *grand*. You can't be blaming yourself."

I asked, "Did he make any phone calls? Get any phone calls?"

Shay's eyes flicked to me for a second, narrow and assessing, but he kept his mouth shut. Carmel said, "He was texting back and forth with some girl—Aisling, was it? I was telling him not to be leading her on, but he said I hadn't a clue, that's not how things work nowadays . . . He was awful snotty with me, so he was. That's what I mean about out of sorts. The last time I saw him, and . . ." Her voice had a subdued, bruised note to it. Any minute she was going to start crying again.

"No one else?"

The girls both shook their heads. I said, "Hmm."

Jackie asked, "Why, Francis? What difference does it make?"

"Kojak's on the trail," Shay said, to the lilac sky. "Who loves ya, baby?"

I said, "Put it like this. I've heard a whole bunch of different explanations for what happened to Rosie and what happened to Kevin. I don't like a single one of them."

Jackie said, "No one does, sure."

Carmel popped paint blisters on the railing with one fingernail. She said, "Accidents happen. Sometimes things just go terrible wrong; there's no rhyme nor reason to it. You know?"

"No, Melly, I don't know. To me that looks exactly like all the other explanations people have tried to shove down my throat: a great big stinking lump of shite that's nowhere near good enough for either Rosie or Kevin. And I'm in no humor to swallow it."

Carmel said, with certainty weighing down her voice like a rock,

"'There's nothing that'll make this better, Francis. We're all of us heart-broken, and there's no explanation in the world that'll fix that. Would you not leave it?"

"I might, except that plenty of other people won't, and one of the top theories has me down as the big bad villain. You think I should just ignore that? You're the one said you wanted me to keep coming here. Have a think about what that means. You want me to spend every Sunday on a street that thinks I'm a killer?"

Jackie moved on the step. She said, "I already told you. That's just talk. It'll blow over."

I said, "Then, if I'm not the bad guy and Kev's not the bad guy, yous tell me. What happened?"

The silence went on for a long time. We heard them coming before we saw them: kids' voices twisting together, a quick hushed running murmur, somewhere inside the dazzle of long evening light at the top of the road. They stepped out of that dazzle in a tangle of black silhouettes, the men tall as lampposts, the kids blurring and flickering in and out of each other. Holly's voice called, "Daddy!" and I raised an arm to wave, even though I couldn't make out which one she was. Their shadows leaped down the road in front of them and threw mysterious shapes at our feet.

"Now," Carmel said softly, to herself. She took a breath and ran her fingers under her eyes, making sure nothing was left of her cry. "Now."

I said, "Next time we get a chance, you'll have to finish telling me what happened last Sunday."

Shay said, "And then it got late, Ma and Da and me headed for bed, and Kev and Jackie headed for home." He threw his cigarette over the railings and stood up. "The end," he said.

As soon as we all got back into the flat Ma kicked things up a gear, to pun-ish us for leaving her to her own terrifying devices. She was doing ferocious things to vegetables and issuing orders at warp speed: "You, Carmel-Jackie-Carmel-whoever-you-are, get them potatoes started—Shay, put that over there, *no*, you simpleton, *there*—Ashley, love, give the table a wipe for your

nana—and Francis, you go in and have a word with your da, he's after getting back into the bed and he wants a bit of company. Go on!" She smacked
me across the head with a dish towel, to get me moving.

Holly had been leaning against my side, showing me some painted ce-
ramic thing she had bought in the Christmas Village to give Olivia and
explaining in detail how she had met Santa's elves, but at that she melted
neatly away among the cousins, which I felt showed good sense. I considered doing the same thing, but Ma has the ability to keep nagging for so
long that it borders on a superpower, and the dishcloth was aimed in my
direction again. I got out of her way.

The bedroom was colder than the rest of the flat, and quiet. Da was in
bed, propped up on pillows and apparently doing nothing at all except,
maybe, listening to the voices coming from the other rooms. The fussy
softness all round him—peach decor, fringed things, muted glow from a
standing lamp—made him look bizarrely out of place and somehow stronger, more savage. You could see why girls had fought over him: the tilt of
his jaw, the arrogant jut of his cheekbones, the restless blue spark in his
eyes. For a moment, in that untrustworthy light, he looked like wild Jimmy
Mackey still.

His hands were what gave him away. They were a mess—fingers swollen
huge and curled inwards, nails white and rough like they were already de-
caying—and they never stopped moving on the bed, plucking fretfully at
loose threads in the duvet. The room stank of sickness and medicine and
feet.

I said, "Ma said you fancied a chat."

Da said, "Give us a smoke."

He still seemed sober, but then my da has poured a lifetime of dedication into building up his tolerance, and it takes a lot to put a visible dent
in it. I swung the chair from Ma's dressing table over to the bed, not too
close. "I thought Ma didn't let you smoke in here."

"That bitch can go and shite."

"Nice to see the romance isn't dead."

"And you can go and shite too. Give us a smoke."

"Not a chance. You can piss Ma off all you want; I'm staying in her good
books."

That made Da grin, not in a pleasant way. "Good luck with that," he said, but all of a sudden he looked wide awake and his focus on my face had got sharper. "Why?"

"Why not?"

"You were never arsed about keeping her happy in your life."

I shrugged. "My kid's mad about her nana. If that means I have to spend one afternoon a week gritting my teeth and sucking up to Ma, so Holly won't see us tearing strips off each other, I'll do it. Ask me nicely and I'll even suck up to you, at least when Holly's in the room."

Da started to laugh. He leaned back on his pillows and laughed so hard that it turned into a spasm of deep, wet coughing. He waved a hand at me, gasping for breath, and motioned at a box of tissues on the dresser. I passed them over. He hawked, spat into a tissue, tossed it at the bin and missed; I didn't pick it up. When he could talk, he said, "Bollix."

I said, "Want to elaborate on that?"

"You won't like it."

"I'll live. When was the last time I liked anything that came out of your mouth?"

Da reached painfully over to the bedside table for his glass of water or whatever, took his time drinking. "All that about your young one," he said, wiping his mouth. "Load of bollix. She's grand. She doesn't give a fuck if you and Josie get on, and you know it. You've got reasons of your own for keeping your ma sweet."

I said, "Sometimes, Da, people try to be nice to each other. For no reason at all. I know it's tough to picture, but take it from me: it happens."

He shook his head. That hard grin was back on his face. "Not you," he said.

"Maybe, maybe not. You might want to keep in mind that you know just under shag-all about me."

"Don't need to. I know your brother, and I know the pair of yous were always as like as two peas in a pod."

I didn't get the sense he was talking about Kevin. I said, "I'm not seeing the resemblance."

"Spitting image. Neither of yous ever did anything in his life without a bloody good reason, and neither one of yous ever told anyone what the reason was unless he had to. I couldn't deny the pair of yous, anyway, that's for sure."

He was enjoying himself. I knew I should keep my gob shut, but I couldn't do it. I said, "I'm nothing like any of this family. Nothing. I walked away from this house so that I wouldn't be. I've spent my whole life making damn sure of it."

Da's eyebrows shot up sardonically. "Listen to him. Are we not good enough for you these days, no? We were good enough to put a roof over your head for twenty years."

"What can I say? Gratuitous sadism doesn't pop my cork."

That made him laugh again, a deep harsh bark. "Does it not? At least I know I'm a bastard. You think you're not? Go on: look me in the eye and tell me you don't enjoy seeing me in this state."

"This is something special. It couldn't have happened to a nicer guy."

"See? I'm in bits, and you're loving it. Blood tells, sonny boy. Blood tells."

I said, "I've never in my life hit a woman. I've never in my life hit a child. And my kid has never in her life seen me drunk. I understand that only a seriously sick sonofabitch would be proud of any of those, but I can't help it. Every single one of them is proof that I have sweet fuck-all in common with you."

Da watched me. He said, "So you think you're a better da than I ever was."

"That's not exactly bigging myself up. I've seen stray dogs who were better das than you."

"Then tell me this and tell me no more: if you're such a saint and we're such a shower of shites, why are you using that child for an excuse to come around here?"

I was headed for the door when I heard, behind me, "*Sit down.*"

It sounded like Da's own voice again, full and strong and young. It grabbed my inner five-year-old around the throat and shoved me back into my chair before I knew what had happened. Once I was there, I had to pretend it was by choice. I said, "I think we're more or less done here."

Giving the order had taken it out of him: he was leaning forward, breathing hard and clutching at the duvet. He said, on short gasps, "I'll tell you when we're done."

"You do that. Just as long as it's soon."

Da shoved his pillows farther up behind his back—I didn't offer to help: the thought of our faces getting that close made my skin crawl—and got his breath back, slowly. The ceiling-crack shaped like a race car was still there above his head, the one I used to stare at when I woke up early in the mornings and lay in bed daydreaming and listening to Kevin and Shay breathe and turn and murmur. The gold light had faded away; outside the window, the sky over the back gardens was turning a cold deep-sea blue.

Da said, "You listen to me. I haven't got long left."

"Leave that line to Ma. She does it better." Ma has been at death's door ever since I can remember, mostly due to mysterious ailments involving her undercarriage.

"She'll outlive us all, just out of spite. I wouldn't say I'll see next Christmas."

He was milking it, lying back and pressing a hand to his chest, but there was an undercurrent to his voice that said he meant it at least partway. I said, "What are you planning on dying of?"

"What do you care? I could burn to death in front of you before you'd piss on me to put me out."

"True enough, but I'm curious. I didn't think being an arschole was fatal."

Da said, "My back's getting worse. Half the time I can't feel my legs. Fell over twice, the other day, just trying to put on my kacks in the morning; the legs went out from under me. The doctor says I'll be in a wheelchair before summer."

I said, "Let me take a wild guess here. Did the doctor also say your 'back' would get better, or at least stop getting worse, if you went off the booze?"

His face curled up with disgust. "That little nancy-boy'd give you the sick. He needs to get off his ma's tit and have a real drink. A few pints never did a man any harm."

"That's a few pints of beer, not vodka. If the booze is so good for you, what are you dying of?"

Da said, "Being a cripple's no way for a man to live. Locked up in a home, someone wiping your arse for you, lifting you in and out of the bath; I've no time for that shite. If I end up like that, I'm gone."

Again, something under the self-pity said he was serious. Probably this was because the nursing home wouldn't have a minibar, but I was with him on the wider issue: death before diapers. "How?"

"I've got plans."

I said, "I'm after missing something, along the way. What are you looking for off me? Because if it's sympathy, I'm fresh out. And if you want a helping hand, I think there's a queue."

"I'm asking you for nothing, you stupid little prick. I'm trying to tell you something important, if you'd only shut your gob long enough to listen. Or are you loving your own voice too much for that, are you?"

This may be the most pathetic thing I've ever admitted: deep down, a speck of me clung on to the chance that he might actually have something worthwhile to say. He was my da. When I was a kid, before I copped that he was a world-class fucknugget, he was the smartest man in the world; he knew everything about everything, he could beat up the Hulk with one hand while he bicep-curled grand pianos with the other, a grin from him lit up your whole day. And if ever I had needed a few precious pearls of fatherly wisdom, it was that night. I said, "I'm listening."

Da pulled himself up, painfully, in the bed. He said, "A man needs to know when to let things lie."

I waited, but he was watching me intently, like he was expecting some kind of answer. Apparently that was the sum total of enlightenment I was going to get off him. I could have punched myself in the teeth for being thick enough to look for more. "Great," I said. "Thanks a million. I'll bear that in mind."

I started to get up again, but one of those deformed hands shot out and grabbed my wrist, faster and a lot stronger than I had expected. The touch of his skin made my hair stand up. "Sit down and listen, you. What I'm telling you is this: I've put up with a load of shite in my life and never thought about topping myself. I'm not weak. But the first time someone puts a nappy on me, I'm gone, because that's when there's no fight left where winning would be worth my while. You have to know what to fight against and what to leave alone. D'you get me?"

I said, "Here's what I want to know. Why do you all of a sudden give a tinker's damn about my attitude to anything?"

I expected Da to come back swinging, but he didn't. He let go of my wrist and massaged his knuckles, examining his hand like it belonged to someone else. He said, "Take it or leave it. I can't make you do anything. But if there's one thing I wish I'd been taught a long time back, it's that. I'd have done less damage. To myself and everyone round me."

This time I was the one who laughed out loud. "Well, color me gobsmacked. Did I just hear you take responsibility for something? You must be dying after all."

"Don't fucking mock. Yous lot are grown; if you're after banjaxing your lives, that's your own fault, not mine."

"Then what the hell are you on about?"

"I'm only saying. There's things went wrong fifty years ago, and they just kept going. It's time they stopped. If I'd've had the sense to let them go a long time back, there's a lot would've been different. Better."

I said, "Are you talking about what happened with Tessie O'Byrne?"

"She's none of your bloody business, and you watch who you're calling Tessie. I'm saying there's no reason your ma should have her heart broke for nothing, all over again. Do you understand me?"

His eyes were a hot urgent blue, crammed too deep with secrets for me to untangle. It was the brand-new soft places in there—I had never before in my life seen my da worried about who might get hurt—that told me there was something enormous and dangerous moving through the air of that room. I said, after a long time, "I'm not sure."

"Then you wait till you are sure, before you do anything thick. I know my sons, always did. I know well you had your reasons for coming here. You keep them away from this house till you're bloody sure you know what you're at."

Outside, Ma snapped about something and there was a placating murmur from Jackie. I said, "I'd give a lot to know just what's going on in your mind."

"I'm a dying man. I'm trying to put a few things right, before I go. I'm telling you to leave it. We don't need you causing trouble around here. Go back to whatever you were doing before, and leave us alone."

I said, before I could help it, "Da."

All of a sudden Da looked wrecked. His face was the color of wet cardboard. He said, "I'm sick of the sight of you. Get out there and tell your ma I'm gasping for a cup of tea—and she's to make it a decent strength, this time, not that piss she gave me this morning."

I wasn't about to argue. All I wanted was to grab hold of Holly and get the pair of us the hell out of Dodge—Ma would blow a blood vessel about us skipping dinner, but I had rattled Shay's cage enough for one week, and I had seriously misjudged my family-tolerance threshold. I was already trying to decide on the best place to stop, on the way back to Liv's, so I could get Holly fed and stare at that beautiful little face till my heart rate dropped back into normal range. I said, at the door, "I'll see you next week."

"I'm telling you. Go home. Don't come back."

He didn't turn his head to watch me go. I left him there, lying back on his pillows and staring at the dark windowpane and pulling fitfully at loose threads with those misshapen fingers.

Ma was in the kitchen, stabbing viciously at an enormous joint of half-cooked meat and giving Darren hassle, via Carmel, about his clothes (". . . never get a job as long as he's running around dressed like a fecking pervert, don't say I didn't warn you, you take him outside and give him a good smack on his arse and a nice pair of chinos . . ."). Jackie and Gavin and the rest of Carmel's lot were in a trance in front of the telly, staring slack-jawed at a shirtless guy eating something wiggly with a lot of antennae. Holly was nowhere. Neither was Shay.

21

I said, and I didn't care whether my voice sounded normal or not, "Where's Holly?"

None of the telly crowd even looked around. Ma yelled, from the kitchen, "She's after dragging her uncle Shay upstairs to help her with her maths—if you're going up there, Francis, you tell them two the dinner'll be ready in half an hour and it won't wait for them . . . Carmel O'Reilly, you come back here and listen to me! He won't be allowed to sit his exams if he goes in on the day looking like Dracula—"

I took the stairs like I was weightless. They lasted a million years. High above me I could hear Holly's voice chattering away about something, sweet and happy and oblivious. I didn't breathe till I was on the top landing, outside Shay's flat. I was pulling back to shoulder-barge my way in when Holly said, "Was Rosie pretty?"

I stopped so hard that I nearly did a cartoon face-plant into the door. Shay said, "She was, yeah."

"Prettier than my mum?"

"I don't know your mammy, remember? Going by you, though, I'd say Rosie was almost as pretty. Not quite, but almost."

I could practically see Holly's tip of a smile at that. The two of them sounded contented together, at ease; the way an uncle and his best niece should sound. Shay, the brass-necked fucker, actually sounded peaceful.

Holly said, "My dad was going to marry her."

"Maybe."

"He was."

"He never did, but. Come here till we give this another go: if Tara has a hundred and eighty-five goldfish, and she can put seven in a bowl, how many bowls does she need?"

"He never did because Rosie died. She wrote her mum and dad a note saying she was going to England with my dad, and then somebody killed her."

"Long time ago. Don't be changing the subject, now. These fish won't put themselves in bowls."

A giggle, and then a long pause as Holly concentrated on her division, with the odd encouraging murmur from Shay. I leaned against the wall by the door, got my breath back and wrenched my head under control.

Every muscle in my body wanted to burst in there and grab my kid, but the fact was that Shay wasn't completely insane—yet, anyway—and Holly was in no danger. More than that: she was trying to get him to talk about Rosie. I've learned the hard way that Holly can outstubborn just about anyone on this planet. Anything she got out of Shay went straight into my arsenal.

Holly said, triumphantly, "Twenty-seven! And the last one only gets three fish."

"It does indeed. Well done you."

"Did someone kill Rosie to stop her from marrying my dad?"

A second of silence. "Is that what he says?"

The stinking little shitebucket. I had a hand clenched around the banister hard enough to hurt. Holly said, with a shrug in her voice, "I didn't ask him."

"No one knows why Rosie Daly got killed. And it's too late to find out now. What's done is done."

Holly said, with the instant, heartbreaking, absolute confidence that nine-year-olds still have, "My dad's going to find out."

Shay said, "Is he, yeah?"

"Yeah. He said so."

"Well," Shay said, and to his credit he managed to keep almost all of the vitriol out of his voice. "Your da's a Guard, sure. It's his job to think like that. Come here and look at this, now: if Desmond has three hundred and forty-two sweets, and he's sharing them between himself and eight friends, how many will they get each?"

"When the book says 'sweets' we're supposed to write down 'pieces of fruit.' Because sweets are bad for you. I think that's stupid. They're only imaginary sweets anyway."

"It's stupid all right, but the sum's the same either way. How many pieces of fruit each, then?"

The rhythmic scrape of a pencil—at that stage I could hear the tiniest sound coming from inside that flat, I could probably have heard the two of them blinking. Holly said, "What about Uncle Kevin?"

There was another fraction of a pause before Shay said, "What about him?"

"Did somebody kill him?"

Shay said, "Kevin," and his voice was twisted into an extraordinary knot of things that I had never heard anywhere before. "No. No one killed Kevin."

"For definite?"

"What's your da say?"

That shrug again. "I *told* you. I didn't ask him. He doesn't like talking about Uncle Kevin. So I wanted to ask you."

"Kevin. God." Shay laughed, a harsh lost sound. "Maybe you're old enough to understand this, I don't know. Otherwise you'll have to remember it till you are. Kevin was a child. He never grew up. Thirty-seven years old and he still figured everything in the world was going to go the way *he* thought it should; It never hit him that the world might work its own way, whether that suited him or not. So he went wandering around a derelict house in the dark, because he took it for granted he'd be grand, and instead he went out a window. End of story."

I felt the wood of the banister crack and twist under my grip. The finality in his voice told me that was going to be his story for the rest of his life. Maybe he even believed it, although I doubted that. Maybe, left to his own devices, he would have believed it someday.

"What's derelict?"

"Ruined. Falling to bits. Dangerous."

Holly thought that over. She said, "He still shouldn't have died."

"No," Shay said, but the heat had gone out of his voice; all of a sudden he just sounded exhausted. "He shouldn't have. No one wanted him to."

"But someone wanted Rosie to. Right?"

"Not even her. Sometimes things just happen."

Holly said defiantly, "If my dad had married her, he wouldn't have married my mum, and I wouldn't have existed. I'm *glad* she died."

The timer button on the hall light popped out with a noise like a shot—I didn't even remember hitting it on my way up—and left me standing in empty blackness with my heart going ninety. In that moment, I realized that I had never told Holly who Rosie's note had been addressed to. She had seen that note herself.

About a second later, I realized why, after all that adorable heartstring-tugging stuff about hanging out with her cousins, she had brought along her maths homework today. She had needed a way to get Shay alone.

Holly had planned every step of this. She had walked into this house, gone straight to her birthright of steel-trap secrets and cunning lethal devices, laid her hand on it and claimed it for her own.

Blood tells, my father's voice said flatly against my ear; and then, with a razor edge of amusement, *So you think you're a better da.* Here I had been milking every self-righteous drop out of how Olivia and Jackie had screwed up; nothing either of them could have done differently, not at any lost moment along the way, would have saved us from this. This was all mine. I could have howled at the moon like a werewolf and bitten out my own wrists to get this out of my veins.

Shay said, "Don't be saying that. She's gone; forget her. Leave her rest in peace, and go on with your maths."

The soft whisper of the pencil on paper. "Forty-two?"

"No. Go back to the start; you're not concentrating."

Holly said, "Uncle Shay?"

"Mmm?"

"This one time? When I was here and your phone rang and you went in the bedroom?"

I could hear her gearing up towards something big. So could Shay: the first beginnings of a wary edge were growing in his voice. "Yeah?"

"I broke my pencil and I couldn't find my sharpener because Chloe took it in Art. I waited for ages, but you were on the phone."

Shay said, very gently, "So what did you do?"

"I went and looked for another pencil. In that chest of drawers."

A long silence, just a woman gabbling hysterically from the telly down-stairs, muffled under all those thick walls and heavy carpets and high ceil-ings. Shay said, "And you found something."

Holly said, almost inaudibly, "I'm sorry."

I almost went straight through that door without bothering to open it. Two things kept me outside. The first one was that Holly was nine years old. She believed in fairies, she wasn't sure about Santa; a few months back, she had told me that when she was little a flying horse used to take her for rides out her bedroom window. If her evidence was ever going to be a solid weapon—if, someday, I wanted someone else to believe her—I had to be able to back it up. I needed to hear it come out of Shay's mouth.

The second thing was that there was no point, not now, in bursting in there with all guns blazing to save my little girl from the big bad man. I stared at the bright crack of light around the door and listened, like I was a million miles away or a million years too late. I knew exactly what Olivia would think, what any sane human being would think, and I stood still and left Holly to do my dirtiest work for me. I've done plenty of dodgy things in my time and none of them kept me awake at night, but that one is special. If there's a hell, that moment in the dark hallway is what will take me there.

Shay said, like he was having a hard time breathing, "Did you say that to anyone?"

"No. I didn't even know what it was, till just a couple of days ago I figured it out."

"Holly. Love. Listen to me. Can you keep a secret?"

Holly said, with something that sounded horrifically like pride, "I saw it ages ago. Like months and months and months, and I never said anything."

"That's right, you didn't. Good girl yourself."

"See?"

"Yeah, I see. Now can you go on doing the same, can you? Keeping it to yourself?"

Silence.

Shay said, "Holly. If you tell anyone, what do you think will happen?"

"You'll get in trouble."

"Maybe. I've done nothing bad—d'you hear me?—but there's plenty of people won't believe that. I could go to jail. Do you want that?"

Holly's voice was sinking, a subdued undertone aimed at the floor. "No."

"I didn't think so. Even if I don't, what'll happen? What do you think your da's going to say?"

Uncertain flutter of a breath, little girl lost. "He'll be mad?"

"He'll be livid. At you and me both, for not telling him about it before. He'll never let you back here; he'll never let you see any of us again. Not your nana, not me, not Donna. And he'll make dead sure your mammy and your auntie Jackie don't find a way around him this time." A few seconds, for that to sink in. "What else?"

"Nana. She'll be upset."

"Nana, and your aunties, and all your cousins. They'll be in bits. No one will know what to think. Some of them won't even believe you. There'll be holy war." Another impressive pause. "Holly, pet. Is that what you want?"

"No . . ."

"Course you don't. You want to come back here every Sunday and have lovely afternoons with the rest of us, am I right? You want your nana making you a sponge cake for your birthday, just like she did for Louise, and Darren teaching you the guitar once your hands get big enough." The words moved over her, soft and seductive, wrapping around her and pulling her in close. "You want all of us here together. Going for walks. Making the dinner. Having laughs. Don't you?"

"Yeah. Like a proper family."

"That's right. And proper families look after each other. That's what they're for."

Holly, like a good little Mackey, did what came naturally. She said, and it was still just a flicker of sound but with a new kind of certainty starting somewhere underneath, "I won't tell anyone."

"Not even your da?"

"Yeah. Not even."

"Good girl," Shay said, so gently and soothingly that the dark in front of me went seething red. "Good girl. You're my best little niece, aren't you?"

"Yeah."

"It'll be our special secret. Do you promise me, now?"

I thought about various ways to kill someone without leaving marks. Then, before Holly could promise, I took a breath and pushed open the door.

They made a pretty picture. Shay's flat was clean and bare, almost barracks-tidy: worn floorboards, faded olive-green curtains, random bits of characterless furniture, nothing on the white walls. I knew from Jackie that he had been living there for sixteen years, ever since crazy old Mrs. Field died and left the place empty, but it still looked temporary. He could have packed up and gone on a couple of hours' notice, without leaving a trace behind.

He and Holly were sitting at a little wooden table. With her books spread out in front of them, they looked like an old painting: a father and daughter in their garret, in any century you picked, absorbed together in some mysterious story. The pool of light from a tall lamp made them glow like jewels in that drab room, Holly's gold head and her ruby-red cardigan, the deep green of Shay's jumper and the blue-black gloss on his hair. He had put a footstool under the table, so Holly's feet wouldn't dangle. It looked like the newest thing in the room.

That lovely picture only lasted a split second. Then they leaped like a pair of guilty teenagers caught sharing a spliff; they were the image of each other, all panicked flash of matching blue eyes. Holly said, "We're doing maths! Uncle Shay's helping me."

She was bright red and wildly obvious, which was a relief: I had been starting to think she was turning into some ice-cold superspy. I said, "Yep, you mentioned that. How's it going?"

"OK." She glanced quickly at Shay, but he was watching me intently, with no expression at all.

"That's nice." I wandered over behind them and had a leisurely look over their shoulders. "Looks like good stuff, all right. Have you said thank you to your uncle?"

"Yeah. Loads of times."

I cocked an eyebrow at Shay, who said, "She has. Yeah."

"Well, isn't that rewarding to hear. I'm a big believer in good manners, me."

Holly was almost hopping off her chair with unease. "Daddy . . ."

I said, "Holly, sweetheart, you go downstairs and finish your maths at Nana's. If she wants to know where your uncle Shay and I are, tell her we're having a chat and we'll be down in a bit. OK?"

"OK." She started putting her stuff into her schoolbag, slowly. "I won't say anything else to her. Right?"

She could have been talking to either of us. I said, "Right. I know you won't, love. You and me, we'll talk later. Now go on. Scoot."

Holly finished packing up her stuff and looked back and forth between us one more time—the tangle of shredded expressions on her face, while she tried to get her head around more than any grown adult could have handled, made me want to kneecap Shay all by itself. Then she left. She pressed her shoulder up against my side for a second, on her way past; I wanted to crush her in a bear hug, but instead I ran a hand over her soft head and gave the back of her neck a quick squeeze. We listened to her running down the stairs, light as a fairy on the thick carpet, and the rise of voices welcoming her into Ma's.

I shut the door behind her and said, "And here I was wondering how her long division had improved so much. Isn't that funny?"

Shay said, "She's no eejit. She only needed a hand."

"Oh, I know that. But you're the man who stepped up. I think it's important for you to hear how much I appreciate that." I swung Holly's chair out of the bright pool of lamplight, and out of Shay's reach, and had a seat. "Nice place you've got here."

"Thanks."

"The way I remember it, Mrs. Field had it wallpapered with pictures of Padre Pio and stinking of clove drops. Let's face it, anything would've been an improvement."

Shay slowly eased back in his chair, in what looked like a casual sprawl, but the muscles in his shoulders were coiled like a big cat's ready to leap. "Where's my manners? You'll have a drink. Whiskey, yeah?"

"And why not. Work up an appetite for the dinner."

He tilted his chair so he could reach over to the sideboard and pull out a bottle and two tumblers. "Rocks?"

"Go for it. Let's do this right."

Leaving me on my own put a wary flash in his eye, but he didn't have a choice. He took the glasses out to the kitchen: freezer door opening, ice cubes popping. The whiskey was serious stuff, Tyrconnell single malt. "You've got taste," I said.

"What, you're surprised?" Shay came back shaking ice cubes around the glasses, to chill them. "And don't be asking me for a mixer."

"Don't insult me."

"Good. Anyone who'd mix this doesn't deserve it." He poured us each three fingers and pushed a glass across the table to me. "*Sláinte,*" he said, lifting the other one.

I said, "Here's to us." The glasses clinked together. The whiskey burned gold going down, barley and honey. All that rage had evaporated right out of me; I was as cool and gathered and ready as I had ever been on any job. In all the world there was no one left except the two of us, watching each other across that rickety table, with the stark lamplight throwing shadows like war paint across Shay's face and piling up great heaps of them in every corner. It felt utterly familiar, almost soothing, like we had been practicing for this moment all our lives.

"So," Shay said. "How does it feel, being home?"

"It's been a hoot. I wouldn't have missed it for the world."

"Tell us: were you serious about coming around from now on? Or were you only humoring Carmel?"

I grinned at him. "Would I ever? No, I meant it, all right. Are you delighted and excited?"

A corner of Shay's lip twisted upwards. "Carmel and Jackie think it's because you missed your family. They're in for a shock, somewhere down the line."

"I'm wounded. Are you saying I don't care about my family? Not you, maybe. But the rest of them."

Shay laughed, into his glass. "Right. You've got no agenda here."

"I've got news for you: everyone always has an agenda. Don't worry your pretty little head, though. Agenda or no, I'll be here often enough to keep Carmel and Jackie happy."

"Good. Remind me to show you how to get Da on and off the jacks."

I said, "Since you won't be around as much, next year. What with the bike shop and all."

Something flickered, deep down in Shay's eyes. "Yeah. That's right."

I raised my glass to him. "Fair play to you. I'd say you're looking forward to that."

"I've earned it."

"You have, of course. Here's the thing, though: I'll be in and out, but it's not like I'm going to be moving in here." I shot an amused look around the flat. "Some of us have lives, you know what I mean?"

That flicker again, but he kept his voice even. "I didn't ask you to move anywhere."

I shrugged. "Well, someone's got to be around. Maybe you didn't know this, but Da . . . He's not really on for going into a home."

"And I didn't ask for your opinion on that, either."

"Course not. Just a word to the wise: he told me he's got contingency plans. I'd be counting his tablets, if I were you."

The spark caught, flared. "Hang on a second. Are you trying to tell me my duty to Da? *You?*"

"Christ, no. I'm only passing on the info. I wouldn't want you having to live with the guilt if it all went wrong."

"*What* bloody guilt? Count his tablets yourself, if you want them counted. I've looked after the whole lot of yous, all my life. It's *not my turn* any more."

I said, "You know something? Sooner or later, you're going to have to ditch this idea that you've spent your life being everyone's little knight in shining armor. Don't get me wrong, it's entertaining to watch, but there's a fine line between illusion and delusion, and you're bouncing along that line."

Shay shook his head. "You don't have a clue," he said. "Not the first fucking clue."

I said, "No? Kevin and I were having a little chat, the other day, about how you *looked after* us. You know what sprang to mind—Kevin's mind, not mine? You locking the pair of us in the basement of Number Sixteen.

Kev was what, two, maybe three? Thirty years later, and he still didn't like going in there. He felt well looked after that night, all right."

Shay threw himself backwards, chair tilting dangerously, and burst out laughing. The lamplight turned his eyes and mouth into shapeless dark hollows. "That night," he said. "My Jaysus, yeah. Do you want to know what happened that night?"

"Kevin pissed himself. He was practically catatonic. I ripped my hands to coleslaw trying to get the boards off the windows so we could get out. That's what happened."

Shay said, "Da got fired that day."

Da got fired on a regular basis, when we were kids, up until people more or less quit hiring him to begin with. Those days were nobody's favorites, specially since he usually ended up with a week's wages in lieu of notice. Shay said, "It gets late, he's still not home. So Ma puts the lot of us to bed—this was when the four of us were all on the mattresses in the back bedroom, before Jackie came along and the girls went into the other room—and she's giving out seven shades of shite: this time she's locking the door on him, he can sleep in the gutter where he belongs, she hopes he gets bet up and run over and thrown in jail all at once. Kevin's whingeing because he wants his daddy, fuck only knows why, and she tells him if he doesn't shut up and go asleep, Daddy won't come home ever again. I ask what will we do then, and she says, 'You'll be the man of the house; you'll have to look after us. You'd do a better job than that bollix, anyway.' If Kev was two, what would I have been? Eight, yeah?"

I said, "How did I know you would turn out to be the martyr in this story?"

"So Ma heads off: sweet dreams, kids. I don't know what time of night, Da comes home and breaks the door down. Me and Carmel leg it out to the front room and he's throwing the wedding china at the wall, one bit at a time. Ma's got blood all down her face, she's screaming at him to stop and calling him every name under the sun. Carmel runs and grabs hold of him, and he smacks her across the room. He starts shouting that us fucking kids have ruined his life, he ought to drown the lot of us like kittens, slit our throats, be a free man again. And believe me: he meant every word of it."

Shay poured himself another inch of whiskey and waved the bottle at me. I shook my head.

"Suit yourself. He's heading for the bedroom to slaughter the whole bunch of us on the spot. Ma jumps on him to hold him back and screams at me to get the babies out. I'm the man of the house, right? So I haul your arse out of bed and tell you we have to go. You're bitching and complaining: why, I don't want to, you're not the boss of me . . . I know Ma can't hold Da for long, so I give you a clatter, I get Kev under my arm and I drag you out of there by the neck of your T-shirt. Where was I supposed to take yous? The nearest cop shop?"

"We had neighbors. A whole shitload of them, in fact."

The blaze of pure disgust lit up his whole face. "Yeah. Spill our family business in front of the whole Place, give them enough juicy scandal to keep them going for the rest of their lives. Is that what you would've done?" He knocked back a swig of booze and jerked his head, grimacing, to keep it down. "You probably would, and all. Me, I'd've been ashamed of my life. Even when I was eight, I had more pride than that."

"When I was eight, so did I. Now that I'm a grown man, I have a harder time seeing where locking your little brothers in a death trap is something to be proud of."

"It was the best bloody thing I could've done for yous. You think you and Kevin had a bad night? All you had to do was stay put till Da passed out and I came and got yous. I would've given anything to stay in that nice safe basement with yous, but no: I had to come back in here."

I said, "So send me the bill for your therapy sessions. Is that what you want?"

"I'm not looking for any fucking pity off you. I'm just telling you: don't expect me to go running off on a great big guilt trip because you had to spend a few minutes in the dark, once upon a time."

I said, "Please tell me that little story wasn't your excuse for killing two people."

There was a very long silence. Then Shay said, "How long were you listening at that door?"

I said, "I didn't need to listen to a single word."

After a moment he said, "Holly's after saying something to you."

I didn't answer.

"And you believe her."

"Hey, she's my kid. Call me soft."

He shook his head. "Never said that. I'm only saying she's a child."

"That doesn't make her stupid. Or a liar."

"No. Gives her a great old imagination, though."

People have insulted everything from my manhood to my mother's genitalia and I never batted an eyelid, but the idea that I would diss Holly's word on Shay's say-so was starting to get my blood pressure rising again. I said, before he could spot that, "Let's get something straight: I didn't need Holly to tell me anything. I know exactly what you did, to Rosie and to Kevin. I've known for a lot longer than you think."

After a moment Shay tilted his chair again, reached into the sideboard and brought out a pack of smokes and an ashtray: he didn't let Holly see him smoking, either. He took his time peeling the cellophane off the packet, tapping the end of his cigarette on the table, lighting up. He was thinking, rearranging things in his mind and stepping back to take a long look at the new patterns they made.

In the end he said, "You've got three different things. There's what you know. There's what you think you know. And there's what you can use."

"No shit, Sherlock. So?"

I saw him decide, saw the set of his shoulders shift and harden. He said, "So you get this straight: I didn't go into that house to hurt your mot. Never even thought of it, up until it happened. I know you want me to be the evil villain here; I know that'd fit in great with everything you've always believed. But that's not the way it went. It was nothing like that simple."

"Then enlighten me. What the hell did you go in there to do?"

Shay leaned his elbows on the table and flicked ash off his smoke, watching the orange glow flare and fade. "From the first week I started at the bike shop," he said, "I saved every penny I could, out of my wages. Kept it in an envelope stuck to the back of that poster of Farrah, remember that? So you or Kevin wouldn't nick it, or Da."

I said, "I kept mine in my rucksack. Taped it inside the lining."

"Yeah. It wasn't much, after what went to Ma and the few pints, but it was the only way I kept myself from going mental in that gaff: told myself, every time I counted it up, that by the time I'd the deposit on a bedsit, you'd be old enough to look after the little ones. Carmel'd give you a hand—she's a sound woman, Carmel, she always was. The two of yous would've managed grand, till Kevin and Jackie got big enough to look after themselves. I just wanted a little place of my own, where I could have mates around. Bring home a girlfriend. Get a decent night's sleep, without keeping one ear open for Da. A bit of peace and quiet."

The old, worn-out yearning in his voice could almost have made me feel sorry for him, if I hadn't known better. "I was nearly there," he said. "I was that close. First thing in the new year, I was going to start looking for a place . . . And then Carmel got engaged. I knew she'd want to have the wedding fast, soon as they could get the money off the credit union. I didn't blame her: she deserved her chance to get out, same as I did. God knows the pair of us had earned it. That left you."

He gave me a tired, baleful glance, across the rim of his glass. There was no brotherly love in there, barely even recognition; he was looking at me like I was some huge heavy object that kept appearing in the middle of the road and cracking him across the shins, at the worst possible moments. "Only," he said, "you didn't see it that way, did you? Next thing I knew, I found out you were planning to take off as well—and to London, no less; I'd have been happy with Ranelagh. Fuck your family, yeah? Fuck your turn to take responsibility, and fuck my chance to get out. All our Francis cares about is that he's getting his hole."

I said, "I cared that me and Rosie were going to be happy. There's a decent chance we were about to be the two happiest people on the planet. But you just couldn't leave us to it."

Shay laughed smoke out his nose. "Believe it or not," he said, "I almost did. I was going to beat the shite out of you before you went, all right, send you off on the boat all bruises and hope the Brits gave you hassle at the other end for looking dodgy. But I was going to leave you go. Kevin would've been eighteen in three years' time, he'd've been able to look after Ma and Jackie; I figured I could hang on that long. Only then . . ."

His eyes slipped away, to the window and the dark rooftops and the Hearnes' sparkling tackfest. "It was Da that did it," he said. "That same night

I found out about you and Rosie: that was the night he went mad down in the street outside Dalys', got the Guards called and all . . . I could've hacked three years of the same old same old. But he was getting worse. You weren't there; you didn't see. I'd had enough already. That night was too much."

Me coming home from moonlighting for Wiggy, walking on air; lights blazing and voices murmuring all along the Place, Carmel sweeping up broken china, Shay hiding the sharp knives. All along, I had known that that night mattered. For twenty-two years, I had thought it was what had sent Rosie over the edge. It had never occurred to me that there were other people a lot closer to the edge than she was.

I said, "So you decided to try and bully Rosie into dumping me."

"Not bully her. Tell her to back off. I did, yeah. I had every right."

"Instead of talking to me. What kind of man tries to solve his problems by picking on a girl?"

Shay shook his head. "I would've gone after you, if I thought it'd do any good—you think I *wanted* to go yapping about our family business with some bint, just because she had you by the knackers? But I knew you. You'd never have thought of London on your own. You were still a kid, a great thick kid; you hadn't the brains, or the guts, to come up with anything that big all by yourself. I knew London had to be your one Rosie's idea. I knew I could ask you to stay till I went blue in the face, and you'd still go anywhere she told you to. And I knew without her you'd never get farther than Grafton Street. So I went looking for her."

"And you found her."

"Wasn't hard. I knew what night yous were heading off, and I knew she'd have to call into Number Sixteen. I stayed awake, watched you leave, then went out the back and over the walls."

He drew on his cigarette. His eyes through the trails of smoke were narrow and intent, remembering. "I would've worried I'd missed her, only I could see you, out the top windows. Waiting by the streetlamp, rucksack and all, running away from home. Sweet."

The urge to punch his teeth down his throat was starting to build again, somewhere far in the back reaches of my head. That night had been ours, mine and Rosie's: our secret shimmering bubble that we had built together over months of work, to sail away in. Shay had smeared his grubby fingers over every inch of it. I felt like he had watched me kissing her.

He said, "She came in the same way I did, through the gardens. I got back in a corner and followed her up to the top room, thought I'd give her a scare, but she hardly even jumped. She had guts, anyway; I'll give her that much."

I said, "Yeah. That she did."

"I didn't bully her. I just told her. That you had a responsibility to your family, whether you knew it or not. That in a couple of years, once Kevin was old enough to take over, yous could head off wherever you liked: London, Australia, I wouldn't give a damn. But up until then, you belonged here. Go home, I told her. If you don't fancy waiting a few years, find yourself another fella; if you want to go to England, off you go. Just leave our Francis alone."

I said, "I don't see Rosie taking well to you giving her orders."

Shay laughed, a hard little snort, and ground out his smoke. "No shit. You like the mouthy ones, yeah? First she laughed at me, told me to go home myself and get my beauty sleep or the ladies wouldn't love me any more. But when she copped I was serious, she lost the rag. She kept the volume down, thank Jaysus, but she was raging all right."

She had kept it down at least partly because she knew I was just a few yards away, waiting, listening, just over the wall. If she had screamed for me, I could have got there in time. But Rosie: calling for help would never have occurred to her. She had been well able to sort this tosspot all by herself.

"Still see her standing there, giving out yards: mind your own business and don't be annoying me, not our problem if you can't get yourself a life, your brother's worth a dozen of you any day, you dozy bollix, yak yak yak . . . I did you a favor, saving you from a lifetime of that."

I said, "I'll be sure and write you a thank-you card. Tell me something: what did it, in the end?"

Shay didn't ask, *Did what?* We were past that kind of game. He said, and the rags of that old helpless rage were still caught in the corners of his voice, "I was trying to talk to her. That's how desperate I was: I was trying to tell her what Da was like. What it felt like going home to that, every day.

The things he did. I just wanted her to listen for a minute. You know? Just to fucking *listen*."

"And she wouldn't. My Jaysus, the cheek of her."

"She tried to walk out on me. I was in the doorway, she told me to get out of her way, I grabbed hold of her. Just to make her stay, like. From there . . ." He shook his head, eyes skittering across the ceiling. "I'd never fought a girl, never wanted to. But she wouldn't bleeding shut up, wouldn't bleeding *stop*— She was a vixen, so she was, gave as good as she got; I was covered in scrapes and bruises, after. The bitch nearly kneed me in the balls, and all."

Those rhythmic bumps and whimpers that had made me grin up at the sky, thinking of Rosie. "All I wanted was for her to stay still and listen. I got hold of her, shoved her up against the wall. One second she was kicking me in the shins, trying to scratch the eyes out of me . . ."

A silence. Shay said, to the shadows collecting in the corners, "I never meant for it to end like that."

"It just happened."

"Yeah. It just happened. When I realized . . ."

Another fast jerky shake of his head, another silence. He said, "Then. Once I got my head together, I couldn't leave her there."

Then came the basement. Shay had been strong, but Rosie would have been heavy; my mind snagged hard on the sounds of getting her down the stairs, flesh and bone on cement. Torchlight, the crowbar and the slab of concrete. Shay's wild breathing, and the rats stirring curiously in the far corners, eyes reflecting. The shape of her fingers, curled loose on the damp dirt of the floor.

I said, "The note. Did you go through her pockets?"

His hands running over her limp body: I would have ripped his throat out with my teeth. Maybe he knew that. His lip pulled up in disgust. "The fuck do you think I am? I didn't touch her, only to move her. The note was on the floor in the top room, where she put it—that was what she was doing, when I came in on her. I had a read of it. I figured the second half could stay put, for anyone who wondered where she'd gone. It felt like . . ." A soundless breath, almost a laugh. "Felt like fate. God. A sign."

"Why did you hang on to the first half?"

Shrug. "What else was I going to do with it? I put it in my pocket, to get rid of later. Then, later, I figured you never know. Things come in useful."

"And it did. My Jaysus, did it ever. Did that feel like a sign, too?"

He ignored that. "You were still at the top of the road. I figured you'd hang on for her another hour or two, before you gave up. So I went home." That long trail of rustles, moving through the back gardens, while I waited and started to be afraid.

There were things I would have given years of my life to ask him. What had been the last thing she said; whether she had known what was happening; whether she had been frightened, been in pain, tried to call me in the end. Even if there had been a snowball's chance in hell that he would answer, I couldn't have made myself do it.

Instead I said, "You must have been well pissed off when I never came home. I got farther than Grafton Street, after all. Not as far as London, but far enough. Surprise: you underestimated me."

Shay's mouth twisted. "Overestimated, more like. I thought once you were over the pussy blindness, you'd cop that your family needed you." He was leaning forward across the table, chin jutting, voice starting to wind tighter. "And you owed us. Me and Ma and Carmel between us, we'd kept you fed and clothed and safe, all your life. We got between you and Da. Me and Carmel gave up our education so you could get yours. We had a fucking *right* to you. Her, Rosie Daly, she had no right getting in the way of that."

I said, "So that gave you the right to murder her."

Shay bit down on his lip and reached for the smokes again. He said flatly, "You call it whatever you want. I know what happened."

"Well done. What about what happened to Kevin? What would you call that? Was that murder?"

Shay's face closed over, with a clang like an iron gate. He said, "I never did nothing to Kevin. Never. I wouldn't hurt my own brother."

I laughed out loud. "Right. Then how did he go out that window?"

"Fell. It was dark, he was drunk, the place isn't safe."

"Bloody right, it isn't. And Kevin knew that. So what was he doing in there?"

Shrug, blank blue stare, click of the lighter. "How would I know? I heard there's people who think he had a guilty conscience. And there's plenty of people think he was meeting you. Me, though, I figure maybe he'd found something that was bothering him, and he was trying to make sense of it."

He was too smart ever to bring up the fact that that note had shown up in Kevin's pocket, and smart enough to steer things that way just the same. The urge to punch his teeth in was rising, inch by inch. I said, "That's your story, and you're sticking to it."

Shay said, final as a slamming door, "He fell. That's what happened."

I said, "Let me tell you my story." I took one of Shay's smokes, poured myself another slug of his whiskey and leaned back into the shadows. "Once upon a time, long ago, there were three brothers, just like in a fairy tale. And late one night, the youngest one woke up and something was different: he had the bedroom to himself. Both his brothers were gone. It wasn't a big deal, not at the time, but it was unusual enough that he remembered it the next morning, when only one brother had come home. The other one was gone for good—or anyway for twenty-two years."

Shay's face hadn't changed; not a muscle moved. I said, "When the lost brother finally came home, he came looking for a dead girl, and he found her. That's when the youngest one thought back and realized that he remembered the night she had died. It was the night both his brothers were missing. One of them had gone out to love her, that night. The other one had gone out to kill her."

Shay said, "I already told you: I never meant to hurt her. And you think Kev was smart enough to put all that together? You must be joking me."

The bitter snap in his voice said I wasn't the only one biting down on my temper, which was good to know. I said, "It didn't take a genius. And it wrecked the poor little bastard's head, figuring it out. He didn't want to believe it, did he? He just couldn't stand to believe that his own brother had killed a girl. I'd say he spent his last day on this earth driving himself mental, trying to find some other explanation. He phoned me a dozen times, hoping I'd find one for him, or at least take the whole mess off his hands."

"Is that what this is about? You feel guilty for not taking baby brother's calls, so you're looking for a way to put the blame on me?"

"I listened to your story. Now you let me finish mine. By Sunday evening, Kev's head was melted. And, like you said, he wasn't the brightest little pixie in the forest to start with. All he could think of to do was the straightforward thing, God help him, the honest thing: talk to you, man to man, and see what you had to say. And when you told him to meet you in Number Sixteen, the poor thick bastard walked right in. Tell me something, do you think he was adopted? Or just some kind of mutation?"

Shay said, "He was protected. That's what he was. All his life."

"Not last Sunday, he wasn't. Last Sunday he was vulnerable as hell and he thought he was safe as houses. You gave him all that self-righteous bullshit about—what was it again?—family responsibility and a bedsit of your own, same as you gave me. But none of that meant anything to Kevin. All he knew was the facts, pure and simple: you killed Rosie Daly. And that was too much for him to handle. What did he say that got up your nose that badly? Was he planning on telling me, once he could get hold of me? Or did you even bother to find out, before you went ahead and killed him too?"

Shay shifted in his chair, a wild trapped move, cut off fast. He said, "You haven't a notion, have you? Neither of yous ever did."

"Then you go right ahead and clue me in. Educate me. For starters, how did you get him to stick his head out that window? That was a cute little trick; I'd love to hear how you worked it."

"Who says I did?"

"Talk to me, Shay. I'm just dying of curiosity. Once you heard his skull smash open, did you hang about upstairs, or did you go straight out the back to shove that note in his pocket? Was he still moving when you got there? Moaning? Did he recognize you? Did he beg for help? Did you stand in that garden and watch him die?"

Shay was hunched over the table, shoulders braced and head down, like a man fighting a high wind. He said, low, "After you walked out, it took me twenty-two years to get my chance back. *Twenty-two fucking years.* Can you imagine what they've been like? All four of yous off living your lives, getting married, having kids, like normal people, happy as pigs in shite. And me here, *here*, fucking *here*—" His jaw clenched and his finger stabbed down on the table, over and over. "I could've had all that too. I could've—"

He got some of his control back, caught his breath in a great rasp and pulled hard on his smoke. His hands were shaking.

"Now I've got my chance back. It's not too late. I'm still young enough; I can make that bike shop take off, buy a gaff, have a family of my own—I still get the women. *No one's going to throw that chance away.* No one. Not this time. Not again."

I said, "And Kevin was about to."

Another breath like an animal hissing. "Every bloody time I get close to getting out, so close I can taste it, there's one of my own brothers holding me down. I tried to tell him. He didn't understand. Thick bloody fool, spoilt kid used to everything falling in his lap, didn't have a *clue*—" He bit off the sentence, shook his head and jammed out his smoke viciously.

I said, "So it just happened. Again. You're an unlucky fella, aren't you?"

"Shit happens."

"Maybe. I might even fall for that, if it wasn't for one thing: that note. That didn't suddenly occur to you after Kevin went out the window: gee, I know what would come in useful right now, that piece of paper that I've had hanging around for twenty-two years. You didn't trundle off home to fetch it, take the risk of being seen coming out of Number Sixteen or going back in. You already had it on you. You had the whole thing planned."

Shay's eyes came up to meet mine and they were blazing blue, lit up with an incandescent hate that almost knocked me back in my chair. "You've got some neck, you little bastard, do you know that? Some fucking brass neck, getting all superior with me. Of all people."

Slowly, in the corners, the shadows clotted into thick dark lumps. Shay said, "Did you think I'd forget, just because that would suit you?"

I said, "I don't know what you're talking about."

"Yeah, you do. Calling me a murderer—"

"Here's a little tip for you. If you don't like being called a murderer, don't kill people."

"—when I know and you know: you're no different. Big man, coming back here with your badge and your cop talk and your cop buddies— You can fool anyone you like, fool yourself, go right ahead, you *don't fool me.* You're the same as me. The exact same."

"No I'm not. Here's the difference: I've never murdered anyone. Is that too complex for you?"

"Because you're such a good guy, yeah, such a saint? What a load of *shite*, you give me the sick— That's not morals, that's not holiness. The only reason you never murdered anyone is because your dick beat your brain. If you hadn't been pussy whipped, you'd be a killer now."

Silence, just the shadows seething and heaving in the corners and that telly gibbering mindlessly downstairs. There was a tiny terrible grin, like a spasm, on Shay's mouth. For once in my life, I couldn't think of a damn thing to say.

I was eighteen, he was nineteen. It was a Friday night and I was blowing my dole in the Blackbird, which was not where I wanted to be. I wanted to be out dancing with Rosie, but this was after Matt Daly had put the kibosh on his daughter going anywhere near Jimmy Mackey's son. So I was loving Rosie in secret, having a harder time keeping it hidden every week, and bashing my head off walls like a trapped animal looking for a way to make something, anything, change. On nights when I couldn't take it any more, I got as hammered as I could afford and then picked fights with guys bigger than me.

Everything was going to plan, I had just headed up to the bar for my sixth or seventh and was pulling over a bar stool to lean on while I waited to get served—the barman was down the other end, having an in-depth argument about racing—when a hand came in and whipped the stool out of reach.

Go on, Shay said, swinging a leg over the stool. *Go home.*

Fuck off. I went last night.

So? Go again. I went twice last weekend.

It's your turn.

He'll be home any minute. Go.

Make me.

Which would only get both of us thrown out. Shay eyed me for another second, checking whether I meant it; then he shot me a disgusted look, slid off the stool and threw back one more swallow of his pint. Under his breath, savagely, to no one: *If we'd any balls between the pair of us, we wouldn't put up with this shite . . .*

I said, *We'd get rid of him.*

Shay stopped moving, halfway through flipping up his collar, and stared at me. *Throw him out, like?*

No. Ma'd just take him back in. Sanctity of marriage, and all that shite.

Then what?

Like I said. Get rid of him.

After a moment: *You're serious.*

I had hardly realized that myself, not till I saw the look on his face. *Yeah. I am.*

All around us the pub was buzzing, full to the ceiling with noise and warm smells and men's laughter. The tiny circle between the two of us was still as ice. I was stone-cold sober.

You've been thinking about this.

Don't tell me you haven't.

Shay pulled the stool towards him and sat back down, without taking his eyes off me.

How?

I didn't blink: one flinch and he would throw this away as kids' rubbish, walk out and take our chance with him. *He comes home pissed, how many nights a week? The stairs are falling to bits, the carpet's ripped . . . Sooner or later, he's going to trip and land four flights down, smack on his head.* My heart was in my throat, just from hearing my voice say it out loud.

Shay took a long pull at his pint, thinking hard, and wiped his mouth with a knuckle. *The fall mightn't be enough. To do the job.*

Might, might not. It'd be enough to explain why his head was smashed in, anyway.

Shay was watching me with a mixture of suspicion and, for the first time in our lives, respect. *Why're you telling me?*

It's a two-man gig.

Couldn't go through with it on your own, you mean.

He might fight back, he might need moving, someone might wake up, we might need alibis . . . With one guy, more than likely something'd go pear-shaped, along the way. With two . . .

He hooked an ankle around the leg of another stool and pulled it towards us. *Sit. Home can wait ten minutes.*

I got my pint in and we sat there, elbows on the bar, drinking and not looking at each other. After a while Shay said, *I've been trying for years to think of a way out.*

I know. Same here.

Sometimes, he said. *Sometimes I think maybe, if I don't find one, I'll go mental.*

This was the closest to an intimate brotherly conversation the two of us had ever had. It startled me, how good it felt. I said, *I'm going mental already. No maybe about it. I can feel it.*

He nodded, with no surprise. *Yeah. Carmel is, too.*

And there's days Jackie doesn't look right. After he's had a bad one. She goes spaced out.

Kevin's all right.

For now. As far as we can tell.

Shay said, *It'd be the best thing we could ever do for them, too. Not just for us.*

I said, *Unless I'm missing something, it's the only thing. Not just the best. The only.*

Our eyes finally met. The pub had got noisier; someone's voice rose to a punch line and the corner exploded in rowdy, dirty laughter. Neither of us blinked. Shay said, *I've thought about this before. A couple of times.*

I've been thinking about it for years. Thinking's easy. Doing it . . .

Yeah. Whole different thing. It'd be . . . Shay shook his head. He had rings of white around his eyes, and his nostrils flared every time he breathed.

I said, *Would we be able?*

I don't know. I don't know.

Another long silence, while we both replayed our very favorite father-son moments in our heads. *Yeah,* we said, simultaneously. *We would.*

Shay held out his hand to me. His face was white and red in patches. *OK,* he said, on a fast breath. *OK. I'm in. Are you?*

I'm in, I said, and slapped my hand into his. *We're on.*

We both gripped like we were trying to do damage. I could feel that moment swelling, spreading outwards, rippling into every corner. It was a dizzy, sweet-sick feeling, like shooting up some drug that you knew would leave you crippled for life, but the high was so good that all you could think of was getting it deeper into your veins.

That spring was the only time in our lives when Shay and I voluntarily went near each other. Every few nights, we found ourselves a nice private corner of the Blackbird and we talked: turned the plan over to examine it from every angle, fined off the rough edges, scrapped anything that wouldn't work and started over. We still hated each other's guts, but that had stopped mattering.

Shay spent evening after evening schmoozing Nuala Mangan from Copper Lane: Nuala was a hound and an idiot, but her ma had the finest glazed look around, and after a few weeks Nuala invited Shay home for tea and he nicked a nice big handful of Valium from the bathroom cabinet. I spent hours in the Ilac Centre library, reading medical books, trying to work out how much Valium you would have to slip to a two-hundred-pound woman or a seven-year-old kid to make sure they slept through a certain amount of ruckus, one night, and still woke up when you needed them to. Shay walked all the way to Ballyfermot, where no one knew him and the cops would never go asking, to buy bleach for clean-up. I had a sudden burst of helpfulness and started giving Ma a hand with the dessert every night—Da made nasty comments about me turning into a poof, but every day we were getting closer and the comments were getting easier to ignore. Shay swiped a crowbar from work and hid it under the floorboard with our smokes. We were good at this, the pair of us. We had a knack. We made a good team.

Call me twisted, but I loved that month we spent planning. I had some hassle sleeping, every now and then, but a big part of me was having a blast. It felt like being an architect, or a film director: someone with long-range vision, someone with plans. For the first time ever, I was engineering something huge and complex that, if I could just get it right, would be utterly, utterly worthwhile.

Then all of a sudden someone offered Da two weeks' work, which meant that on the last night he would be coming home at two in the morning with a blood-alcohol level that would stop any cop's suspicions in their tracks, and there were no excuses left for waiting. We were on our final countdown: two weeks to go.

We had run over our alibi till we could have recited it in our sleep. Family dinner, finished off with yummy sherry trifle, courtesy of my new domestic streak—sherry not only dissolved the Valium better than water, it masked the taste, and individual trifles meant personalized doses. Up to the disco at the Grove, over on the northside, in search of a fresh pool of lovely ladies to fish in; getting thrown out by midnight, as memorably as possible, for being loud and obnoxious and for sneaking in our own cans; walking home, stopping along the way to finish off our contraband cans on the banks of the canal. Home around three, when the Valium should have started wearing off, to the shocking sight of our beloved father lying at the bottom of the stairs in a pool of his own blood. Then came the much too late mouth-to-mouth, the frantic banging on the Harrison sisters' door, the wild phone call for an ambulance. Just about everything, except the stop for refreshment, was going to be true.

Probably we would have got caught. Natural talent or no, we were amateurs: there were too many things we had missed, and way too many that could have gone wrong. Even at the time, I half knew that. I didn't care. We had a chance.

We were ready. In my head, I was already living every day as a guy who had killed his own da. And then Rosie Daly and I went to Galligan's one night, and she said *England*.

I didn't tell Shay why I was pulling the plug. At first he thought I was having some kind of sick joke. Slowly, as it dawned on him that I meant it, he got more frantic. He tried bullying, tried threatening, he even tried begging. When none of those worked, he got me by the neck, hauled me out of the Blackbird and beat the shite out of me—it was a week before I could walk upright. I hardly fought back; deep down, I figured he had a right. When he finally exhausted himself and collapsed beside me in the laneway, I could barely see him through the blood, but I think he might have been crying.

I said, "That's not what we're here to talk about."

Shay barely heard me. He said, "At first I thought you just chickened out: didn't have the guts, once it started getting close. I thought that for months, right up until I got talking to Imelda Tierney. Then I knew. It had nothing to do with guts. The only thing you ever cared about was what you wanted. Once you found an easier way to that, the rest wasn't worth a damn to you. Your family, me, everything you owed, everything we'd promised: not a damn."

I said, "Let me make sure I've got this straight. You're giving me shit for not having killed someone?"

His lip pulling up in pure disgust: I'd seen that look on his face a thousand times, when we were little kids and I was trying to keep up. "Don't get clever. I'm giving you shit because you think that puts you above me. You listen to me: maybe your cop mates all believe you're one of the good guys, maybe you can tell yourself the same thing, but *I know better*. I know what you are."

I said, "Pal, I can promise you, you do not have the foggiest clue what I am."

"Do I not? I know this much: that's why you joined the cops. Because of what we almost did, that spring. How it made you feel."

"I had a sudden urge to make amends for my wicked past? The sappy streak is cute on you, but no. Sorry to disappoint."

Shay laughed out loud, a fierce burst that showed his teeth and made him look like that reckless bad-news teenager again. "Make amends, my arse. Not our Francis, not in a million years. No: once you've got a badge to hide behind, you can get away with anything you like. Tell me, Detective. I'm only dying to know. What've you got away with, along the way?"

I said, "You need to get this through your thick skull. All your ifs and buts and almosts mean bugger-all. I *did nothing*. I could walk into any station in the country, confess every single thing we planned that spring, and the only thing I'd get in trouble for would be wasting police time. This isn't church; you don't go to hell just for thinking bad thoughts."

"No? Tell me it didn't change you, that month we spent planning. Tell me you didn't feel different, after. Come on."

Da used to say, a few seconds before the first punch, that Shay never knew when to stop. I said, and my voice should have made him back off, "Surely to sweet baby Jesus in heaven you're not trying to blame me for what you did to Rosie."

That twitch of his lip again, halfway between a tic and a snarl. "I'm only telling you. I'm not going to sit in my own home and watch you give me that self-righteous look, when you're no different from me."

"Yeah, pal, I am. We may have had some interesting conversations, you and me, but when you get down to the actual *facts*, the fact is that I never laid a finger on Da, and the *fact* is that you murdered two people. Call me crazy, but I'm seeing a distinction there."

His jaw had set hard again. "I did nothing to Kevin. Nothing."

In other words, sharing time was over. After a moment I said, "Maybe I'm losing my mind here, but I'm getting the sense you expect me to just nod and smile and walk away. Do me a big fat favor: tell me I'm wrong."

That glitter of hate was back in Shay's eyes, pure and mindless as heat lightning. "Take a look around yourself, Detective. Have you not noticed? You're right back where you started. Your family needs you again, you still owe us, and this time you're going to pay up. Only you're in luck. This time, if you don't fancy sticking around and doing your share, all we need you to do is walk away."

I said, "You think for one second that I'm going to let you away with this, you're even crazier than I thought."

The moving shadows turned his face into a wild animal mask. "Yeah? Let's see you prove it, pig. Kevin's not here to say I went out that night. Your Holly's made of better stuff than you, she won't squeal on family; and even if you twist her arm, you can take everything the child says as gospel, but other people might not feel the same way. Fuck off back to your cop shop and get your little pals to blow you till you feel better. You've got *nothing*."

I said, "I don't know where you got the idea that I'm planning on proving anything." Then I slammed the table into Shay's stomach. He grunted and went over backwards with the table on top of him, glasses and the ashtray and the whiskey bottle thudding everywhere. I kicked my chair out of my way and dived after him. That was the moment when I realized I had come into that flat to kill him.

A second later, when he got hold of the bottle and aimed for my head, I realized that he was trying to kill me too. I ducked sideways and felt it split my temple open, but through the burst of stars I got a grip on his hair and banged his head off the floor till he used the table to shove me off him. I went over hard, flat on my back; he leaped on top of me and we rolled, jabbing for soft spots with everything we had. He was as strong as me and every bit as furious, and neither one of us could let go of the other. We were wrapped together tight as lovers, pressed cheek to cheek. The closeness, and the others downstairs, and nineteen years' worth of practice, muffled us almost silent: the only sounds were hard straining breath and the fleshy thuds when something hit home. I smelled Palmolive soap, straight out of our childhood, and the hot-steam smell of animal rage.

He shot a knee at my balls and scrabbled away, trying to get his feet under him, but his aim was off and I was faster. I got him in an armlock, flipped him onto his back and planted an uppercut on his jaw. By the time he could see straight I had my knee on his chest, my gun out and the barrel pressed to his forehead, right between his eyes.

Shay went still as ice. I said, "The suspect was informed that he was under arrest on suspicion of murder and was cautioned accordingly. He responded by telling me to, quote, fuck off, unquote. I explained that the process would run more smoothly if he behaved in a cooperative fashion, and requested that he present his wrists for handcuffing. Suspect then became enraged and attacked me, striking me in the nose, see attached photograph. I attempted to retreat from the situation, but suspect blocked the exit route. I drew my weapon and warned him to step aside. Suspect refused."

"Your own brother," Shay said, low. He had bitten his tongue; blood bubbled on his lips when he talked. "You dirty little prick."

"*Look who's fucking talking.*" The jolt of fury practically lifted me off the ground. I only realized I had almost pulled the trigger when I saw the fear zap across his eyes. It tasted like champagne. "Suspect continued to abuse me and informed me repeatedly that, quote, I will kill you, unquote, and that, quote, I'm not going to bloody jail, I'll die first, unquote. I attempted to calm him by reassuring him that the situation could be resolved peacefully, and requested again that he come to the station with me to discuss it in a controlled environment. He was in a highly agitated state and did not appear to take in what I was saying. At this point I had become concerned that suspect was under the influence either of some drug, possibly cocaine, or of some mental illness, as his behavior was irrational and he seemed extremely volatile—"

His jaw was clenched. "And on top of everything else, you're going to make me out to be a lunatic. That's how you'll have me remembered."

"Whatever gets the job done. I made numerous attempts to convince the suspect to sit down, in order to bring the situation under control, with no effect. Suspect became increasingly agitated. At this point he was pacing up and down, muttering to himself and striking the walls and his own head with a closed fist. Finally, suspect seized . . . Let's give you something more serious than a bottle; you don't want to go down looking like a pussy. What've you got?" I took a good look around the room: tool kit, of course, neatly tucked away under a chest of drawers. "I'm going to bet there's a wrench in there, am I right? Suspect seized a long metal wrench from an open tool kit, see attached photos, and repeated his threat to kill me. I ordered him to drop his weapon and attempted to move out of striking range. He continued to advance towards me and aimed a blow at my head. I avoided this blow, fired a warning shot over suspect's shoulder—don't worry, I'll keep well clear of the good furniture—and warned him that if he attacked me again I would have no choice but to shoot him—"

"You won't do it. You want to tell your Holly you killed her uncle Shay?"

"I'm going to tell Holly sweet shag-all. The only thing she'll need to know is that she's never coming near this poxy stinking family again. When she's all grown up and she barely remembers who you were, I'll explain that you were a murdering fuck and you got exactly what you deserved." Blood was falling onto him from the split in my temple, big drops soaking into his jumper and spattering his face. Neither of us cared. "Suspect attempted again to strike me with the wrench, this time successfully, see medical records and attached photo of head wound, because trust me on this, sunshine, there will be an absolute beauty of a head wound. The impact caused me to pull the trigger of my weapon reflexively. I believe that, if I had not been partially stunned by the blow, I would have been able to fire a nonlethal disabling shot. However, I also believe that, in the circumstances, firing my weapon was my only option, and that if I had refrained from doing so even for an-other few seconds, my life would have been in serious jeopardy. Signed, Detective Sergeant Francis Mackey. And with no one around to contradict my lovely tidy official version, what do you think they're going to believe?"

Shay's eyes had gone a thousand miles beyond sense or caution. "You give me the sick," he said. "Turncoat pig." And he spat blood in my face.

Light splintered across my eyes like sun slamming through shattered glass, dazzled me weightless. I knew I had pulled the trigger. The silence was huge, spreading out and out till it covered the whole world, not a sound left except the rhythmic rush of my breathing. For a vast dizzy freedom like flying, for wild clean heights that almost burst my chest open, nothing in my life had ever compared to that moment.

Then that light started to dim and that cool silence wavered and broke open, filled up with a babble of shapes and noises. Shay's face materialized like a Polaroid out of the white: battered, staring, covered in blood, but still there.

He made a terrible sound that could have been a laugh. "Told you," he said. "I told you." When his hand started scrabbling for the bottle again, I turned the gun around and smacked him across the head with the butt.

He let out a nasty retching noise and went limp. I cuffed his wrists in front of him, nice and tight, checked that he was breathing and propped him up against the edge of the sofa so he wouldn't choke on his blood. Then I put my gun away and found my mobile. Dialing got messy: my hands smeared blood all over the keypad and my temple dripped onto the screen, I had to keep wiping the phone on my shirt. I kept one ear open for feet pounding up stairs, but all I heard was the faint demented gibbering of the telly; it had masked any stray thumps and grunts that might have filtered through the floor. After a couple of tries, I managed to ring Stephen.

He said, with a certain amount of understandable wariness, "Detective Mackey."

"Surprise, Stephen. I've got our guy. Held, handcuffed and not one bit happy about it."

Silence. I was doing fast circles of the room, one eye on Shay and the other one checking corners for nonexistent sidekicks; I couldn't stand still. "Under the circumstances, it would be a very good thing all round if I weren't the arresting officer. I think you've earned first shot at the collar, if you want it."

That got his attention. "I want it."

"Just so you know, kid, this isn't the dream pressie that Santy's leaving in your Christmas stocking. Scorcher Kennedy is going to go through the roof on a scale I can only begin to imagine. Your main witnesses are me, a nine-year-old kid and a severely pissed-off skanger who will deny knowing anything about anything, just on principle. Your chances of getting a confession are somewhere near nil. The smart thing would be to thank me politely, tell me to ring the Murder Squad room, and go back to whatever it is you do on a Sunday evening. But if playing it safe isn't your style, you can come down here, make your first murder arrest, and take your best shot at making a case. Because this is the guy."

Stephen didn't even pause. He said, "Where are you?"

"Number Eight, Faithful Place. Ring the top buzzer and I'll let you in. This needs to be done very, very discreetly: no backup, no noise, if you drive then park far enough away that no one'll see the car. And hurry."

"I'll be there in about fifteen minutes. Thanks, Detective. Thank you."

He was around the corner, in work. There was no way Scorch had authorized overtime on this one: Stephen had been giving the case one lonely last shot. I said, "We'll be here. And, Detective Moran? Fair play to you." I hung up before he managed to untie his tongue and find an answer.

Shay's eyes were open. He said, painfully, "Your new bitch, yeah?"

"That was one of the rising stars of the force. Nothing but the best for you."

He tried to sit up, winced and let himself fall back against the sofa. "I should've known you'd find someone to hang out of your arse. Now Kevin's not around to do it."

I said, "Is it going to make you feel better if I get into a bitch fight with you? Because if it is, I'll go nuts, but I would've thought we were a few steps past the point where it would make any difference."

Shay swiped at his mouth with his cuffed hands and examined the streaks of blood on them with a kind of strange, detached interest, like they belonged to someone else. He said, "You're actually going to do this."

Downstairs a door opened, letting out a burst of overlapping voices, and Ma yelled, "Seamus! Francis! Your dinner's nearly ready. Come down here and wash your hands!"

I leaned out onto the landing, keeping an eagle eye on Shay and staying a safe distance from the stairwell and Ma's line of vision. "We'll be down in a minute, Ma. Just having a chat."

"Yous can chat here! Or do you want everyone to sit around the table and wait till it suits you?"

I dropped my voice a notch and put a pained twist on it. "We're just . . . We both really need to talk. About stuff, you know. Could we take just a few minutes, Mammy? Would that be all right?"

A pause. Then, grudgingly: "Go on, then. It'll keep an extra ten minutes. If yous aren't down by then—"

"Thanks, Mammy. Seriously. You're a star."

"Course I am, when he wants something I'm a star, the rest of the time . . ." Her voice faded back into the flat, still grumbling.

I shut the door, shot the bolt just in case, got out my phone and took photos of both our faces from various artistic angles. Shay asked, "Proud of your work?"

"It's a thing of beauty. And I've got to hand it to you, yours isn't half bad either. This isn't for my scrapbook, though. It's just in case you decide to start whining about police brutality and trying to dump the arresting officer in the shite, somewhere down the line. Say cheese." He gave me a look that could have flayed a rhino at ten paces.

Once I had the gist of things on record, I headed for the kitchen— small, bare, immaculate and depressing—and soaked a J-cloth to clean the pair of us up with. Shay jerked his head away from it. "Get off. Let your mates see what you did, if you're so proud of it."

I said, "Frankly, my dear, I don't give a damn about my mates. They've seen me do a lot worse. But in a few minutes' time they're going to be walking you down those stairs and up the Place, and it had occurred to me that the entire neighborhood doesn't need to know what's going on here. I'm just trying to keep the drama to a minimum. If that's not your style, by all means let me know and I'll be happy to give you another clatter or two, for top-up."

Shay didn't answer that, but he shut his gob and stayed still while I finished wiping the blood off his face. The flat was quiet, just a faint snatch of music I couldn't place coming from somewhere and a restless wind wandering through the eaves above us. I couldn't remember ever looking this closely at Shay before, close enough to take in all the details that only parents and lovers ever bother to see: the clean savage curves of his bones under the skin, the first speckle of five o'clock shadow, the intricate patterns his crow's-feet made and how thick his lashes were. The blood had started crusting dark on his chin and around his mouth. For a strange second I caught myself being gentle.

There wasn't much I could do about the black eyes or the lump on his jaw, but when I was done he was at least a few steps closer to presentable. I refolded the J-cloth and went at my own face. "How's that?"

He barely glanced at me. "You're grand."

"If you say so. Like I said, it's no skin off my nose what the Place sees."

That made him take a proper look. After a moment he jabbed a finger, almost reluctantly, at the corner of his mouth. "There."

I gave my cheek another scrub and raised an eyebrow at him. He nodded.

"OK," I said. The cloth was smeared with great spreading splotches of blood, blooming crimson all over again where the water had revived them, soaking through the folds. It was starting to come off on my hands. "OK. Hang on there a sec."

"Like I've a choice."

I rinsed the cloth a bunch of times in the kitchen sink, tossed it in the bin for the search team to find later on, and scrubbed my hands hard. Then I went back out to the front room. The ashtray was under a chair in a scatter of gray ash, my smokes were in a corner and Shay was where I had left him. I sat down on the floor opposite him, like we were a couple of teenagers at a party, and put the ashtray between us. I lit two smokes and stuck one between his lips.

Shay inhaled hard, eyes closing, and let his head fall back on the sofa. I leaned back against the wall. After a while he asked, "Why didn't you shoot me?"

"Are you complaining?"

"Don't be a bleeding sap. I'm only asking."

I peeled myself off the wall—it took an effort; my muscles were starting to stiffen up—and reached across to the ashtray. "I guess you were right all along," I said. "I guess, when you get down to it, I'm a cop now."

He nodded, without opening his eyes. The two of us sat there in silence, listening to the rhythm of each other's breathing and to that faint elusive music coming from somewhere, only moving to lean forward and flick ash. It was the nearest to peaceful we'd ever been together. When the buzzer yelled, it almost felt like an intrusion.

I answered fast, before anyone could spot Stephen waiting outside. He ran up the stairs as lightly as Holly running down; the stream of voices from Ma's never changed. I said, "Shay, meet Detective Stephen Moran. Detective, this is my brother, Seamus Mackey."

The kid's face said he had already got that far. Shay looked at Stephen with no expression at all in those swollen eyes, no curiosity, nothing but a kind of distilled exhaustion that made my spine want to sag just looking at it.

"As you can see," I said, "we had a little disagreement. You might want to get him checked out for concussion. I've documented this for future reference, if you need pictures."

Stephen was looking Shay over carefully, from head to toe, not missing an inch. "I might, yeah. Thanks. Do you want those back straight away? I can put him in mine."

He was pointing at my handcuffs. I said, "I'm not planning on arresting anyone else tonight. Get them to me some other time. He's all yours, Detective. He hasn't been cautioned yet; I left that for you. You don't want to get sloppy on the technicalities, by the way. He's smarter than he looks."

Stephen said, trying to phrase it delicately, "What do we . . . ? I mean . . . you know. Reasonable cause for arrest without a warrant."

"I figure this story will probably have a happier ending if I don't spill all our evidence in front of the suspect. But trust me, Detective, this isn't just sibling rivalry gone wild. I'll give you a ring in an hour or so for a full briefing. Until then, this should keep you going: half an hour ago he gave me a full confession to both murders, complete with in-depth motives and details about the manner of death that only the killer could know. He's going to deny it till the cows come home, but luckily I've got lots of other tasty nibbles stashed away for you; that's just your starter. Think it'll hold you for now?"

Stephen's face said he had his doubts about that confession, but he also had better sense than to go there. "That's plenty. Thanks, Detective."

Downstairs, Ma yelled, "Seamus! Francis! If this dinner burns on me, I swear I'll malavogue the pair of yous!"

I said, "I've got to split. Do me a favor: hang on here for a while. My kid's downstairs, and I'd rather she didn't see this. Give me time to get her out before you leave. OK?"

I was talking to both of them. Shay nodded, without looking at either one of us.

Stephen said, "No problem. Will we get comfortable, yeah?" He tilted his head towards the sofa and reached out a hand to haul Shay to his feet. After a second, Shay took it.

I said, "Good luck." I zipped up my jacket over the blood on my shirt, and swiped a black baseball cap—"M. Conaghy Bicycles"—off a coat hook to cover the cut on my head. Then I left them there.

The last thing I saw was Shay's eyes, over Stephen's shoulder. No one had ever looked at me like that, not Liv, not Rosie: like he could see right to the bottom of me, without even trying, and without a single corner left hidden or a single question left unanswered along the way. He never said a word.

22

Ma had pried everyone away from the telly and smacked the Christmas idyll back into shape: the kitchen was crowded with women and steam and voices, the guys were being herded back and forth with pot holders and dishes, the air was hopping with the sizzle of meat and the smell of roast potatoes. It made me light-headed. I felt like I had been gone for years.

Holly was setting the table, with Donna and Ashley; they were even using paper napkins printed with perky angels, and singing "Jingle bells, Batman smells." I let myself take about a quarter of a second to watch them, just to stash away the mental image. Then I put a hand on Holly's shoulder and said in her ear, "Sweetheart, we have to go now."

"*Go?* But—"

She was openmouthed with outrage, and stunned enough that it was a moment before she could get in gear to argue. I gave her the five-alarm-emergency parental eye-flash, and she deflated. "Get your stuff," I said. "Quick, now."

Holly banged down her handful of cutlery on the table and dragged herself off towards the hallway, as slowly as she could get away with. Donna and Ashley stared at me like I had bitten the head off a bunny. Ashley backed away.

Ma stuck her head out of the kitchen, brandishing an enormous serving fork like it was a cattle prod. "Francis! And about bleeding time. Is Seamus with you?"

"No. Ma—"

"Mammy, not Ma. You go find your brother, and the two of yous go in and help your father get out here for the dinner, before you have it burnt to a crisp with your dawdling. Go on!"

"Ma. Holly and I have to go."

Ma's jaw dropped. For a second there, she was actually speechless. Then she went off like an air-raid siren. "*Francis Joseph Mackey!* You're joking me. You tell me this minute that you're joking me."

"Sorry, Ma. I got talking to Shay, lost track of time, you know how it goes. Now we're running late. We need to head."

Ma had her chin and her bosoms and her bellies all inflated ready for battle. "I don't give a feck what time it is, your dinner's ready, and you're not leaving this room till you've eaten it. Sit down at that table. That's an order."

"Can't be done. Sorry again about the hassle. Holly—" Holly was in the doorway, coat dangling half-on one arm, eyes wide. "Schoolbag. Now."

Ma clouted me in the arm with the fork, hard enough to bruise. "*Don't you dare fecking ignore me!* Are you trying to give me a heart attack? Is that what you came back here for, because you wanted to watch your mammy drop dead in front of you?"

Cautiously, one by one, the rest of the gang were appearing in the kitchen doorway behind her to see what was going on. Ashley ducked around Ma and hid in Carmel's skirt. I said, "It wasn't top of my agenda, but hey, if that's how you fancy spending the evening, I can't stop you. Holly, I said *now.*"

"Because if that's the only thing that'll make you happy, you go on and leave, and I hope you'll be satisfied when I'm dead. Go on, get out of here. Your poor brother's after breaking my heart, I've nothing left to live for anyway—"

"Josie!" from the bedroom, in a furious roar. "What the bloody hell is going on?" and the inevitable explosion of coughing. We were neck-deep in just about every single reason I had kept Holly away from this shit hole, and we were sinking fast.

"—and here's me, in spite of everything, killing myself trying to make a lovely Christmas for yous lot, all day and all night at that cooker—"

"Josie! Stop your fucking *shouting*!"

"Da! We've the children here!" from Carmel. She had her hands over Ashley's ears, and she looked like she wanted to curl up and die.

Ma's voice was a screech and still rising. I could practically feel her giving me cancer. "—and you, you ungrateful little bastard, you can't even be bothered sitting your arse down to eat dinner with us—"

"Gee whiz, Ma, it sure is tempting, but I think I'll pass. Holly, wake up! Schoolbag. Go." The kid was starting to look shell-shocked. Even at our worst, Olivia and I had always, always managed to keep the bare-knuckle stuff out of her earshot.

"God forgive me, listen to that, just *listen* to the language out of me, in front of those children—*now* d'you see what you're after making me do?"

Another whack with the serving fork. I caught Carmel's eye over Ma's head, tapped my watch and said, "Custody agreement," in an urgent undertone—I was pretty sure Carmel had watched a lot of movies in which callous ex-husbands tortured brave divorcées by playing fast and loose with custody agreements. Her eyes widened. I left her to explain the concept to Ma, grabbed Holly's arm and her bag and steered her out of there, fast. As we hurried down the stairs ("Out, get out, if you hadn't come back here upsetting everyone we'd still have your brother alive . . .") I caught the even rhythm of Stephen's voice above us, calm and steady, having a nice civilized chat with Shay.

Then we were out of Number 8, in nighttime and lamplight and silence. The hall door slammed behind us.

I got a huge lungful of cool damp evening air and said, "Sweet Jesus." I would happily have killed someone for a cigarette.

Holly twitched her shoulder away from me and whipped her schoolbag out of my other hand.

"I'm sorry about all that back there. I really am. You shouldn't have had to be there for that."

Holly didn't deign to answer, or even to look at me. She marched up the Place with her lips pressed shut and her chin at a mutinous angle that told me I was in big trouble as soon as we got ourselves some privacy. On Smith's Road, three cars down from mine, I spotted Stephen's, a pimped-out Toyota that he had clearly picked from the detective pool to harmonize with the environment. He had a good eye; I only caught it because of the elaborately casual guy slumped in the passenger seat, refusing to look my way. Stephen, like a good little Boy Scout, had come prepared for anything.

Holly flung herself into her booster seat and slammed the car door hard enough that it nearly came off the hinges. "*Why* do we have to go?"

She genuinely had no idea. She had left the Shay situation in Daddy's capable hands; as far as she was concerned, that meant it was sorted, over and done with. One of my main ambitions had been for her to go through life, or at least a few more years of it, without discovering it didn't work that way.

"Sweetheart," I said. I didn't start the car; I wasn't sure I could drive. "Listen to me."

"Dinner's *ready*! We put *plates* for you and me!"

"I know. I wish we could have stayed, too."

"So *why*—"

"You know that conversation you had with your uncle Shay? Just before I got there?"

Holly stopped moving. Her arms were still folded furiously across her chest, but her mind was racing, behind no expression at all, to work out what was going on. She said, "I guess."

"Do you think you could explain that conversation to someone else?"

"You?"

"No, not me. This guy I know from work, called Stephen. He's only a couple of years older than Darren, and he's very nice." Stephen had mentioned sisters; I just hoped he had been good with them. "He really needs to hear what you and your uncle were talking about."

Holly's lashes flickered. "I don't remember."

"Sweetie, I know you said you wouldn't tell anyone. I heard you."

A quick, wary flash of blue. "Heard what?"

"I'm going to bet it was just about everything."

"Then if you heard, *you* tell that Stephen guy."

"Won't work, love. He needs to hear it direct from you."

Her fists were starting to clench on the sides of her jumper. "So, tough. I can't *tell* him."

I said, "Holly. I need you to look at me." After a moment her head turned, reluctantly, an inch or two in my direction. "Remember we talked about how, sometimes, you need to tell a secret because someone else has a right to know it?"

Shrug. "So?"

"So this is that kind of secret. Stephen's trying to find out what happened to Rosie." I left Kevin out of it: we were already several light-years beyond what the kid should have been coping with. "That's his job. And to do it, he needs to hear your story."

More elaborate shrug. "I don't care."

Just for a second, the stubborn tilt to her chin reminded me of Ma. I was fighting against every instinct she had, everything I had put into her bloodstream straight from my own veins. I said, "You need to care, sweetheart. Keeping secrets is important, but there are times when getting to the truth is even more important. When someone's been killed, that's almost always one of those times."

"Good. Then Stephen Thingy can go bug somebody else and leave me alone, 'cause I don't think Uncle Shay even did anything *bad*."

I looked at her, tense and prickly and shooting off sparks like a wild kitten trapped in a corner. Just a few months earlier she could have done what I asked her to, unquestioning, and still kept her faith in lovely Uncle Shay intact. It seemed like every time I saw her the tightrope got thinner and the drop got longer, till it was inevitable that sooner or later I would get the balance wrong and miss my foothold just once, and take both of us down.

I said, keeping my voice even, "OK, kiddo. Then let me ask you something. You planned today pretty carefully, amn't I right?"

That wary blue flash again. "No."

"Come on, chickadee. I'm the wrong guy to mess with on this one. This is my job, planning this exact kind of stuff; I know when I see someone else doing it. Way back after you and me first talked about Rosie, you started thinking about that note you'd seen. So you asked me about her, nice and casually, and when you found out she'd been my girlfriend, you knew she had to be the one who'd written it. That's when you started wondering why your uncle Shay would have a note from a dead girl stashed away in his drawer. Tell me if I'm going wrong here."

No reaction. Boxing her in like a witness made me so tired I wanted to slide off my seat and go to sleep on the car floor. "So you worked on me till you got me to bring you over to your nana's today. You left your maths homework till last, all weekend, so you could bring it along and use it to get your uncle Shay on his own. And then you went on at him till you got him talking about that note."

Holly was biting down hard on the inside of her lip. I said, "I'm not giving out to you; you did a pretty impressive job of the whole thing. I'm just getting the facts straight."

Shrug. "So what?"

"So here's my question. If you didn't think your uncle Shay had done anything wrong, then why did you go to all that hassle? Why not just tell me what you'd found, and let me talk to him about it?"

Down to her lap, almost too low to be intelligible: "Wasn't any of your business."

"But it was, honeybunch. And you knew it was. You knew Rosie was someone I cared about, you know I'm a detective, and you knew I was trying to find out what had happened to her. That makes that note very much my business. And it's not like anyone had asked you to keep it a secret to begin with. So why didn't you tell me, unless you knew there was something dodgy about it?"

Holly carefully unraveled a thread of red wool from her cardigan sleeve, stretched it between her fingers and examined it. For a second I thought she was going to answer, but instead she asked, "What was Rosie like?"

I said, "She was brave. She was stubborn. She was a laugh." I wasn't sure where we were going with this, but Holly was watching me sideways, intently, like it mattered. The dull yellow light from the street lamps turned her eyes darker and more complicated, harder to read. "She liked music, and adventures, and jewelry, and her friends. She had bigger plans than anyone else I knew. When she cared about something, she didn't give up on it, no matter what. You would have liked her."

"No I wouldn't."

"Believe it or not, chickadee, you would've. And she would have liked you."

"Did you love her more than Mum?"

Ah. "No," I said, and it came out so cleanly and simply that I was nowhere near sure it was a lie. "I loved her a different way. Not more. Just differently."

Holly stared out the window, winding the bit of wool around her fingers and thinking her own intent thoughts. I didn't interrupt. Up at the corner, a troop of kids barely older than her were pushing each other off a wall, snarling and chattering like monkeys. I caught the glow of a cigarette and the glint of cans.

Finally Holly said, in a tight, level little voice, "Did Uncle Shay kill Rosie?"

I said, "I don't know. It's not up to me to decide that, or to you. It's up to a judge and a jury."

I was trying to make her feel better, but her fists clenched and she hammered them down on her knees. "Daddy, no, that's not what I mean, I don't care what anyone *decides*! I mean *really*. Did he?"

I said, "Yeah. I'm pretty sure he did."

Another silence, longer this time. The monkeys on the wall had switched to mashing crisps in each other's faces and hooting encouragement. In the end Holly said, still in that tight small voice, "If I tell Stephen what me and Uncle Shay talked about,"

"Yeah?"

"Then what happens?"

I said, "I don't know. We'll have to wait and find out."

"Will he go to jail?"

"He might. It depends."

"On me?"

"Partly. Partly on a lot of other people, too."

Her voice wavered, just a touch. "But he never did anything *bad* to me. He helps me with homework, and he showed me and Donna how to make shadows with our hands. He lets me have sips out of his coffee."

"I know, sweetie. He's been a good uncle to you, and that's important. But he's done other stuff, too."

"I don't *want* to make him go to jail."

I tried to catch her eye. "Sweetheart, listen to me. No matter what happens, it won't be your fault. Whatever Shay did, he did it himself. Not you."

"He'll still be mad. And Nana, and Donna, and Auntie Jackie. They'll all hate me for telling."

That wobble in her voice was getting wilder. I said, "They'll be upset, yeah. And there's a chance they might take that out on you for a bit, just at first. But even if they do, it'll wear off. They'll all know none of this is your fault, just like I do."

"You don't know for definite. They could hate me forever and ever. You can't promise."

Her eyes were white-ringed, hunted. I wished I had hit Shay a lot harder while I had the chance. "No," I said. "I can't."

Holly slammed both feet into the back of the passenger seat. "I don't *want* this! I want everyone to go away and leave me alone. I wish I never even *saw* that stupid note!"

Another slam that rocked the seat forward. She could have kicked my car to pieces for all I cared, if it made her feel any better, but she was going at it hard enough to hurt herself. I leaned around, fast, and got an arm between her feet and the seat back. She made a wild helpless noise and twisted furiously, trying to get a clear kick without hitting me, but I caught her ankles and held on. "I know, love. I know. I don't want any of this either, but here it is. And I wish to God I could say that everything'll be all right once you tell the truth, but I can't. I can't even promise that you'll feel better; you might, but you could just as easily end up feeling even worse. All I can tell you is that you need to do it, either way. Some things in life aren't optional."

Holly had slumped back in her booster seat. She took a deep breath and tried to say something, but instead she clamped a hand over her mouth and started to cry.

I was about to get out and climb into the back to hug her tight. It hit me just in time: this wasn't a little kid howling, waiting for Daddy to sweep her up in his arms and make everything all better. We had left that behind, somewhere in Faithful Place.

Instead I stretched out my hand and took Holly's free one. She held on like she was falling. We sat there like that, with her leaning her head against the window and shaking all over with huge silent sobs, for a long time.

Behind us I heard men's voices swapping a few brusque comments, and then car doors slamming, and then Stephen driving away.

Neither of us was hungry. I made Holly eat anyway, some radioactive-looking cheese croissant thing that we picked up at a Centra on the way, more for my sake than for hers. Then I took her back to Olivia's.

I parked in front of the house and turned around to look at Holly. She was sucking a strand of hair and gazing out the window with wide, still, dreamy eyes, like fatigue and overload had put her into a trance. Somewhere along the way she had fished Clara out of her bag.

I said, "You didn't finish your maths. Is Mrs. O'Donnell going to get in a snot about that?"

For a second Holly looked like she had forgotten who Mrs. O'Donnell was. "Oh. I don't care. She's stupid."

"I bet she is. There's no reason you should have to listen to her being stupid about this, on top of everything else. Where's your notebook?"

She dug it out, in slow motion, and handed it over. I flipped to the first blank page and wrote, *Dear Mrs. O'Donnell, please excuse Holly for not finishing her maths homework. She hasn't been well this weekend. If this is a problem, feel free to give me a call. Many thanks. Frank Mackey.* On the opposite page I saw Holly's round, painstaking handwriting: *If Desmond has 342 pieces of fruit . . .*

"There," I said, passing the notebook back to her. "If she gives you any hassle, you give her my phone number and tell her to back off. OK?"

"Yeah. Thanks, Daddy."

I said, "Your mother's going to need to know about this. Let me do the explaining there."

Holly nodded. She put the notebook away, but she stayed put, clicking her seat belt open and shut. I said, "What's bugging you, chickadee?"

"You and Nana were mean to each other."

"Yeah. We were."

"How come?"

"We shouldn't have been. Every now and then, though, we just get on each other's nerves. Nobody in the world can make you crazy like your family can."

Holly stuffed Clara into her bag and gazed down at her, stroking the threadbare nose with one finger. "If I did something bad," she said. "Would you tell lies to the police to keep me from getting in trouble?"

"Yeah," I said. "I would. I would lie to the police and the Pope and the president of the world till I was blue in the face, if that was what you needed. It would be the wrong thing to do, but I'd do it just the same."

Holly startled the hell out of me by leaning forward between the seats, wrapping her arms around my neck and pressing her cheek against mine. I hugged her tight enough that I could feel her heartbeat against my chest, quick and light as a little wild animal's. There were a million things I needed to say to her, every one of them crucial, but none of them would come out of my mouth.

Finally Holly sighed, an enormous shaky sigh, and disentangled herself. She climbed out of the car and hoisted her schoolbag onto her back. "If I have to talk to that Stephen guy," she said. "Could it be not on Wednesday? Because I want to go play at Emily's."

"That's absolutely fine, sweetie. Whatever day suits you. Go on ahead, now. I'll be in to you in a bit; I've just got to make a phone call."

Holly nodded. There was an exhausted sag to her shoulders, but as she went up the path she gave her head a little shake and braced herself. By the time Liv answered the door with her arms open, that narrow back was straight and strong as steel.

I stayed where I was, lit a smoke and sucked down about half of it in one drag. When I was sure I could keep my voice steady, I phoned Stephen.

He was somewhere with crappy reception, presumably deep in the warren of Murder rooms in Dublin Castle. I said, "It's me. How's it going?"

"Not too bad. Like you said, he's denying everything, and that's when he bothers answering me at all; mostly he won't talk, except to ask me what your hole tastes like."

"He's a charmer. It runs in the family. Don't let him get to you."

Stephen laughed. "Ah, God, I'm not bothered. He can say whatever he likes; at the end of the day, I'm the one going home when we finish up. Tell us, though: what've you got? Anything that might get him feeling a bit chattier?"

He was all charged up and ready to keep going for as long as it took, and his voice was bursting with brand-new confidence. He was trying to sound tactfully subdued, but deep down, the kid was having the time of his life.

I gave him everything I had and how I had got it, down to the last rancid stinking detail: info is ammo, and Stephen didn't need any blanks in his stockpile. At the end I said, "He's fond of our sisters, especially Carmel, and of my daughter, Holly. As far as I know, that's it. He hates my guts, he hated Kevin's but he doesn't like admitting that, and he hates his life. He's viciously jealous of anyone who doesn't, almost definitely including you. And, as you've probably figured out what with one thing and another, he's got a temper."

"OK," Stephen said, almost to himself; his mind was going flat out. "OK, yeah. I can use that."

The kid was turning into a man after my own heart. "Yeah, you can. One more thing, Stephen: up until this evening, he thought he was inches away from getting out. He thought he was about to buy the bike shop where he works, dump our da in a home, move out, and finally get his shot at a life worth having. A few hours ago, the world was this guy's oyster."

Silence, and for a second there I wondered if Stephen had taken that as an invitation to get his compassion on. Then he said, "If I can't get him talking with that, I don't deserve to get him talking at all."

"That'd be my general feeling. Go for it, kid. Keep me posted."

Stephen said, "Do you remember," and then the reception went nuts and he turned into a bunch of disjointed scraping noises. I heard, ". . . all they've got . . ." before the line cut out and there was nothing left but pointless beeping.

I rolled down my window and had another smoke. The Christmas decorations were coming out here too — wreaths on doors, a "SANTA PLEASE STOP HERE" sign stuck lopsided in a garden—and the night air had turned cold and glassy enough that it finally felt like winter. I threw my cigarette butt away and took a deep breath. Then I went up to Olivia's door and rang the bell.

Liv answered in her slippers, with her face washed ready for bed. I said, "I told Holly I'd come in and say good night."

"Holly's asleep, Frank. She's been in bed for ages."

"Ah. OK." I shook my head, trying to clear it. "How long was I out there?"

"Long enough that I'm amazed Mrs. Fitzhugh didn't ring the Guards. These days she's seeing stalkers everywhere."

She was smiling, though, and the fact that she wasn't annoyed at me for being there gave me a ridiculous little flash of warmth. "That woman always was a fruitcake. Remember the time we—" I saw the retreat in Liv's eyes and caught myself before it was too late. "Listen, is it OK if I come in for a few minutes anyway? Grab a cup of coffee, clear my head before I drive home, maybe have a quick chat about how Holly's doing? I promise not to overstay my welcome."

Clearly I looked like I felt, or at least enough like I felt to push Liv's pity buttons. After a moment she nodded and held the door wide.

She took me into the conservatory—there was frost starting in the corners of the windowpanes, but the heating was on and the room was snug and warm—and went back to the kitchen to make the coffee. The lights were low; I took off Shay's baseball cap and shoved it into my jacket pocket. It smelled of blood.

Liv brought out the coffee on a tray, with the good cups and even a little jug of cream. She said, settling into her chair, "You look like you've had quite a weekend."

I couldn't make myself do it. "Family," I said. "How about you? How's Dermo?"

There was a silence, while Olivia stirred her coffee and decided how to answer that. Finally she sighed, a tiny sound I wasn't meant to hear. She said, "I told him I didn't think we should see each other any more."

"Ah," I said. The quick sweet shot of happiness, straight through all the dark layers that were wrapped tight around my mind, took me by surprise. "Any particular reason?"

Elegant little shrug. "I didn't think we were well suited."

"And did Dermo agree with that?"

"He would have, soon enough. If we'd been on a few more dates. I just got there a bit faster."

"As usual," I said. I wasn't being bitchy, and Liv smiled a little, down at her cup. "Sorry it didn't work out."

"Ah, well. You win some . . . What about you? Have you been seeing anyone?"

"Not recently. Not so you'd notice." Olivia dumping Dermot was the best present life had given me in a while—small, but perfectly formed; you take what you can get—and I knew if I pushed my luck I would probably smash it to pieces, but I couldn't stop myself. "Some evening, maybe, if you're free and we can get a babysitter, would you fancy going for dinner? I'm not sure I can swing the Coterie, but I can probably find somewhere better than Burger King."

Liv's eyebrows went up and her face turned towards me. "Do you mean . . . What do you mean? As in, a date?"

"Well," I said. "Yeah, I guess so. Very much as in a date."

A long silence, while things moved behind her eyes. I said, "I did listen to what you said the other night, you know. About people wrecking each other's heads. I still don't know if I agree with you, but I'm trying to act like you're right. I'm trying bloody hard, Olivia."

Liv leaned her head back and watched the moon moving past the windows. "The first time you took Holly for the weekend," she said, "I was terrified. I didn't sleep a wink the whole time she was gone. I know you thought I'd been fighting you for the weekends out of sheer spite, but it had nothing to do with that. I was positive you were going to take her and get on a plane, and I'd never see either one of you again."

I said, "The thought had crossed my mind."

I saw the shudder go across her shoulders, but her voice stayed steady. "I know. But you didn't go through with it. I don't fool myself that that was for my sake; partly it was because leaving would have meant giving up your job, but mainly it was because it would have hurt Holly, and you wouldn't do that. So you stayed here."

"Yeah," I said. "Well. I do my best." I was less convinced than Liv that staying put had turned out to be in Holly's best interests. The kid could have been helping me run a beach bar in Corfu, turning brown and getting spoilt rotten by the locals, instead of having her head cluster-bombed by her entire extended family.

"That's what I meant, the other day. People don't *have* to hurt each other just because they love each other. You and I made each other miserable because we decided to, not because it was some kind of inevitable fate."

"Liv," I said. "I need to tell you something."

I had spent most of the car ride trying to find the low-drama way to do this. It turned out there was no such thing. I left out everything I could and toned down the rest, but by the time I finished Olivia was staring at me, huge-eyed, with trembling fingertips pressed to her mouth. "Sweet Lord," she said. "Oh, sweet Lord. *Holly*."

I said, with all the conviction I could find, "She's going to be all right."

"On her own with a— *God*, Frank, we have to— What do we—"

It had been so long since Liv had let me see her in any mode but poised and glossy, perfectly armored. Like this, raw and shaking and wild to find a way to protect her baby, she cracked me wide open. I knew better than to put my arms around her, but I leaned across and folded my fingers around hers. "Shh, hon. Shh. It'll be OK."

"Did he threaten her? Frighten her?"

"No, honey. He had her worried and confused and uncomfortable, but I'm pretty sure she never felt like she was in any danger. I don't think she was, either. In his own incredibly fucked-up way, he does care about her."

Liv's mind was already zipping ahead. "How strong is the case? Will she have to testify?"

"I'm not sure." We both knew the list of ifs: if the DPP decided to prosecute, if Shay didn't plead guilty, if the judge figured Holly was capable of giving an accurate account of events . . . "If I had to put money on it, though, then yeah. I'd bet she will."

Olivia said, again, "Sweet Lord."

"It won't be for a while."

"That's beside the point. I've seen what a good barrister can do to a witness. I've *done* it. I don't want it done to Holly."

I said gently, "You know there's nothing we can do about it. We'll just have to trust her to be OK. She's a strong kid. She always has been." For a needle-stab second I remembered sitting in that conservatory on spring evenings, watching something fierce and tiny bounce off the inside of Olivia's belly, ready to take on the world.

"She is, yes, she's strong. That doesn't *matter*. No child in the *world* is strong enough for this."

"Holly will be, because she doesn't have a choice. And Liv . . . you already know this, too, but you can't talk about the case with her."

Olivia's hand whipped out of mine and her head went up, ready to defend her young. "She's going to need to talk about it, Frank. I can't begin to imagine what this has been like for her, I'm *not* having her bottling it all up—"

"Right, but you can't be the one she talks to, and neither can I. As far as a jury's concerned, you're still a prosecutor: you're biased. One hint that you've been coaching her, and the whole case goes out the window."

"I don't give a damn about the *case*. Who else is she supposed to talk to? You know perfectly well she won't talk to a counselor, when we separated she wouldn't say a single word to that woman— I won't have this damaging her for life. I won't have it."

The optimism of her, the faith that the job hadn't already been done, reached right inside my rib cage and squeezed. "No," I said. "I know you won't. Tell you what: you get Holly to talk as much as she needs to. Just make sure no one ever finds out about it. Including me. OK?"

Olivia's lips tightened, but she said nothing. I said, "I know it's not ideal."

"I thought you were so passionately against her keeping secrets."

"I am. But it's a little late for that to be top priority now, so what the hell."

Liv said, and there was a grating note of exhaustion at the bottom of her voice, "I suppose that translates as, 'I told you so.'"

"No," I said, and meant it. I caught the surprise in the quick turn of her head towards me. "Absolutely not. It means that we both fucked up here, you and me, and now the best thing we can do is concentrate on damage limitation. And I trust you to do a pretty impressive job of that."

Her face was still wary and tired, waiting for the twist. I said, "No hidden meaning this time. I promise. I'm just glad the kid has you for a mother, right now."

I had taken Liv off guard; her eyes flickered away from mine, and she shifted restlessly in her chair. "You should have told me as soon as you got here. You let me put her to bed as if everything was *normal*—"

"I know I did. I figured she could do with a bit of normality tonight."

She moved again, sharply. "I need to check on her."

"If she wakes up, she'll call us. Or come down."

"She mightn't. I'll only be a moment—"

And she was gone, hurrying up the stairs as quietly as a cat. There was something weirdly comforting about this little routine. We used to go through it a dozen times a night, back when Holly was a baby: one squeak on the monitor and Olivia would need to go make sure she was still asleep, no matter how often I tried to reassure her that the kid had a fine set of lungs and was well able to let us know if she wanted us. Liv was never afraid of cot death or of Holly falling out of bed and hitting her head or any of the standard-issue parental boogeymen. All she worried about was that Holly might wake up, in the middle of the night, and think she was all alone.

Olivia said, coming back in, "Fast asleep."

"Good."

"She looks peaceful. I'll talk to her in the morning." She dropped into her chair and pushed her hair out of her face. "Are you all right, Frank? I didn't even think to ask, but my God, tonight must have been—"

I said, "I'm fine. I should be heading, though. Thanks for the coffee. I needed that."

Liv didn't push it. She asked, "Are you awake enough to drive home?"

"Not a problem. I'll see you on Friday."

"Ring Holly tomorrow. Even if you don't think you should talk to her about . . . all of this. Ring her anyway."

"Course. I was going to." I tossed back the last of my coffee and stood up. "Just so I know," I said. "I assume that date is out of the question now."

Olivia watched my face for a long time. She said, "We'd have to be very careful not to get Holly's hopes up."

"We can do that."

"Because I can't see much chance that it would go anywhere. Not after . . . God. Everything."

"I know. I'd just like to try."

Olivia moved in her chair. The moonlight shifted on her face, so that her eyes vanished into shadow and all I could see was the proud delicate curves of her lips. She said, "So that you'll know you've made every possible effort. Better late than never, I suppose."

"No," I said. "Because I'd really, really like to go on a date with you."

I could feel her still watching me, out of the shadows. Finally she said, "I'd like that too. Thank you for asking me."

There was a tumbling split second when I almost moved towards her, almost reached out to do I don't know what: grab her, crush her against me, go on my knees on the marble tiles and bury my face in her soft lap. I stopped myself by clenching my teeth so hard, I almost snapped my jaw. When I could move again, I took the tray out to the kitchen and left.

Olivia didn't move. I let myself out; maybe I said good night, I don't remember. All the way out to the car I could feel her behind me, the heat of her, like a clear white light burning steadily in the dark conservatory. It was the only thing that got me home.

23

I left my family alone while Stephen put together his case, and while he charged Shay with two counts of murder, and while the High Court turned Shay down for bail. George, God bless his cotton socks, let me come back to work without saying a word; he even threw me a new and insanely complicated operation, involving Lithuania and AK-47s and several interesting guys named Vytautas, on which I could easily work hundred-hour weeks if I felt the urge, which I did. Squad rumor claimed that Scorcher had filed an outraged complaint about my general lack of protocol, and that George had surfaced from his usual semicoma long enough to hit him with several years' worth of nitpicky paperwork requesting further information in triplicate.

When I figured my family's emotional pitch might have dropped a notch or two, I picked an evening and got home from work early, around ten o'clock. I put whatever was in the fridge between two slices of bread and ate it. Then I took a smoke and a glass of Jameson's finest out onto the balcony, and phoned Jackie.

"Jaysus," she said. She was at home, with the telly going in the background. Her voice was blank with surprise; I couldn't tell what else was under there. To Gavin: "It's Francis."

An unintelligible mutter from Gav, and then the TV noise fading as Jackie moved away. She said, "Jaysus. I didn't think . . . How're you getting on, anyway?"

"Hanging in there. How about you?"

"Ah, sure. You know yourself."

I said, "How's Ma doing?"

A sigh. "Ah, she's not great, Francis."

"What way?"

"She's looking a bit peaky, and she's awful quiet—and you know yourself, that's not like her. I'd be happier if she was giving out right and left."

"I was afraid she'd have a heart attack on us." I tried to make it sound like I was joking. "I should've known she wouldn't give us the satisfaction."

Jackie didn't laugh. She said, "Carmel was telling me she was over there last night, herself and Darren, and Darren knocked over that porcelain yoke—you know the one of the little young fella with the flowers, on the shelf in the front room? Smashed it to bits. He was afraid for his life, but Mammy didn't say a word, just swept it up and threw it in the bin."

I said, "She'll be all right in the long run. Ma's tough. It'd take more than this to break her."

"She is, yeah. Still, but."

"I know. Still."

I heard a door shutting, and wind catching at the phone: Jackie had taken this conversation outside, for privacy. She said, "The thing is, Da's not the best either. He hasn't got out of the bed, ever since . . ."

"Fuck him. Leave him there to rot."

"I know, yeah, but that's not the point. Mammy can't manage on her own, not with him like that. I don't know what they're going to do. I do be over there as much as I can, and so does Carmel, but she's got the kiddies and Trevor, and I've to work. Even when we're over, sure, we're not strong enough to lift him without hurting him; and anyway he doesn't want us girls helping him out of the bath and all. Shay . . ."

Her voice trailed off. I said, "Shay used to do all that."

"Yeah."

I said, "Should I go over and give a hand?"

There was a startled instant of silence. "Should you . . . ? Ah, no; no, Francis. You're all right."

"I'll get my arse down there tomorrow, if you think it's a good idea. I've been staying clear because I figured I'd do more harm than good, but if I'm wrong . . ."

"Ah, no; I'd say you're right. Not meaning that in a bad way, like; just . . ."

"No, I get you. That's what I thought."

Jackie said, "I'll tell them you were asking after them."

"You do that. And if anything changes down the road, just let me know, yeah?"

"I will, yeah. Thanks for the offer."

I said, "What about Holly?"

"What d'you mean?"

"Is she going to be welcome over at Ma's, from now on?"

"Do you want her to be? I thought for sure . . ."

"I don't know, Jackie. I haven't got that far yet. Probably not, no. But I do want to know exactly where she stands."

Jackie sighed, a small sad flutter. "Sure, no one else knows that either. Not till . . . you know. Till things sort themselves out a bit."

Till Shay had been tried and acquitted, or else convicted and put away for life twice over, either way due at least partly to what kind of job Holly did giving evidence against him. I said, "I can't afford to wait that long, Jackie. And I can't afford to have you being coy with me. This is my kid we're talking about."

Another sigh. "Being honest with you, Francis, if I was you I'd keep her away for a bit. For her own sake. Everyone's a mess, everyone's up to ninety, sooner or later someone's going to say something that'll hurt her feelings— not meaning to, but . . . Leave it for now. Do you think that'd be all right? It wouldn't be too hard on her, like?"

I said, "That I can deal with. But here's the thing, Jackie. Holly's flat-out positive that what happened to Shay is her fault, and that even if it isn't, the whole family thinks it is. Keeping her away from Ma's—not that I have any problem with that, believe me—is only going to leave her more convinced. Frankly, I don't give a fuck if it's one hundred percent true and everyone else in the family's decided she's a leper, but I need her to know that you're the exception here. The kid is in pieces, and she's already lost enough people to last her a lifetime. I need her to know that you're still in her life, that you've got no intention of abandoning her, and that you don't for one instant blame her for the anvil that's after landing on all of our heads. Is any of that going to be a problem?"

Jackie was already making horrified sympathetic noises. "Ah, God love her, the poor little dote, how would I blame her—sure, she wasn't even born when all this started! You give her a big hug from me and tell her I'll be round to see her the second I get a chance."

"Good. That's what I figured. It doesn't matter what I tell her, though: she needs to hear it from you. Can you give her a ring, set up a time to go hang out with her? Put the poor kid's mind at ease. OK?"

"I will, of course. Come here, let me go do that now, I hate the thought of her sitting there getting herself all worried and upset—"

"Jackie," I said. "Hang on a sec."

"Yeah?"

I wanted to smack myself across the back of the head for asking, but it came out anyway. "Tell me something, while we're on the subject. Am I going to be hearing from you again, too? Or is it just Holly?"

The pause only lasted a fraction of a second, but that was long enough. I said, "If that's not on the cards, babe, I'm OK with it. I can see where you'd be having trouble here. I just like knowing what the story is; I find it saves time and hassle all round. Does that not sound fair enough?"

"Yeah. It does. Ah, God, Francis . . ." A quick catch of breath, almost a spasm, like she'd been gut-punched. "Course I'll be back in touch. *Course* I will. Just . . . I might need a little while. A few weeks, maybe, or . . . I'm not going to lie to you: my head's melted. I don't know what to do with myself. It could be a while before . ."

"Makes sense," I said. "Believe me, I know the feeling."

"I'm sorry, Francis. I'm really, really sorry."

Her voice sounded thin and desperate, frayed to the last thread. It would have taken an even bigger sonofabitch than me to make her feel worse. I said, "Shit happens, kid. This wasn't your fault, any more than it was Holly's."

"It was, but. If I hadn't brought her over to Mammy's to begin with . . ."

"Or if I hadn't brought her that specific day. Or, better yet, if Shay hadn't . . . Well, there we go." The rest of the sentence unraveled into the empty air between us. "You did your best; that's all anyone can do.

You go unmelt your head, babe. Take your time. Call me when you're done."

"I will. Honest to God, I will. And, Francis . . . you look after yourself, meanwhile. Seriously, now."

"Will do. You too, honeybunch. See you out there."

Just before Jackie hung up, I heard that fast, painful catch of breath again. I hoped she would go in to Gavin and let him hug her, instead of standing outside in the darkness, crying.

A few days later I went to the Jervis Centre and bought the kind of King Kong telly that you buy if the possibility of saving up for anything more substantial has never entered your universe. I felt it would take more than electronics, no matter how impressive, to stop Imelda from kicking me in the goolies, so I parked my car at the top of Hallows Lane and waited for Isabelle to get home from wherever she went all day.

It was a cold gray day, sky heavy with sleet or snow waiting to fall, thin skins of ice on the potholes. Isabelle came down Smith's Road walking fast, with her head down and her thin fake-designer coat pulled tight against the slicing wind. She didn't see me till I got out of the car and stepped in front of her.

I said, "Isabelle, yeah?"

She gave me a wary stare. "Who wants to know?"

"I'm the prick who smashed your telly. Nice to meet you."

"Fuck off or I'll scream."

And a chip off the old block personality-wise, too. The kid gave me the warm fuzzies all over. I said, "Dial it down a notch there, Penelope Pitstop. This time I'm not here to give you hassle."

"Then what d'you want?"

"I brought you a new telly. Happy Christmas."

The suspicion on her face got deeper. "Why?"

"You've heard of a guilty conscience, yeah?"

Isabelle folded her arms and shot me the filthies. Up close, the resemblance to Imelda was still there, but not as strong. She had the round

Hearne nub of a chin. "We don't want your telly," she informed me. "Thanks all the same."

I said, "Maybe you don't, but your ma might, or your sisters. Why don't you try them and find out?"

"Yeah, right. How do we know that yoke wasn't robbed two nights ago, and if we take it you'll be round to arrest us this afternoon?"

"You're overestimating my brainpower."

Isabelle raised an eyebrow. "Or you're underestimating mine. 'Cause I'm not thick enough to take anything off a cop who's pissed off with my ma."

"I'm not pissed off with her. We had a little difference of opinion, it's been resolved, she's got nothing to worry about from me."

"Better not. My ma's not scared of you."

"Good. Believe it or not, I'm fond of her. We grew up together."

Isabelle considered that. "Then what'd you smash our telly for?" she demanded.

"What does your ma say?"

"She won't."

"Then neither will I. A gentleman never divulges a lady's confidences."

She threw me a withering look to show that she wasn't impressed by the fancy talk, but then she was at the age where nothing I did would have impressed her anyway. I tried to imagine what it was like, seeing your daughter with breasts and eyeliner and the legal right to get on a plane to anywhere she wanted. "Is that yoke meant to make sure she says the right thing in court? 'Cause she already gave her statement to that young fella, what-d'you-call-him, Ginger Pubes."

A statement that she could and presumably would change several dozen times by the time the trial came along, but if I had felt the urge to bribe Imelda Tierney I wouldn't have needed to blow the budget; I could have stuck with a couple of cartons of John Player Blue. I figured I was better off not sharing that with Isabelle. I said, "That's nothing to do with me. Let's get this much straight: I've got nothing to do with that case, or that young fella, and I don't want anything off your ma. OK?"

"You'd be the first fella who didn't. Seeing as you don't want anything, can I go now, yeah?"

Nothing moved on Hallows Lane—no old ones out polishing their brasswork today, no yummy mummies in buggy wars, all the doors shut tight against the cold—but I could feel eyes in shadows behind the lace curtains. I said, "Can I ask you a question?"

"Whatever."

"What do you work at?"

"What do you care?"

"I'm the nosy type. Why, is it classified?"

Isabelle rolled her eyes. "I'm taking a course to be a legal secretary. Is that all right with you, yeah?"

I said, "It's great. Well done."

"Thanks. Do I look bothered what you think of me?"

"Like I told you, I cared about your ma, back in the day. I like knowing she's got a daughter making her proud and looking after her. Now let's see you keep up the good work and bring her this bleeding telly."

I flipped open the boot. Isabelle moved around to the back of the car—keeping her distance, in case I was planning to push her in there and sell her into slavery—and had a look. "'S not bad," she said.

"It's the pinnacle of modern technology. Do you want me to bring it to your place, or do you want to get a mate to give you a hand?"

Isabelle said, "We don't want it. What bit of that are you not getting?"

"Look," I said. "This yoke cost me good money. It's not robbed, it doesn't have anthrax on it and the government can't watch you through the screen. So what's the problem here? Is it just the cop cooties?"

Isabelle looked at me like she wondered how I managed to put on my boxers right way round. She said, "You grassed up your brother."

And there we all were. I had been the big dumb sucker all over again, thinking it might not turn into public knowledge: if Shay had kept his mouth shut there was always the local ESP network, and if that had had an off day there had been nothing to stop Scorcher, in one of the follow-up interviews, from dropping just one tiny little hint. The Tierneys would happily have taken a telly that had fallen off the back of a lorry—probably they would have taken one off Deco the friendly neighborhood drug dealer, if he decided he owed them for whatever reason—but they wanted nothing to do with the likes of me. Even if I had felt like defending myself, to

Isabelle Tierney or to the fascinated watchers or to every living soul in the Liberties, it would never have made one drop of difference. I could have put Shay in intensive care, maybe even in Glasnevin cemetery, and spent the next few weeks collecting approving nods and pats on the back; but nothing he had done was a good enough excuse for squealing on your own brother.

Isabelle glanced round, making sure there were people near and ready to come to the rescue, before she said—nice and loud, so those same people could hear her—"Take your telly and shove it up your hole."

She jumped back, quick and agile as a cat, in case I went for her. Then she gave me the finger to make sure no one missed the message, spun on her spike heel and stalked off down Hallows Lane. I watched while she found her keys, vanished into the hive of old brick and lace curtains and watching eyes, and slammed the door behind her.

The snow started that evening. I had left the telly at the top of Hallows Lane for Deco's next client to steal, taken the car back home and started walking; I was down by Kilmainham Gaol when the first rush came tumbling to meet me, great perfect silent flakes. Once it started, it kept on coming. It was gone almost as soon as it touched the ground, but Dublin can go years without even that much, and outside James's Hospital it had turned a big gang of students giddy: they were having a snowball war, scraping handfuls off cars stopped at the lights and hiding behind innocent bystanders, red-nosed and laughing, not giving a fuck about the outraged suits huffing and flouncing on their way home from work. Later, couples got romantic on it, tucking their hands in each other's pockets, leaning together and tilting their heads back to watch the flakes whirl down. Even later, drunks picked their way home from the pubs with triple-extra-special care.

It was somewhere deep inside the night when I wound up at the top of Faithful Place. All the lights were out, just one Star of Bethlehem twinkling in Sallie Hearne's front window. I stood in the shadows where I had stood to wait for Rosie, digging my hands into my pockets and watching the wind sweep graceful arcs of snowflakes through the yellow circle of lamplight. The Place looked cozy and peaceful as a Christmas card, tucked in for the winter, dreaming of sleigh bells and hot cocoa. On all the street there wasn't a sound, only the shush of snow being blown against walls and the faraway notes of church bells ringing some quarter hour.

A light glimmered in the front room of Number 3, and the curtains slid open: Matt Daly, in his pajamas, dark against the faint glow of a table lamp. He leaned his hands on the windowsill and watched the snowflakes falling on cobblestones for a long time. Then his shoulders rose and fell on a deep breath, and he pulled the curtains closed. After a moment the light clicked out.

Even without him watching, I couldn't make myself take that step into the Place. I went over the end wall, into the garden of Number 16.

My feet crunched on pebbles and frozen weeds still holding on in the dirt where Kevin had died. Down in Number 8, Shay's windows were dark and hollow. No one had bothered to close his curtains.

The back door of Number 16 was swinging open on blackness, creaking restlessly when the wind caught it. I stood in the doorway, watching the dim snow-blue light filtering down the stairs and my breath drifting on the frozen air. If I had believed in ghosts, that house would have been the let-down of a lifetime: it should have been thick with them, soaking the walls, cramming the air, keening and flittering in every high corner, but I had never seen anywhere that empty, empty enough to suck the breath out of you. Whatever I had come looking for—Scorcher, bless his predictable little heart, would presumably have suggested closure or some equivalent chunk of arsebiscuit—it wasn't there. A sprinkle of snowflakes swirled in over my shoulder, lay for a second on the floorboards and were gone.

I thought about taking something away with me or leaving something behind, just for the sake of it, but I had nothing worth leaving and there was nothing I wanted to take. I found an empty crisp packet in the weeds, folded it and used it to jam the door shut. Then I went back over the wall and started walking again.

I was sixteen, in that top room, when I first touched Rosie Daly. It was a Friday evening in summer: a gang of us, a couple of big bottles of cheap cider, twenty SuperKing Lights and a pack of strawberry bonbons—we were that young. We had been picking up days on the building sites on our school holidays, me and Zippy Hearne and Des Nolan and Ger Brophy, so we were brown and muscly and in the money, laughing louder and wider, thrumming with all that brand-new manhood and telling amped-up work stories to impress the girls. The girls were Mandy Cullen and Imelda Tierney and Des's sister Julie, and Rosie.

For months she had slowly been turning into my own secret magnetic north. At nights I lay in bed and was sure I felt her, through the brick walls and across the cobblestones, drawing me towards her down the long tides of her dreams. Being this close to her pulled at me so hard I could barely breathe—we were all sitting against the walls, and my legs were stretched out so near Rosie's that if I had moved just a few inches, my calf would have been pressed to hers. I didn't need to look at her; I could feel every move she made right inside my skin, I knew when she pushed her hair behind her ear or shifted her back against the wall to get the sun on her face. When I did look, she made my head stop working.

Ger was sprawled on the floor, giving the girls a dramatic based-on-a-true-story account of how he had single-handedly caught an iron girder that had been about to plummet three stories onto someone's head. All of us were half giddy, on the cider and the nicotine and the company. We had known each other since we were in diapers, but that was the summer when things were changing, faster than we could keep up. Julie had a stripe of blusher down each plump cheek, Rosie had on a new silver pendant that flashed in the sun, Zippy's voice had finally finished breaking, and all of us were wearing body spray.

"—And then your man says to me, 'Son,' he says, 'if it wasn't for you, I wouldn't be walking out of here on my own two feet today—'"

"D'you know what I smell?" Imelda asked no one in particular. "Bollix. Lovely fresh bollix."

"And you'd recognize those," Zippy said, grinning at her.

"Dream on. If I ever recognized yours, I'd top meself."

"It's not bollix," I told her. "I was standing right there, saw the whole thing. I'm telling yous, girls, this fella's a real-life hero."

"Hero, me arse," Julie said, nudging Mandy. "The state of him. He wouldn't have the strength to catch a football, never mind a girder."

Ger flexed a bicep. "Come over here and say that, you."

"Not bad," Imelda said, lifting an eyebrow and tapping ash into an empty can. "Now show us your pecs."

Mandy squealed. "You dirtbird, you!"

"You're the dirtbird," Rosie said. "Pecs is just his chest. What'd you think it was?"

"Where'd you learn words like that?" Des demanded. "I never heard of these pec yokes before."

"The nuns," Rosie told him. "They showed us pictures and all. In biology, you know?"

For a second Des looked gobsmacked; then he copped on and threw a bonbon at Rosie. She caught it neatly, tossed it into her mouth and laughed at him. I thought about punching him, but I couldn't come up with a good excuse.

Imelda gave Ger a little cat grin. "So are we seeing them or not?"

"D'you dare me?"

"I do, yeah. Go on."

Ger winked at us. Then he stood up, wiggled his eyebrows at the girls and inched his T-shirt coyly up his belly. All of us whooped; the girls started giving him the slow clap. He peeled off the T-shirt, whirled it around his head, tossed it at them and struck a muscle-man pose.

The girls were laughing too hard to keep clapping. They were collapsed together in the corner, heads on each other's shoulders, holding their stomachs. Imelda was wiping away tears. "You sexy beast, you—"

"Ah, God, I think I'm after rupturing myself—" from Rosie.

"That's not pecs!" Mandy gasped. "That's a pair of diddies!"

"They're grand," Ger said, injured, dropping the pose and inspecting his chest. "They're not diddies. Here, lads, are they diddies?"

"They're gorgeous," I told him. "Bring them here to me and I'll measure them for a lovely new bra."

"Fuck off, you."

"If I had those I'd never leave the house again."

"Fuck off and die. What's wrong with them?"

"Are they meant to be all squishy?" Julie wanted to know.

"Give us that back," Ger demanded, waving a hand at Mandy for his T-shirt. "If yous don't appreciate these, I'm putting them away again."

Mandy dangled the T-shirt from one finger and looked at him under her lashes. "Might hang on to it for a souvenir."

"Janey Mac, the smell off that," Imelda said, batting it away from her face. "Mind yourself: I'd say you could get pregnant just touching that yoke."

Mandy shrieked and threw the T-shirt at Julie, who caught it and shrieked louder. Ger made a grab for it, but Julie ducked under his arm and jumped up: "'Melda, catch!" Imelda caught the shirt one-handed on her way up, twisted away from Zippy when he got an arm around her and was out the door in a flash of long legs and long hair, waving his shirt behind her like a banner. Ger went thumping after her and Des held out a hand to pull me up on his way past, but Rosie was leaning back against the wall and laughing, and I wasn't moving until she did. Julie was tugging down her pencil skirt on her way out, Mandy threw Rosie a wicked look over her shoulder and called, "Hang on, yous, wait for me!" and then all of a sudden the room was quiet and it was just me and Rosie, smiling a little at each other across the spilled bonbons and the near-empty cider bottles and the curls of leftover smoke.

My heart was going like I had been running. I couldn't remember the last time we had been alone together. I said—I had some confused idea about showing her I wasn't planning a lunge—"Will we go after them?"

Rosie said, "I'm grand here. Unless you want to . . . ?"

"Ah, no; no. I can live without getting my hands on Ger Brophy's shirt."

"He'll be lucky to get it back. In one bit, anyway."

"He'll survive. He can show off his pecs on the walk home." I tipped one of the cider bottles; there were still a few swigs left. "D'you want more?"

She held out a hand. I put one of the bottles into it—our fingers almost touched—and picked up the other. "Cheers."

"*Sláinte.*"

The summer stretch had come into the evenings: it was gone seven, but the sky was a soft clear blue and the light flooding through the open windows was pale gold. All around us the Place was humming like a beehive, shimmering with a hundred different stories unfurling. Next door Mad

Johnny Malone was singing to himself, in a cheerful cracked baritone: "Where the Strawberry Beds sweep down to the Liffey, you'll kiss away the worries from my brow . . ." Downstairs Mandy shrieked delightedly, there was a tumble of thumping noises and then an explosion of laughter; farther down, in the basement, someone yelled in pain and Shay and his mates sent up a savage cheer. In the street, two of Sallie Hearne's young fellas were teaching themselves to ride a robbed bike and giving each other hassle— "*No*, you golf ball, you've to go *fast* or you'll fall off, who cares if you hit things?"—and someone was whistling on his way home from work, putting in all the fancy, happy little trills. The smell of fish and chips came in at the windows, along with smart-arse comments from a blackbird on a rooftop and the voices of women swapping the day's gossip while they brought in their washing from the back gardens. I knew every voice and every door-slam; I even knew the determined rhythm of Mary Halley scrubbing her front steps. If I had listened hard I could have picked out every single person woven into that summer-evening air, and told you every story.

Rosie said, "So tell us: what really happened with Ger and the girder?"

I laughed. "I'm saying nothing."

"Wasn't me he was trying to impress, anyway; it was Julie and Mandy. And I won't blow his cover."

"Swear?"

She grinned and crossed her heart with one finger, on the soft white skin just where her shirt opened. "Swear."

"He did catch a girder that was falling. And if he hadn't it would've hit Paddy Fearon, and Paddy wouldn't've walked out of there tonight."

"But . . . ?"

"But it was sliding off a stack down in the yard, and Ger caught it just before it fell on Paddy's toe."

Rosie burst out laughing. "The chancer. That's typical, d'you know that? Back when we were little young ones, like eight or nine, Ger had the lot of us convinced that he had diabetes, and if we didn't give him the biscuits out of our school lunches, he'd die. Hasn't changed a bit, has he?"

Downstairs Julie screamed, "Put me down!" not like she meant it. I said, "Only these days he's after more than biscuits."

Rosie raised her bottle. "And fair play to him."

I asked, "Why would he not be trying to impress you, as well as the others?"

Rosie shrugged. The faintest pink flush had seeped onto her cheeks. "Maybe 'cause he knows I wouldn't care if he did."

"No? I thought all the girls fancied Ger."

Another shrug. "Not my type. I'm not into the big blondie fellas."

My heart rate went up another notch. I tried to send urgent brainwaves to Ger, who in fairness owed me one, not to put Julie down and let people head back upstairs; not for another hour or two, maybe not ever. After a moment I said, "That necklace's lovely on you."

Rosie said, "I'm only after getting it. It's a bird; lookit."

She put down the bottle, tucked her feet underneath her and got up on her knees, holding out the pendant towards me. I moved across the sun-striped floorboards and knelt facing her, closer than we had been in years.

The pendant was a silver bird, wings spread wide, tiny feathers made of iridescent abalone shell. When I bent my head over it I was shaking. I had chatted up girls before, all smart-mouthed and cocky, not a bother on me; in that second, I would have sold my soul for one clever line. Instead I said, like an idiot, "It's pretty." I reached out towards the pendant, and my finger touched Rosie's.

Both of us froze. I was so close I could see that soft white skin at the base of her throat lifting with each quick heartbeat and I wanted to bury my face in it, bite it, I had no clue what I wanted to do but I knew every blood vessel in my body would explode if I didn't do it. I could smell her hair, airy and lemony, dizzying.

It was the speed of that heartbeat that gave me the guts to look up and meet Rosie's eyes. They were enormous, just a rim of green around black, and her lips were parted like I had startled her. She let the pendant drop. Neither one of us could move and neither one of us was breathing.

Somewhere bike bells were ringing and girls were laughing and Mad Johnny was still singing: "I love you well today, and I'll love you more tomorrow . . ." All the sounds dissolved and blurred into that yellow summer air like one long sweet peal of bells. "Rosie," I said. "Rosie." I held out my hands to her and she matched her warm palms against mine, and when our fingers folded together and I pulled her towards me I couldn't believe it, I couldn't believe my luck.

All that night, after I shut the door and left Number 16 empty, I went looking for the parts of my city that have lasted. I walked down streets that got their names in the Middle Ages: Copper Alley, Fishamble Street, Black-pitts where the plague dead were buried. I looked for cobblestones worn smooth and iron railings gone thin with rust. I ran my hand over the cool stone of Trinity's walls and I crossed the spot where nine hundred years ago the town got its water from Patrick's Well; the street sign still tells you so, hidden in the Irish that no one ever reads. I paid no attention to the shoddy new apartment blocks and the neon signs, the sick illusions ready to fall into brown mush like rotten fruit. They're nothing; they're not real. In a hundred years they'll be gone, replaced and forgotten. This is the truth of bombed-out ruins: hit a city hard enough and the cheap arrogant veneer will crumble faster than you can snap your fingers; it's the old stuff, the stuff that's endured, that might just keep enduring. I tilted my head up to see the delicate, ornate columns and balustrades above Grafton Street's chain stores and fast-food joints. I leaned my arms on the Ha'penny Bridge where people used to pay half a penny to cross the Liffey, I looked out at the Custom House and the shifting streams of lights and the steady dark roll of the river under the falling snow, and I hoped to God that somehow or other, before it was too late, we would all find our way back home.

Author's Note

Faithful Place did exist once, but it was on the other side of the River Liffey—northside, in the warren of streets that made up the red-light district of Monto, rather than southside in the Liberties—and it was gone long before the events of this book. Every corner of the Liberties is layered with centuries of its own history, and I didn't want to belittle any of that by pushing an actual street's stories and inhabitants aside to make way for my fictional story and characters. So, instead, I've played fast and loose with Dublin geography: resurrected Faithful Place, moved it across the river, and added this book into the decades when the street doesn't have a history of its own to be pushed aside.

As always, any inaccuracies, deliberate or otherwise, are mine.

Acknowledgments

I owe enormous thank-yous to the usual suspects, and then some: the
amazing Darley Anderson and his team, especially Zoë, Maddie, Kasia,
Rosanna and Caroline, for being several million miles beyond what any
author could expect from an agency; Kendra Harpster at Viking, Ciara
Considine at Hachette Books Ireland and Sue Fletcher at Hodder &
Stoughton, three editors who regularly take my breath away with their passion, skill, and immense soundness; Clare Ferraro, Ben Petrone, Kate Lloyd
and everyone at Viking; Breda Purdue, Ruth Shern, Ciara Doorley, Peter
McNulty and everyone at Hachette Books Ireland; Swati Gamble, Katie
Davison and everyone at Hodder & Stoughton; Rachel Burd, for another
razor-sharp copy-edit; Pete St. John, for his beautiful love songs to Dublin
and for his generosity in allowing me to quote from them; Adrienne Murphy, for remembering McGonagle's even through the haze; Dr. Fearghas O
Cochláin, for the medical bits; David Walsh, for answering questions about
police procedure and sharing insights into a detective's world; Louise Lowe,
for coming up with such a great title (and cast) for that play, all those years
ago; Ann-Marie Hardiman, Oonagh Montague, Catherine Farrell, Dee
Roycroft, Vincenzo Latronico, Mary Kelly, Helena Burling, Stewart Roche,
Cheryl Steckel and Fidelma Keogh, for various invaluable kinds of warmth
and love and support; David Ryan, *braccae tuae aperiuntur*; my brother
and sister-in-law, Alex French and Susan Collins, and my parents, Elena
Hvostoff-Lombardi and David French, for more reasons than I have room
to list; and, as always, last but so far from least, my husband, Anthony
Breatnach.